MASTERS OF WAR

Cherry Tree Publishing Co.

Special thanks:
Laurie Rosin, book editor
Rick Barry, copy editor
Greg Gubi, interior design
Steve Hall Creative, cover design

ISBN-10: 0985266007
ISBN-13: 9780985266004

Library of Congress Control Number: 2012935126

Printed in the United States of America

MASTERS OF WAR

by

CONRAD JOHN

AUTHOR'S NOTE

As with any major event such as World War II, its secrets tend to leak out afterward, often over many decades. Some were reported contemporaneously, so they were never really secret, but often were relegated to the back pages of newspapers, their significance not realized without the context and broader perspective of hindsight.

This novel is based on facts and historical events, some of which trickled into public view many years after they occurred. Some remain obscure though well documented.

Sadly, nowhere are all these incidents compiled, placed in context, and given the historical treatment they deserve. The Rise and Fall of the Third Reich: A History of Nazi Germany, written by William L. Shirer in 1960, doesn't mention many of them, including one of the most fateful episodes in Hitler's rise to power: a little-known deal that saved Hitler's regime in its infancy, a deal between Zionists (Jews dedicated to the creation of a Jewish state) and the Nazis.

To remind readers, Hitler was appointed Chancellor of Germany in January 1933. He assumed full dictatorial power in March. A growing worldwide boycott of German goods was threatening to topple the Nazi regime. The boycott gained momentum following a steady series of accounts of Nazi atrocities committed against Jews in Germany that were smuggled out and printed in Western newspapers.

By the summer of 1933, the impact of the boycott on Germany's economy was reaching critical mass. A commonly expressed opinion by those who followed these events was that Hitler would not last through the winter.

The Nazi-Zionist deal changed all that. Sealed in August 1933, the agreement was a complex arrangement that enabled the emigration of Jews and the transfer of their frozen assets out of Germany and into Palestine, largely in the form of German manufactured goods, which were resold there. In essence, Palestine became a sales agent for German goods in the Mideast and elsewhere. As part of the deal, the Zionists agreed to use their political influence to end the worldwide boycott of German goods, which they did to great effect.

For a full treatment of the Nazi-Zionist deal, I recommend the meticulously researched and well written 1984 book by Edwin Black, The Transfer Agreement, which was invaluable in my research, or visit the book's website: www.transferagreement.com.

This deal is just one of many little-known episodes from WWII used in the setting of this novel. For references used by me for other "secret" facts and events, please refer to this book's website, at: http://www.mastersofwarbook.com.

Though the setting of Masters of War is historically accurate and it ties together many obscure WWII incidents and hidden alliances, this book is fiction, not history.

Enjoy.

PROLOGUE

Rioters banged on the boarded-up windows and doors on all sides of the house. Inside, a young boy clung to his mother's dress in the midst of relatives and neighbors who had gathered to provide a common defense. Spurred on by the ranting rabble in the street, the assailants screamed and shouted in Russian, a language the boy recognized but did not understand. He knew it all had something to do with him being Jewish and them Christian, as he had overheard the adults say the day before when the riot first began, but it made no sense. The only thing clear to him was the hatred the rioters had for them.

Many of the men inside prepared to make a stand and brandished knives, kitchen utensils, narrow boards, even pieces of furniture, or scrambled to arm themselves with something. Someone hollered that a defense would be futile; they had to escape. "To where?" another replied scornfully. "We're surrounded." A feeling of dread filled the air. It was evident to the boy, though he was just six years old, that an attack could not be averted and, absent a miracle, that blood would spill and people would die.

Suddenly, a man cried out, "Bring the children. We can put them on the roof," and the boy's mother immediately grabbed him and shoved him toward the door leading to a bedroom.

"Quickly," she said, hustling him into the room, where, in the far corner, sunlight spilled onto the floor through a freshly cut hole in the ceiling. A man standing beneath the hole grabbed the first child to reach him, a girl, and lifted her onto his shoulders. Two other children stood in line ahead of the young boy.

"What do I do after I get up there?" he asked his mother, as the man who had summoned them joined the other man to help heave the girl on his shoulders through the hole onto the roof.

"Lie there and be still. Wait for them to leave," she said.

A woman ahead of them turned and said to the boy's mother, "The attackers will look on the roof when they see the hole and then kill the children to get rid of witnesses." Then she told the boy upon whose shoulders her hand rested, "Jump off the roof when no one is looking and run to the outhouse."

From the other room the loud sound of wood splintering startled them. The boy turned and saw the infuriated mob barge through the front door wielding cudgels hewn from tree branches, which they immediately began swinging viciously at the men in the house. But they stood their ground and fought back. His mother shoved him forward. Another child had been pushed through to the roof and the two men helping the children grabbed for the boy in front of him.

"What are you going to do, Mother?"

"Don't worry about me. Worry about yourself."

The men in the corner grabbed him and started lifting, tearing him from his mother. In that instant, the intruders burst into the room, heading straight for them. Thrown into the air, he instinctively grabbed for the rim of the hole just as a second boost to his feet threw him upward onto the roof. Rather than scurrying away, he peered back down the opening.

The two men who had thrown him through the hole grabbed his mother in an attempt to lift her toward the hole when three or four of the attackers came at them. "Mother," the boy cried, and reached out for her outstretched hand. One rioter grabbed his mother's dress just as the two men began to lift her and the dress ripped, leaving the raider with a scrap of cloth in his hand. The boy grabbed his mother's arm and pulled with all his might. Her other hand grabbed for the roof, and then she screamed and fell back, her arm slipping from the boy's grip.

"Run, Isidor," she screamed.

He hesitated, but then more rioters poured in and overcame the two men defending his mother. They beat the two men badly while other men tore the clothes off his mother and began fondling her. Overwhelmed with a sense of doom and the urge to escape, Isidor rose to his knees and scanned the rooftop and surrounding area. Three children crouched on the roof. He didn't see the boy who had gone before him, but spotted the outhouse he must have escaped to.

He saw frenzied crowds in the streets watching and cheering on others who stormed homes and destroyed and looted every structure in their path. The city square was littered with broken glass and other debris. On a side street, he spied a patrol of soldiers, and was about to scream to them for help when it occurred to him that they could see the same things he was seeing – and were doing nothing to stop it. He looked around, spotted another patrol on another street smoking and talking amongst themselves, and then saw a policeman sitting idly on the corner of the street, right in the middle of it all.

His mother's piercing scream jolted him. He spun around and looked at the hole. He felt the urge to return and rescue her, but knew he was powerless to do anything. And, afraid of what he might see, thought better of it. He scrambled to the lower edge of the roof in the front of the house, jumped down, and ran into the street. Rioters who saw him trying to escape shouted out to stop him, and two men chased him. Isidor ran for his life, jumping over puddles from the weekend's rains. Beyond a courtyard which marked the boundary of the Jewish quarter he stepped into a very deep puddle – and fell.

PART I

January - September 1933

CHAPTER ONE

Isidor Franks held up a glass of champagne. "Mazel tov," he said, toasting Ben Komorosky, who smiled proudly, held up his own glass, and tapped Isidor's.

"Thank you, Isidor. And thank you for coming."

"Only for you. Normally, I don't celebrate days like this one," Isidor said, cocking his eye in obvious reference to the news that President Von Hindenburg had named Adolf Hitler Chancellor of Germany earlier in that day, January 30, 1933.

Ben sighed. "That's all everyone is talking about," he said with a sweep of his glass at the crowd of twenty-five or more people milling about in the spacious room decorated specially for the occasion. Large letters on one wall, hanging above a table filled with gifts, signified the occasion: "Congratulations, College Graduate."

"Your good fortune has been overshadowed by our misfortune," Isidor said, and Ben agreed with another sigh.

"Do you plan on doing anything now?" Isidor asked.

"I'm going to graduate school in America. I leave the end of July. Until then I plan to help out at the store."

"I meant about Hitler. If he's not stopped, there will be no store to work in. Haven't I been right so far?"

"You have," Ben said. "I'm amazed, actually."

"My dear friend," he said, putting a hand on Ben's shoulder. "The words of an English philosopher come to mind," and he switched from the German they had been speaking to English: *The only thing necessary for evil to triumph is for good men to do nothing.*"

The tapping sound of a spoon against a glass grabbed their attention.

"Please be seated everyone," Adam, Ben's older brother, called out to the gathering.

"I left you a gift on the table," Isidor whispered. "I have something else for you if you are interested in stopping evil. Something..." He paused, giving Ben a knowing look. "...personal."

"I am interested," Ben said.

Isidor grinned. "Good for you," he said and slapped Ben on his shoulder.

* * *

In the faint glow of the hallway light, Ben crossed the oval rug in the living room, leaned over a sofa, and drew the window shades on two side-by-side windows. Only then did he flick the switch of a lamp next to the sofa, lighting the room just enough for him to see. He had done as Isidor had instructed; it was not his normal routine. By the time he turned on a second lamp, Isidor had materialized in the doorway bearing a wrapped package. Rectangular, maybe an inch deep, he guessed it might be a framed photo or a painting.

"Come in," Ben said. "I'll show you around." After closing the door behind him, Isidor set the gift on an armchair and dropped his hat beside it. Fifteen years older than Ben, Isidor was a chubby fellow with a cropped beard and a ready smile. His attention fell on the shelves against the near wall. "What are all the trophies about?"

"Marksmanship. It's one of my two hobbies."

"May I?" Isidor said, reaching for one. Ben nodded.

Isidor read from the trophy. *"1932 Bavarian Three Hundred Meter Rifle Championship. First Place."* An impressed look showed on his face. "Hmm. You must be good." He set it back on the shelf. "Now I'm curious. What's your other hobby?"

Ben grinned mischievously. "Women," he said, winking.

"Oy," Isidor muttered, rolling his eyes.

"And now I'm free to enjoy the nightlife here in Munich as I did in Paris, only no homework." He motioned for Isidor to follow him.

"Be careful, my friend. This isn't Paris."

Ben finished the tour of his three-room apartment, then pointed to the package. "What have you got for me?"

Isidor handed it to him, and Ben removed the paper. The red-orange glow of the nearby lampshade was reflected in a piece of glass in a walnut frame. He read the banner headline over an article clipped from the *Volkischer Beobachter* (*Racial Observer*), a Nazi gossip sheet published by Alfred Rosenberg: "Mach Ganze Arbeit Mit Den Juden," it read ("Clean Out The Jews Once And For All"). The date of the article, March 10, 1920, gave him an eerie feeling. He turned an inquiring eye to Isidor.

"When I was a boy," Isidor said, "my mother took me on a trip to visit her family in Kishinev, which was then part of the Russian province of Bessarabia but is now in Romania."

"I know about Kishinev," Ben said. "Were you there during the pogrom?"

"I was. My mother was raped and killed by an angry mob of Christians. They probably would have killed me, too, but I escaped...with her help."

"Please," Ben said, motioning to his sofa. "Sit and tell me about it."

Isidor took a seat and related the story. At the point where Isidor tripped and fell in the puddle, Ben was on the edge of his chair. "So how did you escape?" Ben asked.

"I was rescued by, of all things, a Christian family. I broke both my arms in the fall. One was a compound fracture. I still have the scar," he said, standing to slip off his coat. He pulled up the sleeve on his left arm, and Ben rose to his feet to look.

"The family that rescued me was as generous and kind as the rest of the city was cruel and bigoted. They paid for my medical care and, after confirming that my mother had been killed, notified my father who returned to bury her and take me to Berlin.

"Later, when I was old enough to do so, I researched the Kishinev pogrom, and learned that the riot was precipitated by the murder of a Christian boy in a nearby town on the Orthodox Easter holiday." Isidor's face tightened and his voice turned bitter. "Even though it was clear to anyone interested in the truth that the boy had been killed by a relative who was later arrested. A Russian-language, anti-Semitic newspaper, much like the one you hold in your hands, insinuated that the boy was killed by Jews. Another one alleged Jews had killed the boy to use his blood to prepare matzo." He threw his eyes upward.

"I took two lessons from the experience," he said, holding up two fingers. Then he curled the middle one down and spoke intently. "One, hatred toward Jews lies deep within our culture and, once stirred into action, its people will commit the most heinous crimes in expressing that hatred."

The second finger reappeared, along with a telling look. "And two, most people will stand by and let it happen.

"The same thing is happening today in Germany. I clipped and framed that article when I saw it in 1920 because it reminded me of the articles that preceded the Kishinev pogrom."

A reflective smile came to Isidor's broad, bearded face as he placed an arm across Ben's shoulders. Determination showed in his eyes. "So, today I fight so others will not have to suffer their own pogrom. I could use your help."

"What kind of help?" Ben said.

"Something easy for you that I have neither the talent nor the time for."

CHAPTER TWO

Isidor splashed his face with water from the bathroom sink in a guest suite at Berlin's Askanischer Hof hotel. He gazed in the mirror at his bearded face, stroked the black hairs, not a one of which was gray even though he expected to see one any time now, and pondered whether he needed a trim. Not quite. He rubbed his thick eyebrows, and tousled his wavy black hair into place, then ran a brush through it. A big smile revealed his white teeth, perfectly aligned on top, slightly jagged below. He reached for his toothbrush, and began brushing.

A telephone rang. His brow furrowed, then he rinsed his mouth. Still in his underwear, he strode across his suite to a writing table in the far corner as the phone rang twice more.

"Herr Franks?" Isidor acknowledged the voice he recognized to be the clerk's. "A cable from London marked urgent just arrived. Should I send a bellman to your room?"

"Yes, please." Isidor slowly lowered the receiver onto its cradle, pondering, then quickly stepped into a pair of trousers. A messenger rapped on his door a few moments later. Isidor accepted the cable and tipped the young man. The moment the door closed, he tore it open.

He decoded the encrypted message as he read:

Göring has called an emergency meeting in his private office with German Jewish leaders for noon today. No Zionists were invited. Get invited or at least find out what happened and report back as soon as possible.

Isidor crushed the note in his hands and then rushed to the phone.

CHAPTER THREE

Adam wore a resolute expression, gently tapping a copy of *Der Sturmer* (The Stormer) in his left hand. Germany's most vehemently anti-Semitic newspaper, *Der Sturmer*, was not the periodical of choice for a Jew. Eight years Ben's senior, Adam was the oldest of the four Komorosky brothers and Ben's and Michael's guardian away from home. He had called a family meeting. Obviously something troubled him greatly. For the first time Ben found his dark, rugged features unattractive.

Ben sat in one of the cushioned arm chairs next to Adam's large oak desk. Michael was the youngest brother at nineteen. He was baby-faced and thin, with delicate features. Seated in one of the chairs in front of David's desk, he had scooted it next to Ben's. David sat in his high-backed leather chair behind his desk. At twenty-six, he was four years younger than Adam and four older than Ben. His hair and skin tones were similar to Ben's, his eyes almost hazel-colored. He was fit and trim, warm natured, and easy going. While Adam ruled with a heavy hand, David tended to lead by example, working efficiently and intelligently.

They were gathered in the large office in the back of David and Adam's store, Komorosky Brother's Clothiers, an upscale men's clothing store on Munich's fashionable Maximilian Boulevard. A picture window looked out on the empty showroom. Above the window, which was a mirror on the showroom side, were bulletin and chalk boards, setting forth to-do lists, sales targets, monthly projections, and the like.

"I'm taking Lara and the kids back to Leningrad," Adam announced, referring to his wife and four small children. He turned to David. "I think you and Michael should go, too."

The news struck David like a punch to the gut. "And do what?" he said. "Work in a factory the rest of our lives?"

"At least the Soviets tolerate Jews and will leave us alone. My kids can't even walk home from school without being taunted and called names. Yesterday, some German boys called Elena a dirty Jew and said she wasn't born, that her mother shit her out. She's only six, for Heaven's sake."

David winced. "Why don't you send Lara and the kids back and stay in Munich alone, like you did when you first came here?"

Adam waved the *Sturmer*. "It's going to get worse." He unfolded the newspaper and pointed to the front-page article. "The Nazi party is calling for a boycott of Jewish businesses starting next Saturday, the first of April," he said, handing the paper to David.

"Hitler will be gone by winter," Michael said. "That's what I hear everybody saying."

"That's pie in the sky," Adam shot back. "The same people also said he would never get elected."

Ben started to say something, but Adam cut him off. "I'll get to you in a minute."

"Michael's right," David said. "The worldwide boycott of German goods is growing rapidly and a boycott of Jewish businesses will only make it worse for Hitler. Not to mention the millions of reichsmarks in lost taxes." He flicked the newspaper, *Der Sturmer*. "This is suicide for the Nazis. Pure lunacy," and then tossed the paper onto the desk.

Adam raised his voice, "It might be suicide for them, but it's *murder* for the business."

"I admit they can hurt us," David replied. "There'll be ups and downs, perhaps. But, we've had a good run of profits; we can weather it."

Adam ran his fingers through his hair in obvious frustration. He sighed, then spoke softly. "It's closer to home than that." His eyes shifted toward Ben. David and Michael's attention followed. Adam reached inside his jacket.

He produced an article from the British *News Chronicle*.

David looked befuddled, perhaps because he couldn't read English and neither could Adam. Ben got Adam's point, though; he saw the byline and lowered his head in his palms.

Adam read aloud, "by A.D.S. Rosenberg." He shot a glance at Ben, and then turned to David: "A.D.S stands for Alfred Das Schwein (Alfred the Pig). It's a parody of Alfred Rosenberg." He was referring to the high ranking Nazi official and former editor of the *Racial Observer*. "Ben's publicly calling a top Nazi official a pig."

Michael snickered at Ben who said to Adam, "I told you that in confidence. No one else knows I'm writing articles using that name." Under his breath he added, "Except Izzy."

Adam fired back, "This is a family matter now. They have a right to know. I warned you that your actions could endanger the business. Just because you chose to take that risk does not make it only about you."

A look of understanding replaced David's quizzical expression.

He motioned for Ben to back off and said to Adam, "What if he were to write under another name?"

"That's only half the problem," Adam said. "What he writes below the byline is the other half."

Ben frowned as Adam continued speaking to David, wondering how Adam could know what the English words meant. "It's about Nazi abuses against Jews," said Adam.

Ben interjected, "How do you know what...," but he was cut off by David, who said to Adam, "Isn't that a good thing he's doing?"

Adam angrily replied, "No. These are the kind of stories that are riling up the Nazis."

"Maybe they should be riled into stopping the abuses," David said.

"If the stories are true, perhaps" Adam said. "The Nazis claim they are false."

"They're true," Ben said.

"According to Isidor Franks," Adam said to Ben.

"Why would you believe the Nazis over Izzy?" Ben replied.

"Because they are the government," Adam said, almost shouting, as though he needed to raise his voice to emphasize the same point he had made privately earlier that morning to Ben, and then he leaned from his seat and grabbed the *Sturmer* sitting on the desk in front of David. "The abuse stories being written and shipped out of the country are the sole reasons given for the call to boycott Jewish businesses," he said, repeatedly stabbing the newspaper with his finger.

Adam then zeroed in on Ben. "What you write stirs them up whether the stories are true or not. They *agitate* them. And since the Nazis now run the German government, whether you agree or disagree, you truly are an anti-German agitator. And you know what the Nazis do to agitators – and to their supporters." He then flung the newspaper back onto the desk.

After a moment of silence, Adam spoke to David in a lowered tone. "You know our agreement. We stay out of politics. That's one of the reasons for our business success."

"True, but this is not his business," David said.

Adam jumped on his comment, almost cutting him off. "As long as he's living off the business, at least while he's living in Germany, he should respect our policy. We don't mix politics with business."

"Okay, I see your point," David said.

Adam eased back in his chair as David considered the matter. His eyes turned to Ben, then shifted toward Michael, then toward Adam.

Finally David looked at Adam and said, "Didn't you just tell us that you were going back to Leningrad?"

Adam stared at him blankly.

"If you're leaving and I'm staying, then I become the head of the business *and* of the family in Germany," David said.

"Until we finalize a deal, I'm still the leader."

David drew a deep breath. "What all do you want? Let's take Ben first. You want him to stop writing altogether, number one. Is there anything else?"

"Two things. I'd like him to leave early for America and I want him to stop sleeping with German girls."

Michael's eyes and ears perked up.

"I already promised you that," Ben interjected.

"In case you don't leave early, I want to make sure David holds you to it when I'm gone," Adam said.

"Isn't that why we leased the apartment for him," David said to Adam, "so he could have some privacy?"

Adam turned to Ben. "Do you want to tell him what I walked in on this morning or should I?"

Michael's jaw dropped, and Ben threw his head back in disbelief.

"No," David barked. "I don't want to hear about it. And further, I will not impose any restrictions on him. I intend to treat him as an adult, which he is."

Adam started to lash back as Ben jumped up. "This is silly. We went over this, Adam. I made a promise to you about what you saw this morning and I intend to keep it. I've also decided that I'm not dating again until I get to America, not German girls, not Jewish girls, not French girls. No dating whatsoever."

Adam calmed down and said, "Good. That's smart of you."

Ben settled back into his chair.

"So what about Michael?" David asked. "You want him to return to Leningrad with you. Anything else?"

Michael chimed in. "Do I have any say in this?"

David turned to Adam for an answer.

"You can study music in the Soviet Union," Adam said.

"But Germany is the home of the greats. Beethoven, Brahms, Mozart ..."

"Tchaikovsky," Adam shot back.

Michael flashed a grin. "I'll give you four German greats for every Russian you can name. Handel, Bach, Strauss, Schubert."

He rolled his hand toward Adam facetiously signaling it was his turn.

Adam tightened his jaw, then said to Michael, "What are you going to do if they pass the law they've proposed to limit the number of Jewish students?"

"Five percent can be Jewish, even with the law," Michael said. "I like my chances."

"First it's 5 percent, then it's zero percent," Adam replied. "And other laws after that. Mark my words."

"I don't want to return to the Soviet Union if I have any say in the decision. Even if I can't go to school here, I want to stay and help David run the store so I can help him make enough extra money to send me to New York. There's a famous school of music there." He glanced at Ben before continuing his reply to Adam, "...'The Juilliard School.' It's not far from Columbia University where Ben's going. That's my second choice. Ben said I could live with him and that he'll help support me once he finishes his studies and starts making money. He's already teaching me English."

Adam cocked his head at Ben, the meaning of which was apparently lost on David but not on Ben. Adam often ended his lectures during the past year by reminding Ben that Michael regarded him as a hero and that anything he did Michael might copy.

"Frankly," David said to Adam, "with you leaving, I'll need Michael to help out at the store. At least for a year. Then we can take another look at the situation. I'll keep your opinions in mind. Honestly. The fact that you're leaving doesn't change my high regard for you. You're a wise man. You're the main reason for our success. I've said that privately to both of them, too."

Ben and Michael both nodded their heads in agreement.

"And I mean it," David continued. "In the meantime, I'll talk to Ben separately about leaving early for America. How's that?"

Adam became lost in thought, staring at David but not focused on him. Finally, he shook his head and rose. "I've got a lot to do."

Ben jumped to his feet and stretched out his arms to Adam, offering him a hug. "I'm really sorry about what you and the kids are going through."

Adam nodded appreciatively and let Ben embrace him. "And thank you for all you've done for me," Ben said. "You've been a great guardian and I'll miss you."

"Thanks, Ben."

Michael gave Adam a hug, too.

David started around his desk to join them but held up when Ben waved him off and as Adam shied away and headed out of the office with tears beginning to well up in his eyes.

"I'll talk to you later," David said to Adam's back.

CHAPTER FOUR

Isidor and Rabbi Langenberg entered the anteroom to Herman Göring's private office in the Prussian Ministry of the Interior, causing a stir among the guests who were already assembled.

Huge framed portraits of Hitler and Göring hung on one of the white walls. Standing regally between them was a large Third Reich flag on a pole topped by a spectacular gold Nazi Eagle over a black, gold-circled swastika. The room was clean and simple, furnished in rustic-looking natural wood.

Rabbi Langenberg was the head of the German Zionist Federation, of which Isidor was a member. In addition to being a colleague of the Rabbi's, Isidor was a confidant. Isidor knew everyone and everything, or so the rabbi had once said to him. Isidor was fond of giving those words back to the rabbi, as he had done that morning when Langenberg had asked him how he found out about the meeting. "Remember, my dear friend. I know everyone and everything."

The men they joined in the anteroom were:

Dr. Julius Brodnitz, the venerable chairman of the Central Verein, Germany's largest Jewish organization, which comprised many Jewish business owners and had been formed in 1893 with the intention of unifying German citizens of the Jewish faith. Its members saw themselves as primarily German and, consequently, repudiated Zionism;

Heinrich Stahl, the newly elected chairman of the Berlin Jewish Community;

Dr. Max Naumann, founder of the Association of National German Jews, a passionately patriotic group that sought the total assimilation of Jews into German society and the self-eradication of the Jewish identity.

All the men rose to their feet with varied looks of surprise, bewilderment, and in the case of Naumann, red-faced outrage at the presence of the Zionists. His angry eyes locked onto Rabbi Langenberg's.

The hostility between Langenberg and Naumann was palpable, as though sending off sparks and an eerie hum like two high voltage lines that had come too close together. Naumann was an easy man to dislike. The former German officer came out in support of Hitler after his appointment as Chancellor in January 1933 and was an avowed enemy of the Zionists, who, by definition, desired a separate Jewish state and therefore saw themselves as Jews first and foremost, not Germans. Naumann, and for that matter the overwhelming majority of German Jews, opposed Zionism because they considered themselves to be assimilated, loyal Germans. Only about one percent of German Jews were Zionists.

"Hello gentlemen," Langenberg said, flashing Naumann a crooked smile before directing his attention to the others. "I see we haven't missed anything."

"What are you doing here?" Naumann demanded. "This is a meeting between the government and *legitimate* representatives of German Jews. Zionists are not Germans by your own declarations. Go to your Palestine and stop meddling in our affairs."

"Well, the government apparently doesn't share your parochial views," Langenberg retorted before Isidor could intervene. "We're on the guest list," he said.

A young soldier interrupted them. "Mr. Göring is ready to see you," he snapped, then did an about-face and marched into Göring's office. Langenberg smugly stepped in front of Naumann.

Out of view of the two men, Isidor rolled his eyes in frustration and wondered what lay on the other side of the door, where they would meet a Nazi leader who, more or less, shared Naumann's views of the Zionists.

Insouciance, he reminded himself. *We've made it to the meeting. That's the main thing. Now ad lib and hope for the best.*

Göring stood regally in front of his large, burnished oak desk. He struck an imposing figure with piercing blue eyes, a square jaw, and slicked-back brown hair. Most striking, he wore his Nazi dress uniform. Isidor felt a chill and judging from the furtive glances and subdued looks he saw from the other guests, everyone got the same message.

"So much for the distinction between the government and the party," he whispered to Langenberg, in reference to Hitler's repeated excuses for the government's supposed inability to rein in overly zealous party members.

"Indeed," Langenberg whispered back.

Göring, commander of the Stormtroopers, the private army of the Nazi party, displayed a row of medals above the left pocket of his brown uniform. Isidor recognized the Iron Cross. Much more prominently, the *Pour Le*

Merite hung from a ribbon around his thick neck. Prussia's highest military order, the blue-enameled Maltese Cross with eagles between its arms enhanced the aura of power and leadership and reminded Isidor of the man's storied career as a fighter pilot during the Great War.

The other guests gathered in the center of the room. Like Göring, they stood. Obviously, they should; not only was the Reich Minister standing, but chairs had been pushed off to the sides.

The aide introduced the Jewish leaders, giving the names of both the individual and the organization he represented. Göring received each with careful attention. "Rabbi Langenberg, Director of the Zionist Federation of Germany, and Isidor Franks, his colleague," the aide gave as the final introduction. Göring's eyes narrowed as he scanned the crowd.

"You are the ones who bear full responsibility for the malicious, false and derogatory headlines in the English and American press. The false reports malign the German government, and instigate protests against the purchase of German goods which, in turn, strikes at the German economy and the German people.

"In the past I have accommodated you. I have even apologized to some of you present today for the actions of zealots within the party, and what do I get in return? You betray me. I cannot be responsible for actions against your people if you continue to inflame the outside world against us."

Heinrich Stahl, head of the Berlin Jewish Community spoke first. "Herr Göring, I can only speak for myself and my organization, but I can honestly state that we do not sanction communications concerning the German government or the Nazi party to outsiders, and I know of no such unofficial actions."

Isidor felt uneasy with Stahl's disjointed stand. The problem was that he was telling the truth and was credible. Minister Göring even seemed to believe Stahl, although he didn't acknowledge his statement. Rather, he scrutinized the rest of the room. It was easy for Isidor to predict how the drama might play out. Göring would not reasonably suspect that Naumann or his League of German Jews could be behind such articles. That left the Central Association or the Zionist Federation for suspicion if fingers were to be pointed or a scapegoat identified.

Brodnitz had apparently come to the same conclusion. He jumped in. "Herr Göring, what articles are you talking about? We're not aware of any."

The *Reichsmarschall* glared back, then turned to his aide and snapped his fingers. The aide departed and returned with a stack of newspaper clippings. Göring displayed the news articles, one at a time. "*London Times*, February 16, 1933, 'Nazis Storm Jewish Businesses;' *New York Daily News*, March 8, 1933, 'Nazi Thugs Given License to Attack Jews.'" He grew angrier, and his voice louder, as he progressed through the articles. "*New York Times*, March 21, 1933, 'Synagogues Disrupted and Pillaged in Berlin,'" His face seething with anger, he violently threw the articles onto his desk, knocking off a cigar box.

"Unless you put a stop to these libelous accusations immediately, I shall no longer be able to vouch for the safety of German Jews," he thundered.

A hush fell upon the guests. With eyes transfixed upon the speaker, no one moved a muscle. Minister

Göring stared back, boring into the souls of each of them, one-by-one. Not once, but three times. On each round he relaxed the force of his glare a little, until at last, he drew a deep breath, and let it out.

Brodnitz was the first to break the silence. "Herr Göring, we can't control the British and American press. I can get with my people and advise them that we must do all we can to discourage complaints ..."

"No. You must go immediately to London and from there to America, and convince Jews in both places, and the press, that German Jews are not being physically abused, and that the stories they hear and read are despicable lies. You must do this. For the safety of your people, you must.

"The most important thing is for you to make sure that the protest meeting called in New York by Dr. Stephen S. Wise is canceled." Göring was referring to the upcoming protest at Madison Square Garden where a proclamation for a global boycott of German goods was planned. "That assembly must not take place. Dr. Wise is one of our most dangerous and unscrupulous enemies."

"Herr Göring, we have no influence over Dr. Wise or other leaders of American and British Jews; a trip would be futile," Brodnitz said. Stahl and Naumann nodded their heads in concurrence. In the case of Naumann and Stahl, their assessments were probably true, but Isidor knew that Brodnitz had significant connections and influence in both cities. It was an honorable lie, however. Who could blame a person for refusing to assist in his own demise?

Rabbi Langenberg spoke. "Herr Göring, the German Zionist Federation is affiliated with Jewish leaders in other countries because it is part of a worldwide organization. We alone are capable of assisting the German government in the manner you propose."

Isidor felt the wind knocked out of him. Naumann's face was contorted in a barely restrained rage. The other Jewish leaders exchanged astonished looks.

Göring gazed at Langenberg with an odd, curious expression. Isidor yanked the rabbi's pant leg.

"Excuse me," Langenberg said to the Reich minister, then leaned in to Isidor.

"What are you doing?" Isidor whispered.

"We've talked about opening a dialogue with the government. Now's our chance."

"Yes, but not on these conditions." Langenberg threw him an incredulous glance. Isidor spelled it out. "We can't disavow abuses that are real and atrocious."

"Of course," he said, straightening to address their Nazi host.

"My colleague reminded me to clarify our position. While we are uniquely capable of speaking with Jewish leaders from other countries, we must speak truthfully about the treatment of German Jews. The minister himself acknowledges..."

"What is there to tell?" Göring shouted.

"The Minister is not well informed if he is not aware of a marked change for the worse in the treatment of Jews," Langenberg replied. He recounted numerous incidents of physical attacks on Jews, violent beatings and even murder.

"Where one uses a plane, shavings will fall," Göring said with a dismissive wave of his hand. He paused. "I don't care what is said to get the rally in New York called off. Perhaps it is even beneficial for them to understand the grim situation in Germany so they are motivated not to provoke us and make the situation worse. Nor do I care who goes to London as long as those who go agree to report regularly to the German embassies."

"I want to be part of the delegation you send," Isidor said to Langenberg the moment the two of them were out of earshot of the other Jewish leaders.

"I'll pass it on."

* * *

Isidor boarded the train for Munich late that evening, still reeling from the news given him by Langenberg two hours earlier: "London picked a delegation that, I'm sorry to say, does not include you." By "London," Langenberg meant the worldwide Zionist headquarters in London, the Office of the Zionist Executive.

Isidor found an isolated seat and fell into it, staring into the darkness through the window. A feeling of betrayal continued to gnaw at him as he reviewed past observations and events in an effort to reconcile his feeling with reality. Something was awry. He reminded himself to go over his escape plan when he got to Munich; Ben's too. He then settled into his seat, pulled the brim of his hat over his forehead, and closed his eyes.

CHAPTER FIVE

Ben pounded on the keys of his English language typewriter, then paused to re-read what he had just written: *May 21, 1933. In Hannover, stormtroopers broke into the home of a* Jewish *doctor in the middle of the night, supposedly in search of weapons and anti-Nazi literature.* He referred to Isidor's handwritten notes lying to his left. The man was beaten to death when he refused to confess to having possession of the illegal items not found. He wanted to emphasize that point before he got to the grisly beating. Back to the keys. He tapped away.

Four completed articles were strewn on the right side of his desk. In place of a byline, "From Nazi Germany" separated headlines and text. Penciled abuse reports, scratched in German and Yiddish, were scattered about the floor, having been pushed out of his way when they had served their purpose.

Dressed in gabardine pants, an undershirt and socks, Ben paused to gaze at the graduation present Isidor had given him, the framed page from the *Volkischer Beobachter* hanging on the wall above his desk. "Clean Out The Jews Once And For All," the headline still blared.

The Nazi intention had crystallized in his mind over the past four months. Why had it? Because he was informed. And now he was doing something to help inform the rest of the world. Feeling a burst of inspiration, he hit the keys to pound out the last paragraph of the final article.

His corpse was taken to the hospital where doctors observed boot prints on his stomach, fist-sized holes in his back with scraps of cotton fabric stuffed into them. The autopsy's official finding: "Cause of death: dysentery, which is frequently accompanied by premature age spots."

Ben pulled the story from the carriage and proofread the entire article. Satisfied, he scooped up all the news stories, shuffled them into order, and placed them inside his rifle case.

* * *

"Good shooting," Isidor said, as Ben sauntered into the Munich range. He motioned to the far corner of the pavilion. "Over there," he said, leading the way. "How much did you see?"

"I saw the last six shots. Impressive, all bull's-eyes."

Ben beamed as a rifle shot rang out from the firing range. "Stick around for the award ceremony and you can see them award me the winner's trophy."

"I don't have any choice. Someone dropped me off, so I need you to drive me home. But don't the others still shooting have a say in that?"

Another round fired, as Ben shook his head. "No, this is the final round. They can't catch me." Reaching his station, he opened the rifle case. "There are the articles."

Isidor peeked over his shoulder. They couldn't be heard by other participants or spectators. "Excellent. I'll look at them after we get in the car."

Ben began breaking down his rifle, first by disengaging the telescopic sight. Shots from the rifle range crackled.

"I've decided to shut down your end of the operation," Isidor said.

Ben shifted his eyes to Isidor for an explanation. Isidor's grim face matched the tone of his voice. "It's too dangerous."

Ben cased the telescope and reached for the bolt of his Mauser 98K, removing it. He could tell that Isidor had more to say, so he kept silent.

"The Zionists are negotiating with the Nazis."

A shock wave reverberated through Ben's mind. "Negotiating?" he asked too loudly. He lowered his voice. "For what?"

"For a deal that would allow German Jews to emigrate to Palestine and transfer their frozen assets there in the form of German-made goods."

Ben set his rifle onto a wooden rack, the muzzle pointing downward, and sifted through his thoughts. He reached for his cleaning kit. "What do the Nazis get in return?" His eyes were riveted on Isidor's.

"An end to the worldwide protest and boycott against German goods."

Ben almost dropped his kit. "You can't be serious."

Isidor's expression told Ben otherwise. His normally jovial face was woodenly glum. "It's much worse than it sounds, my friend. The assets will be used to buy German goods and then transferred to Palestine. So, not only will Zionists actively work to end the boycott against German goods, their assets will buy goods in Germany which they will then re-sell throughout the Middle East."

Ben extracted a cleaning rod and a cotton patch from his kit. "How can they do that? What gives them the right to speak for other Jews?" He uncapped a jar of solvent.

"They seized an opportunity. The Nazis are desperate to stop the boycott."

Ben doused the cotton patch with solvent. "But I helped build the boycott. The Central Verein helped. Jews from around the world helped." He rammed the cotton swab down the rifle barrel. "The leverage they're using to bargain with does not belong to them."

Isidor's face lit up. "I like that: *'The leverage they're using to bargain with does not belong to them,'*" he repeated. "I'll remember that for my trip."

"What trip?" Ben said, pulling the cleaning rod out.

"I'm going to Berlin, and then to London." He pointed a stern finger at Ben. "That's for your ears only."

"Of course," Ben said. He checked and saw the swab in his hand was covered with black residue and tossed it aside.

"I need to gather some intelligence, find out who's pushing the deal and figure out a way to stop it – if it can be stopped," Isidor said, as Ben reached for a clean swab.

"Meanwhile, you should go over your emergency escape plans and be alert. Now that the Zionists are working with the Nazis they might be inclined to make us part of a package deal."

Ben flashed a scowl at Isidor and jammed the fresh swab down the muzzle of his rifle.

"Why not?" Isidor said. "They're selling out the rest of Germany's Jews."

CHAPTER SIX

Isidor stood on the cobblestones of the ancient, pedestrian bridge, his hands settled on the concrete railing that was adorned with colorful streamers for the year-end festivities known as May Week, a name given the event when it was actually held in May, before final exams, rather than after, as it was now. He gazed down at the River Cam before him, at the ducks gliding along on its shimmering waters, and at the reflection of overhanging branches and the river's manicured grassy banks. It was a fine, balmy spring day, with throngs of people strolling along the river, and throughout The Backs, as the park-like area behind many of the colleges comprising Cambridge University is called. Isidor absorbed it all, reminiscing about his college days.

"Ah, there you are, Mr. Franks."

Isidor turned to the familiar voice. The man was tall and dark, dressed in a beige double-breasted suit and a dark hat. He carried himself in a gentlemanly, almost stiff manner and approached with an extended hand and an affable smile on his face. Isidor ignored the hand and responded instead with a hearty hug.

"Oh my, Mr. Franks. What a jolly fellow you are," he said with a titter, blushing. Isidor laughed as he let go, slapped the man on the back, and gestured sweepingly at the Backs.

"Just like the good old days, eh?" Isidor said.

Sir William agreed and said he was pleased Isidor enjoyed the setting, given his long trip and all.

His name was William, but Isidor had dubbed him "Sir William" as part of a failed effort to instill the informality of addressing him as Isidor, or even Isidor, rather than as Mr. Franks. William had missed the point and instead was flattered, so the moniker stuck.

"I must thank you for the splendid intelligence you provided me," Sir William said. "Sir Philip Cunliffe-Lister, who is the British Colonial Secretary with direct purview over England's colonies and the Palestine Mandate, has confirmed that the Zionists have indeed struck a deal with the Nazi government." He was referring to Britain's authorization – mandate – to oversee the administration of the territory in the Mideast known as Palestine. The authorization was issued by Allied powers at the end of the Great War (1914 - 1918) in favor of the establishment of a national home for Jewish people while, at the same time, honoring the rights of existing non-Jewish communities in Palestine. Prior to the war, Palestine was part of the Ottoman Empire (Modern Turkey), which had entered the war in 1914 aligned with Germany and lost control of Palestine during the war.

"The deal has not been finalized," Sir William continued. "As a matter of fact, there is some political infighting within the Zionist leadership and they are currently trying to modify its terms.

"Either deal being proposed is most distressing to the interests of Great Britain," Sir William went on. "Think of it. Jews will become the blasted agents for the export and sale of German goods in the Middle East. German goods will be sold in the place of British goods. Not to mention of course the fact that the deal will bail out the Nazis and impede, if not entirely destroy, the boycott movement against German goods and all our efforts to topple that not-so-jolly fellow, Hitler."

A phalanx of rollicking students approached the bridge, and Isidor gave Sir William a subtle nod toward them. Without looking back, Sir William steered Isidor by an elbow.

"Let's take a stroll.

"I hope you don't mind me prying," Sir William said, "but I imagine this development...the Zionist Organization striking a deal with the Nazis, I mean...creates a strain on your loyalties?"

"I am loyal to my principles, not to political organizations," Isidor said. They stepped off the bridge and turned right, onto the pathway leading toward Trinity College. "I seek a homeland for my people, true, but I believe for it to be worthy of our quest, and lasting, it must be built on peace and honor, not force and treachery. The vast majority of Zionists and German Jews agree with me, by the way."

"Yes, of course. I suppose they do. Or, at least they should, if you want my view of it. If they knew what I know, they would bloody well revolt."

Isidor perked his ears, hoping he'd elaborate, but Sir William moved on. "So, tell me, how do we put the kibosh on this dreadful deal?"

Isidor explained the current politics inside both the Zionist Organization and Palestine, and then offered a plan to defeat the deal at the Zionist Congress that

August in Prague. After hearing him out, Sir William promised financial and logistical support. Just then, a canon shot shook the air, sounding the four-minute warning for the first rowing race of the day.

"Good show on all your work, by the way," Sir William said. "Now, if you don't mind, I would like to watch the races from the Trinity Bridge. I see there are still some spaces. If you hold them, I'll fetch us a drink. I'm dying for a cup of tea. Would you care for one?"

* * *

After the boat races, in which the two Trinity College racing teams lost out to the Pembroke College team, Isidor and Sir William leisurely strolled the Backs, ultimately destined for the Fellows' Garden party at Trinity College. Sir William asked him about his trip to London.

Isidor gave him a summary of his meetings and interactions with friends and associates at the Zionist Organization's headquarters and Sir William listened attentively. Isidor didn't have to brief Sir William about his trip to Berlin, which preceded the one to London, because he had already reported to William by mail upon his arrival in London.

Isidor noticed through occasional questioning that Sir William thoroughly understood every detail.

"It sounds like you have good relations there and are respected in spite of it all," Sir William said when Isidor had finished.

"I do. After my trip to Berlin, I resolved that the existing Zionist hierarchy was bound and determined to make a deal of some kind with the Nazis and that since I couldn't stop it internally I might as well accept it and concentrate on maintaining good relations."

"First rate diplomacy, indeed. I applaud you." Turning his attention to the large, festive gathering at the garden party fifty or so paces ahead of them, he added. "Ah, I see some of the old chaps have made it. Shall we join them?"

* * *

After a couple of hours, they migrated off campus with two other Trinity alumni to the beer garden of the Eagle Pub on Bene't Street. Not until almost six o'clock that afternoon did they find themselves alone again and free to talk "business." The opportunity occurred when they took a river ride in a punt, a narrow, flat-bottomed boat similar to a gondola of Venice without the curved bow and stern. A college student steered the punt with a pole, standing on the back of it, and they were the only two passengers, seated near the water line in the bottom of the punt.

Sir William asked Isidor where he planned to go in the unfortunate event they were unable to topple Hitler.

"London," Isidor immediately replied. He owned a house there, the vast bulk of his assets were in England, and he had a permanent visa, all of which Sir William knew. "Not to Palestine, if that's what you wondered."

"You are a Zionist, after all."

"There's a lot of work to do in London."

"Yes, I suppose so," Sir William said, then dropped the subject.

* * *

After the river ride, and during their second trip to the Eagle Pub, they ordered fish and chips and a pint of Greene King Indian Pale Ale for old times' sake. They sat at a small wooden table in the corner of a back room. Lamplight cast a glow over a burnt orange wall that was separated into sections by uneven, rustic oak vertical beams. The lower half of the wall was paneled with dark-grained hardwood. The air was stuffy and smoke-filled.

The pub was packed, ale was flowing, and a din from the boisterous crowd made it difficult to think, let alone hear the person across the table. Sir William leaned over the table, with a glint in his eye.

"I noticed that your writing skills vastly improved rather suddenly in February," he shouted into Isidor's ear, then leaned back and took a swig from his pint, his eyes fixed playfully on Isidor.

Isidor faltered and recognized that he had let down his guard, which he attributed to the sense of security he had developed being around Sir William all day, and the ale.

Sir William leaned back over the table. "It would be grand if you could bring that asset with you to London, should that event transpire," Sir William said.

Isidor collected his wits. "Perhaps my friend assumes too much," he said, leaning over the table with a grin. He leaned back, lowered his eyes disinterestedly, took a bite of the fried cod sitting before him, and glanced up at Sir William, who sported an amused, studied look.

"Then I shall reveal my assumptions and allow you to be the final judge," Sir William said, obviously delighted in the gamesmanship.

"I assume that he is Jewish, that he is fluent in German...he is quite obviously fluent in English, and I assume further that he is trustworthy, at least in your opinion, which is all that matters to me since I do not have to meet the fellow. He can remain unknown to me and me to him."

"You also assume that the *asset*, as you call it, is not me," Isidor said, leaning closer. "Hitler was appointed Chancellor at the end of January. Perhaps urgency motivated me to put more into my work. The asset could also be female. You referred to it as a male." With that, Isidor reached for his ale, lifted it, tipped it toward Sir William and winked.

"Ah, you are quite right on both counts. Once again, I'm afraid I must stand corrected. I shall point out to you, however, in defense of my faculties, that neither of the assumptions alters the conclusion upon which my request was based. For if it was you alone, and you were to come to London, then naturally the asset would accompany you. And if it were a female, it is doubtful that you would entrust a mere secretary or clerk with matters involving such a degree of risk , so I suppose the chances are rather good that she would accompany you as well," Sir William countered. He reached for his own pint, and lifted it.

"You have such a low opinion of the opposite sex, my friend." Isidor said. "She could be a colleague without being my mate."

Hoping to end the contest, he rested his arms on the table. "Yes, I suppose you are right on that one, Sir William said, putting down his ale. "I really should not inquire into your affairs. I would be remiss, however, if I did not disclose two important facts that led me to make my remark. One, it could be most helpful to have such skills available to us, and, two, if this asset both lives in Germany and is Jewish, then he...or she, as you point out might be the case, needs to go somewhere, because, in the event this transaction between the Nazis and the Zionists is consummated, that person, along with all other German Jews, will be condemned to a most miserable fate."

Isidor was well aware of the consequences and didn't need a British gentile to explain it to him. His attention, however, was stuck on Sir William's allusion to the two of them working together in the event he came to London, as though they would still share some common interests. Isidor saw none. They had come together to defeat Hitler, it had expanded into defeating also the Zionist-Nazi deal, and if they failed in both those efforts, he saw nothing mutual remaining beyond friendship.

Isidor quickly reviewed the entirety of their conversations that day and a broader picture of Sir William's intentions began to emerge.

Sir William leaned over the table, gestured with his finger for Isidor to come closer. "War," he said and then pushed back and nodded his head, confirming that Isidor had heard him correctly.

He leaned back over the table. "When we leave," he said, gesturing to the crowd, which Isidor interpreted to mean there was more to discuss and that what he had to say was too confidential to be discussed there.

* * *

They emerged from the pub about eight-thirty and walked along a narrow sidewalk. The welcomed silence and fresh, cool air invigorated Isidor. He took a deep breath and exhaled toward the darkening sky. Sir William took his arm and gestured toward the other side of the street, which was devoid of pedestrians. "Let's cross. I parked near Trinity. I'll give you a lift to the station."

They settled into a comfortable pace heading west. Sir William stuck his hands in his pants pockets. "You should know that Hitler promised his financial backers to rearm Germany and go to war over the terms of the Versailles Treaty. The difficult part to understand – because it is so brazen, I suppose – is that the very people who negotiated the Versailles Treaty represent his financial backers."

Isidor listened attentively, fully aware of the facts and issues. The treaty of which Sir William spoke was signed in June 1919 in Versailles, France ending the Great War between Germany and the Allied Powers. The treaty's terms were extremely harsh, exacting enormous reparations in the form of currency, coal, steel, and other property. The payment of reparations led to massive hyperinflation in postwar Germany and civil unrest, creating a political climate ripe for a nationalist like Hitler who promised to right the wrongs of Versailles.

Sir William continued speaking. "Two of the participants at Versailles – and I submit to you, the two most important men present – were Paul and Max Warburg. Paul created America's central banking system and was its chairman at the time. He represented the interests of the American bankers at Versailles. His brother Max – we know him today as the chairman of IG Farben and a major German banker in his own right – sat on the other side. He represented the interests of the German central bank. Together, they negotiated terms for the treaty that they began to violate before the ink was dry, a remark I shall clarify if you bear with me."

Nearing King's Parade, a major boulevard and turning point, Sir William gestured with his head for Isidor to cross Bene't Street, putting them on the east side of King's Parade.

"First I'll introduce Adolf Hitler, the poor corporal – and I mean that literally – he was destitute and living in impoverished conditions when the treaty was signed. He had an important connection, however. Max Warburg. They were both part of German Intelligence. In 1920 Hitler suddenly began living like a wealthy man, with plush apartments, mansions, expensive suits, luxury cars, servants and body guards. In the same time period, he had gotten involved in the fledgling German Labor Party that he had been sent to spy on for German intelligence. He took over the party, of course, and it became the infamous Nazi Party.

"American Wall Street bankers and the companies they controlled were pouring money into Hitler's personal accounts, as well as into the accounts of the Nazi Party and other high-ranking Party officials from the outset.

"Beginning in 1924, the Bank of England and various Wall Street banks made a deal with the Nazis through Hjalmar Schacht, who was then the Reich's Commissioner for National Currency, and is now, of course, President of Germany's Central Bank, the Reichsbank. The Bank of England provided half the capital for the Reichsbank. Wall Street Banks have funneled thirty-two million dollars to the Nazi Party through various European banks since 1929, which is partly to blame for America's depression, incidentally; much of its capital went to Germany. Prior to that, three Wall Street houses handled seventy-five percent of the war reparation loans that were used to build German cartels, including the chemical giant, IG Farben – Max Warburg's company – and United Steel Works. All of these funded German cartels, which make up its military industry, and have also heavily donated to the Nazi Party since the mid-1920s.

"You see, Hitler promised his financial backers he would rearm Germany, which is, itself, a flagrant violation of the Versailles Treaty. The same treaty ..."

Isidor nodded his understanding.

"They want another war, is the upshot of it all," Sir William said. "Their plan called for the Nazis to take control of Germany...by election, if possible; by revolution, if not.

"After Hitler lost the election last year, some of Germany's top business leaders – many of whose companies were beneficiaries of the Wall Street loans – petitioned President von Hindenburg to appoint Hitler Chancellor, giving him a limited leadership role. A deal was cut on January 4 at the home of banker Baron Kurt von Schroder. Allen and John Foster Dulles were present at the meeting. The Dulles brothers are corporate lawyers with the New York law firm for the Schroder Bank, and they are two of three key intermediaries between Nazi leaders and Wall Street. The other one is Prescott Bush, of W.A. Harriman & Company, a New York banking firm."

They had reached Green Street. Sir William pointed. "I'm parked right around the corner."

They climbed into Sir William's car, a spiffy two-toned Austin touring car, and motored off, easterly to Sidney Street where he turned south. Isidor sat silently, contemplating the information Sir William had thrown at him and piecing it together with information of his own.

"What can you share with me about the Zionist-Nazi deal?" Isidor asked.

"Ah. This is precisely the point where you come into the picture. As you surely know, Schacht traveled to America in early May."

"Yes, I followed it closely," Isidor said, recalling news of Schacht's trip, which coincided with huge public protests against the Nazi regime for its abuses of its Jewish citizens. One hundred thousand people showed up in New York alone. Schacht met with President Roosevelt, the Secretary of State, and other government officials, all of whom reportedly pleaded for tolerance. "Schacht defiantly defended Hitler while he was there," he added.

"Publicly – and to a point he did," Sir William replied. "At the end of his trip, and before he boarded a liner to return to Germany, he received an urgent call for a meeting to be held on behalf of John Foster Dulles, who, as I stated earlier, is an agent for Wall Street bankers. After the meeting, Schacht cabled Hitler with an urgent, but cryptic warning."

Sir William turned left onto Station Road. "We know from other messages we intercepted that Schacht met with James McDonald of the Foreign Policy Association that day.

"The FPA is an organization formed by Dulles. McDonald flatly told Schacht that Germany was living on borrowed time, that France was calling for the permanent partition of Germany, and that Czechoslovakia and Poland have allied for a preemptive strike against Germany.

"Of course, the story behind the story is what precipitated McDonald's urgent call. A few days earlier, Schacht had threatened President Roosevelt, and others present, that Germany would stop making interest payments on loans from American banks if the boycott against German goods continued. The loans total two billion dollars."

Sir William slowed the car, pulled into the Cambridge Railway Station, and parked, leaving the motor running. He turned to Isidor.

"Because of your splendid intelligence work inside Germany, we were able to interpret Schacht's warning to Hitler. The date of Schacht's meeting with McDonald, and his subsequent telegram to Hitler, was on the thirteenth, the same day that Hitler accepted the Zionist offer.

"The same financial interests who are backing Hitler and pushing him to rearm are pushing the Zionist-Nazi deal."

CHAPTER SEVEN

Isidor threw his travel bags together near the door to his Munich apartment and scurried to the phone. He called the Komorosky store one more time. As the phone rang, he scanned the apartment, checking to see if he had forgotten anything. He noticed the unfinished afternoon coffee and cake on the kitchen table, and thought it told a tale of a man leaving suddenly and considered whether to clean it up. The phone continued to ring, unanswered. To hell with the cake. Warning Ben and disposing of the coded telegram in his pocket were of much greater concern.

He slammed down the phone, rushed to the open gabled kitchen window, and looked out below onto Raffini Street, hoping to see his taxi and no sign of Nazi soldiers or police. A few pedestrians ambled up and down the sidewalks on either side of the street and automobiles glided east and west without any more ado than an occasional gentle honk from one of them. He detected no signs of either Nazis – or his taxi. He heard a distant rumble of thunder, looked up at the threatening cloud cover, and realized it could start raining at any moment. For some reason, it added to his sense of urgency. Anxiety began to set in, but he quickly reminded himself, out loud and in Yiddish, "Make no more haste than good speed."

He pulled the wadded telegram from his pocket and read his decoding of it penciled above the typed encryption one final time. Dated that day, June 23, 1933, it read: "Get out of Germany immediately. Orders for your arrest have been issued." He then strode to the stove, lit a match to the telegram, and held it over the sink. As the flame burned toward his fingertips, followed by blackened ashes curling and dropping into the sink, the triple blast of an automobile horn sounded from the street. He abruptly dropped the scarred remnants of the telegram into the drain and flushed it with a gush of water from the faucet.

He scrambled to the window, looked out and saw his taxi sitting by the curb. As he picked up his hat from the table, an idea struck him and he let go of it. He then grabbed his bags and raced out the door, hastily locking it behind him.

"The train station," he said to the driver after he stuffed his large frame into the backseat of the cab. "Go by way of Maximilian Street, please. I need to buy a hat."

The driver acknowledged him and sped off.

As they neared the Komorosky store, Isidor instructed the driver to slow down, pointing out the store. The driver slowed. A car with Nazi emblems sped past them, veered to the curb in front of the store, and came to a screeching stop. Two men wearing black shirts jumped out of either side of the car. The soldiers were part of the new SS (*Schutzstaffel*, defense echelon), a political police unit that Isidor had read about but not yet seen. He also noticed a large yellow-on-black spot in the window. Such displays had become commonplace in

Munich lately and signified Jewish ownership. It had not been there the last time Isidor had been in the vicinity, nor had Ben said anything to him about it, which caused Isidor to surmise that it had been placed there during the past week.

As the taxi driver began to pull to the curb, behind the Nazi car, the soldiers ran straight for the door of the Komorosky store.

"No, don't stop," he hollered out. "That store is owned by Jews. I didn't know that."

The driver seemed to understand, and sped off. Isidor turned in his seat and tried to see inside the store as the taxi went by, but couldn't make out anything. He slumped back into his seat and prayed that Ben wasn't inside.

CHAPTER EIGHT

Ben fitted a suit jacket on Wilhelm Schuessler, David's business lawyer. Dressed in a brown suit with a red plaid waistcoat, the sixth generation Bavarian and war hero was a massive figure who projected self-confidence, wealth and wisdom. David stood nearby, holding Schuessler's walking stick. He was finishing up a conversation with Schuessler about the yellow dot that had been placed on the store window two days earlier and David's idea to bring in a German Christian as a partner. Michael was in the front of the store behind the counter.

"Giving up fifty-one percent of the business will certainly solve the immediate problem of ridding yourself of that terrible nuisance in front of the store, that much I can guarantee. If you're serious about it, I recommend that you authorize me to spend some time researching the legal mechanisms used by others who have done it in order to determine precisely what has worked and what hasn't. It will cost you more, but it will give you peace of mind and may actually be less expensive in the long run."

"Do whatever you think needs done. The sooner, the better."

Ben finished his work and invited Schuessler to look in the mirror.

Schuessler gestured for his walking stick and David handed it to him. With his exquisite stick in hand, Schuessler posed before the mirror.

"What do you think?" Ben said.

"I like it." He glanced at David. "Do you agree?"

"Indeed," David said, and Schuessler turned inquiringly to Ben.

"It looks perfect on you." He added playfully, "And to celebrate my coming departure, it's on the house."

"What a generous gesture," Schuessler said to David.

David's eyes bulged, having apparently just caught on. "Oh...well, fortunately for me, Ben and I have an understanding. The way it works is, you pay the store for the suit and then redeem the offer from him."

A commotion outside drew Ben's attention. Dressed in the black uniforms of the newly-formed SS, two men rushed the front door. Ben fell to his knees behind a rack of dress jackets. The front door flew open, followed by the sound of trampling boots.

"We're looking for Ben Komorosky," one of the officers sharply demanded.

Ben stared uneasily at Schuessler. David's eyes darted from Ben to Schuessler.

Schuessler's left hand, which was resting against his pant leg, motioned for Ben to leave. "Let me handle this," he whispered to David.

Ben spun around and stole his way toward the open door to the back room, about ten feet away, crawling on his hands and knees.

He heard the booming voice of Schuessler. "Gentlemen, may I introduce myself. I'm Wilhelm

Schuessler, Attorney and German national." The confident, slow pace of Schuessler and his walking stick, followed by David's lighter steps, sounded on the hardwood floor as they moved toward the officers. Ben darted behind a circular rack of men's pants and peered around it.

The attention of the SS officers was riveted completely on Schuessler, who was taking an arcing approach to them, drawing their field of vision away from the back of the store.

Ben dropped below the line of sight of the soldiers and slithered on his belly to the next, and final, clothes rack.

"I represent the legal interests of the proprietor, David Komorosky."

Ben reached the rack, got to his knees, and stole another glance.

"Herr Schuessler," the SS officer said. "This is an urgent matter of state security." Ben scurried on hands and knees for the doorway. "We are looking for Ben Komorosky, who we understand works at this store and perhaps is a relative of your client."

"Officer, Ben Komorosky left for America to finish his education," Schuessler said.

Ben made it through the doorway. He rose to his feet, set his sights on the back door, and proceeded slowly and softly on the tips of his loafers.

"Yes, we are aware of his plans," Ben heard the lead officer reply. "However, his ship is not scheduled to depart for another month."

Ben reached the door, carefully settled his right hand on the brass door knob and placed his left hand on the door itself. He slowly turned the knob.

"He changed his plans and left early." Schuessler stated boldly. "I personally witnessed his early departure. You have my word on that, gentlemen."

"When did he leave?"

The door latch moved free of the strike plate, and Ben froze. Stiffly and silently, he stood, wondering and waiting for the next move of the soldiers. He felt his heart pounding and noticed for the first time that his pulse was racing.

"Earlier today, as a matter of fact," Schuessler said.

"By what means?"

Ben felt Schuessler walking into a trap and decided he should risk making noise. He reached for the doorknob and slowly turned it. He heard David's voice but it was too muffled to make out his words.

"Ben didn't say," Schuessler said. "He left rather abruptly and unexpectedly is what my client meant to convey. Is that correct, Mr. Komorosky?"

As he spoke the latch to the back door clicked. Ben halted, wanting to make sure the noise hadn't been heard by the officers.

"Yes," David said. "He didn't say."

Ben put both hands on the doorknob and readied to pull on it when the officer spoke.

"Thank you for your time, Herr Schuessler."

Ben relaxed as he listened to the rustling sound of footsteps, followed by the sound of the front door opening.

He waited for the front door to close, then pulled the back door open with both hands, stepped across the threshold, and began softly closing it behind him. The final words he heard were David's.

"The suit, sir, *is* on the house."

The alley behind the store emptied onto a side street. Ben checked both ways for police, saw none, and headed right, walking away from the boulevard fronting the store. Lightning lit the darkened skies, and a drop of rain struck his face, then another. A loud thunderclap split the air, and rumbled. He noticed the temperature drop abruptly and realized that the dark clouds were about to unload. He was wearing summer fabrics, a cotton shirt and linen pants and sports jacket. In his rushed departure, he had left his hat, and he hadn't taken an umbrella to work. He looked at his watch: 5:40 p.m. He had plenty of time to go by David's apartment, grab his packed belongings, and still get to the Central Train Station to catch the evening through train to Berlin. He would grab an umbrella and one of David's hats. He picked up his pace.

He walked ten blocks to go four, avoiding major streets and intersections. Rain began to pour down. Lightning and thunder split the air every minute or so. The thunder, which originally followed the lightning by eight seconds, was down to five, placing the last bolt about a mile away and closing fast. He turned onto Pfister Street, his soaked jacket pulled over his head. Parked in front of David's townhouse was a Nazi vehicle. He spun in his tracks and started running. Absolutely drenched, and the storm center closing in on him, he spotted a taxi two blocks into his run and hailed it.

"Marienplatz," he told the driver, referring to the public square a half-mile away.

* * *

Ben reached the train platform at 8:40 p.m. Breathing in the pungent smell of diesel fuel, he reached a line of about fifteen passengers stretched toward his train. He spotted an SS officer at the front of the line, peering over the shoulder of a boarding clerk and scanning the faces of the boarding passengers suspiciously. Ben felt an adrenalin rush and an urge to run, but resisted it. His instincts told him to board. He turned his back to the passengers and looked at his watch. He didn't see the dial; he was buying time. He took a deep breath and let it out slowly.

"Insouciance," he whispered, reciting Isidor's training instruction to himself.

"*Control your emotions,*" he recalled, Isidor's voice replaying in his mind. "*Insouciance will get you out of as many predicaments as panic will get you into. Project an air of innocence, not guilt, even in the most compromised circumstances. Then improvise – and hope for the best.*"

He placed his boarding pass on top of a *Der Sturmer* newspaper he had picked up after buying his train ticket, and got in line. The train let out a blast of steam and the second boarding whistle blew. The boarding clerk, with the SS officer hovering over him, reached the passengers in front of him, a young couple. Together, they carried three bags of luggage, the man two, the woman one. The clerk checked their papers. The eyes of the SS officer passed over them and locked onto Ben.

A chill shot through him and his blood drained from his head. The fingers on his left hand fidgeted with the boarding pass and newspaper, raising it slightly in an attempt to inconspicuously draw the officer's attention to his reading material.

The clerk returned the papers to the young couple and Ben moved forward.

He stuck out his left hand to the clerk, revealing both the Nazi paper and the boarding pass. He then quickly reached for the newspaper with his right hand. "Oops, sorry," he said.

The SS Officer squinted, boring forcefully into Ben's skull. Ben felt his muscles tense. He fought to maintain his poise but noticed his knees quivering. The officer's attention seemed to follow Ben's to his knees. A puzzled look flashed across the officer's face. He grabbed the boarding papers from the clerk's hand and quickly inspected them.

"Where are your travel bags, Mr. Schwartz?" the officer demanded sharply.

The question startled Ben. He had forgotten the phony name he was using. Moreover, the oddity of a traveler without any bags struck him. He felt his bladder weaken.

"My bags?" He flashed the masthead of *Der Sturmer*, as he looked down at his feet. "No, I don't have bags."

"I know you don't have any? I can see. My question was *where* are they?"

Ben's heart pounded. He felt trapped. Running was pointless. He may as well turn himself in. He pounded into his brain the lesson given him by Isidor.

"Confident behavior, not logic or common sense, convinces people. One merely needs to be plausible and assertive. Be confident at all times, even in bizarre situations. Mean it and project it. Whether there is a factual basis for your confidence is irrelevant."

"My travel bags are in Berlin. I didn't bring them with me to Munich, so I can't take them back, officer."

"How long have you been in Munich?"

"I arrived this morning on the through train from Berlin, for a business meeting."

"No briefcase?"

"I didn't need one today."

"I find that strange." Again his glare bore into Ben.

"Strange perhaps, but practical. I left home with my favorite hat, an expensive one, and I'm returning without it."

"Yes, I noticed you aren't wearing one. Where is it?"

"I don't know. I only discovered it missing when I got caught out in the rain."

The officer mulled over the papers. He raised his eyes. By then Ben was relaxed and fully composed. He casually stuck the Nazi paper inside his sport coat's outer pocket, patiently awaiting the officer's approval.

The officer handed the papers to Ben. "Very well. You may go," and he turned his attention to the next passenger in line.

"Thank you, officer." He boarded the train.

Looking for a seat, he walked completely through one car and down the aisle of a second one when something ahead of him, caught his attention. To his right, a seated passenger had suddenly turned away from him. Ben pretended he hadn't noticed and casually walked on. As he came even with the row in which the passenger was seated, he sneaked a peek. It was Izzy! Their eyes momentarily met, but Isidor had not acknowledged him in any way. Ben passed several more empty seats and into the next car, somehow confident that Isidor would have wanted him to keep his distance.

CHAPTER NINE

A damp, chilly sea breeze cut through Ben's thin summer clothes as he lingered outside the Hamburg train station in the darkness waiting for Isidor. The streets were wet and water dripped from the leaves of trees and a sign post, suggesting it had been raining only minutes earlier.

Ben shivered impatiently, unsure what to do given Isidor's presence on the train. Should he wait or proceed alone to the designated address his escape plan called for?

Just when Ben had decided to search for a taxi and go to the address, Isidor emerged from the train station, toting two bags and, Ben noted enviously, wearing a warm-looking overcoat. Their eyes met, and Isidor headed toward Ben, who stood on a sidewalk near the intersection of two streets, shivering with his hands in his pants pockets.

As Isidor neared, a surprised look on his face transformed into a sympathetic one. When he reached Ben, he dropped one of his bags, and threw the other on top of a rock wall adjacent to the sidewalk.

"Where are your bags?" Isidor said, as he opened the bag atop the wall.

"In Munich," Ben said. "Nazi police were parked in front of David's apartment."

Isidor extracted an overcoat from the bag, and handed it to Ben. "Here. Put this on. You're making me cold just looking at you."

Ben snatched the coat and gratefully wrapped it around himself. Though several sizes too big through the chest and too short in the sleeves, Ben relished the relief and comfort it brought him.

Isidor hoisted the bag onto his shoulder, and headed off, leaving the other bag on the sidewalk. "You can carry one of mine," he said.

"Follow a little behind me," Isidor said over his shoulder. "We can talk later."

They walked, hopped on a bus, walked some more, and wended their way through the streets of Hamburg to a harbor filled with fishing boats. A fishy, salt water smell filled the air. The sky in the east had lightened enough to reveal dreary, gray skies. Seagulls cawed and sailed over sea, shoreline, and boats. An unobstructed sea breeze blew from the north at a steady twenty-five knots, and cut against Ben's face.

Isidor signaled to a scruffy-looking man on one of the boats and, moments later, Ben followed him aboard. Isidor introduced the three men already onboard by first names only: Bernard, the scruffy one, with a weathered face, probably fifty years old; Joachim, short and stocky, with a friendly, bearded face, about thirty; and Toby, a young, clean-shaven fellow with blond, wavy hair and sky-blue eyes. Isidor referred to Ben as "Jacques, my friend from Paris."

His new name and nationality were a complete surprise to Ben, but he instantly adapted. He set down the bag he was carrying and exchanged greetings in a shivering French accent.

No sooner had he finished shaking hands than Isidor snappily said, "Let's go," and the fishermen instantly sprang into action and began to make ready for sea.

"Follow me," Isidor said to Ben, then stepped quickly onto a staircase leading below deck, and dropped out of sight.

Confused, Ben lingered for a moment, then rushed after him, leaving the bag on the deck. He caught up to Isidor in the cabin below.

"Wait a minute. Where are we going?"

"To England," Isidor said.

"All the way to England on this?"

Isidor nodded and dropped his bag next to a table in the middle of the cabin. "What did you expect, my friend, a liner?"

"A liner would be nice."

"Nice and dangerous. They expect us to leave Germany and will be monitoring the ports." He motioned to two bunks before Ben had accepted his fate. "Take your pick."

Ben surveyed the cabin, disheartened at the sight. There were six bunks, six lockers, and the table in a space smaller than his former apartment's bedroom. Moreover, the boat was bobbing in the water like a cork – and they were still in the harbor.

"Don't worry about it," Isidor said. "The company you'll be keeping will make up for any discomfort."

Ben snorted and smiled.

"Eh?" Isidor said, as he slapped his arm around Ben's shoulders. "I'm glad you agree. Now, go get my other bag," and he gave Ben a playful shove in that direction.

After they had settled in, with the diesel engine of the vessel chugging rhythmically in the background, Ben related his experience. Isidor told him that he had received a tip. "I tried to alert you but no one answered the phone and I got to the store just after the SS officers were leaping out of their car."

Ben's attention shifted to the rolling and pitching of the boat, which had become more pronounced, tossing them about roughly. Mimicking Isidor, he had braced himself with his hands and feet in an attempt to ride the waves, which worked – to a point. He glanced uneasily at Isidor, obviously wondering if it would get worse. Isidor flashed a knowing smile.

"Let me give you something to take your mind off the seas. I have a friend in London I've never told you about. He works with Britain's Secret Intelligence Service, SIS for short. I met him as a student in the early '20s at Trinity College."

Ben perked up, both confused and intrigued. Confused because he thought Isidor hated the British. Intrigued because Isidor had never before talked about such connections. He took Isidor's disclosure as license for him to inquire. "Is he the source for your tip?"

"Between you and me, yes. He's been helping me get your articles published as part of an operation to defeat the plans of Hitler's financial backers, who want war." Isidor then told Ben what Sir William had shared with him at Cambridge, ending with Sir William's final point that the same players behind Hitler's rise to power are behind the Nazi-Zionist deal.

Ben was fascinated. Everything Isidor said resonated with him and had indeed taken his mind off the rough seas.

"He wants me to infiltrate Zionist Headquarters in London as his spy," Isidor said. Just as Ben had begun to digest his comment, Isidor added, "He didn't say that, but I think that's his angle."

Ben greeted the information with mixed emotions. He felt a sense of the importance of the mission, a chance to right a wrong, but his confusion over Isidor's loyalties resurfaced.

"Do you trust him?"

Isidor scowled. "In this business, I don't trust anyone."

After a moment's thought, clarity came to Ben. Isidor had his own agenda, a personal calling that arose out of the Kishinev pogrom, a calling that Ben could barely begin to understand. "So, what are you going to do?"

Isidor said he was still thinking about it. "When I get to London, I plan to meet with him, ask him some tough questions, and see how he responds."

Isidor paused, probing Ben. "He also inquired about my *asset*?"

Ben cocked his head, puzzled.

"He assumed I had one because my English writing appeared to improve so dramatically in February." Ben grinned broadly, knowing that was when he began writing for Isidor. "That's the problem working with intelligence officers," Isidor said. "They notice too much."

Ben asked for the nature of the man's interest in him, and Isidor shrugged.

"Nothing specific. It might be too late for us to kill the Zionist-Nazi deal, but perhaps we can expose their treachery and find another way to remove Hitler," he said with a wink.

Isidor's wink instilled in Ben a kindred sense of destiny, making him feel more a part of something larger, as though they had worked together for a worthy cause for years. How fitting that their paths had crossed despite the differences in their ages, politics, and lifestyles, and that events were unfolding as they were.

Isidor grinned and slapped Ben's shoulder. "Let's see how my talk with him goes, then we can discuss it further," he said, then stood. "I'm going to check on the crew. Feel free to join me...Jacques," he added with another grin and then ambled off, using his hands along the way to steady himself.

"Hey," Ben hollered to Isidor when he reached the staircase. "Thanks for confiding in me."

"My dear friend, look at us," Isidor said, gesturing with outstretched arms at their surroundings. "We're in the same boat."

CHAPTER TEN

They met at a pub on Campden Hill Road in West London and found an isolated table in a large garden in the rear, cloistered behind ivy-covered walls. Over English lamb chops and ale, Isidor thanked Sir William for the warning of the Nazi's arrest warrant and told him that his escape from Germany was uneventful. Sir William did not inquire whether Isidor's *asset* had come with him to England.

Next, they discussed the political campaign Isidor had been working on to defeat the Nazi-Zionist deal on the floor of the Zionist Congress being held in Prague at the end of August, now only two months away. The campaign between rival Zionist parties had become extremely bitter. The leader of the ruling Labor Party was assassinated ten days earlier and his party was calling for murder charges to be filed against the leader of the Revisionist Union. The Labor Party had negotiated the deal with Hitler and was pushing for its passage. The Revisionist Union opposed the deal and was campaigning for the Congress to vote it down. All other differences between the two parties had merged into this one issue: deal or no deal, and the Zionist Congress had become the final battleground.

"Mr. Franks, do you believe the Revisionists assassinated Chaim Arlosoroff?" Sir William asked, referring to the Labor Party leader. "Not that it matters much at this point. Criminal charges alone may prove to be sufficient to undo the Revisionists and spoil our campaign to defeat the deal, but I'm curious as to your thoughts on the matter."

Isidor dug into his gravy-covered, roasted root vegetables. "No."

"Then whom do you suspect? I'm dying to hear."

Isidor looked him straight in the eye. "The British crossed my mind."

Surprisingly, a sparkle appeared in the Englishman's bluish-gray eyes. "Oh, please, do explain."

"I know the British like to rule their colonies with the Roman policy of *divide et impera* (divide and rule)," Isidor said. "Arlosoroff's attempt at coexistence with the Arabs conflicts with that policy."

Sir William, who had broken into an amused grin when Isidor mentioned the Roman policy, now feigned outrage. "I'm offended by your accusation."

"You should be ashamed."

Sir William laughed. "On the other hand, if I am to criticize the Zionists for making a deal with the Nazis, I suppose it is only fair for me to grant you the right to criticize the Crown, which is, to put a fine point on it, the proper target of your censure."

Now it was Sir William's turn to explain himself. Isidor gave him time.

Sir William stuffed his mouth with a forkful of meat, then shoved his unfinished plate away and reached for his glass of ale. He glanced from side to side and scooted his chair closer to the table.

"What we are up against in Palestine," Sir William said, "is not much different than what we are up against in Germany. Indeed, the same forces are behind both. Allow me to explain.

"Jack Philby and Ibn Saud, for instance." He was referring to the King of Saudi Arabia. Isidor's knowledge of Jack Philby was limited, but he had the two men connected. Philby had tried to broker a deal with the Zionists to have unlimited Jewish immigration to Palestine if Palestine was allowed to come under Saudi domination. That deal blew up when it was leaked to the press.

"Jack Philby is Saud's confidential adviser. He used to be an agent for SIS until he was fired a few years ago. He ran the SIS station in Transjordan beginning in 1921, but double-crossed us by backing Saud in his conquest of the land we now call Saudi Arabia. Saud is the leader of the fanatical Wahhabi branch of Islam. Enter Amin al-Husseini, a Wahhabi follower. Saud funds Husseini.

"Enter Allen Dulles. Philby and Dulles met in the Middle East the same year you and I met at Trinity College, in 1922. Dulles worked in the Diplomatic Corps in America's State Department, stationed in Constantinople at the time. You might recall that he was one of the representatives for Wall Street interests at Versailles, negotiating the treaty at the end of the world war, prior to that."

Sir William checked his surroundings again and leaned in, his arms and elbows spread on the table. "We believe that Dulles recruited Philby at that time. In 1926, with military secrets provided him by Philby, Ibn Saud completed his military victories and established his kingdom. Philby became his confidential adviser, while still on the payroll of SIS, mind you. We assumed that he would use his connection to advance British interests, so we overlooked his transgressions. Meanwhile, Allen Dulles returned to Washington and became the State Department's Division Chief for Near East Affairs. In 1926, he left the State Department and joined his brother John Foster at the Wall Street law firm of Sullivan & Cromwell. Philby converted to Islam and began brokering deals for Saudi oil, receiving commissions on each deal he arranged."

Isidor finished his plate without taking his eyes off Sir William, fully engrossed.

"Through Dulles and, unknown to us, Philby brought in American oil money, Standard Oil of California, and brokered a deal with Saud for all of Saudi Arabia's oil production, forming the Arabian-American Oil Company, Aramco as they call it. The devious bastard continued to negotiate with the British Petroleum Company for Saudi oil after Aramco already owned it.

"During that period, Dulles began establishing international cartels on behalf of Sullivan & Cromwell clients and funneling huge blocks of capital into Germany, depressing the American capital markets in the hope of reaping huge profits during the planned rearmament and subsequent rise of the German economy.

"I touched on these findings during our meeting at Cambridge. Socal, by which I mean Standard Oil of California, hired Philby who remains the King's confidential adviser. Both Philby and Dulles stand to reap millions off the Saudi oil deal.

"We fired Philby, which only means that we stopped paying him a salary and officially declared him to be a traitor. He still has access to many of his acquaintances inside SIS and, in some respects, it appears as though he never left the agency."

"Why don't you stop that?" Isidor said.

"It isn't as though we haven't tried," Sir William said. "Besides, sometimes it is more profitable to allow a spy to operate and monitor him than it is to shut him down."

Isidor bobbed his head, unconvinced but willing to move on.

"So where was I?" Sir William asked. "Oh yes. Philby is the one who orchestrated the appointment of Amin al-Husseini," the Palestinian Arab nationalist and Muslim leader who actively opposed Zionism. "Somewhere between him and Dulles they are profiting off the sales of arms to both al-Husseini and the Haganah," the underground Jewish military.

"In other words, they are funding both sides of the conflict, the Arabs *and* the Jews. It's a splendid racket if you can pull it off, don't you see? So, naturally, a person like Chaim Arlosoroff, who sought peaceful coexistence with the Arabs, would be very bad for business."

"You think Philby and Dulles were behind his assassination?" Isidor asked.

"I'm not sure how it works out precisely, but my point is that we have to go down this track in order to find the correct answer. There is nothing wrong with your perceptions, but when you see those policies in play, one side being pitted against the other, whether it is with political parties, factions within a country, or between countries, know that one or more people who profit by the conflict are hidden in the background somewhere keeping the conflict alive.

"You see, Mr. Franks, the basic problem is who controls the military and its intelligence apparatus: the duly constituted government run by elected representatives, or private interests such as this financial oligarchy, the City of London and its Wall Street cousin? At Cambridge, I told you that the Bank of England and Wall Street financed Hitler and his Nazi Party. We know that. With that intelligence we were able to predict their rise and take steps to prevent them from attaining their objectives. We made splendid progress, I must say, with the worldwide boycott of German goods and all that. And then from out of nowhere came this deal between the Nazis and the Zionists. It was a complete surprise. We had a working relationship with the Zionists and thought everything was under control.

"Due to your splendid intelligence, we were able to re-group and quickly mount a counterintelligence plan to kill the deal at the Zionist Congress. Then Arlosoroff was assassinated and the fellow we are supporting gets charged and convicted for his murder in the Jewish Press before Arlosoroff's blood had even dried.

"The primary role of intelligence is to predict future events in order to take preemptive action and prevent the occurrence of situations that might harm the organization it serves. We failed to predict these harmful events because we lacked intelligence from the right places. We assume that the financial backers of Hitler are somehow behind these events, not only the deal with the Zionists, but also the assassination of Arlosoroff and the framing of the Revisionist Zionists. We also assume there is a network somewhere...that there are links among these financial interests to the Zionists and Nazis. If our assumptions are correct, all three connect somehow to each other and to these events.

"We must find the links."

Isidor saw this coming back in Cambridge. Sir William had designs on using him as an agent inside Zionist headquarters in London. An agenda that once troubled him no longer did now that he was better informed and believed he understood its purpose.

"You appear to include me in your future plans," Isidor said.

"Mr. Franks, I believe we share a common goal or two and none in opposition, don't you agree?"

Isidor nodded. "We do. It's your agency and government I'm concerned about."

"And I about yours, but then we repeat ourselves," Sir William said. "Please permit me an opportunity to satisfy your specific concerns."

"How did you learn that the Nazis planned to arrest me?" Isidor said.

"We have a friend or two within different echelons of the Nazi Party who routinely provide us with reports about Nazi activities directed against anti-German agitators, and I saw your name on one of the reports."

"Do these *friends* know about my relationship with British Intelligence?" Isidor asked.

"Not from us," Sir William said. "You see, our request for information is quite general. We informed them of our interest in information related to internal dissent for the ostensible purposes of, one, possibly assisting the agitators or complementing their actions, and two, assessing the priorities of Nazi police activities."

"How many names were on the list?" Isidor said.

"Twenty-six." Sir William said.

"May I see the list of names?" Isidor asked.

Sir William smiled. "Mr. Franks, I happen to have that list with me." He reached for a briefcase at his feet and set it on his lap. From it, he took out a sheet of paper and slid it across the table.

Isidor couldn't focus on list of names. Something else on the sheet grabbed his attention and struck him like a lightning bolt of betrayal. The list was on German Zionist Federation letterhead.

He had the distinct feeling of coming to after having been unconscious: gradually his perceptions returned. When he looked up, Sir William was sitting with his arms on the table, emotionless. Isidor then remembered he was about to read the names on the list. He glanced back at it and everything came into focus, including Ben's name.

"As I was saying," Sir William said, "I believe we share a common goal or two."

Chapter Eleven

Isidor arrived on time, and Ben ushered him into the sitting room of his new home, a brick duplex in the City of Westminster section of West London. Ben's travel bags and all his worldly goods covered two sofas and practically filled the room. They had arrived the week before and had been carted in and stacked where they now lay.

"In my bedroom," Ben said. "Follow me." He guided Isidor toward the back of the house.

"What do you think of the place?" Isidor said.

"I like it. You have good taste."

Isidor snorted. "Now I'm broke. It's the only thing I could find that suited our purpose. A little privacy and a long view of the street in either direction. Did you see the garden in back?"

Ben said he had, and that he liked it as well, adding: "It's peaceful."

"It's got the high walls so I can access the property through the back without people from the street or your neighbors seeing me," Isidor said.

"Except for the neighbors beside us," Ben said, in reference to the unit on the other side of a common wall, and which shared the garden. Known in England as a "semi-detached house," the street had rows of them on both sides.

"I bought the whole thing," Isidor said. "They will be moving out soon, and I'm not concerned with replacing them."

They reached a bedroom and Ben pointed to a dresser. "There it is."

The room was sparsely furnished with a bed, a desk and chair, two lamp stands and lamps in addition to the dresser. The beds were made, but there was nothing on the walls and none of the little things that make a room look lived in.

"Good. Let's see what you've done," Isidor said when he spotted the letter. He rested an elbow on the dresser and began reading in German:

"Dear David, I have changed my plans. I decided to stay in London and postpone my trip to New York indefinitely. I have applied for a British visa and cannot make permanent plans until it has been approved. You can correspond to me at the address given below."

Isidor's voice trailed off and he continued reading silently, nodding his head occasionally. When he finished, he looked up and said, "Perfect. I'll mail it. I'll also get a rumor started in Munich that you are living in London. Tell it confidentially to a few select people I can depend on to tell only *someone they really trust*."

Ben laughed, and Isidor joined in. "They all have two or three, eh?" Isidor said.

"Yes, that's true," Ben said.

"But I'll personally sneak into Munich and see David during my trip to the Zionist Congress in August, as I promised you."

Ben thanked him.

Isidor reached inside his jacket. "Here's your boarding pass. The *Mauritania*. It's a luxury liner. You'll like this boat." Ben grinned, thinking of the boat they took from Hamburg to Hull, England. Isidor continued, "As you can see, it's not in your real name. It departs Southampton in four days. I have a ride scheduled to pick you up the day before the ship departs, and a hotel room in Southampton reserved for that evening. It's in another name as well. I will encrypt all that and drop it in the letter box in the next day or two. You can practice your code."

Ben nodded. "Okay."

Isidor pulled a large, folded envelope out of an inner jacket pocket, and handed it to Ben. "Guard this with your life until you've memorized it, then burn it."

Ben nodded in agreement. He knew what was inside; they had already discussed the code and how they would communicate with each other.

"The mailing address will be easy to memorize, but I would still practice writing it out a number of times before you burn it, just in case. The code will take a lot of practice to remember. It's like learning a different language. Err on the side of holding onto the code too long."

Isidor wagged his finger. "Just don't let it lie around, or else..." and he swiped the tip of his finger across his throat.

"Understood," Ben said.

"Meanwhile, make your face known around here over the next few days. Take some walks; visit the local pubs, that sort of thing. Keep it low key. Don't overdo it. Remember your cover story."

"I remember," Ben said.

"Tell it to me."

"I'm a writer. I work odd hours and often travel for my research. I'm thinking about buying a country cottage where I can split my time."

"Good," Isidor said. "And I'll get you back here every once in a while so you can show your face."

Isidor reached out and gave Ben a big hug. "Shalom, my friend."

"Shalom," Isidor said, returning the hug.

CHAPTER TWELVE

David spied Isidor across the wide boulevard as he was opening the door of the darkened store, and signaled for him to cross over. It was only then that Isidor knew for sure that he was at the right place. The storefront was completely different from the one he had seen the day he and Ben fled Munich almost three months earlier. Even the name had been changed. "Maximilian Clothiers," a sign now read. The ignominious yellow dot had been replaced by a red poster: "Recognized German-Christian Enterprise."

Isidor first made a security check, then nodded. David slipped back inside. He then pulled the brim of his hat down and raised the left side of his jacket with his arm, shielding his face from a cold, wind-driven mist that blew viciously, unobstructed and almost horizontally down the boulevard. The odd weather condition known as an *Alpenstau,* had preceded him to Munich by just a few hours.

Safely inside, David ushered him back to the office through the still-dark store, assuring Isidor in soft tones that Michael was home, completely unaware of his visit, and that there was absolutely no chance that he or anyone else would appear.

David turned on a light after he had closed the office door, and Isidor asked about the remodeled store-front. David explained that he had sold a majority share of the business to a German national for a nominal amount of cash. In return he had given up a small percentage of the profits but no real control.

"A German Christian?" Isidor said, drawing attention to the sign in the window.

"It's better than a swastika."

Isidor got David's point: Many German businesses displayed a Swastika on their storefronts in an effort to clarify their loyalties.

The changes had been worth it, David reported enthusiastically. He told Isidor that he had netted more profit during the month of August than he had during any of the prior "Hitler months." Isidor regarded both the news and David's demeanor with dismay, which prompted him to end the small talk and get down to business.

"I came into Germany at considerable risk with a message from Ben that can only be relayed to you in person. Let me deliver it and be on my way."

"Is he okay?" David said, with an alarmed look.

"He's fine," Isidor said, and then swore David to secrecy before continuing.

"He's in New York, going to school, just as he had originally planned. The London address is a facade meant for his protection, in case the Nazis pursue him. We want people in Germany to think he lives in London but Ben wants you to know the truth."

David asked a few questions, which Isidor answered within the framework of the cover story he had fabricated, without disclosing the true purpose of the ruse. David seemed to find his explanation satisfactory and agreed to cooperate fully.

"Ben also wanted me to ask you to leave Germany," Isidor said. "Actually, he was more insistent than that. He made me promise to use my *full weight* on you. As you can see, that would be gruesome, so I suggest you yield."

Isidor laughed with David, but only for a moment. "I've just come from Prague where I attended the Zionist Congress. Have you heard anything about the Transfer Agreement?" he asked, mentioning the name given to the Zionist-Nazi deal, and reaching inside his jacket.

David said that German newspapers had carried the story a couple of weeks ago and that he had read about it. Isidor pulled some papers from inside his jacket and handed them to David.

"Here's a copy of the actual agreement in German. You can keep it."

"I heard from other sources that it was not finalized," David said while accepting the papers. He immediately set them aside.

"You are misinformed, my friend. It was signed by both parties on August 28 and is being implemented as we speak."

David looked befuddled. "I heard that an action committee was established to review it further and that the World Jewish Conference, which just met in Geneva, passed a resolution to condemn *any* trade agreements with the Reich and to create a committee to coordinate the worldwide boycott. You're saying that's not true?"

"Actually, I came here from Geneva. I went there from Prague. There was an action committee established at Prague, that part is true. It did not convene, though, due to the lack of a quorum. Not enough people showed up. It will never convene. As for the Geneva resolution, that is also true. It was proposed, anyway. But the final wording omitted the creation of a committee. Rabbi Wise backed down."

Rabbi Stephen Wise was the honorary president of the American Jewish Congress and a staunch proponent of the boycott of Nazi Germany. Wise organized the Madison Square Garden protest that Minister Göring had tried to stop.

David sighed. "I was hoping for a better outcome, but thank you for the news. I'm disappointed, but not inclined to leave Germany. This business is my life."

"Your *life* will be worth a lot more in London or New York," Isidor said.

"I'm not so sure. The feeling among people I know, including German nationals, is that Hitler won't last the winter. It may be too late to stop the boycott. This deal may backfire on the Zionists; it is very unpopular to the vast majority of Jews."

"As I said, I have come to you at great risk. I took the risk only because you are the brother and a loved one of someone who is very dear to me. Ben wants you and Michael to leave Germany while it is not too late. That's my message."

"Don't you feel that Jews and decent people in the rest of the world will continue the boycott in spite of this deal?" David said.

"When I was in Geneva, while Dr. Wise spoke against commercial relations with Hitler's Germany, the Reich and the Jewish Agency were busy finalizing negotiations on all matters of business, not just oranges, which you may have heard about, but also steelworks, cement factories, irrigation systems, printing presses, medical facilities, the list goes on and on. A momentum has been created by organized forces on both sides that will run its course irrespective of the will and best efforts of individuals."

David looked away, apparently wrestling with his dilemma. Isidor sat silently. He glanced at his watch and decided he could spare a little more time.

"If I sell the business," David said, "I can't transfer my assets to London or New York and ..."

"I can," Isidor interjected.

David kept talking, as though he hadn't heard. "I don't want to go to Palestine, especially now, if my assets would be used to buy German goods under this agreement," he said, motioning with disgust to the papers Isidor had given him. "I wouldn't do that as a matter of principal, even if I could force myself to go there." He paused. "Wait, you can do that? Legally?"

"Legally?" Isidor said. "I follow a higher power than Hitler, my friend. Of course it'd be legal. I wouldn't have it any other way."

David laughed, and Isidor checked his watch again. His time had run out.

"Here's my recommendation: Do as I did. Transfer your assets out of Germany and plan to emigrate in case things don't work out the way you'd like them to. Apply for a visa to England or America, or both. Maybe I can help push them through on my end. If Hitler doesn't survive the winter as you hope, what have you lost? Nothing."

David nodded, but remained noncommittal.

"Let me know what you decide," Isidor said, as he rose from his chair. "I've got a schedule to keep."

David rose as well.

"To get mail to me," Isidor said, "just address it to Ben at the London address and mark a small 'x' anywhere on the envelope. If it has an 'x' on it, I'll know it's for me. Otherwise, I'll forward it to Ben without opening it."

David thanked him for delivering Ben's message and for his generous offer and then doused the office light and led Isidor to the back of the store. David opened the door for him, and Isidor groaned.

Before him, in near total blackness, was the foreboding, howling wind and slashing mist. He pulled his coat over his ears, took a deep breath, and plunged into it.

PART II

May 1938 - May 1939

CHAPTER ONE

Papers strewn before him, Ben held a pencil over a notepad. Once again, his attention had drifted to Germany. Worry over the plight of his brothers turned into something approaching paranoia. They had been shot escaping. Isidor, too. Despair gripped him. No, that was impossible. Isidor was too resourceful, too well connected, too clever. He was the Houdini of espionage. People like Izzy didn't get caught or killed. If someone didn't tip him off at the last second, and he were arrested and clutched tightly in their grasp, he would simply evaporate. Poof! A bit of glee accompanied that absurd image. Ben snatched himself back to reality. He was not in Germany. He was in New York, sitting at a table in Columbia University's Butler Library, trying to get some work done, but obviously failing. He grimaced and tossed the pencil down.

He strummed his fingers and looked around. No one was staring at him. A library assistant was nearest him, sitting at an information desk, quietly engrossed in her work. Students ambled through the stacks to his left and studied at tables ahead of and behind him. A couple strolled down the aisle whispering and smiling to each other.

He grabbed the telegram from beneath the notepad and re-read his decoding of it:

May 19, 1938. Soviet papers en route to Berlin. Every reason to believe they will be allowed to emigrate within days. No need to go to Germany. Besides, the borders are sealed. Would be almost impossible. Please be patient. Top people are working on this. Everyone is doing their best.

Soviet papers were required before Germany would allow them to travel since they were Soviet citizens. Germany would release them to the Soviet Union, and from there they planned to emigrate to Britain. But their Soviet papers had not arrived.

Ben was angry with himself for not having done more to get them out earlier. What could have been carried out with ease in 1933 became very difficult in 1936, dangerous in 1937, and "almost impossible," according to Isidor, in 1938. Ben was also angry with David for not selling the business sooner. He and Michael had obtained British visas in 1934, but David wanted to wait for a more opportune time to sell. They found a buyer in 1937, but soon after, before David had transferred all of his assets to London, mail service between Germany and England was cut off, severing communications with him.

Finally, a breakthrough occurred earlier in 1938. The Reich issued an expulsion decree for a large number of Soviet Jews inside Germany. David and Michael's names were designated for expulsion. The only snag: they still needed their Soviet entry permits. Twice the date of expulsion had been extended to accommodate the Soviet bureaucracy, which was exceedingly inefficient. Additionally, helping Jews was not high on the Soviet agenda. Pressure had been brought to bear on the Soviet machine from every conceivable source: Jewish Resistance, the SIS, family connections inside the Soviet Union, and Mr. Schuessler, David's German lawyer.

Ben crumpled the cable and stuffed it into his pants pocket, then put his elbows on the table, clutching his head with both hands, wondering what he could possibly do to find some inner peace and get something done. He had classes to prepare for. He had tried working in his office. That hadn't worked. He had gone for a stroll through Morningside Park, but never reached the park. Now even the relative silence of the library was no help. He considered target practice, but figured he might turn the gun on himself. At least he still had a sense of humor.

He found himself absently tapping the pencil on his notepad. He flipped it in the air and sat back in his chair. Trying to work was pointless until he heard that David and Michael were on the train bound for the Soviet Union. At least his final exam questions were prepared and all he had to do was monitor his students. The introductory lectures for his fall literature classes...forget about it. He would have to wing them. He had volunteered to give them, anyway; he hadn't been asked and wasn't being paid.

His attention somehow drifted to the library assistant's desk and he gradually focused on a figure standing in front of the desk, a girl. Just seeing her face brought him a hint of peace. When he fully realized the effect she was having on him, lifting him from his doldrums if only for a moment, he exhaled deeply and a smile involuntarily crossed his face. He sat up straight and then, with little awareness of his actions, reached for the pencil and began tapping it again. The sensation he felt was new and uplifting. He stared at her, intrigued and curious.

She was brunette with shoulder-length hair swept back on the sides, and sparkling blue eyes. She had a look that was intelligent and acutely aware of her surroundings, yet somehow playful, as though she didn't take herself too seriously. She was certainly pretty. But Ben had known many pretty girls, so it wasn't that alone. And there were plenty of bright young people on this campus. There was something down-to-earth, approachable about her.

Her dress was simple, even plain, but its rust-colored fabric perfectly complemented her hair and skin tones. Her appeal was undeniable, but he couldn't really explain it, which intrigued him all the more.

He knew he wanted to know more about her. Was she a student? Obviously. But where? Here, or at Barnard, the women's college nearby?

He started searching clumsily for some way to approach her before she could slip away. But he also found himself suddenly shy and a bit confused, which was also a new condition.

Then he heard her address the assistant, holding two books in her arms. "I wonder if you can help me?" she asked, with a sweet southern accent. "I want to read one of these books. Which one would you recommend?"

The librarian took the books from her, and Ben craned his neck to see their titles. "Let's see. That one's supposed to be decent. I haven't read it, but I've heard ..." and she stopped and turned toward Ben. The girl's attention followed.

"You should ask him. He teaches Russian literature. He would know."

For the first time in his life Ben blushed as the girl flashed him a big grin.

"Oh, really?" she said. Her gaze shifted from Ben to the papers on the desk in front of him, and back, as though asking whether he minded the intrusion.

Ben smiled back and stood quickly. "I'd be happy to help. Let me see what you've got." He reached for the books as the assistant librarian pushed them at the girl. She handed them to Ben.

They were two of his favorites, *The Brothers Karamazov* and *Anna Karenina*. He was on solid ground.

"Is this for class, or..."

"No, just for pleasure. Something I read recently about Russia sparked my interest. Maybe I'll take a course in Russian literature next year if I read a couple of books in the meantime and like them."

"I see." He earnestly considered the two books and passed back *The Brothers Karamazov*.

"This one will bore you for the first half of the book if you don't have some knowledge of Russian culture. It's a great book, though...*in Russian*. This translation's not that good."

She brightened, looking impressed.

"Now this one, *Anna Karenina*, I highly recommend. Great book. Excellent translation, too."

Ben glanced at the assistant who gave him a dubious look before walking off. Fortunately for Ben, the girl didn't notice.

She accepted the book gratefully.

"Thank you very much. This is perfect. I never thought of checking...I mean...I guess you know the language." She opened the cover.

"Yes. I grew up there."

"Oh, really? That's really interesting." She had half her attention on the book. "Oh, there it is. Translated by Benjamin Komorosky."

"What's your name?" Ben asked.

"Marsha. Marsha Thomas. I'm from Rocky Mount, Virginia. I go to Barnard. What's yours?"

"Ben. Ben Komorosky."

She did a little double take, and an amused grin took shape and a glint appeared in her now-inquiring eyes. He confessed with a sheepish shrug, and she shook her head, playfully reproaching him. "*Excellent* translation, huh?"

"I could be biased, of course."

She giggled and he laughed with her, perhaps too loudly. He furtively checked as she put a hand to her mouth. As he suspected, they had the attention of a few students close by.

"Would you like to get a soda?" Ben whispered. "I could use a break."

She hesitated and then nodded, and Ben reached for his blue blazer, which was draped over the back of his chair. He was wearing a shirt unbuttoned at the top and a loosened red-and-blue silk tie.

They agreed to walk to a café in her residence hall and talked animatedly on the way. She was a junior, an education major. She had initially planned to teach elementary school in her hometown but an anthropology course she had taken the previous year caused her to have second thoughts and take some more courses outside her major, which would extend her stay at Barnard a full semester.

"So, you have another three semesters to go?" Ben asked.

"Um-hmm. That is, if I don't take any more courses outside my major. Maybe I should put Anna Karenina back," she joked.

She asked how long he had been teaching at Columbia and Ben told her he had taught some as a graduate student but began teaching full time after he received his doctorate two years ago – in Russian literature and translation. He was now teaching courses in both subjects.

She asked where he had done his undergraduate studies.

"At the Sorbonne, a university in Paris."

"Oh," she said, and asked if he also spoke French. He said he did, learned it as a child.

After they were seated in a corner of the sparsely-populated café and had ordered drinks, she asked if he would say something in French.

He fumbled for a moment, then rattled off the first thing that came to his mind. She asked him what it meant and he replied. "I asked if you have ever gone into a room and felt your spirits lifted without knowing why, then realized it was a beautiful bouquet of flowers that did it."

She lowered her eyes, as if picking up on the reference to his spotting her in the library, and she seemed put off by it. That gave him some insight into her earlier reaction, the hesitation when he asked her to join him for a soft drink and the distancing he thought he had sensed when he told her he had a doctorate and had studied in Paris. He figured she was intimidated by his age and accomplishments – or maybe thought him pretentious – and wondered why she had taken him up on his offer.

He also noticed that he really cared what she thought, another first for him.

She raised her lashes, a thin smile on her face.

He wondered if he should apologize or let it pass, re-examining his own intentions. He was interested in getting to know her and now saw as a bad habit a romantic trick he had developed after arriving in America, where, to his surprise, he found that women were enthralled with the French language. He had only meant to emphasize his French background to deflect attention from the German portion of his eclectic accent. After a year or so, the foreign accent in his English had dissipated enough that he no longer needed to rely on French – or Russian – as a cover. Now his use of French was purely recreational. Flirting and French were great allies, although he hadn't consciously meant to flirt with Marsha.

"The only foreign language I ever studied was German," she said. "My grandmother was German and I had to take a foreign language, so I took that one. I don't remember much about it, though. Do you know German?"

The waitress arrived with their drinks. Ben used the distraction as an excuse not to answer. He searched for a new topic but she barged ahead the moment the waitress left.

"Do you speak any other languages besides Russian and French? And English, of course."

"Norwegian."

"Norwegian? What led you to learn that language?"

"Actually, there are two forms of Norwegian. I speak one of them, it's called Book Norwegian. I learned it because I have a cousin who moved there from Russia and I spent two summers with him when I was a teenager."

"Oh. Why didn't you just speak Russian?"

"Because I wanted to learn a different language. I liked the idea of learning a language I had never heard before."

"That's why I studied German for two semesters, but I still didn't learn it," Marsha said. "I mean, I remember some words, but that's about it."

"You can't learn to speak a foreign language at school. I tried learning English that way and it doesn't work. They have you conjugate verbs and all kinds of things you aren't ready for. Babies learn a language without even knowing what a verb is, let alone its different forms."

Marsha eyes bulged. "Wow. That's so true, and German has three different words for the word *the*. One is masculine, one is feminine, and one is neutral. They use a different one for different nouns, without any rhyme or reason to it. I nearly went crazy studying it."

Ben knew only too well but didn't let it show.

"So, tell me. How do you learn a foreign language? Your English is really good, by the way. I can't even tell you're from a foreign country."

Ben thanked her and then explained his method. He learned the sounds of the alphabet and basic words for numbers, verbs, nouns, prepositions, and the articles, just enough to get by on a preschool level, and then by going to a place where the language is used, and speaking, hearing, and reading it, exclusively.

"It took me three weeks to learn enough Norwegian to understand someone and get my point across. I built upon that base, just the way a child naturally learns a language. I learned to conjugate verbs, and everything else, in time. Actually, I haven't really mastered that language, but then, some of my students haven't mastered English, either."

Marsha clung to every word, which both baffled and intrigued him. None of his past experiences or rules applied to this woman.

Never had a woman he'd been attracted to been truly interested in his pursuits. Some female students had feigned interest, but their interest in him had been apparent. He wondered whether she knew the effect she had on him or how attractive he found her. It seemed not.

"I learned to read and write English in college," he said. "Mainly through literature. I learned to speak and understand the spoken language in college, but not well. I really only learned to speak it by following the Yankees."

Marsha's face lit up. "Do you know baseball?" he asked.

"Of course, everybody in America knows about baseball and the Yankees."

"Have you ever been to a game at Yankee Stadium?"

"No," she said.

"I'll have to take you some time."

"Perhaps." A guarded look returned to her face. "Please finish your story. I'm fascinated by it and you left me hanging. I can't imagine how you learned to speak English by going to a baseball game."

"Well, you see, I lived in a hotel in the Bronx near Yankee stadium when I first arrived in America. And I noticed that everyone talked about the Yankees. So I went to a game in order to understand what they were all talking about. One of the first things I heard at a game was someone hollering out: 'Whad'ya mean, ya' bum?'

Marsha laughed.

"You won't find that in a text book," Ben said. "*Ain't* is another word you won't find. 'He ain't got a lick o' sense.' A man sitting next to me said that about one of the players who had made a bad play. Actually, I didn't even know a good play from a bad play, but I heard the crowd groan, and he spoke in a hostile tone. 'He ain't got a lick o' sense,'" Ben imitated the man's voice. "I knew the word *ain't* from a Mark Twain book. 'Lick' was a new one for me, but I figured it out. I said to him, 'He is a bum,' and from that moment forward the guy treated me like I knew all about the game and I was his best friend."

Giggling throughout, Marsha was fascinated.

"It was helping me learn the culture and idioms so much that I went to a lot of games, and began listening to games on the radio, too. Wherever I went, I could easily start a conversation talking about the Yankees. I paid close attention to the way people spoke, the words and phrases they used, their accents. I learned more about speaking English in a month that way than I did in all my classes at the Sorbonne."

"That makes perfect sense to me." She paused, a gleam in her eye. "Perfect sense, which of course is way more than a lick," which caused Ben to laugh heartily.

"That's what I want to do some day," Marsha said dreamily. "Learn a foreign language and then travel where they speak it. But I'll probably end up teaching elementary school in Rocky Mount and never get the chance."

"No, that's not true. Not if you don't give up on your dream."

She shrugged, smiling. "Right now, I just want to learn about other places through books, like this one," she said, tapping *Anna Karenina*. "After listening to you talk about learning languages, I can tell that you're a good teacher and I bet I'd learn a lot if I took one of your classes."

"You can sit in on my class anytime, if you want. Right now, we're studying Chekhov, who, by the way, I highly recommend. He's my favorite Russian writer. Next semester, I have a class on three works by Tolstoy: *Anna Karenina, War & Peace...* "

"*War & Peace*! I saw that book. It's fifteen hundred pages long. It would take me all semester just to read it – if that's all I did."

"The class is for students who read it over the summer, or have read it before. I give introductory classes on each of the books at the end of the spring semester...beginning tomorrow, in fact, to orient students to the books. They read them over the summer and we study them in the fall. But you're welcome to sit in."

"I might just do that." She glanced at her watch and gasped. "Oh my God, it's been over an hour and I've taken you from your work. I feel so bad." She reached for her purse.

Ben reached out his hand, and she pulled away.

"The truth is, I'm not on a break," Ben said. "I took the day off and have plenty of time to spare."

She cocked her head.

"No, really. It's true. I was in a jam...a mental block you might say, and I had just decided to take the day off when I saw you." As he recalled his "mental block," he realized that he hadn't once thought about the situation with David and Michael since he first saw her.

"Maybe we can go for a walk. If you'd like, I'll even take you to dinner tonight." The moment the words left his lips, he tried to reel them back in, holding up his hand, prepared to apologize profusely.

Her facial muscles instantly tightened. Like a dam ready to burst, she finally did.

"Do you pursue all your students?"

Rather than act defensively, or apologize, he opted for another tactic.

"No, not the males," he said, with as straight a face as he could muster.

She threw her head back and put both her palms on the table, as though she were ready to bolt. Ben thrust a hand on hers. "I'm joking. I've never pursued any of my students, not even the females."

She relaxed her grip and eased back into her seat. "I'm a female student."

"Not mine, you're not."

"You invited me to take one of your classes, and...," softening further, "and I was thinking about doing it."

Ben quickly mulled over the situation.

"Alright. Maybe I was *pursuing* you. I don't know. I wasn't conscious of it, but I can see from your perspective how it came across that way. Let me explain something. When I saw you in the library...forget about the bouquet of flowers, but the truth is you brightened my day. You see, I've been going through a lot of personal...stress ..."

"Oh," she said with a sympathetic frown. "I saw that your papers were all mussed up."

"More than my papers were mussed up." He was thinking of his mental state.

"If it's personal, don't tell me. I don't want to pry."

"It is personal and I won't go into it except to say that I have been troubled lately and I was in that condition when I saw you. You're very pretty in case you don't know it, and something else about you grabbed my attention ...."

"What was that?" she said meekly.

"I don't know exactly, but, you know, I'm trying to explain something that I haven't quite figured out. So stop interrupting me," he said playfully.

"Okay. I'll just listen."

"Good. Now, as I was saying...you took my mind off my trouble. And I guess it was just my nature that I tried to charm you...a little bit. Believe me, I've pursued before and this was nothing. I've had my face slapped. More than once."

"I believe that."

"I thought you were going to just listen."

"I'm sorry. I will now."

Ben looked at her, grinned, and shook his head incredulously. She tried to suppress a laugh, but failed, and he broke up, too. Then he composed himself and started over. "What I'm trying to say is, if you don't want to be *pursued*, that's fine with me. Now that I know it, I'll mind my manners, but I've enjoyed meeting you and spending time with you. I was just thinking a little while ago that an hour had gone by without me being troubled by...the things that were...troubling me. We seem to have a mutual interest in a few subjects. We can leave it at that. You probably wouldn't like my baseball friends, anyway. They curse and smoke ..."

Marsha laughed. "They sound like my daddy and his friends." After a pause, she said, "Oops," and put her hand to her mouth. "Were you done?"

"I'm done now."

"Okay, may I say something in response?"

"Please do."

"Do you promise not to interrupt?"

Ben chuckled; she laughed, too. He found her laugh incredibly attractive.

"I enjoyed my time with you, too, and I would like to be friends on the terms you mentioned. You're older than me. You've been all over the world. And I can tell you're, well, experienced with women, if I can be straight about it. And I don't have a problem with that. I'm just not interested in being one of them." She paused. "Now that I've said that, I also want to thank you because I can see that you accept me for who I am and aren't offended by my ways."

"No, I'm not offended. Not at all."

"I'm ready for that walk now," she said. "Is it possible we can walk to Morningside Park and you give me your introduction to *Anna Karenina*?"

"I'd love to do that."

CHAPTER TWO

"Do you have a moment?" Eli Traynor said to Isidor through a partially open door. Traynor was a recent addition to the Zionist Executive staff, the director of a new section called Intelligence & Special Task, with offices in the basement. He had a professional, well-heeled look, with unique features: a cleft chin, square jaw and dark complexion with silver hair, thick black brows, and a salt-and-pepper Hitler style moustache. Each hair was trimmed and brushed.

Sir William had asked Isidor to find out what he was doing there, so of course he had a moment. He invited Traynor in.

Isidor's office was small and in the back of the Zionist headquarters. It had one window, one guest chair, one wooden filing cabinet, and one plant in a corner. A green glow radiated from a banker's lamp, its yellow rays splashing onto papers spread out on the desk. The morning sun illuminated the rest of the office. He switched off the lamp and rotated his chair to face Traynor, who had taken the guest chair.

Isidor was Director of European Jewish Resistance. He was appointed to the position in 1935, when Dr. Chaim Weizmann became president. Prior to that, Isidor had been active in the Jewish Resistance, doing basically the same thing without an office and the bureaucracy around him.

"I'm working on something rather sensitive," Traynor said. "It mustn't go beyond these walls, not even to Dr. Weizmann."

"Most of what I do doesn't go beyond these walls," Isidor said. "Some of it doesn't even make it inside."

Traynor choked back a laugh. An arched brow signaled that they spoke the same language. "We need Jewish men who have experience or skills in urban warfare," he said. "Resistance fighting. Courageous young men who are committed to our cause and have a bit of a chip on their shoulders."

"I have plenty of them," Isidor said.

"Good. I need names, qualifications, contact information and ..."

Isidor cut him off. "They work for me. I can't turn them over without the proper introductions or assurances."

"As I said, the project is quite sensitive."

"So are my contacts," Isidor said.

Traynor cleared his throat, nonplused. It seemed as though he was used to getting his way and struggled to maintain his composure in the face of disagreement. Traynor's weakness was Isidor's strength; he held his position without the slightest concern over pleasing or turning away the man.

Traynor's resistance melted. "You've heard of the Special Night Squads in Palestine?"

Isidor nodded. The squads either defended Jews or terrorized Arabs in Palestine, depending on one's perspective. "We're expanding the program."

"You need men to go to Palestine?" Isidor said.

"Not necessarily."

Isidor waited for an elaboration that did not come. He calculated his next move, and then switched on the banker's lamp. He picked up his pen and tore out the sheet of paper beneath the one on which he had been writing. He scooted the pad out of his way to avoid leaving impressions on paper beneath it.

"What qualifications are you looking for?"

Isidor took down Traynor's answer verbatim:

Young, single, multi-lingual – ideally one of the European languages – fighting expertise of some kind, explosives, night combat, and sniper skills.

* * *

Later that day, Isidor pushed an entrance buzzer beside the double doors that led to Traynor's office, carrying a manila envelope.

A male voice he didn't recognize asked for his name and the nature of his business. Isidor gave his name and said he had something specially requested by Eli Traynor to deliver.

He heard a click on the door and wondered what had just happened. He ventured to turn the door handle, and it opened. He went inside. The male receptionist asked him to sign-in, handing him a clipboard. The form asked for a name, times of arrival and departure, and the name of the person being visited. He filled it out and returned the clipboard.

The receptionist then had him take a seat, indicating a sofa and two chairs across from his desk. The entire area was small, perhaps twelve-by-eight, with bare walls except for a keyed double steel door opposite the entrance. A ceiling fan stirred the air. The level of security was beyond anything Isidor had ever seen. Even the president's office was more accessible.

After only a few minutes, one of the steel doors opened, and Traynor emerged, the thick door closing behind him with a thud. Isidor held up the envelope.

"You should have called," Traynor said. "I would have come to you."

Isidor handed him the envelope. "I've never been down here and wanted to see it," he said. "Besides, I can use the exercise," and he patted his ample torso with both hands.

"Well then, let me give you a tour."

Traynor took him down a wide hallway and pointed out offices along the way. They reached another double-steel door on the left side of the hall that Traynor said led to the central filing room.

He unlocked the door using a key he selected from a set of keys he pulled from his pocket, and ushered Isidor inside.

The room was huge, filled with rows of steel filing cabinets and two large work tables. A clipboard sat on an unmanned desk beside the door. "Files have to be checked out to leave the room," Traynor said when Isidor glanced at the sheet.

They ended up back in Traynor's office, which was twice the size of Isidor's. A fan in one corner of the room hummed. It was furnished with a desk and chair; a credenza with pictures of a woman and children on top and shelves extending over it; two guest chairs, an unoccupied secretarial desk with a typewriter on top, and a row of four steel cabinets next to the credenza butting up against the far wall. The filing cabinets were different from those in the central filing room in only one respect: a heavy padlock secured a vertical metal bar that blocked access to all four drawers on each cabinet.

Traynor tossed the envelope Isidor had given him on his desk. "Have a seat. Let's get to know each other. I have a feeling we're going to be doing a lot of work together."

* * *

Isidor hopped off a bus in the City of Westminster and stepped into a telephone box. He was anxious to schedule a meeting with Sir William. He called a number and hung up when the call was answered. He immediately called back, hung up again, and left the box. He walked north on Seventon Street, heading in the general direction of Ben's London home. In addition to taking Sir William's call there, in exactly one hour – Sir William was always precisely on time – he wanted to check the mail.

Isidor never took the same route to the house or came at the same time of day. The one constant was the length of his approach: two streets minimum, unless it was raining. He liked to survey the traffic near the house, both pedestrian and vehicular. On this day, he zigzagged his way to the house, going up one street, turning down another.

He was one and a half blocks from the house when he saw two men seated in a black sedan parked on the opposite side of the street, about five houses south of Ben's.

The closer he got to the car, the more he was convinced that they were on a stakeout. He was not close enough to make out the men's features, and didn't want to get that close out of concern that they might recognize him. But he did note that both men appeared to be dressed in dark suits and hats. He couldn't make out the number on the vehicle's registration.

Isidor turned right at the next corner, aborting his planned approach. He would enter the house through the back garden.

Inside, he rushed upstairs and grabbed a pair of binoculars and peered through a curtain. He wrote down the registration number.

Only then did he concern himself with the mail, and go downstairs. There were three letters scattered on the floor beneath the letter box. He picked them up. All three were from Ben. He sighed, and began opening them.

As usual the telephone rang precisely one hour after Isidor had signaled Sir William that he needed to talk. "I have news," Isidor said. They agreed to meet that night.

"One other thing," Isidor said. "We have visitors...An automobile." After a pause: "Yes, I wrote it down. I'll bring it with me."

* * *

"Eli Traynor worked in SIS as an intelligence officer in Palestine for General Orde Wingate," Sir William said, referring to the British Army officer who trained the *Haganah*, the Jewish paramilitary organization. "He's Canadian, and went to law school at Cambridge."

The horn of a barge sounded, followed by the caw of a seagull and the flapping of wings. Isidor and Sir William were sitting alone on the patio of a pub on the bank of the river Thames, drinking ale after having eaten a late supper inside. A thick fog under a night sky obstructed their view of the river. Sir William was holding a pocket notepad in one hand, a pen and his glass of ale in the other.

He referred to his notes, then said, "Sounds like they intend to train saboteurs and send them into Germany, don't you think?" He frowned. "Too bad we didn't have a chance to discuss this before you gave him your list of names."

"He won't find anyone on that list until they want to be found, and they don't want to be found until I clear it with them. Sooner or later Traynor will figure out that if he wants my men, he'll have to go through me."

A large grin crept onto Sir William's face. "Good show, Mr. Franks."

After taking a long draft of ale, he asked Isidor for the layout of Eli's office while it was fresh in his mind, saying he wanted to send a team inside, pick the file cabinet locks, and photograph the contents. "I'd like to know what-all our boy is up to."

"I'm ahead of you, my friend," Isidor said, pulling a folded piece of paper from his coat pocket. He unfolded what was obviously a detailed diagram of the office. As Sir William reached for it, Isidor withdrew it and returned it to his pocket.

Sir William twisted his face. "I promise to proceed with caution, if that's your concern. I shall hold off for an appropriate period of time and first make a dry run or two."

"I want to talk about Ben, first," Isidor said. "He's writing daily about his brothers. I got three more letters today."

"You told him about the Soviet papers, right? Surely he can wait a blasted week."

"He's all-consumed by the delays," Isidor said. "He's been let down too many times and is now talking about coming here and doing something himself."

Sir William blurted out a laugh. "That's ridiculous. There's nothing he can do."

"True, but he's a loose cannon in his current state."

"What do you propose we do, Mr. Franks?"

"I have in mind a joint operation using my Jewish Resistance resources and yours to spring them next week if the Soviet papers don't arrive or they aren't released for some reason."

Sir William's jaw dropped. "Are you mad?"

"Perhaps," Isidor said.

Sir William rolled his eyes, exasperated. "For one thing I would have to run it by C," he said after calming down. C was the code name for the head of SIS.

"I'm sure you can persuade C that the value of gaining access to Traynor's intelligence files outweighs the risks and costs involved," Isidor said, patting his coat pocket.

Sir William gasped. "This is bloody extortion, Mr. Franks."

Isidor smiled. "I call it a working relationship."

CHAPTER THREE

David was just finishing up with a customer when he heard the man's voice. "Are you David Komorosky?" He looked up and saw a tall, lanky man addressing Hans Brenner, who was the store's new manager and co-owner, a young red-haired man.

"No, he's with a customer. May I assist you?"

"I was recommended to David Komorosky," the man said, looking around. His eyes landed on David.

"I'm David Komorosky," he said. "I'll be with you in a moment. Please look around."

The man nodded, "Thank you, I will."

David joined the man in the suit section against the far wall. He was inspecting the inventory hanging on a rack of woolen suits.

"Are you looking for a woolen suit?" David said as they neared the rack.

"Wool would be fine," the man said. He rubbed the fabric of a dark blue suit between finger and thumb. With his head down, his eyes scanned the showroom floor. "You have very nice clothes here."

"Yes we do, thank you. The finest in Munich, we believe. That's very nice Italian wool..." David cut himself short. "Who recommended me to you?"

"Isidor Franks."

"Oh, really," David said, as he recovered from his initial shock. "I haven't seen him in many years. That suit would look very nice on you. Would you like to see?"

"Perhaps." He pulled back the jacket and inspected its lining. In his hand was a folded piece of paper. He glanced at David, as though wanting to ensure he saw the note, and then slipped it inside the left pocket of the suit. "Your instructions. We leave tonight."

David felt a rush. "Excuse me."

"I'm taking you and Michael out of Germany tonight."

David was dumbstruck.

The man shifted his hand to another suit, a light charcoal wool blend. He lifted it off the rack and held it high. "I like this one. What size is it?"

David's mind was on the man's earlier comment. He muttered something before composing himself. "What size are you?" he said as he stepped back to get an overview of the man. "Ninety-four, correct?"

"Yes," the man said, arching his brows, impressed.

"I've been doing this for a long time." David took the suit. "Let me show you the same suit in your size." He replaced the one suit with another one.

Just as he handed the man the suit, a commotion broke out in the front of the store. David turned to see a Nazi police van screech to a halt in front of the store. Three SS officers stormed out of the vehicle, reminiscent of when the SS came looking for Ben. Except this time, David knew they were coming for him and Michael.

The man next to David reached into the pocket of the dark blue suit, extracted the instructions, and crammed them down the front of his trousers.

The SS officers burst through the door. Two of the men held pistols. Everyone froze. The lead officer, a burly man, announced in a booming voice to no one in particular, "We're here to arrest David and Michael Komorosky."

David stepped forward, as Hans headed toward the back of the store. "I'm David Komorosky."

"Stop!" hollered the officer at Hans. The armed officers instantly whipped their guns in his direction. Their willingness to shoot was unmistakably etched in their faces. "Where are you going?"

Hans stopped. A deep voice sounded from the back door. "Excuse me, officers. Why are you disrupting my business in this manner? Surely the guns and shouting aren't necessary." His name was Max Bechting, a middle-aged, heavy-set, balding man.

"Who are you?" The office said.

"I'm the principal owner, a Christian German and a war veteran. What's this all about?"

"We have orders to arrest David and Michael Komorosky."

Bechting spoke calmly. "They are here," he pointed them out, "unarmed and willing to cooperate fully. Do you have to use guns and scare my customers?"

The lead officer instructed his men to put away their weapons. As soon as they did so, a customer who had been viewing swatches at a table in the center of the store, a round-faced, middle-aged man, stepped forward, clutching his hat in both hands at the waist. "May I be excused, sir."

The officer waved his hand brusquely. "Go."

The customer with Michael in the center back of the store also asked for permission to leave, which was granted. "Another time," he said to Bechting. The only remaining customer in the store was the man there to rescue David and Michael. He had his back to the officers, his head buried over the rack of suits.

"What have the Komoroskys done, officer?" Bechting asked. David knew he was stalling. They had all discussed what to do in such an event.

"They are Soviet Jews who have been ordered to leave Germany."

"It's my understanding that they are awaiting their Soviet papers, but my lawyer is on the way," Bechting said. "He can explain it."

His comment drew a sharp rebuke from the officer. "My orders are to arrest them. There's nothing to explain."

"Officer, you drive my customers away. Do you also take my employees before I first replace them? Can't we do this in an orderly fashion that does not harm our own citizens? My lawyer is in touch with Moscow, and...well, here he is now."

Schuessler entered the store carrying a satchel. Bechting introduced him to the Nazi officer in charge, who identified himself as Lieutenant Dohring.

"Herr Schuessler, as I have told your client I have orders to arrest two of his employees."

"Yes, yes. I understand, Lieutenant. But there is an administrative error. I have been in touch with Werner Best, Deputy Chief of the Security Police, regarding this matter. The Komoroskys are awaiting their Soviet entry permits that will allow them to leave. The permits were sent from Moscow last week, but apparently got lost in the mail. Duplicates have been issued and are being delivered by courier whose train is presently en route. I have papers verifying all this." He opened his satchel. "You don't need to arrest them."

The officer clenched his jaw and drew an impatient breath.

Schuessler presented the papers. The Lieutenant looked down his nose at them for a moment and then snatched them, and looked them over.

"Well now, that explains it. Your affidavit is dated the twenty-seventh." He shoved the papers back at Schuessler. "My orders are dated the twenty-eighth."

"I understand, Lieutenant. All I'm asking is that you first phone Herr Best. He is personally aware..."

The Lieutenant's patience was exhausted. "Herr Schuessler, my orders come from Reinhard Heydrich, the Chief of the Security Police. Herr Best cannot countermand his orders and I won't waste my time with such nonsense."

To his men, he shouted: "Arrest them!"

The two soldiers sprang into action. "Besides, Herr Schuessler, based on what you're saying they will be released in two days."

The soldiers took David and Michael by their arms, and began pushing and shoving them toward the door. David gestured his appreciation to Schuessler on his way by.

"Lieutenant Dohring, please, I beg of you, may I speak with someone?" Schuessler said as he scrambled toward the officer.

The officer stopped short of passing through the door, and turned to Schuessler. "Yes, you may. They will be taken to the Dachau concentration camp. You may speak with the camp commandant." He then spun on his heels and stormed out the door.

Running through the door after him, Schuessler said, "What about their belongings?"

"They will be provided all they need," the Lieutenant said, without looking back.

CHAPTER FOUR

A gentle tapping on the door stirred Ben. Groggy from sleep, he raised his head, not yet fully aware of what had awakened him. He saw the coded telegram lying on the desk and felt the wetness of his sleeve. His memory of the morning flashed into view. He rubbed the residue of tears from his eyes and shook his head, trying to clear away the fog. Wondering how long he had slept, he glanced at his watch. Ten thirty-five. He heard the doorknob turn, and snatched the message. The door opened slightly, then abruptly closed.

"Who's there?" He stuffed the message into a pants pocket.

The door opened wide this time and Marsha's beaming face appeared. "It's me."

With words on her lips, she abruptly held up. The grin disappeared, replaced by a look of surprise. Her gaze drifted to his shirt sleeve, then her soft eyes fell upon his. Her expression of sympathy pleased and comforted him and for a brief moment he yearned to embrace her and share his grief.

"I must have dozed off," he said.

"Someone said that you were still here, but I...if this is a bad time, I can ..."

"No, please." He gestured to the wooden chairs in front of his desk. His office was small, with full bookshelves behind his chair and framed pictures on the wall with his degrees from the Sorbonne and Columbia on one wall.

Two open windows brought in the smell of freshly mown grass and the sound of a bird chirping. His hat and blazer hung on a hat rack in a corner.

"I just wanted to stop by to tell you how much I enjoyed your introductory class on *War and Peace* before I go home for the summer," she said, sitting on the edge of the chair closest to the door.

"You certainly inspired me to read the book. I mean, I *really* want to read it now, and I will, too, as soon as I finish your book." She corrected herself, "*Anna Karenina*, I mean."

Ben noticed his morale rising as he listened to her.

He thanked her. "I saw you in class and wondered where you ran off to. I was hoping for a chance to say hello."

"Oh, I had to run. I barely fit it in with my final exams. You know what it's like to be a student this time of year. And your book is so interesting. I read all of Part One and had to force myself to put it down so I could study. I can't wait to get on the train so I can read it straight through."

She looked around the room and her eyes settled on the artworks. "That's Russian isn't it?"

"Yes. That's Michael's Castle in St. Petersburg – now Leningrad – my hometown and the portrait is Count Tolstoy when he was young."

"Oh. He's handsome. And the other one?"

"A painting by Sergey Gerasimov."

She looked at him compassionately. "Would you like to get a soda or go for a walk?"

"Yes." Ben jumped to his feet. "I need to get out of this office." He had the idea that Marsha knew he had been grieving and was going out of her way to cheer him up.

They decided to reprise their initial meeting, go to the café and then for a walk, but this time to go in the opposite direction once they got to Morningside Drive. On the way to the café they chatted about the class.

"Everyone I heard talk about them really likes your classes."

"Oh, really? That's good to hear. None of the girls complained about me pursuing them, did they?"

"Uh-uh. None of the boys, either." She flashed a mischievous grin.

Ben laughed. "See, I told you."

"I did hear some of the girls saying things that suggest your task would not be too difficult if you put your mind to it."

"You didn't by chance get any names, did you?"

Marsha gasped in mock disgust.

At the café, Marsha spoke admiringly about Ben's translation, telling him about a discussion she had with another student over the Russian names of the characters and the title of the book. "You explain it so well in your introductory notes that I was able to correct her and explain to her why it is Anna Karenina in Russian but should be translated to Mrs. Karenin, or Anna Karenin, in English. I gave her your name as an example. Tell me if I'm right. If you got married in Russia, say you married Jane Doe, her name would become Jane Komoroskaya, right?"

"That's correct."

"But if you moved to America, after you married her, her name would be Jane Komorosky, just like if you had married her here, right?"

"Exactly."

"And I'm glad you went over all the nicknames for *War and Peace*, so I'll know that when I come across the name Natalie the author is talking about the character he introduced as Natasha. Or Masha for Maria. A samovar is a kind of tea kettle, a troika is a carriage drawn by three horses, and Christmas mummers dress up in costumes and sing or perform sketches for their neighbors. Those are the sort of things I want to learn and I might have missed without your help. It's lucky I ran into you. Otherwise, I probably would have missed out on a lot of what I wanted to learn."

"One of the early American translations of *Anna Karenina*," Ben said, "which should be titled *Anna Karenin* to begin with, has Anna telling her lover that she is "beremenna." The translator gives a reader the impression that Anna has some strange disease or something. Actually, it is the Russian word for–"

Ben cut himself short, realizing that she hadn't read that far into the book. "Sorry. I don't want to ruin it for you."

"Oh, but you've already let the cat out of the bag. Now I want to know what beremm ..." She botched the word badly and started laughing. "See, I can't even say it."

Ben repeated the word and helped her pronounce it, then asked her what she thought it meant.

"It sounds awful, like...like a bad dream. If I was reading it, though, I would think about the context. I assume that she and the Prince will become lovers, so what does a woman tell her lover? Oh no! She's pregnant!"

"Well, that wasn't so tough," Ben said. "Perhaps I should stop criticizing the translator."

"Women will get it easier than men," she said. Ben nodded in agreement.

"But your criticism is valid," she said. "A translator should translate and not mince words."

After sodas, they strolled along Morningside Drive by the Hudson River. They talked about Russian books and Russian culture. Only once did their conversation veer into anything personal. It occurred when Ben asked her what she planned to do over the summer.

"Work as a secretary in a lawyer's office."

"Is that what you do every summer?"

"No. The lawyer's secretary is *beremenna*," she said with a glint in her eye. Ben laughed. "How did I do that time? It sounded pretty good to me."

"Much better."

"She's married, though, so it's okay. Lucky for me, she has her babies in the summer. This will be the second time I've replaced her since coming to Barnard, and that job pays better than anything else in town."

"Do you pay for your own schooling?"

"I pay for everything. My own room and board, tuition... You name it, I pay for it."

"With a summer job?"

"No, I have a small trust fund. My daddy left it for me when he died. That's how I met the lawyer I work for. My daddy had a lawyer, imagine that. I sure didn't know it. Neither did mother."

"What about your mother?"

Her smile suddenly faded. "What about her?"

Ben shrugged, not wishing to push it. He was on thin ice as it was, aware that asking her personal questions entitled her to delve into his background. He hadn't intended to ask about her family to begin with, and was searching for another subject when she answered.

"I moved out several years ago. I rent a room with an elderly widow who has been really lonely since her husband died. She likes my company and I like making her life a little better."

Ben looked at her expecting more, but it didn't come.

"What about you? Did your family help you through school? It must be awfully expensive to study and live abroad."

"My two older brothers paid for my education. All of it – expenses, everything. I worked in the family store when I wasn't going to school in Paris." He wondered – too late – whether she was familiar with the nationalization of businesses in the Soviet Union; a family store in Russia was a thing of the past. His father's clothing store and small factory had been taken away under Lenin's War Communism policy, returned in 1921, and retaken in 1928 under Stalin's first five-year plan, and is what drove Adam and David to Germany. Luckily, it appeared to have gone over her head.

"I've already paid them back with the money I've made from my job and the translation. It's a nice feeling to be financially independent of your family, isn't it?"

"Yes," she said. "It sure is."

She then said that she had to get back to her room so that she could study for her remaining final exam later that afternoon, and they returned to the Barnard campus. Ben asked her when she planned to leave for Rocky Mount.

"Tomorrow. I need to pack my things after the exam because some of the girls are having a going away party tonight and I want to go."

"So I guess I'll see you next fall, maybe in my class." Ben fumbled for words, uncertain how he should part with her.

"Yes, I definitely will attend your class. Oh, that reminds me. I wanted to ask you for a huge favor, if you don't mind. That's why I stopped by your office and here we've spent all this time together and I almost forgot to ask you."

"Please. Ask away."

"I thought of writing you in case I had any questions about the books I'm reading. Would you mind terribly if I did that?"

"No, not at all. I'd enjoy it, actually."

CHAPTER FIVE

After breakfast, David and Michael lined up for roll call with the other prisoners. They were dressed in gray-and-blue-striped denim trousers held up by suspenders over their own shirts. The prison uniforms included a striped shirt, but since they weren't required to wear them most prisoners didn't. Their prison number was on a white rectangular patch that was stitched into their right pant legs. The prison guard called out numbers, not names, and gave out the day's work assignment.

Except for the first day of indoctrination, David and Michael had been assigned each day to a detail in the porcelain factory adjacent to the camp.

When their numbers were called, they answered up.

"Return to your barracks and await further orders," the guard said. A nervous twinge jarred David's nervous system. He stole a glance at Michael to his left and saw a repressed jubilation. David also sensed encouragement from the prisoners around him who, in a variety of gestures, silently congratulated them.

Afraid of the effect on Michael of letdown after false hopes were raised, David elbowed him and scowled. The glee on Michael's face was replaced by an annoyance.

They were escorted to their barracks where they waited under guard for nearly an hour. Another guard arrived. He checked the prisoners' numbers on their denims against a sheet of paper he held in his hand. Satisfied, he released the barracks guard.

"Follow me," he said to them.

"Where are you taking us, sir?" David asked.

"To the gatehouse. Quickly." He marched off.

Michael gloated. David knew he had reason to be encouraged. Every prisoner goes to the gatehouse before their release. Not only had they been told that by the other prisoners but they had witnessed it.

The timing was right as well. The courier with their Soviet entry papers should have arrived two days after their arrest. This was their seventh day. Taking into account the red tape involved, another five days was about right. In spite of the positive signs, David was determined to keep Michael's enthusiasm in check. If they were released, there would be plenty of time to celebrate.

As they marched across the compound, the gravel crunching beneath their feet, Michael leaned into David with his buoyant face.

"We're going home."

"No," David shot back. "We're going to the gatehouse."

At that moment David spotted a German soldier peering down at them over the sights of a machine gun in the tower atop the gatehouse. "Don't look now, but the guard in the tower has his gun pointed at us," David whispered.

Moments later Michael glanced up, and wiped the glee off his face.

The white, two-storied gatehouse, with its red roof, black tower above and black wrought-iron gate below, was surrounded by dark green trees. Under a deep blue sky, the Dachau prison was actually sort of picturesque. David noted the irony. Although, if indeed they were about to be released, it had not been that bad. Beyond their shaved heads – hair which would grow back – they were physically no worse off than when they had arrived. They had been well fed, were reasonably well-rested, and, though the hours had been long, not abusively overworked.

David recalled the bleak image of his first view of the gatehouse, from the admitting side of the building, and his first sighting of the gate's ominous sign, *"Work Brings Freedom."* The possibility of freedom, he discovered, had caused him to completely forget the degradation of their communal quarters, the limited sleeping space and bathroom facilities, and the humiliation to which they had been subjected: the roll calls, the marches to and from work and to and from meals, the dehumanizing reference to each prisoner by numbers instead of names, and the guards' arrogant, demeaning attitude toward them by the guards, who regarded the Jewish prisoners as filth and beings who must be tolerated.

And freedom to where? To the Soviet Union, at least temporarily. What he formerly viewed as an intolerable place to live had become his dreamland. He laughed at the irony.

They reached the gate, and a guard on the other side opened the pedestrian portion of the gate for them to pass and released the guard who had escorted them there.

The gate guard ushered them toward the gatehouse where David's attention was grabbed by the sound of a speeding vehicle approaching the gatehouse from outside the camp. He and Michael simultaneously spun. Soldiers rushed toward the gate while a limousine bearing little Nazi flags on the front fenders came to an abrupt halt. The guard behind David rammed the broadside of a rifle into his back, knocking him forward and off-balance. He winced in pain.

The guard shoved the two of them inside the gatehouse and into a small room with only a work desk and three wooden chairs. Atop the desk were two boxes marked with their inmate numbers, apparently containing their personal belongings. Michael snuck David a triumphant grin. The guard shoved his rifle against Michael and ordered them both to sit.

A minute later, the door flew open and two SS officers strode into the room. The guard snapped to attention and saluted. He then filed out of the room and closed the door behind him. Both officers were very intimidating. One was the Camp Commandant Hans Loritz, a young, thick-jawed, fire-breathing man. His very presence made David shiver. All the Jews in the prison instantly hated and feared him. David didn't recognize the other man. He was middle-aged, with gray hair at his temples and a stern, serious demeanor. Clearly he was in charge. Loritz stood behind him, holding two files in crossed hands.

The man in charge glared at David and Michael, as if insulted by their very presence, shifting from one to the other, back and forth, for almost a minute without saying a word. Loritz gently rocked on his heels silently with a smirk on his face.

The senior officer then reached inside his uniform jacket and pulled out some folded papers and approached David. Towering over him, he shoved the papers in front of his face and ordered him to look at them. They were newspaper articles. David's fingers trembled as he unfolded one. A chill shot through his body when he recognized an English-language article written by A.D.S. Rosenberg, the pen name initially used by Ben, where A. D. S stood for Alfred Das Schwein (Alfred the Pig), a parody of the Nazi official and former editor of the anti-Semitic *Racial Observer*.

David sifted through the articles, buying time, and decided to claim ignorance of the language just when the officer shouted, "They are articles written by your brother." He then yanked the articles from David's hands, and leaned into David.

"Tell me. Do I look like a pig?" he shouted. David trembled as he realized the man was Alfred Rosenberg.

"Ben stopped writing a long time ago, Herr Rosenberg," he said.

"Of course. Under that name." Practically on top of David, Rosenberg spoke through gritted teeth, sputtering. "Where is he now?"

"He was in London, the last I knew."

"Why do you think that?"

"I corresponded for years to his London address," David said.

Rosenberg asked for the address, and David said he didn't remember it by heart, only that it was in London.

"Do either of you know a Jew by the name of Isidor Franks?"

Michael and David exchanged glances then nodded in unison.

"How would you describe his relationship with your brother?"

David shrugged. "I'm not sure they had one."

Rosenberg turned to Michael, who nodded.

"Do you speak?" Rosenberg shouted.

Michael cleared his throat and sat taller in his chair. "Yes, sir. I don't know of any relationship between them, either."

David interjected, "Everyone knows Herr Franks. He has that kind of a personality."

Rosenberg took a step closer and glared at David. "Let me make myself clear. Your brother has engaged in intelligence activities against the Reich on behalf of a foreign government which is treason, and for that he can be put to death. Anyone who aids or comforts him or helps hide his activities or current whereabouts will suffer the same fate. Or worse."

Rosenberg stepped back, snapped his fingers, and pointed at the file folders Loritz was holding. Loritz extracted some papers from the folder and handed them to Rosenberg.

While his back was turned, David looked at Michael and saw him nervously fidgeting with the edge of his chair, his lips quivering. In hope of easing the tension, David spoke:

"Herr Rosenberg, there must be some mistake. Ben was a college student. Like a lot of people his age, he was young and idealistic when he wrote those articles. He had just graduated from the Sorbonne in Paris and planned to spend only a few months in Munich before going to America to finish his studies..."

As David spoke, Rosenberg slowly revolved on his heels, his head curiously tilted, with a wry, half smile on his face. David's voice trailed off. His attention had drifted onto the papers in Rosenberg's hands. They bore the marks of official Soviet documents.

Rosenberg's eyes followed David's stare to the documents.

They locked eyes and Rosenberg gloated. "Oh, don't let me interrupt you. These are just your Soviet entry papers. They are of no value to you unless and until we find your brother and you were saying something about him going to America to study."

"I was just saying that I don't think he's a threat to the Reich," David said.

"Did he go to America to study?" Rosenberg, said.

"I thought he went to London," David said.

"What do you think?" Rosenberg snapped at Michael.

Michael stiffened, then shook his head and replied softly. "No."

"No, what?" Rosenberg hollered, causing Michael to cringe. "No, you don't think? Or, no, he didn't go to America?"

"I don't think he went to America," Michael said.

"Yet he applied for and obtained a visa to America." Rosenberg spoke satirically, in a singsong voice, and began to pace in front of them. "In his application he offered evidence of his admission to a university in New York, Columbia University. He also purchased a ticket for a liner from Hamburg to New York. He never boarded the liner. Just to be safe, we also checked with the school and discovered that he never attended the university. Not in 1933, the year for which he had applied, and not in any subsequent year."

David became puzzled and fought to keep a straight face.

"Now, why would a person go to all that trouble and not follow through?"

David shrugged. Rosenberg turned to Michael. "Huh? Why is that?"

When Michael also shrugged, Rosenberg jumped in his face and screamed: "Why did he do that?"

Michael shook his head and mouthed the words, "I don't know."

Rosenberg composed himself, then resumed speaking in the singsong manner. "Because he's a spy and that's what spies do. They build covers and misdirect people into thinking they did something else or went somewhere else."

He paused, as though wanting his message to sink in and then leisurely strolled to the boxes sitting on the desk. He swept a hand over them.

"These are your personal belongings." He displayed the Soviet papers for their view. "These are your Soviet papers. An automobile is standing by outside ready to transport you to the train station. All that remains is your cooperation with me, with the Reich.

"Our job is to look past all the smoke and mirrors and determine where this spy against the German people is currently located. Your freedom depends on it. Your very lives may even depend on it."

He moved closer and stared, first into David's eyes, then into Michael's. He spoke softly and intently, speaking alternately to one brother and then the other.

"I'm going to leave you two alone for ten minutes. Think about it. Put your heads together. Decide what is more important to you: your freedom or the freedom of an enemy of the Reich? Do something noble for German people, and for your own people, who suffer because of the acts of a handful of anti-German agitators. Show me that you deserve your freedom."

He rose and straightened the jacket of his uniform with a tug. "When I return, I want straight answers. I won't waste my time with any more of your evasive nonsense."

He motioned to Loritz, and they left the room.

Michael turned to David, his eyes on the verge of tears. "You were right; we were only going to the gatehouse."

David put his hand on Michael's shoulder. He knew he possibly held the key to their freedom – that is, if Rosenberg could be trusted and the opportunity to be released really existed. He considered telling Michael the truth, but decided against it. For one thing, Rosenberg might be listening in: The whole exercise seemed to have been staged. For another, the decision was not Michael's to make. David was the one entrusted with the information.

"I should have sent you back to Moscow with Adam," he said.

Michael sat up straight. "You? It was my decision. Remember?"

David reached out and put his hand around Michael's head, pulled it to him, and kissed his forehead. "Be strong, Michael."

"I will."

When Rosenberg and Loritz returned, David said: "We have already told you everything we know. Michael added, "We don't know where he is."

Rosenberg's face tightened, then he abruptly spun on his heels and addressed Loritz: "Put their papers away. Classify them as political prisoners and treat them as such. Call me if they come to their senses and decide to cooperate."

With that, he marched out of the room.

CHAPTER SIX

Isidor walked through a forest outside Dover, England, looking for a one-story thatched cottage. Tucked away among giant fir, redwood, and swamp cypress, the thatch-roofed, red-brick dwelling was still not visible after a quarter-mile trek off the country lane on which his driver had let him out.

Dimly lit and cool under nature's umbrella, it felt like an autumn evening rather than the warm summer day it was beyond the forest; the midday sun was completely obscured. All he heard was the gentle chatter of birds and his crunching footsteps. He enjoyed the stroll, which calmed him and gave him an opportunity to reflect.

His curiosity had been building ever since he received Sir William's phone call three days ago. He had vital news to deliver at a new clandestine rendezvous. The location and directions for reaching it were passed separately through an encrypted message dropped at a time and spot previously designated for circumstances requiring extreme security.

Isidor had taken considerable precautions in covering his tracks and reaching the spot, having traveled to Dover, then to Calais, France and back to Dover, conducting a bit of business with the Jewish Resistance as he went. No one at Zionist headquarters ever questioned Isidor's need to handle his affairs secretively; it had been part of the terms of his affiliation. They also knew that tailing him in those circumstances was dangerous; that Isidor's men were on orders to shoot first and ask questions later.

At last, the cottage came into view. There was no sign of Sir William, or anyone for that matter. The two windows of the cottage were dark, their curtains drawn. Only when Isidor was fully upon the cottage did he spot the rear end of Sir William's silver and black Austin.

Inside, Sir William took him to a back room that was lit by a single candle that rested on a wooden table. The table was flanked by two arm chairs. The remaining space was mostly filled by a single-sized bed, the top third of which was snugly enclosed by narrow chests of drawers on each side with a shelf above it. A white embroidered skirt and a folded-back blue and white checked throw covered the bed. The walls were paneled in darkly stained wood. The floor was a lighter hardwood with two non-matching patterned rugs that helped give the room a cozy warmth.

Sir William picked up a notepad from the table and motioned for Isidor to take a seat. "Perhaps we should get started." After they were seated, he said, "Well, Mr. Franks, you have done it again. Your diagram led us to the mother lode. I will cover it all in due course. I want to start and end with Ben, however. When does our boy arrive in London?"

"In three days."

"Splendid," Sir William said. "That gives us time to warn him that his life is in danger."

Sir William explained that he had traced the registration number of the automobile involved in the stakeout of Ben's London address to a Londoner who did not match the description of any of the men seen in the vehicle. He's British, but is a known Nazi sympathizer on the British Security Service's dangerous persons list.

"We have also learned that Alfred Rosenberg, who is the head of the Nazi Party's foreign office, is engaged in a campaign to locate known spies for foreign governments.

"What he has done to those persons he has found varies. We have recent reports of German agents kidnapping persons off the streets in England and America and either killing them or carting them off to a ship and taking them back to Germany for interrogation and imprisonment."

"That explains why Ben's brothers are being held as political prisoners now," Isidor said, and he gave Sir William information he had received two days earlier from a Soviet Jew who had recently been released from Dachau prison.

"The same warning could apply to you except they do not appear to be looking for you and, even if they were, you are easy to find," Sir William said.

Isidor was prepared, he assured Sir William.

"But you should warn Ben," Sir William said. "Have him arm himself, buy a gun and learn how to use it."

Isidor laughed. "I will warn him, but he knows how to use a gun. He's a European match caliber marksman."

Sir William looked intrigued. "I didn't know that." He lost himself in thought for a moment, then said, "Aha! That further confirms our analysis that Traynor's request for names for snipers with European...however he worded it, is a trap."

Isidor looked at him quizzically.

Sir William crossed out the first item on his notepad with a pencil. "I shall move on," he said. On looking up and seeing Isidor's reaction, he said, "I'm sorry, Mr. Franks. I jumped ahead. Please permit me to continue. I will clarify my remark in due course."

Isidor nodded.

"Thank you. Now, before I get into the heart of my briefing, I want to share with you some intelligence I have intentionally withheld due to security concerns." He scooted to the edge of his seat. "You have complained to me in the past about Britain's policy of appeasement with the Arabs in Palestine," referring to Britain's decision to abandon support for a plan to partition Palestine into two states, one for Arabs, one for Jews.

"Britain's recent foreign policy positions are all about oil, Mr. Franks.

"You might remember me telling you in '33, after your escape from Germany, about Jack Philby and his role as confidential adviser to King Ibn Saud, and Allen Dulles's role in bringing in Standard Oil to form Aramco to develop Saudi oil." Isidor nodded. He did. "Good, let me bring you up to date.

"I told you that Allen Dulles was running Wall Street capital into Germany, building up its military infrastructure through his law firm, Sullivan & Cromwell. Well, one of the cartels was a huge deal marrying Germany's I.G. Farben chemical conglomerate with Standard Oil of New Jersey, a Sullivan & Cromwell client. Standard gave Farben technology for the production of synthetic oil and rubber. The deal made Farben the number two shareholder of Standard Oil of New Jersey, second only to John D. Rockefeller, Jr.

"In '36, Dillon Read, a Wall Street investment bank, brought Texaco into the Saudi deal, forming Caltex, the current owner of Aramco. Two other oil companies have negotiated secret deals to ultimately merge with Aramco, Mobil Oil and Standard Oil of New Jersey, which undermined an anti-trust order by the United States Supreme Court at the turn of the century, breaking up Standard Oil, incidentally.

"In that same year, another Sullivan & Cromwell client, Schroder Bank of Germany, of which Allen Dulles is a director, merged with Rockefeller family interests to form Schroder, Rockefeller & Co. Dulles sits on its board, too. So does Edsel Ford, one of Henry's sons. All of its capital has been funneled into German cartels.

"As we speak, Germany's electrical equipment industry is merging with two major U.S. firms: International General Electric and International Telephone and Telegraph. Within a year, the entire German electrical industry will be concentrated in a few major corporations linked to an international cartel by stock ownership in those U.S. corporations. Most of Germany's war munitions are manufactured by companies owned by Swiss corporations in which capital from Wall Street and City of London banks are invested. They are reaping millions in profit and will reap millions more when war breaks out. They have structured their multinational holdings to legally make a profit from both sides in the inevitable war.

"Aramco was a huge success. Massive oil reserves were discovered in 1935. Of course, with product, a company needs markets, which brings me to the information that caused Britain to change its foreign policy and abandon the plan to partition Palestine. You might want to brace yourself."

Isidor took a deep breath.

"Aramco is concluding a deal to supply the Third Reich with a virtually unlimited supply of Saudi oil in the event of war," Sir William said. The air went out of Isidor's lungs in spite of the warning.

"Yes, I'm afraid it's true," Sir William said. "*Neutral* Saudi Arabia will ship the oil through *neutral* Spain. Jack Philby is selling Saudi Oil to clients of Allen Dulles with John Foster Dulles representing the Spanish financiers.

"The survival of our nation is at stake here. We are forced to proceed differently. We can't afford to lose access to our own oil fields in the Middle East, especially now, given the growing tensions with Japan over the availability of oil. If we are forced to defend our assets in Asia, we will need ready access to the Suez Canal.

"So Britain plans to issue and stand by policy that basically abandon's our pledge to help build a Jewish homeland.

"On the surface, yes, it's being done to appease King Saud and his Arab extremists. Privately, we remain committed to some form of partition. We want to hold a round table sometime in the fall and bring leaders of both Jews and Arabs to London. The diplomatic groundwork is in the planning stage."

Isidor was visibly distraught, as Sir William took his pad and struck a line on it with his pencil, presumably concluding another item on his briefing agenda.

"Please reserve your judgment," Sir William said, putting aside the notepad. "I have a lot more ground to cover, but I prefer some refreshment first, if you don't mind."

Isidor, too. They left their seats for the kitchen, where on a wooden table there were two bottles of wine, a loaf of bread, and cheese. Sir William reached for the wine, and Isidor, the bread and a knife.

When Sir William finished his snack, he washed his hands over a sink, pouring fresh water from a metal pitcher, and resumed his briefing. "Eli Traynor is running a secret intelligence operation out of Zionists headquarters independent of Dr. Weizmann reporting to David Ben-Gurion." Ben-Gurion was the head of the Labor Party and Chairman of the Jewish Agency in Palestine, while Weizmann was the president of the Zionist Executive. "The intelligence unit is known as the..." he paused to refer to his notes, "...Mossad Le'aliyah Bet. Bet is the letter B in English, so we're calling it the Mossad, Section B.

"With this information, we can predict that a power shift is in the works, moving Zionist leadership from London and Dr. Weizmann to Palestine and Ben-Gurion." Sir William, who was drying his hands on a towel, paused and gave his full attention to Isidor. "Obviously, you can't share that with Dr. Weizmann."

"Of course not," Isidor said.

Sir William invited Isidor to help him clear the table so he had a surface on which to present his documents. He was ready for that part of the briefing.

Sir William brought in a box of documents and his briefcase. He placed the box on the kitchen counter, his briefcase on the table. Sir William's presentation lasted several hours and included copies of fifty-one documents from Traynor's files. They revealed collaboration between Nazi intelligence and Mossad's secret Section B, with which Traynor's unit was affiliated.

Sir William also presented photographs of many of the agents named in the documents. Prominent among the Nazi agents was an officer by the name of Adolf Eichmann, who attended the 1937 Zionist Congress *incognito*. Eichmann was a member of the Jewish Section of the Nazi party's SD, the Security Service, under the leadership of Reinhard Heydrich, and the intelligence branch of the SS (Elite Guard, under the leadership of Heinrich Himmler). Eichmann's Zionist counterpart was Fievel Polkes, the commander of the *Haganah*, and a close associate of Ben-Gurion's.

"Polkes was sent on an intelligence mission in February of last year to meet with Eichmann," Sir William said. "He offered to provide intelligence to the Nazis and find sources of oil for them in the event of war, in exchange for Nazi assistance in the emigration of young, able-bodied Jews from Germany." He showed Isidor a photograph of a report from Nazi Security Service officer Franz-Albert Six detailing the Polkes-Eichmann conversations. "Six is Eichmann's superior. The report is directed to Traynor."

He paused, then added, "Apparently, Polkes came through with the oil."

With that, he cleared the table and went back to his notepad. "The point of my briefing is to show you the extent of the connections among Nazi intelligence, Traynor's unit, and Wall Street." When Isidor signaled his grasp of interconnections, Sir William crossed another item off his list. "Let's take a break. I could use some fresh air," Sir William said.

They took a stroll through the woods, off the beaten path, and discussed how to deal with Traynor should he attempt to recruit Isidor for his intelligence unit, which Sir William predicted may occur.

Upon their return to the cottage, they settled into the armchairs and Sir William resumed.

"What I am about to tell you is one of the most highly guarded secrets in the entire SIS," he said, pausing for Isidor's assurance that the secret was safe with him, before continuing.

"After learning about the flight of capital from Wall Street to Germany's military-industrial base, we set up shop in New York. Among other things, we have a special unit eavesdropping on conversations in the financial district...wiretapping. The principal objective of that office is to expose the financial support of Hitler, leak the information to the press, and instigate government investigations, that sort of thing.

"You need to understand something about American intelligence. They don't have a centralized agency run by government employees and overseen by elected officials like we do in Britain. The closest thing to a central intelligence agency is the Wall Street law firm of Sullivan & Cromwell, which is run by the Dulles brothers. Another private intelligence network is run by a consortium of Union Bank and Brown Brothers Harriman, both Wall Street banks. Union Bank is heavily involved in the laundering of Nazi money and Brown Brothers Harriman specializes in Nazi investments, being an agent for both American investment in German industries and Nazi investments in American firms. We're not sure of that network's organizational structure. Union Bank is headed by a fellow named Herbert Walker, and Brown Brothers Harriman by his son-in-law, Prescott Bush.

"Another intelligence network is run out of Rockefeller family offices in the Rockefeller Center in New York. It is closely aligned with Sullivan & Cromwell, the law firm for Rockefeller interests, although we don't understand the precise chain of command or lines of operations.

"Our intelligence operation in New York is not authorized by the American government. The reason we have not taken any steps to legitimize the operation is simple: Sullivan & Cromwell is a revolving door with the State Department. Both the Dulles brothers started out in the State Department, for example.

"We suspect this Wall Street intelligence apparatus has discovered our operation and are behind a recent spate of assassinations of our operatives. We have had five people on the ground disappear, die of mysterious circumstances, commit suicide and the like since we set up shop six months ago. We exhumed the body of a man who supposedly died of a brain hemorrhage, and discovered a bullet hole in his skull. This leads us to conclude that they have either established an assassination unit or have access to one.

"Because of its ties to this Wall Street apparatus, we further suspect that the twenty snipers fluent in European languages that Traynor's looking for are for this assassination unit, where ever it might be centered."

Sir William referred to his notepad again, then tossed it on the table. "That brings me to the last item on my agenda." He drew a deep breath and then said, "No, I think I shall first pour me another glass of wine. Would you like one, Mr. Franks?"

Sir William poured two glasses of wine and returned to his arm chair.

"Reports from the wiretaps in New York mention Ben's name." Sir William paused as Isidor raised his head. "They looked into his background and discovered his records at Columbia University had been falsified, and they suspect SIS had a hand in it." Isidor groaned. "Yes, I'm afraid it's true. What's more, Mr. Franks, the same report was found in Traynor's files."

Isidor fell back into his chair, fully comprehending the threat to his own security.

"For your safety and the security of our operation, not to mention the security of Great Britain itself, we must cut him loose."

CHAPTER SEVEN

"Here, use this while you're in London." Isidor handed Ben a semi-automatic pistol, a Walther PPK. "Careful, it's loaded."

Isidor had just returned from his visit with Sir William.

"Do you really think this is necessary?" Ben said.

"Yes, I do." Isidor told Ben that there had been incidents where German agents kidnapped their prey on city streets and either killed them or threw them on a boat to Germany.

"Why would they come after me and leave you alone?"

"I don't know," Isidor said. "I work for the Zionist Executive. Maybe the Nazis think I'm on their side now." Ben knew that the Zionists had ratted him and Isidor out to the Nazis in 1933, which was enough information for him to interpret the snide remark. Isidor had not passed on the intelligence recently given him by Sir William, and didn't plan to.

He took Ben by the shoulder and guided him toward one of the sofas in the sitting room of Ben's London home.

"Here, let me give you some news."

Ben placed the gun on the lamp stand next to the sofa as he went by it. Isidor asked Ben if he knew Peter Tripensky, a businessman in Munich. Ben said he had heard the name but didn't know him.

"He was one of the Soviet Jews ordered expelled to the Soviet Union. He, too, was imprisoned in Dachau until his Soviet entrance papers arrived." Ben straightened, fully engrossed. "Peter was released when his papers arrived. I met up with him last week in France."

"Are David and Michael okay?"

"He said they were holding up well and are healthy. That's the good news."

Ben braced himself, and Isidor reached out a comforting hand, placing it on Ben's arm. "Peter said they were not released because they are now being treated as political prisoners."

"What? Did he say why?"

"He didn't know why. They aren't talking to anyone about it. He only knows that they were told to report to the gatehouse one morning at roll call and everyone expected them to be released, but they weren't. A few days later there were red triangle patches on their prison uniforms signifying that they were political prisoners. The prison uses different colored patches to identify each class of prisoner."

Ben sighed and threw his head back. "This is a nightmare."

"You asked me why they are after you. I believe our plan for you has come back on David and Michael. Alfred Rosenberg is tracking down foreign spies against Germany in advance of their plans for war. The illusion we created of your living in London rather than going to school in America has convinced them you are engaged in espionage against them. And you are, one could say, even though you are doing nothing presently."

Ben looked thoughtful. After a few moments, he said, "Okay, I get the picture."

"We think they have given up trying to find you in London and you can expect them to show up in New York and dig deeper to find you," Isidor said. "You should prepare for that. Be on the lookout for anyone tracking you. When they came here, it was always in a nondescript car, a black car. There were always two men inside, and both wore dark-colored suits and brimmed hats. Arm yourself at all times, and don't let them subdue you or throw you into the car. These men are dangerous. Don't hesitate to defend yourself."

"Don't worry," Ben said. "I can take care of myself now that I know what's going on."

"I know you can," Isidor said. "Immediately report to me anything out of the ordinary."

"Okay. I will. "

"Now, this is important. Listen carefully," Isidor said. "We have a plan that might put their minds at ease about you, maybe change their attitude toward your brothers and ..."

Ben's spirits rose, and he cut Isidor off. "This is what I need to hear, a plan."

"I said *might*," Isidor said. "Don't get your hopes too high."

"What is it?" Ben said.

"Once we have a clear signal that you have been discovered and are being tracked in New York, we are going to start doing things differently. We come out into the open. We stop using code. We only converse about the plight of your brothers in case anyone ever opens our mail. We stop using this address. I'm even going to sell the house. We begin using our home addresses. We make them see that you are not engaged in espionage, that you are not building a cover for future activities, that you had only been trying to protect yourself."

"I like it," Ben said.

"This means your days as a spy are over. You are no longer an asset of British intelligence. Their plans for you have ended."

"That's fine by me. I only want to get my brothers out of Germany. That's all I care about now. I'm fed up with the whole thing. Even Roosevelt has betrayed us."

Isidor knew what Ben was talking about. President Roosevelt had called for an international conference to solve Europe's "Jewish problem." The conference was held earlier in the month, in Evian-les-Bains, France on Lake Geneva, in the French Alps, and became known as the Evian Conference. It quickly turned into an unmitigated disaster when countries around the world, including Britain and America, refused to increase their immigration quotas.

Isidor patted Ben's leg and began to stand up. "I have something for you on that," and he retrieved his briefcase from the other sofa. "When I was in France, I got my hands on this and brought it back for you." He handed Ben an issue of the *Volkischer Beobachter*, the Nazi newspaper that Alfred Rosenberg was once ran.

The headline in German read: "No one wants them."

"That's my point," Ben said. "The ones with the power to do something aren't doing it. The message to the Nazis is, 'Do what you will with Jews.' I just want David and Michael out of there and be done with it."

Isidor sighed, slapped Ben's leg, and began to rise. "Well, let's pray it works."

Ben jumped to his feet, and embraced Isidor. "Thank you. This gives me hope."

"You're very welcome, my friend. And if this plan doesn't work, and I get another idea, I'll let you know."

"There's something else I want to go over before you leave London," Isidor said, and he pulled a deck of cards from his shirt pocket. Ben gave him a puzzled look.

"A little card trick," Isidor said. He fanned the deck. "Here, pick a card. Look at it, but don't tell me what it is." Ben took a card and looked at it.

"Now give it to me," Isidor checked the card and put the rest of the deck away.

Ben smiled. "What kind of trick is this? You get to see the card?"

Isidor took the card with a grin. "Patience, my friend." The card was the Ace of Hearts. Isidor tore it in half and handed Ben one half. "Here, don't lose it." He stuck the other half in his pants pocket, and started toward the door.

"Grab your hat. I'll treat you at the best alehouse in England."

"Wait. What was the trick?"

"I'll explain it later," Isidor said over his shoulder.

CHAPTER EIGHT

Ben caught up with Marsha after his class let out. She was clad in a burgundy short-sleeved cotton dress that barely covered her knees, with a bow at the waist in front with a matching ribbon in her hair. Fall semester had just begun and this was the first time he had seen her.

"You look very nice," he said, after they had exchanged greetings. Smashing was more accurate, but nice worked alright, too.

She beamed, and thanked him. "I enjoyed your Tolstoy class," she said. She took him up on his offer for her to audit the class studying *War and Peace*.

"I'm glad you did. Do you have time for a walk?"

"Sure, I'll just drop off my books."

Ben had a particular route in mind, and a plan. He held off talking about the book. Instead, he asked about her summer.

"It was good," she said. "It buzzed by. Usually I get pretty bored in the summertime. Nothing much happens in Rocky Mount. I guess I had a lot going on myself, what with all the reading I did, my job and all. But I enjoyed the book... well, except for his essays, but at least you warned me about those."

"Tell me about the job," Ben said. "I've never even been in a lawyer's office. What's that like?" She took up the topic, and he held her to it all the way to her dormitory.

After she dropped off her books, Ben led her up Broadway to 120th Street, where he turned left and then right on Claremont Avenue. All the while, they talked about the book. When the place he wanted to point out was in sight, he steered the conversation to the book's customs, food and drink.

As he passed by the landmark, he interrupted the conversation and turned to point. "By the way, that's where I live."

She pulled up, turning.

"There, on the second floor," he said, pointing to the red brick building with three stories. "Those are my windows on the south side."

"Oh, that looks comfortable. I like the street."

"And that's my car." He pointed at a two-toned, red over black Pontiac coupe with white-walled tires parked against the curb, about twenty-five feet behind them. As he was looking in that direction he spotted something in the background.

"Oh," Marsha said, her voice barely registering on Ben. His attention was stuck on the black sedan that was parked about forty feet behind his car. Two men were inside, their heads turned away, as though they were looking for some house address down the street. He couldn't make out their features but could tell they were dressed in dark-colored suits and hats with brims.

When he turned back, Marsha was ahead of him. He made a final check on the men to see them still looking away and then rushed to catch up. He tapped the back of his hand against the sturdy metal of the 9 mm pistol in the small of his back under his blazer.

As he and Marsha turned right at the next street corner, Ben stole another peek. The car was gone. Not on the street, not parked somewhere else. Gone. It had either pulled into a driveway or done a U-turn and driven away. He returned his attention to Marsha and collected his thoughts. They had been talking about his class on the book, and what was it?

It finally came back to him. He was going to ask her a question. But the timing was all fouled up. Her mind was on something else. She was humming. When he paid closer attention, he liked the sound.

"What's that tune?" he asked.

"Deep Purple," she said. "Have you heard it before? It's my favorite song."

"It sounds familiar. How does it go?"

She began singing:

When the deep purple falls over sleepy garden walls
And the stars begin to twinkle in the sky —
In the mist of a memory you wander back to me
Breathing my name with a sigh.

"I have heard it," he said. Very nice. You have a pretty voice."

"Thank you."

She returned to humming the tune.

"Say, I was thinking," he said. She stopped humming and listened. "When we were talking about the book, I could tell you were really interested in Russian culture, its unique customs, dress, and food ..."

She nodded her head. "Yes, I enjoy all that. And Tolstoy gives so much detail, I feel like I'm there. Sometimes I can almost taste the food."

"I've got an idea. I could make you a traditional Russian meal."

"Oh, you cook?" she said.

"Not all the time, but yes. I specialize in Russian dishes." That wasn't exactly true, but he knew someone who did.

She smiled and bit her lower lip as her eyes drifted. She started to say something, but held back and then looked at him, a demure smile on her face. "That's tempting."

"Take your time," he said. "It's an open offer."

She placed her hand on his arm. "Thank you. Maybe after the class is over."

That let the air out of Ben's balloon. By an open offer, he didn't mean open for four months! He buried his disappointment.

"All I need is a week's notice."

* * *

Back in his apartment, Ben encrypted a report to Isidor:

Nazis agents showed up near my apartment. Same as in London. Dark car. Two men. Dark suits and hats. Disappeared soon after I spotted them. This is all. Last coded message. Last use of London address. Will let post office box expire. Hope this works.

CHAPTER NINE

Isidor left the Zionist headquarters on Russell Street at six o'clock. He had to get back to his office for a six-thirty meeting. He would either grab a quick bite to eat or guzzle down ale at a favorite pub. The decision would not be his to make. He saw the red telephone box up ahead and squinted, but he couldn't see what he was looking for. It was too dark; he was too far away. The night air was damp and cold. He picked up his pace and buttoned the top button of his winter coat. As he closed on the public phone box, the window panes on the box became more visible. He drew closer yet. And then he saw it – a brown smudge on the topmost pane. He was going to the pub.

He entered the pub, took off his hat, and placed it on the top rung of the hat rack. He approached the bar and ordered a pint of ale. He began gulping it down while he took a careful survey of the other patrons, looking for anything amiss. There wasn't. He finished his drink and left enough money for the drink and a tip. He headed toward the front door, stopped by the hat rack, and took one from a lower rung that looked just like his.

He visited the men's room. Inside a stall, he removed the hat liner. He decoded it as he read. *Londoner who owned the auto used for stakeouts: Dead. Made to appear as boating accident. Likely shot. Be alert.*

* * *

"Your people are very loyal to you," Eli Traynor said to Isidor. They were sitting in Traynor's office. "I admire that. The more I get to know you, the more I find to admire."

"I'm loyal to them. That's why they're loyal to me," Isidor said.

"Then I admire that, too," Traynor said.

"Thank you." Isidor felt his stomach growl, reminding him it was late and that he hadn't eaten. "Did any of the names I gave you work out?" He knew they hadn't. He just wanted to get to the point of the meeting. Traynor had found Isidor leaving for the night and had asked if he could have a few minutes of his time. When Isidor agreed, Traynor added that he wanted to meet in his office, citing a need for privacy.

"Not a one," Traynor said. "Each of them said they would talk to you about it and get back to me. No one got back. I'm curious whether they even spoke to you or whether they did and you discouraged them."

"I was asked what I knew about your project and I told them I didn't know any more than you had told them.   Perhaps   you   should   give   them   more information."

"I can't do that in the screening stage due to the nature of the project," Traynor said.

"The complaint I received back from some of the men is that they came away from their interviews unsure of what they would be called upon to do, but that you required a commitment from them before telling them of their mission. Is that true?" Isidor said.

Traynor cocked his head, his attention riveted on Isidor. He had a calculating look on his face. "Would they follow you without knowing such details?"

Isidor considered the question and answered with a half-hearted shrug, "Perhaps."

"Do you have any interest in joining my organization?"

Isidor contemplated his question. He recalled the words of Sir William on their stroll in the forest outside Dover. "If they suspect you are an agent for SIS, as we believe they do, they might draw you in to a situation where they can monitor you. That may have been Traynor's real intent the very first day he came into your office," Sir William had said to Isidor. "Anyone who knows Mr. Isidor Franks also knows he will not turn over control of his contacts. He is a man who demands a quid pro quo."

Upon learning that the owner of the car used in the stakeout of Ben's London address was dead, Isidor was sure Sir William's suspicions had intensified: the owner's death ended the SIS investigation into his movements and connections.

Because Isidor did not want to lose his autonomy and freedom of movement, his interests aligned with Sir William's proposed strategy: "Drag out the recruitment and find out as much as you can about his organization and its plans," Sir William had said. "Allay their suspicions about you and Ben and make them accept you on your own terms."

"I only joined the Zionist Executive after Dr. Weizmann assured me of a great deal of independence," Isidor said. "I'm not ..."

Traynor cut him off. "I can be flexible as well."

Isidor's stomach growled again. "What time is it?" he said, reaching for his pocket watch. "Ah, ten-thirty. No wonder I'm so hungry."

A sudden clamor erupted in the hallway. The sound of shouting and fists banging on the steel doors. Their heads jerked simultaneously toward the commotion.

"Pogrom! Pogrom! Pogrom!"

CHAPTER TEN

Ben lay on his sofa, listening to the *CBS World News Roundup*, a thermometer in his mouth, a box of tissues on the coffee table in front of the sofa, and a trash can filled with used tissues next to it. William Shirer was reporting from Berlin on the aftermath of what had been dubbed, *Crystal Night*, a pogrom against Jews throughout Germany and Austria that began two nights ago and had finally ended. Civilians and both the SA and SS had destroyed thousands of Jewish homes, leaving streets filled with shards of glass.

In addition, Jews were beaten to death, thirty thousand Jewish men were imprisoned in concentration camps, and hundreds of synagogues were ransacked or set on fire. Ben was horrified, and clung to every word of the broadcast.

He heard the faint sound of a tapping on his door and cursed under his breath. He reached for his wristwatch lying on the coffee table. Eight-twenty-three, which meant another seven minutes of the newscast. It also meant his temperature reading was long past ready. He pulled out the thermometer and read it. 99.1 degrees. Good, it was still falling from its high of 103.0 last night. No wonder he was starting to feel human again.

Another series of raps sounded, reminding him what had distracted him the first time. The sound was coupled with a female voice calling out his name, probably Mrs. Donnelly checking in on him again, he thought. She was the matronly tenant living adjacent to him who had shown concern during his illness. He decided to ignore her. Maybe she would get the idea that he had fallen asleep listening to the radio and leave. He pulled the blanket up to his neck, closed his eyes, and concentrated on the newscast.

Another series of raps – louder this time. So was the voice. "Ben, are you in there?" It didn't sound like Mrs. Donnelly. He thought of Marsha, but discounted it. Surely she wouldn't come to his apartment.

"Ben, it's Marsha. Are you there?"

Both surprised and annoyed, he felt his jaw clench. Once again, he cursed quietly. The only thing in the world that mattered to him at that moment was information out of Germany, and what precious little of it that was available in the American media would come through the speakers of his RCA during the next six minutes.

She knocked again. "Ben, it's Marsha."

He exhaled a hopeless sigh and threw back the blanket. He trudged to the radio and turned down the volume.

"Just a minute," he hollered.

He hastily removed the trash can of used tissues to his bedroom and grabbed the robe draped across the armchair and slipped into it. On his way to the door, an after-thought struck him. He dipped into the half-bathroom just inside his apartment and glanced in the mirror. He didn't like what he saw. He had a two-day growth, bleary eyes, rumpled hair, and, generally, a half-dead look.

He thought about asking her to come back the next day, when he would look better, but took stock of his condition and what he had been through during the past few days. The horror of Crystal Night reverberated like a jackhammer through his mind. His infatuation with Marsha, which was on the decline over his frustration that she had yet to accept his dinner invitation, seemed trivial in the overall scheme of his life now. Suddenly he didn't care what he looked like. He stole a final look on his way out, then amended his decision. He cared a little. He ran a comb through his hair, rubbed toothpaste on his teeth, and splashed water in his face.

"Marsha, I'm not feeling well." He spoke through the door.

"Oh, I thought perhaps...I just wanted to check on you. You weren't in class today, or on Wednesday, and I didn't have your phone number. We can talk some other time. Are you okay, though?"

"You can come in. I'm just warning you that I don't look my best."

"Oh please don't worry about that. I just want to know if you're okay...or if there's anything I can ..."

Ben opened the door. She flinched. Whether it was because the door had opened unexpectedly or because of what he looked like, he wasn't sure. She looked great, though. Her blue eyes sparkled even in the dim hallway light.

"I'm getting better. I should be back in class on Monday. You may as well come in, since you walked all the way here."

"I tried to find a phone number but you're not listed. I even went by Columbia's administration office and the lady there said she couldn't find a record on you ..."

Ben took her arm and tried to guide her in. "Please, come in," he said. "Let's not talk in the hallway." Startled, she stepped in. Ben popped his head out the door and scanned the hallway, making sure she hadn't been overheard, and then closed the door, his heart racing.

"Obviously, she was mistaken," Marsha said, as he turned to face her.

"Obviously," he said, ushering her inside ahead of him. He rolled his eyes behind her back. "Have a seat."

She pulled up before sitting, wide-eyed. "Wow, this is nice." She was scanning the apartment. The RCA console stood against the south wall, its cherry wood brought out by the cherry in the coffee table, the soft cinnabar pattern of the matching sofa and arm chair, and the maroon leather recliner, which were positioned by the console on a large rectangular, thick-piled, tan rug. A dark walnut pathway between the back of the sofa and the north wall separated the sofa from a wall of trophies. Beyond the trophies, an open archway to the right led to the kitchen/dining area, and doors to the left and right of the RCA led to Ben's bedroom and a study. She complimented Ben on the decor and asked about the trophies. "Marksmanship, one of my hobbies." One of two, he remembered telling Isidor. He assumed that she wasn't interested in hearing about the other one.

"Oh. You'll have to tell me about it some time." She gave him a compassionate look, then asked about his illness. He gave her a rundown, saying he hadn't missed a day of class since childhood. He ended with the good news that his fever had broken and was almost normal again. "When's the last time you ate?"

"I've lost track," Ben said.

"You should eat, especially now that your fever is almost gone. You know what they say, 'starve a fever.'"

"Well, it must be true because I'm just now beginning to get my appetite back. I'll fix something later."

"Nonsense," Marsha said. "Go lie down and I'll find something in the kitchen."

He thought of resisting, but a warm, fuzzy feeling overtook him; he relished the idea of her taking care of him. "Okay, sure. Make yourself at home. The kitchen's in there," he pointed. "While you're doing that, I'll duck into the shower."

"Do you have any chicken soup?" she asked over her shoulder, already to the kitchen archway. "That would be best for you."

"There might be a can in the cupboard."

He didn't hear a response.

When Ben finished showering and shaving, he dressed in a sweater, slacks, and slippers. The smell of chicken soup had wafted all the way to his bedroom, and the thought of chicken soup really appealed to him. Feeling fresh and more alive, he left the bedroom and headed for the kitchen.

On his way, he caught the sight of Marsha leaning over the dining table. A bolt of terror struck him and blood rushed from his head. He felt his knees wobble. On the table in front of her was an open scrapbook containing news clippings and random thoughts involving not only Crystal Night but the summer's Evian Conference. *Without Evian, Crystal Night does not happen*. That opinion, and who knows what else, filled the scrapbook. Another bolt walloped him when he remembered something else: the copy of *Volkischer Beobachter* covering the Evian Conference that Isidor had picked up for him in France. In German, a language Marsha once studied and would recognize.

Marsha looked up. A guilty, dumbfounded look crossed her face, her jaw sagging. She relaxed her grip on an item she had been viewing and it fell to the table.

"I'm sorry. I didn't know. I was...prying." Her voice trailed off as she spoke.

"No, no. It's not your fault."

Tears welled up in her eyes, as he approached the table. "This is what's been troubling you, isn't it?"

Ben rustled the papers together and didn't take up her question. "I shouldn't have left it out." He stuffed everything back into the scrapbook. "I'll put it in the study and be right back."

He heaved a deep breath and let it out once inside the study, composing himself. He dropped the scrapbook on his desk and contemplated what damage had been done. No doubt, she now knows he's Jewish, which was no longer as important to hide now that the Nazis had found him, other than the mere fact he had been hiding it. She'd probably determined that his brothers were in a concentration camp. Same conclusion: no longer important except that he had been hiding it from her.

She probably saw the German newspaper and now knows he reads German. That one struck a deeper cord, as it touched on his activities inside Germany, which touched on his role with British intelligence, which brought to mind her comment about the administration records.

"Brother!" he cursed. All because he had taken to a girl, a girl who wouldn't even go to dinner with him. He thought of how simple his dating life was: Go out. Dance. Have a few drinks, a little of this, a little of that, and move on. He sighed, and went back to the problem at hand. The only explanation he could come up with was cultural prejudice. The rest he would have to wing. With that decision, he went back to mop up the mess he had made.

"So," he said upon returning to the kitchen, "you know I'm Jewish."

"There's nothing wrong with being Jewish."

"To a lot of people, there is."

"Ben, I know there's more to it than that. You don't have to tell me, but ..."

"Marsha, I really ..."

"... if you want to, I'd like to listen. That's what friends are for, isn't it?"

"To be honest, I really don't know how to define our relationship."

"We're friends."

"I'd like to think a friend would go to dinner with me."

"There are many different kinds of friends."

"Oh. And what kind of friends are we exactly?"

"The kind who can talk to each other."

Ben snickered.

"See. You're feeling better already." She grinned broadly, and its warmth broke down Ben's defenses. He suddenly yearned to open up to her about David and Michael and felt some relief with just the thought of doing so. He had no one in America to talk to about it.

"Marsha, how good are you at keeping secrets?"

"Oh, extremely good. The best."

He eyed her dubiously.

"Honest," she said. "Cross my heart." She crossed her heart with a finger.

He mulled it over. "Let's sit. This might take a while." He motioned to the living room chairs, then glanced at the stove.

She anticipated his question. "Chicken noodle soup. It's ready now, but I can heat it later if you want to wait."

He said he could wait and escorted her into the living room where he revealed to her his time in Munich, the store and his brothers, telling her that David and Michael had decided to stay in Germany. And then he told of their arrest.

"Oh no!" Marsha gasped and threw her hands to her face. Tears came to her eyes, as she bit her lip and shook her head dreadfully. "Ben, don't tell me..."

"Do you remember the first time you came to my office?"

She nodded, and Ben lowered his eyes and choked back tears. "I learned it that day."

He broke down, and Marsha, who had been sitting in the armchair, rushed to his side on the sofa and put an arm on his shoulder. "Ben, I had no idea."

He eventually told her that he had heard nothing more after learning that their Soviet entry permits had arrived, explaining that Germany had closed its borders and ceased mail service, making it impossible to get information into or out of the country.

She stayed until late into the evening, until after they had both eaten. He told her all about his and Adam's family, showed her pictures of everyone, and, when it was all over, thanked her for listening. "You really are a friend," he said.

She flashed a big grin and gave him a gentle hug. Her soft skin and the smell of her hair made him want to hold her tightly, but he resisted the urge. She let go and said she had to get going. On her way out the door, she suddenly stopped, turning to face Ben.

"Do you have a phone number you can give me?"

CHAPTER ELEVEN

Ben placed his rifle case and ammunition bag in the trunk of his car and reached to close the lid. As he did, he saw the bright blue sky over the budding shade trees that lined his street. The warm spring breeze soothed his face, invigorating him. He drew a deep breath. The air tasted fresh. He remembered his date in the park with Marsha later that afternoon and thought what a great day for it. He closed the trunk.

When he reached the car door, he heard his name and looked up. The mail delivery man was walking his way. "I've got something for you." Out of the corner of his eye, Ben thought he noticed something else. He ignored it in favor of the mailman, and brightened, running toward him. "Great," he said.

He met the man who handed him a package from Isidor, saying, "Nice day, huh?"

Ben agreed. "I put an outgoing letter in my box," he said, referring to a letter he had written to Isidor.

He jumped in the car and opened the package. Inside was a letter from Isidor and a large envelope marked from Adam. Ben knew that Isidor had planned to visit him on a trip to Leningrad. He opened the envelop first and saw, not only a letter from Adam, but letters, photographs of him and his family, and crayon pictures from his nephews and nieces. He was overcome with joy. What a treat. He set the package aside. He would read the letters later.

He opened Isidor's letter. It was written in plain language, not code. Isidor always wrote the words as they came to his mind, in Yiddish, German, and English, not in any one language. His letter said he had no news from Germany and that he was forwarding a package from Adam. He had given Adam Ben's New York address, so Ben should, in the future, expect to receive letters from him directly. Isidor said that he had explained to Adam that the London address was set up only to protect Ben from the Nazis and that they didn't find the charade necessary any longer. Isidor also talked about Adam and his family. Ben only scanned that part, then set the letter aside for later.

He started the car. Since a car was parked in front of his, he used the rear view mirror to back up, taking the opportunity to investigate the cars behind him. He spied a black car with two men inside, which is what he suspected he had seen earlier. The car was parked about fifty feet behind him. Two cars and two empty spaces separated them. From what he could see of the car and the men, they looked exactly like those he had seen before. That was in September, seven months ago. He had not seen them in the interim, and found that odd. He wished he could report this to Isidor and get his response, but Isidor had forbidden any mention of subjects not familial or personal.

Ben acted as though he hadn't seen them. He backed up and cranked his front wheels to the left and then pulled away from the curb and drove off. A few seconds later, the black car entered the street. He was being followed. He placed his pistol on the seat beside him.

The car followed Ben all the way to the rifle range. When he turned in to the range parking lot, the car kept going.

* * *

The sun danced white and sparkled off the riffled surface of the Hudson River. Ben and Marsha soaked in the view from their perch on a grassy slope near a majestic oak tree. Marsha was talking about spring in the Appalachians when the subject drifted to her family and religion. It reminded him that she once showed a sore spot on the subject of her mother and he decided to steer the conversation to it. She told him that her family were Baptists but that her mother had taken it too far for both her and her father.

"Really? How so?"

"My daddy didn't see eye-to-eye with her and the preacher...mostly on the subject of liquor, let me just say out of respect to him since he's passed."

Ben plucked a fresh blade of grass and stuck it between his teeth, then leaned back on his elbows. "I can see how that could happen."

She shook a strand of wind-blown hair out of her face and smiled wistfully into the distance. "Yeah, well. Notice I said 'her and the preacher,' because my momma spent an awful lot of time down at the church, if you know what I mean. Oh, it got to be so embarrassing, even for a twelve-year old. And then the preacher, one day when my daddy showed up at church, which was only once in a blue moon, because like I said, they didn't see eye-to-eye, he decided to talk about liquor. And on and on he went, laying into that sermon, sometimes looking straight at my daddy, like it was all meant just for him, like the preacher was going to push the devil right out of him and save his soul that very day.

"Well, I knew my daddy, and I knew he wasn't going to take that sitting down, not even in church. Some people think of the church as the Lord's house, but not my daddy. It was just another building to him, depending on who was doing the preaching.

"He finally raised his hand to speak, and did it politely like he was asking permission, but standing at the same time so that everybody knew he was going to speak anyway. So there was nothing the preacher could do but hear him out."

"'Mister Reverend,' my daddy says, 'is what you're saying about liquor in the Ten Commandments?' The ol' preacher didn't know what to make of that question, but he knew my daddy was up to something. Everybody in the church could tell something was up, and all of a sudden people were on the edge of their seats, all wound up tighter than a spring over what was going to happen next.

"'Why no, it isn't,' the preacher says. 'What's that got to do with anything?'

"My daddy shot back: 'Because fornicating with another man's wife is, and I was a-wondering who should be doing the preaching betwixt you and me.' And he turned and walked out of that church and never went back to either the church or my momma."

"Oh, my," said Ben. "What did the preacher do?"

"Well, I know my momma fainted. There was such a commotion; I didn't really notice what he did."

"Did you ever see your dad again before he passed away?"

"Oh sure. All the time. I loved my daddy and he loved me."

"But you moved away from your mother?"

"Not then. She ended up marrying the preacher when I was in high school. I couldn't stand the man. He kept harping on how I dressed myself, saying I was tempting the boys...I think he was the one being tempted, to tell the truth. I dressed myself the same way then as I do now. There's nothing wrong with the way I dress, is there?"

"No, no. Nothing at all," he said, while thinking to himself that he could understand what the preacher meant.

"It wasn't just that. He preached to me like my daddy was going to hell and that some of him had rubbed off on me, like he was trying to get me to turn my back on my daddy and cleanse me of his influences."

At the end of the day, Ben walked Marsha to her dormitory. They were talking about the end of the school year drawing near when Marsha said, "You know what I'd like to do before I go home for the summer?" Ben cocked his head. "I'd like you to fix me that Russian dinner you once talked about."

Her comment stopped him in his tracks.

"That is, if the offer's still open."

Ben managed to restart his mental processes enough to respond. "Sure it is. All I need is a week's notice."

CHAPTER TWELVE

"Did you win all these shooting a rifle?"

Wearing an apron, Ben finished setting a dish on the dining table and joined her. "All but a few. He picked one of the trophies off the shelf. "This is my favorite. Skeet shooting. Have you ever heard of that?"

She shook her head, she hadn't.

"Machines fling a clay disk about five inches in diameter into the air at high speed from a variety of angles. You only have a few seconds to track and shoot it with a shotgun. It's meant to simulate the action of bird hunting. I used to hunt birds when I was a boy. Quail, pheasant, snipe, that sort of bird. Skeet shooting is much easier than hunting birds, though, especially snipe, which dart all around like this." He ran his hand rapidly through the air in a herky-jerky motion. "I learned to skeet shoot in '33 when I came to America. This trophy is for the course record, just two years later. I gave it up after that. Most of what you see here is from long distance rifle matches. That's my specialty."

"Oh," she said.

"I'll only be another five minutes. Check out my study if you want. It's the door on the right." Ben rushed back to the kitchen.

"Okay, I think I will," she said.

Later, and with Tchaikovsky's *The Nutcracker Suite* playing on the phonograph, Ben turned out the lamps and escorted Marsha with her hands over her eyes to the candle-lit dining table.

"Okay, you can look now," he said.

She dropped her hands, and gasped. A fresh table cloth, china, silverware, food and drink lay before her. "That's incredible. It looks as good as it smells, like something from a fancy restaurant."

"Everything's Russian - except the wine; it's French. I couldn't find any Russian wine, which is okay because it's not that good anyway."

She laughed. "Should I sit down?"

"Not yet. First, a little Russian tradition. It goes with the meal."

He bowed to her, and motioned for her to do the same. A playful glow radiated from her. She bowed. He then leaned in and kissed her cheek. Afterwards he poured a small amount of wine in his glass, tasted it, and handed it to her. Her eyes sparkling, she took a sip. Ben reached out for her to return it, and she handed it to him. He had her bow again, he returned the bow, and seated her.

"Oh my, this is so romantic."

He flashed a smile as he seated himself, the soft, fluttering candlelight illuminating Marsha's face made her look somehow elegant in her simple, skipper blue dress. As he gazed at her, their eyes met and he suddenly saw her special mix of beauty, femininity, innocence, and playfulness in a new light. It seemed she had let go of something protective, or was it that he had let go of something. He felt as though he had won her over; that now she trusted him. Upon realizing that, he felt guilty and undeserving. An image of Adam popped into his mind followed rapidly by memories of his own escapades in Paris and Munich and – he cringed – in New York.

"You'll have to tell me what it is. I hardly recognize a single dish."

He pointed to a large bowl. "This is soup, borscht."

"What's in it?"

"Just about everything. Potatoes, cabbage, beets, tomatoes, onions, carrots, beef...those are the main ingredients."

His hand swept to a small bowl. "This is sour cream. Put as much of it as you want on top of the borscht. The bread is called 'cherniy.' It's a fresh-baked Russian rye bread, really dark, as you can see."

"Did you bake it?"

"No, it's from a bakery. I special-ordered it, though. It was delivered hot from the oven about a half-hour ago." He then gestured toward a golden liquid in a shapely glass mug. "That's a malt beverage, call *kvas*. It's very popular in Russia, like a cola here. I made it from scratch out of malt, rye flour, and water, with a touch of honey."

"Oh, sounds interesting."

He moved to a pastry. "This is dessert. It's called *Kharoset*. It's made out of apples and walnuts, with a little wine, sugar, cinnamon, and, of course, flour."

"Umm," she said.

"This is also a dessert. It's called *Tzar nalivka vishniak*, which is a cherry liqueur made out of cherries and honey, and also a touch of vodka. I didn't ask if you minded alcoholic beverages."

She shrugged. "A little's okay."

"Good, I think you'll like it. It takes months to ferment and another professor in my department, who is from Moscow, makes it in his basement. We barter. I have to take him some *Kharoset* and borsht tomorrow." She laughed.

After eating, and while chatting over coffee to the sound of Tchaikovsky's *Piano Concerto No. 1*, Ben leaned over and kissed her softly on the lips. She didn't resist. He kissed her again. She responded by putting an arm on his shoulder and joining in. The kiss, which had begun lightly and tenderly, turned passionate in an instant. He pulled her against him and she wrapped her arms around him.

Just minutes later, it was clear to him that she was aroused. So was he. Another few moments passed and she suddenly pulled away from him. She paused to catch her breath.

"Do you want to stop?" he asked.

"I want to ask you a personal question. And I want an honest answer."

Ben tilted his head. He had a funny feeling in the pit of his stomach.

"Have you been with another woman lately?"

He felt trapped, his mind muddled.

"Well, have you?"

"No," he mumbled. His first thought was purely defensive. His second thought was a mishmash of dozens that materialized as, "What do you mean by lately?"

As those words rolled off his tongue, her baby blues turned a fiery red. She made a grunt-like shriek and blurted:

"What do you take me for, a whore?" and tears began to roll down her cheeks.

"How could I possibly think that?" He rose. "You're anything but ..."

Her eyes shifted to his trophies. In a flash, she was there. She grabbed his favorite skeet shooting trophy with an angry determination. Ben's jaw dropped. She had some sort of intention. He could sense it. He started backing away from her while trying to discourage her, waving his palms and shaking.

"I'm *not* one of your trophies," she screamed. She cocked her arm.

"No, Marsha. Don't. Please don't do that."

She let loose with a mighty heave. Ben ducked as the trophy sailed over his head and crashed through the window. When he looked up, she was halfway to the door. She grabbed her sweater from a coat rack and flew out.

He began to take chase, but concern over someone having been struck by the trophy entered his mind. He peered through the broken window. The yard below was clear, except for shards of glass and the trophy, which was in two pieces.

Marsha burst out the door of the building and broke into a run.

"Marsha, please stop," he called. She didn't.

He bolted towards the front door, but came to a sliding stop when he realized he was in his stocking feet. He recalled that he had kicked off his shoes when he was sitting on the sofa. He raced over, crammed his feet into them, and then dashed out the door.

He caught up to her about a block shy of her residence hall. "Please, stop and talk."

She turned, crying. "I can't believe you did that. You planned that didn't you? The dinner, the wine, the liquor, the music ..."

"No, I promise. I didn't plan the last part."

"I told you when we first met that I didn't want to be like other women to you."

"And you're not. You're very different than any other woman I've ever met. I've never made a Russian dinner for another ..."

"I don't mean that. I mean you seeing other women and kissing me like...like you did back there."

"But, this is the first time. We've just been friends, you know, who could talk to each other. This was a new development for us."

"It should be obvious to you that you don't kiss a lady like that when you're seeing other women."

"I'm not seeing other women presently, and I'll stop–"

"When's the last time you've been with another woman?"

"I don't know, it's been several weeks, before you accepted my dinner invitation, if that counts for anything."

She whimpered and shook her head disapprovingly. "Ben."

"You're right. I know I have some bad habits. I realized that just tonight. Before we kissed, when we were at the table. Marsha, you're the first female friend I've ever had. I've grown to really, really like you. As a person, as a friend. And I wasn't thinking about kissing you or anything like that when the evening began. Tonight, I realized the way I feel about you is the way Adam always said I should feel before I start thinking about...you know, kissing someone like that.

"I don't go out as much as I used to. I've been losing interest in that way of life. I prefer the company of someone I can talk to, laugh with, and have fun together. And that's you. And only you. There's no one else who makes me feel that way."

She stood with her arms crossed, her eyes filled with tears, wearing an expression that showed skepticism, but also a desire to believe him, and to reconcile.

"I promise I won't see other women. Cross my heart," he crossed it like she had once done for him, bringing a hint of a grin to her face. "Never again."

She sniffled and wiped her tears.

"This was the best date I've ever had," Ben said. "Before I ruined it at the end, that is. I should have just walked you home. I think I would have stopped going to night clubs anyway. And I honestly think I would have stopped seeing other women, too. I really believe that."

She gazed at him earnestly. He had laid himself open, and meant what he said. After perhaps a half-minute, she softened.

"Was it really your best date ever?"

"Yes, it really was."

A smile crept onto her face. "It was mine, too."

He reached out his hand for hers. "May I walk you the rest of the way to your dorm?"

She nodded and extended her hand.

Outside the dorm, she thanked him for the wonderful meal, and kissed his cheek.

When Ben returned to his apartment building, he went to retrieve his trophy but discovered it missing. The shards of glass were still there. He scratched his head and looked all around. He viewed his broken window. Obviously the trophy had been launched from it. He finally gave up trying to find it and went inside to fetch a wastebasket and broom.

PART III

September 1939 - July 1940

CHAPTER ONE

Ben read the daily newspapers over breakfast at a local diner. Britain and France had issued an ultimatum to Germany in response to the German Army's invasion of Poland the day before. In one of the front page stories, President Roosevelt pledged to keep the U.S. out of the war.

He paid for his meal, tucked the sports section under his arm, and headed toward Central Park on foot. He wanted to get some exercise and think through all the news he had absorbed over the past day, both from newspapers and from the radio.

On Manhattan Avenue almost halfway between 116th Street and Cathedral Parkway, he became aware of the sound of a car coming to a stop behind him and a door opening.

An alarm went off inside him. He spun and reached under his jacket for the pistol wedged at the small of his back. Parked next to the curb, about twenty feet away, was a black car with a man behind the wheel and another man stepping out of it. Ice shot through his veins.

He observed both men's hands, and saw no weapons. He relaxed his shooting hand.

Two things stood out about the man behind the wheel: he had a thick neck and appeared to be disinterested.

The man stepping out of the car was in his early thirties. Dressed in a dark gray seersucker suit, he had a military air about him, with piercing dark eyes, a thin mustache, and a wiry physique.

Fully out of the car, the man gave Ben a half smile.

Ben turned and resumed walking without acknowledging him. Hearing the man's footsteps behind him, he picked up his pace.

When the steps behind him also quickened, he walked even faster.

The man hollered out, "I'd like to talk with you, Ben."

Ben slowed his pace and drifted to the right, allowing the man to come alongside him on his left. When he had, Ben spoke without looking. "Who are you?"

"I'm with American military intelligence, but I'll deny that to anyone else."

Ben stared at him, trying to place the accent. It wasn't British, American, or German. He was multi-lingual, with a blend Ben hadn't encountered before.

"I have news from Germany."

Ben stopped.

The man motioned the driver to pull forward. "Let's go for a ride?"

Ben responded in German, "I would rather walk."

The man grinned. "The Gestapo would have shot you. I only want to talk."

He reached for the back door of the car that had pulled up next to them, opened the door, and gestured for Ben to get in.

Ben didn't budge.

The man opened his jacket wide. "See? No gun. You have the advantage."

Ben made a final calculation, then relented. The man smiled.

Once they were both seated inside, the driver pulled away from the curb. The man silently gazed at Ben, his lips slightly curled.

"Your brothers, Michael and David, are in a concentration camp in Dachau."

"How do you know that?"

"Let's just say that I have reliable sources."

"They were supposed to be released when their Soviet entry papers went through. What happened?"

"Do the Nazis need reasons?"

The driver made a left turn onto Cathedral Parkway. Ben saw the two men make eye contact through the rear view mirror. The wiry man nodded, then turned to Ben.

"Let's go where we can talk privately."

The car pulled over at the northern edge of Central Park, and Ben got out. They walked into the park. "You can do something about it – to help your brothers, I mean. In fact, a man with your extraordinary skills can do a lot."

"Do what? Get them out of Germany?"

He lit a cigarette and shoved the pack at Ben. "Cigarette?"

"I don't smoke."

"You can help defeat Hitler and his Nazi war machine, which is the same thing." He took a drag on his cigarette and exhaled.

"I was under the impression that America wasn't involved in the war."

"In politics, nothing is the way it seems."

Ben chuckled and the man proudly smiled back. He was insinuating that the President's publicly-stated policy regarding the war in Europe was a sham. Ben was both annoyed and intrigued by his cynical manner.

"Which of my *extraordinary skills* interest you?"

The man motioned to an empty picnic table adjacent to a playground, and they headed toward it.

"Languages, to begin with. Russian, French, German." He took another long drag on his cigarette and exhaled without taking his eyes off Ben. "I'm particularly interested in your skills as a marksman."

Ben felt a chill. This sounded real. He believed this man had the authority to order the killing of others, and not be fazed by it. He could see it in his eyes, in his whole makeup.

"You see, on the battlefield, soldiers kill soldiers. However, the men who win or lose wars are not on the battlefields. They are in strategic places: high positions in governments, military command headquarters, and the boardrooms of key industries ..."

"You want me to become an assassin," Ben said, his remark laced with contempt.

"Well, that's putting it harshly."

"How would you put it?"

"I want you to help eliminate specially selected targets behind enemy lines to ensure a speedy and successful outcome of the war."

Ben laughed.

The man stood his ground. "What's the matter?"

Still laughing, and shaking his head, Ben turned to leave. "Look, mister. I'm a marksman, not a killer. You'll have to find someone else."

He began walking off.

"I can also help you get your brothers out of Germany, if that's what it takes to get your services." Ben halted, turning slowly. "When the time is right, of course. Obviously, now is not the time."

The man gestured for him to return to his seat, and crushed out his cigarette on the ground with his shoe. Ben sat, and the man lit another cigarette and dropped the package on the table. He exhaled and picked a piece of tobacco from his lip, his eyes fixed on Ben.

"How do I know you work for American military intelligence?"

"You don't, and this is your first lesson. If you decide to work for me, you'll be told only those things you must know in order to do your job. At all times, we must have the capability of plausibly denying anything you might say in the event you are ever captured or compromised."

"That doesn't convince me of your credentials."

"Naturally. Of course, you'll see first-hand the power and resources of our organization and in short order you'll be convinced. Not only can we protect you from the Nazis but we will get you behind enemy lines with detailed plans that can only come from a very thorough and competent military intelligence organization."

"Help me get my brothers out of Germany first and I'll do whatever you require to help defeat the Nazis."

The man laughed. "And put our entire intelligence network at risk for the release of two men? We might get your brothers out and lose the war. Don't be foolish. I'd be dismissed for suggesting such a ludicrous proposition. I'm giving you an opportunity to help bring a quick demise to the Nazi regime. When we can afford to help you rescue your brothers, then I will. That's the best I can offer you."

Ben meditated on the proposition for a minute or so, occasionally glancing at the man, who had finished that cigarette and was lighting another one.

"I don't know that I can bring myself to kill someone."

"The first time might be difficult, but you'll get over it. That's what people do in wars, ordinary people like you. They kill and they get over it."

"But they usually know who they're killing, and why – if only generally."

"If you're ever captured alive, one of the first questions you'll be asked is, 'Why that target?' That's important intelligence to the enemy and therefore it's important that it not be revealed to you. The surest way to prevent you from revealing it is to never tell you."

"That's not good enough for me."

The man stared at Ben thoughtfully, smiled respectfully, and then nodded his head. "I'll be honest with you. I need a man like you. I'm willing to stick my neck out a little bit to help you overcome your moral qualms. I'll share some information with you in the beginning and give you a chance to develop trust in me."

"What about training?"

"You already know how to handle guns. I'll personally train you on everything else."

Ben nodded.

"There's one other thing you need to consider. The slightest breach in security could expose our operation and result in your death." He spoke more like a trainer than the recruiter he had been only a moment before. "You must change apartments, change cars...," he paused and crushed out his cigarette, leaving his thought in midair. His studied glare remained on Ben. He then spoke measuredly. "You must not develop or maintain any relationships, including the one with the Barnard student, Marsha."

Ben's head spun like a top. It took him a moment to recover. "Is there anything about me you don't know?"

"Nothing of any significance," the man responded. He seemed to take a certain measure of delight in Ben's discomfort.

Ben held his stare, sending his own subliminal message that he had could not be intimidated and would hold him to any deal they reached.

The man relaxed. A smile crossed his face. He reached for yet another cigarette.

Ben already hated the man, but also respected him. He would learn from him, impress him with his ability, and gain his trust. And then he would use him to get what he wanted: his brothers' freedom.

"If you want some time to think it over..." the man said.

"I'd like to say goodbye to her."

"Of course. As long as I approve the story you give her."

Ben nodded, and the man extended his hand. "Welcome aboard, Ben."

As Ben shook his hand, he realized something. "I don't even know your name?"

"Field...Chester Field."

Ben glanced down at the package of cigarettes lying on the table. *Chesterfield.* He looked back at the man who smirked and blew out a puff of smoke.

* * *

Chester's car pulled up to a curb four buildings south of Ben's apartment. Ben got out and began to close the door. Chester called out. "One more thing."

He leaned over and reached beneath the driver's seat. He pulled out the trophy Marsha had thrown at Ben earlier in the year and handed it to Ben. "I had it fixed."

Chapter Two

A moving van arrived after dark on Sunday in front of Ben's apartment. Two men carted away all his belongings to an apartment in Greenwich Village. The next morning, on Labor Day, he dropped off a message at Marsha's dormitory, postponing the reunion from her summer vacation they had scheduled for that evening. On Tuesday morning, Ben gave his invented story to University administrators and was granted an emergency, indefinite leave. The sudden departure left him reeling and feeling empty, not unlike the sensation he experienced when chased out of Munich. Except now, he didn't see Isidor in Greenwich Village, as he had seen him in Hamburg; he had no safety net. And he still had to say goodbye to Marsha.

He paced outside her residence hall, rehearsing his cover story. The sound of distant thunder disquieted him further, and also seemed fitting; it had been stormy when he left Germany, too. The possibility of rain offered an excuse to keep the meeting short. Just say it, console her if need be, and move on, he decided, totally rejecting every other approach he had practiced.

He saw her. She emerged from the dormitory, and their eyes met. A terrible grief engulfed him. She rushed to his side, beaming at the sight of him. He fought back tears and had only barely managed to repress his sadness when she jumped into his arms. She embraced him and immediately turned to a girl following her. "This is my roommate, Betsy," she said to Ben with some fanfare, as if showing him off.

Ben put on his best face and exchanged greetings with Betsy. Marsha engaged them in conversation. Ben absently went through the motions. His attention was stuck on Marsha. She was effervescent. As Ben kept up his part of their small talk, Marsha affectionately wrapped her arms around one of his. He decided to remember her in that moment and was then pleased that she had introduced her roommate.

A loud thunderclap and a few drops of rain interrupted them. Betsy said goodbye and scurried inside.

Marsha talked about getting her umbrella, but Ben took her by the arm, and escorted her away. "No, please don't. I only have a few minutes."

They strode arm-in-arm. "So what's kept you so busy?" she asked.

Wanting to clear the quad before dropping his bombshell, he diverted her by asking about her summer and then talking of the war in Europe. He steered her onto Riverside Drive and turned west. Raindrops forced the issue.

His heart raced, as he opened the bomb bay doors. He took a deep breath and let loose. "I came to tell you I'm going away."

She abruptly stopped. Astonishment showed in her face. It turned into consternation as she muttered, "What do you mean, going away?"

"I have a family emergency that requires me to return to Leningrad right away. My father's really ill. All my teaching assignments have been transferred. I leave tomorrow on a ship to the Soviet Union."

"But, you'll be back..., won't you?"

"Maybe someday, but...honestly I don't know." She drifted into a stony silence. A loud thunderclap jolted him. Sporadic rain suddenly turned into a shower. Marsha did not budge. Her painful, pleading expression gave way to tears.

Ben took off his jacket, raised it over their heads and moved close to her.

"I'm so sorry," he said. "This is very hard for me. I was looking forward to spending a lot of time with you this semester."

She put an arm around Ben and dropped her head against his chest. They cried until the rain-soaked jacket began to leak. "Let's get out of the rain. My car's parked just down the street." Chester's disapproving voice whispered in his mind's ear. *Don't be drawn into answering a lot of questions. You'll only make matters worse for both parties.* But he was in no mood to heed his advice.

"But it has to end one way or the other, doesn't it?" she inquired in the car. "Hopefully, he survives, of course, but why wouldn't you return?" The rain pounded on the car.

He embellished on the story constructed by Chester. "I don't know. I want to translate another novel and I can do that in Leningrad and be near my mother. She's suffered a lot this past year with David and Michael being arrested, and now this." Chester's voice barked inside his head. *See, you've spun a web that will soon entrap you. Stick to the story and let it be.* "I really need to be going. My ship leaves first thing in the morning."

"Will you write to me?"

"Yes, after I get settled. I'll send you my address."

"Well then, that's not so bad," she whimpered. Ben took her hand, content that her spirits had lifted but tormented over the false hope he had given her. He drove her to her dormitory, and parked against the curb. The rain had slackened, and now pattered lightly against the car.

She reached for the door handle but then threw herself at Ben. They kissed and she wrapped her arms around his neck, squeezing tightly. Tears ran down Ben's cheeks, as he held her in his arms.

"Ben Komorosky, don't you cry like that. It makes me think I won't see you again and I know better." She wiped away her own tears. He stroked her hand. "I'm sorry, but I really have to go now."

She hurriedly kissed him again, then scrambled out of the car. Before closing it, she leaned back inside, tears flowing. "I love you."

She slammed the door and ran off.

CHAPTER THREE

"Here's your driver's license. Nicholas Stevens. Ben Komorosky boarded a Norwegian merchant ship in New York harbor and set sail for Murmansk. You are officially and for the record at sea in the Atlantic," Chester said.

Ben felt a sinking sensation. Checking the physical description and address given on the license, he slid it into his billfold. Unofficially, he was in a safe house on the West Side of Manhattan, near the Garment District, a long walk and a short car or subway ride from his new digs in the Washington Square South area of Greenwich Village.

"This is where you will receive your training and future assignments, and give your debriefings, receive your pay, and meet with me for any reason."

As Chester spoke, Ben gave the small apartment a once-over. A threadbare sofa sagged against a bare, faded white wall. A single bed was pushed up against the hallway wall. Across from the sofa, a door concealed a bathroom and shower on one end and opened into a kitchenette on the other. With no visible dishes, towels, pots, or pans, it appeared to be unused. Three wooden, straight-backed chairs surrounded a round table, perhaps four feet in diameter. An ashtray on the table contained three cigarette butts, all of them Chesterfields. The table was between two windows that were cracked, their shades half-drawn. A floor fan in the corner of the room stirred the musty, smoke-filled air. A telephone on top of a lamp stand at one end of the sofa seemed out of place in the lifeless space, causing Ben to wonder whether it was functional.

"Now for the first lesson." Moving in front of the sofa, Chester gestured for Ben to have a seat. After Ben had settled in, Chester frowned, his hands outspread. "Look at you."

Ben squinted, befuddled.

"Look at me," Chester said; touching his chest as if he set some sort of example. "What's the difference?"

"I know how to dress," Ben said, being flippant. He had no idea what point Chester was trying to make.

"Agreed. But you stand out. I, on the other hand, *blend in*. People in the neighborhood will notice and remember you, the fancy Dan who visited the building from time to time. They won't remember me because the majority of people don't even notice me. I'm like everyone else on the street. I blend in with the masses."

He motioned Ben to come to the closest window, and raised the shade. "Look at them," referring to men on the street below. "Notice the colors and styles they wear. During the next couple of days, pick up a Sears catalog and mingle with ordinary working people. Pay close attention to the fabrics they wear, their hairstyles, everything about their appearances, down to their..." He paused, eyeing Ben's fingernails. "You have your nails done, don't you?"

Ben gawked at Chester.

"Stop," Chester said, and turned from the window. "I will pay for your new wardrobe, of course."

Ben laughed. "Well, that shouldn't cost you much." He returned to the sofa.

"You might not like it but it's vitally important for you to blend in, for two reasons. One is obvious and I've already touched on it: you don't want to be noticed. Two, when you blend in, you can then pay attention to those who notice you, because, if they notice you, they are too observant – and that's unusual.

"Notice how people respond to you both before and after you dress to blend in, and you'll see a world of difference. Do that as an additional exercise and we'll discuss it as we progress in training. One other thing while we're talking about out-of-class exercises. I need you to change vehicles. People can spot that fancy car of yours from three blocks away. It sticks out like the Empire State Building. Trade it in for a popular brand, a black sedan without whitewall tires, like a Ford."

"I refuse to buy a Ford," he said. Chester seemed startled. "I'm Jewish, remember." Surely Chester read the papers and knew of Henry Ford's anti-Semitic publications and financial backing of Hitler in the early twenties, and, if not that, his acceptance the year before of the only Nazi decoration for distinguished foreigners ever given in the United States. There was a huge public outcry. Ben's incredulous stare must have jogged the trainer's memory.

"Well, if it makes any difference, I'm paying for it."

"It doesn't make a difference. I won't drive a Ford."

"Then buy a Chevrolet, I don't care. Just make sure it's black, at least a year old, and no whitewalls. Do it on your way home if you can afford to."

Ben said he could.

"Good. Use cash and bring me a receipt. I'll take care of the registration and reimburse you for the cost of the car. I'll also give you cash in the amount of the trade-in value of your car."

Chester spent the rest of the two-hour session giving Ben a personality makeover, too, teaching him, in tiresome detail, how to give up his distinctive appearance in order to *blend in* with *them* and appear as *they* appear, referring to the average Joe. He stripped Ben down and remade him from his gait, to his facial expression, down to his fingernails.

When they had finished for the day, Chester scheduled the next training session for a different hour on Friday, three days later, and marked it in a pocket-sized notebook. Ben paused at the door. Raising his head, Chester did a double-take and stared back coldly at Ben. It made him feel as though he had done something wrong, but didn't know what it was, unless...by then it was too late, but he had formulated a response.

"I was waiting for you," Ben said.

"Why? Do you want people to see us leaving together?" Chester said.

"No. I was just..." Chester's glare bore into his skull. "Forget about it," Ben said, and spun to leave. Chester hollered for him to stop, and Ben pulled up and closed the door behind him. Glaring, Chester inched forward.

"We never arrive together. We never leave together."

"I'm sorry. I wasn't thinking," Ben said.

"Well then, think," Chester said, his voice booming even though he was only five feet away. His eyes were glassy, his fingers quivering. "I can't teach you how to think. I can only make it unpleasant for you not to think."

"I understand," Ben said. "It won't happen again."

Chester relaxed and fluttered his fingers. "Good. Now off with you."

On his way out of the building, his pulse racing, Ben wondered what he had gotten himself into and how much of Chester he could take. Someone using his identity was on a ship headed for Russia. Chester had taken care of all the arrangements for the apartment: its selection, the application, the down payment, as well as responsibility for the monthly payments. Ben had not even met the Landlord. Chester probably had his own copy of the key. And now Chester wanted to register his new vehicle. A trapped feeling took hold of him. No one, not even Isidor, knew his new identify or that he had taken a job for a man using the brand of the cigarettes he smoked for a name. A disturbing realization struck him. Chester could get rid of him without leaving a trace.

* * *

In a dour mood, Ben parked his new bland car, a black '38 Chevrolet, on Sullivan Street, the closest available space to his apartment, and commiserated over his situation, trying not to think of his once comfortable life and his affection for Marsha – and hers for him. But then he thought of his brothers and the plight of Jews in Germany. Returning to his former life was not an option. He steeled himself, resigned to suffer a miserable few months or a bit longer, and tried to think of a brighter future. He got out of the car.

"Shine, Mister?" a voice interrupted his thoughts. "Only a nickel." Ben turned and saw the boy standing on the corner, next to a makeshift shoeshine stand, about twenty feet up the street. He examined his shoes, then nodded.

The boy flashed a broad grin, which told Ben he'd made the right decision.

He took a seat in a metal folding chair and the boy grabbed a can of polish from a small wooden crate sitting inside a wagon next to the chair. He propped one of Ben's shoes on top of it, slapped on some polish, and began whistling "Sweet Georgia Brown." He rubbed the polish in with gusto and to the rhythm of the song, lifting Ben's spirits. What the boy lacked in equipment, he made up for with energy and style.

"What's your name?" Ben asked.

"Billy Ray Williams. What's yours?"

"Nicholas, but I go by Nick. Have you been working this corner long?"

"'Bout a year, I guess. Longer 'n you been here, that's for sure." He had a glint in his eye.

"Well, that wouldn't take much. I'm new here."

"That's what I mean." He caught Ben's look of puzzlement. "I seen you drivin' that smart-looking coupe yesta'day."

Thinking of Chester's lesson, "Oh, you saw me in my red and black car?"

"Yep, sure did. You parked it down the street, past the '38 Chevy you got today."

He gave a flamboyant double-tap on the toe of the shoe, signaling he had finished with it, and reached out for the other one.

Ben cocked his head, impressed not only with Billy Ray's slick shoe-shine skills, but with his keen powers of observation.

"I'm a workin' man. Gotta keep my eyes peeled for customers and fetch them nickels. Most folks don't go lookin' for a shine."

"So you can tell the difference between a '38 Chevy and a '37 from this far away?"

"Yep, sure can." Billy Ray spoke without looking up. "I can tell between a '37 Ford and a '37 Chevy, too."

Ben got the sense the boy's comment had some special meaning. He stared at Billy Ray, who finished polishing his left shoe before looking up with an impish look, and then snapped the lid on the polish tin and flipped it into a box full of polish. Pulling out a shoe brush, he reached for Ben's right shoe.

"That's what's been followin' you. One in front and one in back."

Ben's jaw dropped.

"They switch off. Yesta'day, the Ford was followin'. Today, it's the Chevy. You can tell 'em by the antennas, they's bigger 'n normal ones, like on some police cars."

"Are they following me now?"

"Yep, 'cept they's parked now. One's way down the street and the other's behind me a ways. They rev up when you go someplace...'least when I been here."

"Have you told anyone about this?"

"Nope. It don't have ta go nowhere neither, now you's my customer." He raised his brows with a telling look.

Ben laughed. "You know, with eyes like yours and that kind of thinking, you could own this city some day."

Billy Ray beamed, then double-knocked the handle of the brush against the sole of the shoe. Ben switched feet, his mind whirling.

"Are there any other new people living in my building?"

"I ain't seen 'em if they is and, being that school just started back up yesta'day, I been here mosta the time."

While mulling over the situation, an idea struck Ben. "Tell me Mister Working Man, if you don't mind me prying into your business affairs, how much do you make in a week shining shoes?"

"In the summertime, 'bout a fin on a good week." He lifted his head. "That's five dollars."

"Yeah, I know what a fin is."

"Now's school's back up, 'bout a buck fifty so long as the weather holds up. I got to shut down in the winter and hope it snows so I can shovel the rocks." He smiled at Ben, "You know what that is?"

"Sidewalks?" Ben said, taking a stab at it.

"That's right. I do all my shovelin' and shinin' on the rocks.

"How would you like to make an extra fin each week?"

"Doin' what?"

"Doing the same thing you're doing now. Watching my back and letting me know what you see every now and then when you shine my shoes. Can you do that without telling anyone?

"Five dollars? Every week? Jus' for spillin' to you?"

"Yeah, every week you work the street with your shine cart. I might have an errand or two for you to run also. If I do, I'll pay you extra for that."

"Aw, man. That's crazy."

"But it's got to be our secret, just between you and me, or the money stops. That's important. If the people following me are on to what we're doing, they'll get real sneaky and what you see won't be worth five cents to me."

CHAPTER FOUR

Ben caught sight of the '37 Chevy's antenna as he turned left onto Houston Street. On the driver's side of the car, it was noticeably thicker and longer than other cars' antennas, now that he paid attention. Many cars didn't have one at all. Through his side mirror, he also noticed the headlights above the fender, and the rounded grill, two features that set the Chevy apart from the Ford, according to Billy Ray. The driver was skinny, dark-haired, and clean-shaven, just as the boy had described him. The car was two cars lengths behind Ben's.

Having not seen the Chevy on his morning stroll for breakfast, Ben wondered when it had arrived. And, he still had not seen the Ford. If it started out ahead of him, which way did it go when it got to Houston, and how would it find him again?

The skinny man offered a clue to the second question. His right hand went to his mouth. A good fifty feet behind him and only partially visible through the intervening car windows, the man appeared to be talking into a device. To Ben's knowledge, police and taxis were only able to *receive* communications, not send them, but Billy Ray's description of the antennae and the way he had been followed – a car in front and one behind – made him conclude that two-way radio communication was now possible.

Ben turned left onto Fourth. The Chevy followed. It was right behind him, but then another car dropped between them. Soon after Ben crossed Fourteenth Street, the Chevy changed lanes and picked up speed, passing Ben a block later. The driver kept his eyes straight ahead and Ben was careful not to ogle him as he went by. Turning left on Seventeenth, Ben lost the Chevy but picked up the Ford, noting its larger antenna, the pointed grill, distinctive hood ornament, and headlights housed in the fenders. Burly and sporting a black mustache, its driver also fit Billy Ray's account. His left arm held out straight, he signaled to turn. A cigarette dangled between his fingers. He negotiated the turn two cars back of Ben.

Ben turned right on Broadway, and right again on Fifth Avenue. The Ford remained on his tail, now only one car back. At Forty-second, Ben spotted the Chevy. Headed west, it crossed Fifth Avenue while Ben came to a stop for a red light. Almost two minutes passed. When the light turned green, Ben hooked left and the Ford went straight through the intersection. Interesting, Ben thought. And smooth, like a ballet on wheels. No wonder he hadn't noticed them.

He parked at the first parking garage, the same one he had parked in the day before, and walked to the public library. Inside the Forty-second Street entrance, a skinny man wearing the same shade of gray as the driver of the Chevy, stood before the building directory. About five-eight, his hat was tilted back, his hands in his pockets. Ben proceeded to the Newspaper Room without looking back. By the time he had settled himself into a chair to read the London dailies, the skinny man sauntered into the room and took a seat on the far side of the room, three broad tables away, and buried his face behind a newspaper.

Ben took his time. He scoured the London papers, the *Times*, the *Daily News* and *The Jewish Chronicle*, for every article about Germany and the war. When he finished, the Chevy driver was gone. On his way out the door, Ben looked for the Ford driver, thinking perhaps they had switched off, but didn't see him. He grabbed a sandwich at a deli two doors east of the parking garage and took it with him. The cars followed him back to his apartment.

After eating his sandwich, he set out on foot, to the Fourth Street-Washington Square subway station. The burly man followed him into the station and hopped the same train, one car back of Ben's. Paying him scant attention afterward, Ben spotted him again outside a Yankee Stadium ticket booth but didn't notice whether he actually purchased a ticket. The next time he saw him, he was with the skinny guy outside the Seventy-second Street Theater, where Ben had stopped to catch a matinee showing of the latest Universal newsreel. The sun was setting and the sky was gray as he walked to the station. He didn't bother to determine whether either one followed him; he had already accomplished what he set out to do.

The next morning he took a different route to the library, drawing a similar pattern of surveillance from the same drivers and cars. This time he stopped to eat his sandwich and played a game of chess in Bryant Park, next to the library. He stopped at an office supply store on the way back to the apartment and purchased three boxes of typing paper and a box of carbon paper. Back at the apartment, he pulled out a stack of Russian language Chekhov stories he had set aside for a rainy day. He opened the first one, *The Case*, and began translating it into English.

Before leaving to meet Chester on Friday morning, he spread his translated pages next to his typing desk, giving his new project a clear, "in progress" look. He then dug a piece of scrap paper out of the trash can, tore it in half and folded into a small wad. After checking the hallway and finding it empty, he closed the door and fitted the wad inside the hinge. He opened the door, watching for the paper to drop. Too wide. He unfolded the paper, tore off a piece, and tried it again. Back and forth he went until he could squeeze through a crack in the door without the wad falling but sure that it would fall when the door was opened wide.

He arrived at the safe house before Chester. He made sure he was alone, checking the other rooms, and then lifted the telephone. He got a dial tone. He put it down.

Chester arrived one-half hour later. Ben handed him the receipts for his car and clothes, and Chester rifled through them. "Where's the car?"

"On the street," Ben said, gesturing nearby.

Chester asked him to point it out, and complimented Ben after he had seen it.

"You've done well with the clothes you're wearing as well," Chester said as he put the receipts inside a folder he carried into the apartment with him. "Have you done the exercises I gave you."

Ben had, and went over his experiences and observations.

Chester spent another fifteen minutes covering mundane security principles that mainly stressed alertness. He didn't delve into anything secretive, compromising, or indicative of a high degree of trust. He then scheduled the next meeting for the following Tuesday, and Ben left.

The Ford picked up his trail on Twenty-Fifth Street and followed him up Fifth Avenue several streets before turning off. The Chevy then fell in behind him and followed him to the library. Ben drove to the ballpark afterwards to see a Yankee game, and returned to his apartment around four. Billy Ray hustled him for a shine the moment he stepped out of his car, and Ben took him up on it.

"Did you see anyone go into my apartment today?"

"Nope."

"What time did you get here?"

"'Bout an hour ago."

Billy Ray reported on the surveillance he had seen over the past three days and didn't tell Ben anything he hadn't observed himself. "I'll see you next Friday," he said when paying for his shine.

Back at his apartment, Ben squeezed through the door and anxiously checked the floor. The wad of paper was on the floor. Someone had entered his apartment while he was gone.

CHAPTER FIVE

The trees of Washington Square Park were ablaze with fall colors. The sky above was overcast, and a gentle breeze wafted through the open window. The Ford and Chevy were not in sight. Ben felt a sense of freedom. It had been almost five weeks since he had met Chester, seven days since he had last been followed, and ten days since anyone had been inside his apartment. Chester still had not revealed any truly sensitive information, but Ben sensed that he had already won his trust; that revelations would come when Chester needed to make them.

He glanced at his watch. One-thirty. Another half hour before his meeting with Chester. A Friday, it was also another pay day for Billy Ray. On Monday, it would be November. Both the radio and newspapers predicted a cold front moving in over the weekend. He wondered how much longer Billy Ray would be available, and then pondered all these factors and many more. Ultimately, he relied on his senses. He decided to make a move.

He pulled out a piece of typewriter paper and typed: *Four and twenty blackbirds baked in a pie.* He pulled the paper out, cut off the top third containing the letters, and folded it. He crumpled up the unused portion and pitched it in the trash can sitting next to his desk. He closed the window in case it rained while he was gone, and then set off on foot for the subway station.

He had calculated correctly.

"You're now ready to learn how to do the job I hired you to do," Chester proclaimed. "As with every other subject, there are tried and true techniques and basic principles. For each assignment you're given, certain points will be tailored to fit that particular assignment, at which time I will address them. The basic principles, however, will not change, and you must get those down cold. I will delineate them today, and we will go over them until you know them forward, backward, and scrambled. In the coming weeks, we will take up each of the points, one-by-one, and expand on them. I expect you to be ready for an assignment by January. That's only three months."

Ben felt a surge of adrenalin.

"And trust me, the time will go quickly." Chester paused to light a cigarette.

"Point one, a security point that you know well: Blend in with the culture you are in. Dress how they dress, look like they look, and talk how they talk. From the moment you cross the border of a foreign country, speak only the language of that country. Always. Never deviate. Not for a single word.

"Point two, a technique: There will always be three people on every assignment with specific responsibilities and obligations. They are designated by numbers. Number One, Number Two, and Number Three.

"Point three, a security rule: You will know one another by the numbers assigned to the role given for the assignment, never by name. If you have the role of

Number One, you will be known by your colleagues as "Number One."

"Point four, a security sanction: If you breach any of the security rules relating to the identity of the other participants, you will be dispatched. Refer to your dictionary for the various meanings of the word *dispatch*. That means you don't give, you don't ask, you don't pry, you don't so much as wonder about the identity of the others, where they came from, or anything else about them. To each other, you are numbers and nothing more.

"Point five, a security rule: You are required to report the slightest breach of any security rule by the other two.

"Point six, a security sanction: The failure to report a breach of security will result in the same sanction given in point four.

"Points seven through nine, techniques: Number One has primary responsibility for the elimination of the target. Number Two has secondary responsibility for the elimination, and Number Three is there to ensure that Numbers One and Two are not taken alive.

"Point ten, a security rule: Each participant will have upon his person a cyanide capsule, which he must bite in the event of his capture."

Ben flinched, and Chester paused and crushed his cigarette into an ashtray on the table. His eyes remained on Ben. A silent give-and-take ensued. Chester seemed to say, *Take as much time as you need.* He was resolute, with no empathy, as if the procedure had been implied in his initial offer. Ben went through a series of emotions and attitude changes, beginning with the revolting thought of suicide and ending with a simplistic moral:

getting captured was not an option. He must do his job and get out safely. He nodded for Chester to continue.

"Point eleven, a security sanction: Refer to point four. In the event a captured participant fails to take the cyanide capsule, Number Three will carry out the sanction.

"Point twelve, a technique: Numbers One and Two are to triangulate their target, which means to form a triangle such that Numbers One and Two are two points on the triangle and the target is the third. Form an equilateral triangle, if circumstances allow, or the closest thing to one, if they do not. By this technique you maximize the chances of success.

"Point fourteen, a technique: You rendezvous with the other participants at a preselected time and place. You will be shown pictures of your co-participants prior to each assignment. At least within twenty-four hours of target elimination, all three participants will connect and acknowledge each other's presence, either by gesture or words, as the circumstances dictate. Say nothing more to each other, and do not mingle from that point until after completion of the assignment when you will rendezvous according to a predetermined exit plan.

"Point fifteen, a technique: Separately visit the preselected site of the elimination, study it, and look for alternative vantage points in the event the preselected stations are unavailable. Visualize your role in the plan given. Note any necessary adjustments based on your onsite observations.

"Point sixteen, a technique: Meet discreetly. Numbers One and Two will decide in the presence of Number Three their exact positions and work out any problems that exist or have arisen. Review the final plan. Number Three will decide on his position based on what he learns from Numbers One and Two. He will not reveal it.

"Point seventeen, the final point, is a technique: Do the job, do it quickly, leave the area and dispose of the weapon used as securely and as quickly as possible. Follow the exit strategy you are given, and don't get captured alive."

He reached for a cigarette. "Let's go over it again."

* * *

"I need you to run an errand for me. Do you know where the News Building is?"

Billy Ray didn't.

"Don't look now but you can see the top of it from here. It's the tall building with the dark and white vertical stripes."

"Oh, yeah. I know that one."

"It's on East Forty-Second Street. I need you to go there, go inside, and tell someone you're a delivery boy and want to place an advertisement." Ben went over the errand until Billy Ray grasped all that was required of him.

"I'll give you an envelope when you finish. There's more than enough money inside for the ad. You can keep the change. On top of that, I'll give you another five dollars when I see the advertisement in the paper. How's that?"

Billy Ray's eyes lit up. "Five dollars?"

"If you encounter any problems, you know what to do," Ben said, referring to the signals they had worked out. Billy Ray was to wave his hand if everything was okay or he had no news to report, and wave his polish rag otherwise. Ben would get to him when it was safe to do so.

"Ain't gonna be no problems. I can tell you that right now. Five chollies? Are you serious? Uh-huh. Ain't gonna be no problems."

The next day Billy Ray waved his hand. On Sunday, Ben bought a copy of the New York *Daily News* and saw the personal ad.

CHAPTER SIX

"This is our final training session," Chester said in late December 1939. "When I have an assignment for you, or need to reach you for any reason, I will raise the shade of this window before five p.m. for a meeting the following day." He pointed to the kitchen window. "All the way up, like this." He raised the window shade. Outside, snow fell under leaden skies.

"I will change the meeting each time we meet but for now it is set for 2:00 p.m.

"The same applies for you needing to meet me. I have a copy of the key to the apartment here."

Chester reached into his folder, and handed Ben the key. "Leave this in a secure place in your apartment when you go on an assignment. Do not take it with you. Signal your return to New York by raising the shade. Do the same thing if you need to meet with me for any reason.

"Check the window each day after 5:00 p.m."

* * *

A month later, Ben saw the window shade up. He bundled himself in gloves and an overcoat the next day and headed toward the subway station, passing the corner where Billy Ray had once been a fixture. Gone was the shoeshine stand, and gone was any sign of surveillance.

He reached the safe house ten minutes early, and waited another twenty for Chester, who carried himself in a military manner, striding briskly, wearing what must have been his mission face. He was carrying an attaché case in one hand, a rifle case in the other. His gaze barely noted Ben's presence. He set the rifle case on the floor without coming to a complete stop, then set the attaché case on the table. Ben rose from the sofa and joined him, having perceived some signal that Chester expected it.

"You did say you spoke Norwegian, didn't you?" Chester said while opening his case.

Ben said he had but that it had been many years since he last spoke it.

"Good. You have two weeks to brush up on it." He first pulled two large photographs out of his case and dropped them on the table. He then extracted a small paper package and two maps.

Referring to one of the photographs, he said, "Here's your Number One. What is his responsibility?"

"Number One is primarily responsible for the elimination of the target." As he spoke, the reality of what he was about to do struck home, causing a chill to shoot up his spine. In two weeks he would sit face-to-face with the man in the photograph and work out the final details for an assassination. Feeling a little dizzy and weak-kneed, Ben took a corner of the picture in his fingers, and used the heel of his hand on the table to stabilize himself. He focused on the details of the man's features. Dark, short-cropped hair, a forced scowl on an otherwise friendly face that seemed vaguely familiar. He scanned his memory banks but was interrupted when he got to Paris during his college days.

"Very good. And this is your Number Three," Chester said, flipping a second photo onto the table. "His job?"

He let go of the first picture and lifted the second one off the table. Prominent cheekbones highlighting penetrating eyes, exuding a cold confidence; the kind of guy you wanted on your side.

"To ensure that Numbers One and Two escape, and, if they don't, to make sure they are not taken alive." Ben felt his composure returning, his confidence rising.

"Correct." Chester picked up the small paper packet and pointedly displayed it. "Inside is your cyanide capsule. If you cannot escape, immediately remove the capsule and place it between your teeth. Bite down on it if you are captured." He handed the packet to Ben. "Save Number Three the trouble and risk of finishing the job."

Ben nodded, pocketing the tablet.

"You're Number Two. What's your role?"

"Secondary responsibility for the elimination of the target. Take no more than one shot, make it good, and leave the area quickly."

"Exactly. Don't count on Number One. Help him but get out quickly. Worst case, we leave two men down and one returns."

Chester grabbed one of the maps and spread it on the table. "Your target will leave a hotel here," he said, pointing to an "X" marked on one of the streets, "at about eight in the morning. He will cross the street to walk toward an office building on the other side.

"You will fire from here," he said, dragging his finger diagonally southwest to the next block. "There is a four-story office building on this street," he said, pointing to another "X" on the map. "The third floor has a vacant suite of offices that should provide you with a clean shot at just over one hundred yards. Number One will perch on the top of a building over here," he said, pointing to the street on which the hotel was located. "It's not the best of angles, but it will do."

"What are the wind currents like at eight in the morning?" Ben said, drawing a blank stare from Chester. "If they're from the south, they will cut across my line of sight at about...it looks like seventy-five degrees. That could make a difference, depending on wind speed and the distance from here to here," he said, pointing to the two sides of the street between his perch and the target.

"Doesn't the wind constantly change?" Chester asked.

"Yes, but there are patterns. And the distance across that open space won't change between now and then. I like to make calculations based on normal conditions and work out variables ahead of time. Besides, I might be nervous that day."

"I'll do the best I can," Chester said, and turned his attention to the briefcase, extracted another photograph and handed it to Ben. "This is your target. When we met, I promised to tell you who and for what reason you would be asked to eliminate a particular target. Ordinarily I would – and at some point I will – only show you the photograph. His name is Oskar Krager, a Norwegian shipping tycoon. Norway has become the focal point of the war. Germany gets fifty percent of its iron ore from the upper part of Sweden. Germany needs iron of course to maintain its war machine."

Chester reached for the other map and laid it before Ben, showing the North Atlantic and the Scandinavian Peninsula. He pointed to the uppermost portion of

Norway. "This is Narvik. The iron ore is trucked here from Sweden and then loaded on ships that sail down and around the coast." His finger tracked a route to Germany.

He straightened and paused: "On Krager's ships."

"Diplomatic efforts to encourage the King of Norway to voluntarily cease shipping the ore have failed. The British and French, therefore, devised plans to disrupt the flow of iron ore by other means, and we have just discovered that Germany has learned about the plans and is working furiously to thwart the British and French with an attack on Denmark and Norway in order to control these shipping lanes and maintain the flow of iron ore.

"Your assignment is part of a multi-pronged plan to preempt Germany's strategy. By removing Krager, we send two messages. One is to other shippers who might take his place and the other is to the King of Norway. We prefer not to target heads of state if it can be avoided."

Chester picked up the map, began folding it, and gestured toward the rifle case.

"That's the gun I want you to use, a German Mauser. I'm told it's very reliable. Take a look at it and tell me if you approve." As Ben went for the case, Chester added, "If we need to change it out, we can – with anything but an American brand."

Ben grabbed the case, opened it, and looked inside. It was a German Mauser Kar. 98K, his favorite long distance match rifle. There was also a 6X telescopic sight inside.

He lifted the rifle out of the case, checked it out, and gave Chester a nod. It would do nicely.

"What about the ammunition?" he said, as he put the gun back in its case.

"Use anything you like that's not American-made. I'll reimburse you for it."

Ben returned to the table, where Chester had finished re-packing his attaché case. "I like to use match-grade 857 Mausers with that rifle," he said. "With them, what is hit, stays hit – as the saying goes."

"Good," Chester said. He pulled a pack of Chesterfields from his shirt pocket and tapped one free.

"I'll need to practice with both the rifle and the ammunition I'll be using," Ben said.

"It's yours to take, so do with it what you must," Chester said, lighting his cigarette and exhaling. "Have a seat. I want to go over the details."

* * *

Ben boarded a twin-engine plane with U.S. Army Air Corps insignia. The two weeks had flown by and he was now in Washington, D.C., having arrived during the middle of the night on a train from New York. He was special cargo, alone in the hold of the plane. They flew to Gander, Newfoundland and, from there, to Prestwick, Scotland on the central west coast where he left the plane carrying a travel bag and his rifle case. The sky was shades of gray, lighter in the east from the morning sun. A fine, light drizzle cast a sheen on the tarmac.

A British Army uniform caught Ben's attention from perhaps eighty yards. The man turned, and pointed him to a single-prop cabin biplane. Ben waved to the soldier, who gave him the okay sign and walked off toward a nearby hangar. Ben did not get a close enough look to describe the man who wore the uniform. Not that it mattered. He was cold. He ran to the plane.

The military uniforms and planes satisfied two of Ben's concerns about Chester. True to his word, the man had tremendous resources at his disposal; he also appeared to be working for the right side in the conflict. The evidence of the two nations' militaries working together also helped instill in Ben a sense of the mission's importance, as if both countries depended on him. Had he been patriotic, it might have meant a heightened sense of his own importance. He settled for a boost in his resolve.

When he reached the plane, he stepped up onto the lower wing. The pilot opened the cabin door and motioned for him to sit next to him in the front. Ben dropped his bag and rifle case in the back and dropped into his seat. The plane took off as he buckled himself in.

The pilot, a young man in his mid-twenties, was the first person Ben had encountered on his trip who spoke to him. Like the others, however, he displayed not the slightest inkling or curiosity about Ben or his mission. He talked about flying and the landmarks they passed over.

"There she is," he finally said. "Straight ahead." The city of Bergen, Norway, had come into view. From the air, the coastal city looked spectacular, set among a number of sweeping, snow-covered hills, near stunning fjords. Ben had never been to Bergen.

After they touched down, and Ben was dropped off, he changed his clothes before boarding a bus to the train station where he was scheduled to rendezvous with his mission counterparts.

By the time he arrived it was dark, even though it was still afternoon. The combination of the early nightfall and the frigid temperature reminded him of his childhood years in Petrograd, as Leningrad was then known.

Dressed to blend in with the natives, and carrying both his travel bag and rifle case, Ben found the Oslo line, set down his things, and discreetly searched for Numbers One and Three. He located Number One sitting on a bench, his bag and case at his feet. The man's eyes passed over Ben as if he had failed to recognize him or catch his eyes. But then he pushed back the brim of his hat with one finger and returned the glance. Ben immediately scratched the side of his face with two fingers and looked away. The connection was made.

Now that he had seen him in person, an image of the man he bore a striking resemblance to popped into view, an artist Ben had befriended in Paris. He recalled eating on the sidewalk of a bistro when he noticed a man sitting behind an easel, peeking around it at Ben. After he had finished eating, he discovered that the artist was painting a street scene that included a likeness of Ben sitting at the table. Something about that pleasant reminiscence caused Ben to think of Number One as "Frenchie."

This mental familiarity touched something inside him, raising his morale. He felt liberated to a small degree from Chester's claustrophobic security rules, and it distracted him a bit from the gruesome task awaiting him in Oslo. He decided to name each of the men he worked with, based on the first image that came to mind upon meeting them. In a state of heightened anticipation, he sought out the man who would help them escape – if it came to that, Number 3.

It didn't take long. Less than a minute later, the final point of the triangle ambled into the station. Ben immediately recognized the cool, beady eyes from the picture Chester had shown him. He didn't expect to see them so high off the floor, though; Chester had not mentioned his height. But on second thought, he was only about two inches taller than Ben, which made him about six foot four. What had thrown Ben was the odd proportion of the man's legs compared to his torso. His waist was easily five inches higher than Ben's. The final confirmation came when the man changed his grip on the bag he was carrying to display three fingers. Turning away, Ben hung two fingers from his coat pocket. He nicknamed this man "High Pockets."

Ben became restless on the train. Rather than sleep, his mind drifted to Oslo, still eight hours away. The assassination. The cyanide tablet inside his travel bag. And adrenalin began creeping into his veins, and his excitement mounted. Rocked gently to and fro, he closed his eyes and tried to concentrate on the rhythmic sound of the churning wheels. He began to nod off when a rifle shot rang out, and for an instant he thought he was in Oslo. His eyes snapped open.

He was still on the train; apparently he had been dreaming.

In the near-darkness he glanced at Frenchie, who was in the same car. He was fast asleep. High Pockets was seated in another car, and had once walked through their car. He had strolled by, picking up those long legs, stretching them out, and setting them down again, apparently carefree, as though he owned the train. Ben got the distinct impression that both of them had done this before.

He tried a different tack. He thought of Marsha. He pictured her leaning against him, proudly showing him off to her roommate, Betsy. He was in New York, outside her dormitory. He could smell her hair and felt her arms affectionately wrapped around his arm. His nerves began to relax. He skipped to his last memory of Marsha leaning inside his car, the rain pounding on the roof, drowning out sound of the steel wheels on steel tracks. "*I love you,*" she said, in clear tones, tears flowing from her eyes. He felt his eyes grow heavy, as endless images of Marsha meandered through his mind.

He awoke to the sound of the train whistle. Through the chilled window pane, he saw the pale hint of dawn – and the outskirts of Oslo. He sat up straight and shook the cobwebs from his head. He wondered about the time and instinctively looked to his wrist. It was bare. Then the purpose for his presence in Oslo struck him. If it was dawn, it was about seven in the morning, just twenty-five hours before the planned execution. Suddenly, he was wide awake.

* * *

Having committed to memory the street map Chester had shown him, Ben located the hotel from which his target would emerge, the first stop on his site survey. So much open space. The buildings in the downtown district were only four or five stories high, along wide boulevards. Another difference from New York he noticed: The people were more extroverted and friendly. Many of the people he passed on the street not only noticed him, but greeted him.

"Good day," a gentleman dressed much like himself, in a brown suit, overcoat and hat, said as he passed by Ben. "Good day," Ben said, blending in with the culture.

Foot traffic in the area was heavy and brisk. That bothered him. Too many witnesses. Chester had drummed into his head, however, that shots fired from different directions would create a commotion and confusion which would feed on itself and spiral into a frenzy. Thus, the more people, the better. Ben pushed aside his concern.

He was soon standing where he expected his target to be the next morning, on the sidewalk near the curb in front of the hotel. From there he spotted the office building from which he would fire. An abundance of wide open space separated the two locations. Morning had broken but the sun had yet to rise above the buildings behind him. But already the area was bright enough for sighting a target. He observed the cloudless sky and guessed that it was about ten minutes before eight. He wondered what difference a heavy cloud cover might make but didn't dwell on it; the weather was consistent with the forecast and more of the same was forecast for the next day. He took note of the orange glow in the sky over his left shoulder, which suggested to him that the sun would rise to the north of his line of sight and not be a problem.

Two people greeted him in quick succession, reminding him to keep moving. He didn't want to get caught in a conversation. "Good day," he said to each of them, letting them pass.

On the other side of the street, he counted his steps from the edge of a three-story building across the intersection, observing a light northerly breeze from the Oslo Fjord, which he gauged at about five miles per hour from the feel of it on his face. Thirty-two steps later, he reached the edge of a building across the street. He made a mental note of the width of the exposed area. He would calculate for windage settings on his sight when he returned to his hotel room.

He turned around and faced the hotel, viewing the target area from that perspective. The sun still had not risen over the roof of the hotel. The lighting was terrific; visibility was crystal clear. The bustle of cars and pedestrians in the streets and on the sidewalks frequently interrupted his view of the target site from ground level, but he knew they would have no bearing at all on his view from thirty feet above the street.

Next on his list was an inspection of the building containing the vacant office suite. He walked to it and went inside, running into numerous men and women dressed in business attire who treated him as though he no doubt worked there. His comfort level rising, he proceeded to a staircase as though it were part of his daily routine.

He saw no one on the third floor. He found the first door on the north side of the hallway and turned its crystal handle. It opened. He slipped inside. The interior office was empty. He quietly closed the door. He flipped a latch above the knob, locking it.

A counter approximately four-feet high took up most of the back portion of the office. It was devoid of furniture. A closed door was on the west wall. Boxes were stacked throughout. Curious, he looked inside one. Books. A quick check of another box: more books.

He gazed out a window behind the counter to the street below and saw a clear view of the hotel up the street. He looked over his shoulder to the interior door. According to Chester the office he was in was part of a vacant suite. Windows on the other side of the door likely would not afford him a better view but he decided to check them out, anyway. The door opened to a hallway and four other offices, two on either side. The offices on the north side each had a window. Good views, but nothing extraordinary. Both were filled with boxes. So was the hallway. The entire suite was apparently being used solely to store books.

Ben settled on the space he concluded was once a reception area for the suite. He liked the counter. It acted like an enclosure. The longer distance to the target was not a factor. A few yards added to one hundred were insignificant. The short distance to the hallway door, on the other hand, appealed to him.

He opened the window, knelt in front of it, and studied the view to the hotel. The sun now peeked over the skyline, slightly north of his line of sight. Not a factor. In March or April, it would be, but not in February.

He observed a woman on the sidewalk in front of the hotel, walking as though she planned to cross the street on a course similar to the one Ben expected his target would take. He dropped into a shooting position, envisioned her as the target, and tracked her in the sights of his imaginary rifle as she stepped off the curb and into the street and then began crossing it. He had a splendid, unobstructed view. The position was perfect. He dropped his arms.

Sitting on his haunches, he felt secure tucked behind the counter. He considered storing his rifle overnight there rather than carrying it into the building and up the stairs in the morning, something he and Chester had discussed. There were advantages and disadvantages to each, so Chester had left the decision up to Ben. After mulling it over, he opted for overnight storage. He would return later that afternoon.

Before leaving, he visualized himself shooting the rifle and then pulling it inside. He shut the window and then second-guessed whether he should do that the next day. He decided he should and went through the motions of shoving his rifle aside, grabbing his travel bag, and scurrying with it toward the door. He would practice again that afternoon with the real thing. He acted it out again. Fire, pull the rifle in, close the window, ditch the rifle, grab the travel bag, and scurry away from the window on his hands and knees, dragging the travel bag.

He had come to the last item on his site survey: exiting the building.

Swiftly and quietly. He reached the latch. It took too long to unlatch it. Besides, if he was nervous, he might fumble. He made a mental note: don't latch the door. In the hall, he walked with a measured briskness, westward, away from the staircase he had taken up to the suite. He followed it around a corner to the back of the building, past offices that were occupied, according to Chester's report. Ben could not tell. The doors were closed and he saw no one in the hallway.

He found the staircase Chester said was there and scampered down it, keeping up his brisk but reasoned pace. The staircase was vacant. It emptied into an alleyway. In spite of its disuse by morning commuters, Chester had instructed him not to use it as an entrance for fear of standing out, telling him that it was better to blend in with the mass of arrivals. The exit was different. The attention of the occupants would be drawn to the front of the building, possibly clogging the front staircase and entryway.

Ben took the alley west to the street, then turned south, toward the Oslo Fjord, and practiced the efficiently-casual gait Chester had taught him. He tried to instill in himself the raging urge to flee so he could practice tempering his emotions and recalled his flight from Munich, particularly the moment at the train platform when he felt most threatened.

* * *

"I'll be in the first window," Ben said to Frenchie in the presence of High Pockets over food and drink that evening at a lively pub on Karl Johans Gate, a major artery in Oslo. He spoke Book Norwegian. Frenchie disclosed his location, the same spot identified by Chester.

"Any problems we need to talk about?" Frenchie said.

"No," Ben said, and told him he had already stowed his rifle behind the counter. Frenchie nodded and said it made sense. High Pockets listened intently, but said nothing. Ben smiled and arched his brows, inviting a reaction. High Pockets's lips tightened into a half smile. For a man who might have to shoot him the next day, Ben thought he seemed pretty sociable.

"Anything else?" Frenchie said.

Ben thought about mentioning the temperature. It was twenty-eight degrees Fahrenheit at eight that morning and the low that night was forecast to be fourteen degrees. Lower temperature affects muzzle velocity, making a bullet strike lower, requiring a higher elevation setting. He got the idea Frenchie didn't need instruction or reminders and might regard it as idle chatter. He shook his head.

"Very well." Frenchie lifted his glass. "Good luck."

Both Ben and High Pockets lifted their glasses.

They finished their meals in relative silence, with only an occasional word spoken, such as the grunt that came from High Pockets. "Good," he had said, pointing his fork to his smoked salmon, causing Ben to wonder whether he could really speak Norwegian. Frenchie, who Ben knew could speak the language well, simply nodded. Ben felt inclined to start a conversation but felt constrained by all the security rules against getting personal. It occurred to him that Frenchie felt the same restrictions. He said only what he had to say. Chester would be pleased.

When they had finished eating and paying for their meals, Frenchie broke his silence, speaking for the first time in a quarter hour.

"Tomorrow," he said.

Ben and High Pockets nodded. They exited the pub and parted.

CHAPTER SEVEN

B en tossed and turned that night. Anxiety struck him soon after separating from his cohorts, and had intensified as the evening wore on. He was haunted, not so much by the fear of getting caught or harmed, but by the reality of taking another man's life. He wondered about the target. Was he really Oskar Krager, a shipping tycoon greedily assisting the Nazis? Did he have a wife and family? Was he anti-Semitic? And what about Chester? What was his agenda? What had Ben gotten himself into, after all? Would any good come of this? A myriad of questions churned his consciousness despite his efforts to ignore or calm them. He needed sleep, not moral certitude, but discovered that one was not possible without the other, and managed only to drift in and out of a twilight sleep.

He recalled one special Sabbath and, finding comfort in the recollection, pursued it. He and his brothers were seated around their father in the living room near the fire, listening to his instruction from the Torah, the lighted Friday night candles on the mantle, and yarmulkes on their heads. Ben was ten years old, and it was no longer safe to practice their religion publicly in the Soviet Union. Synagogues and Jewish schools had been shut down by the government, and religious books had been confiscated. Jewish religious and communal life had been almost completely eliminated. Thus, religious training occurred in their living room, led by their father, with the windows closed and the shades drawn.

"And the next one," his father said: "Thou shalt not kill."

Next to him lay a cane which reminded Ben that his father was lame from being wounded during a battle against German forces in the Great War, when even men too old to fight had been forced into service to defend the nation from annihilation.

"But, papa," Ben said, "You killed."

Adam, who was seventeen at the time, said, "That was war. War is different."

"It says 'don't kill'," Ben shot back. "It doesn't say it's okay if there's a war."

Adam was ready to tear into Ben when their father said, "No, Adam. That's a fair question. Ben has a good mind. Always reading books and asking tough questions. This is a good thing. Let him think. Let him challenge me."

He turned to Ben. "This commandment is not the only word of God. He doesn't answer every question a mortal mind can dream up. What I and many people decided is that you have to protect yourself and your family. We were chosen to live on this earth and only God has the right to end it. You can't allow other people to violate what God has given you."

Ben decided then that his father was probably right. "I don't want to kill people," he said. "I hope there won't be any more wars when I grow up."

His father smiled at him, ruffled his hair and said, "So do I, Ben. So do I."

Ben got out of bed, walked to the window, and parted the curtains, staring out into the deep velvet, starry night, having come to the crux of the problem. He did not and could not know whether his target was a threat to him or his family, or whether his victim was truly aligned with the Nazis. He was certain only of that uncertainty. He was also certain that he and Frenchie would end the man's life in the morning: The die was cast; there was no turning back.

In the darkness of the Norwegian night, a haunting image of Chester appeared. "Field," Ben recalled him saying, smug and cocksure, "Chester Field." He recalled Chester returning his skeet shooting trophy and saying, in the same arrogant manner, that he had fixed it. Then he replayed Chester giving him a driver's license in the name of Nicholas Stevens and telling him that Ben Komorosky was officially at sea in the Atlantic. Ben resolved to remedy his predicament. He released the curtain and began formulating a plan. As the plan took shape he drifted off to sleep and didn't stir until the ring of his six o'clock alarm.

He jumped to his feet and immediately checked the weather. Stars filled the still-dark sky, meaning it would be light enough to shoot. He touched the icy-cold window pane and got a general sense that the forecast had been accurate. He then began the pre-dawn routine he had planned for himself, which included a shower and breakfast in the hotel's restaurant.

He reached the intersection between the hotel and his perch at the break of dawn and observed the lighting and wind conditions, both of which were ideal: it was clear and the frosty air was virtually still. He proceeded to the vacant suite and, on his way, noticed that he was calm and fully alert, which surprised him, given his lack of sleep and the task that lay before him, but which he also welcomed and did not dwell upon.

Inside the building, he halted before opening the door to the vacant suite and looked for the rolled match cover wedged between door and jamb, near the top. He had placed it there when he returned yesterday afternoon to stow his rifle and travel bag, the red edge of the cover's lettering aligned precisely with the edge of the door. It was still there, apparently undisturbed. He dislodged it and buried it in his coat pocket.

Once inside, he pulled the travel bag out from behind the counter and tossed it onto the counter top. From his coat pocket, he took his pocket alarm clock and placed it on the counter, facing the window. It was seven forty. He began undressing, down to his undergarments, and changed into his travel clothes. He stuffed the business clothes into the bag and zipped it. He then grabbed his rifle case, set it down next to the window, opened it, and attached the telescopic sight. He set the range on the sight for one hundred twenty-five yards, the distance derived from his calculations the day before. He slid one bullet into the chamber.

It was seven forty-five. He decided to wait five minutes before raising the window in order not to chill himself, causing him to shiver.

At seven-fifty, he raised the window about eighteen inches and positioned the rifle along the sill such that only three or four inches of the barrel extended outside, and settled into a comfortable position steadied by his elbow on the sill and his shoulder against the window jamb. He set his telescopic sight on the front doors to the hotel, and waited.

The moment arrived. The man Chester identified as Oskar Krager emerged from the hotel surrounded by an entourage of four men, and walked toward the street. Then an odd thing happened. The world slowed down. Krager and his men moved in slow motion. So did the people on the street. Everything slowed down, as if subject to his command. Rather than jittery nerves, Ben felt only calm. He was locked in. Just like at a shooting match, when he was able to block out the muffled chatter of a crowd, the bustle on the street. The sounds of traffic and pedestrians disappeared and a confident silence overtook him.

He settled the cross hairs of his telescope on Krager's right temple, and tracked it, steadily, smoothly. Pedestrians walking to and from the sidewalk came into view on the outer edges of the sight, as Krager neared the curb. The rifle, his target, the distance between them, and the pressure of his finger against the trigger absorbed his complete attention. He had connected with his target, attaining a sense that it was ready to receive the bullet intended for it.

He tightened his trigger finger, wishing mightily for Frenchie to fire.

A shot rang out. The man immediately in front of Krager's left threw his arms up and fell backwards. Frenchie had missed. In the split second that followed, chaos erupted around Krager, who stood frozen. Pedestrians visible in his telescope either dropped or ran from sight.

Two men in the entourage lunged for Krager in an apparent effort to force him to the ground.

Ben fired.

Krager's head exploded.

The three men fell to the ground in a heap.

Ben jerked the rifle inside with his right hand and rammed shut the window with his left. A hazy wisp of smoke, the acrid smell of gunfire. He scooted away from the window on his haunches, set the rifle on the hardwood floor, and slid it with a strong heave up against the far wall, behind the counter. He grabbed the travel bag and scrambled to the door, rising from his hands and knees once he had passed the counter and sprinting.

He opened the door and peered out into the hallway. It was empty. He went out and quietly closed the door behind him.

He walked briskly down the hall, turned the corner, and hustled toward the back staircase.

An office door next to the stairway opened. Ben abruptly slowed into a casual pace. A young woman darted out from behind the door. "What was that noise?" she said to Ben. Startled, not suspicious, her hand on the inner door knob.

Ben pulled up. He was prepared to plead ignorance of a noise when a door behind him opened. The inquiring woman glanced in that direction, at an older woman with her hair in a bun, also curious. A chorus of agreement had built for a noise having occurred.

"It came from the street," he said to both of them. The older woman's eyes lingered on him. Ben was uncertain whether he detected suspicion, but knew he had overstayed his visit. "I think it was a car."

The two women looked at each other, reluctantly satisfied, he hoped.

"Oh," the young woman said and Ben took that as his cue. He left.

Once through the door, he hit the staircase and bounded down it, taking two and three steps at a time. At the bottom, he slowed and assumed the demeanor of an innocent man and then threw open the door. The sound of sirens filled the crisp, cold air in the alley.

He strode down the alleyway in his practiced, efficiently casual gait. He turned the corner, headed south while peeking over his right shoulder. Traffic filled the east-west street, with motorists jumping out of their stuck vehicles, straining their necks to view some spectacle east of them and talking excitedly with one another. The sirens, the bustle and buzz of the gathering crowd, mixed with the sound of frustrated auto horns, all of which combined to create a curious commotion that, like a magnet pulling iron, drew even his attention. He found the pull of a safe harbor even more attractive, though. He pushed forward toward the Oslo Fjord.

Taking side streets, Ben crossed a stone pedestrian bridge to a parkway adjacent to an inlet of the fjord and met Frenchie and High Pockets on the other side. "Good job," said Frenchie. High Pockets nodded his concurrence.

"What happened with your shot?" Ben said, looking at Frenchie.

"My 'scope was off," he said, shrugging.

Ben wondered if he had forgotten to adjust it high to account for the cold temperature, and wished he had spoken up.

Within a minute or two, a small boat passed beneath the bridge and did an abrupt U-turn. That was their signal. They scurried down the embankment and hopped aboard. The boat whisked them out into the harbor to a large fishing boat, which they climbed aboard and it sailed away. That evening they boarded a British destroyer in the North Sea.

After being fed in the officers' mess and given an officers' cabin to sleep in, Ben became restive and was again unable to sleep. The morning's events replayed unevenly in his mind like an annoying melody. Jumbled and fragmented pictures intertwined inexplicably with the emotions he expected to encounter during the event: anxiety, fear, even terror. He recoiled with the image of Krager's head exploding. Cold sweat beaded on his forehead and his heart raced with the recollection of the young woman barging out of her office door. The older one was wise to him, he was now fairly certain. And even though he had made a clean getaway, never to return, pieces of him remained in the building: a rifle he had fired, the spent casing, and his image etched in the minds of the two women. By now they knew. He would escape justice, in a literal sense – but they knew. And somehow it mattered.

Lying on the single bed he had been awarded by unanimous decision of his comrades in arms, who shared the bunk bed on the other wall of the tiny cabin, he turned to High Pockets and Frenchie. With his eyes peacefully closed, High Pockets appeared to be enjoying a well-earned rest, like a Russian peasant from a Tolstoy novel who had finished a hard day's harvest topped off with a big meal and vodka. Frenchie was engrossed in a magazine, rolled up and held above his head. A contented smile graced his face, too. Both men appeared to have nerves of steel. Ben was grateful that he had gained an upper hand on his emotions when it mattered most, but his composure had gone in a flash. He envied their ability to remain composed throughout, to sleep and relax. Or did he, really?

He wondered what kind of people they were. Were they citizen soldiers like himself, otherwise gainfully employed in some socially acceptable activity? Had they been raised in a religious family, instilled with a conscience about right and wrong conduct? Chester said that normal people "get over" taking another person's life. So far, he hadn't.

Just then, Frenchie caught Ben staring at him. Ben collected himself. "Good idea," he said in Norwegian, pointing to the magazine. "I should have brought something to read."

Frenchie half-smiled and half-nodded and then returned to his reading material.

"I think I'll get some fresh air," Ben said, kicking his legs off the bunk. He grabbed his coat off the hook next to the door and left the cabin.

CHAPTER EIGHT

Ben turned the lock in the door of his Greenwich Village apartment, and squeezed through the door. The wad of paper was on the floor. Someone had entered in his absence. He surveyed the apartment searching for signs of intrusion, and found none; everything was as he left it. He cracked the front windows to freshen up the air, which had a warm, musty smell to it.

Only then did he take his coat and hat off, hanging them on the rack near the front door. He grabbed his watch out of a dish on the living room mantle and looked in the mirror above it. He ran his fingers through his hair. He needed a trim. He needed a lot of things. A rub-down. News. Food. Society. He realized he could use a night on the town. It was Thursday; he would do that on Friday night.

He picked up the tail as soon as he pulled away from the curb. They took turns following him all the way to the safe house. Same boys, same cars. He wondered what had brought it on – nothing he could think of – and how long it would last. At the safe house, Ben raised the window shade all the way, just as Chester had instructed him. He then headed for the library.

Ben rifled though the personal ads of the New York *Daily News*, and found what he was looking for. An ad that read: *Sing a song of sixpence, A pocket full of rye.* He breathed a sigh of relief and felt the connection. Isidor knew he was living in New York, undercover. He didn't know where in New York, the name he was living under, of what he was doing, only that it was not safe to make contact, but it was a start.

* * *

"Here," Chester said, handing him an envelope. "Three thousand bucks."

Ben raised his brow. "An added bonus. You did a great job."

Ben pocketed the money, nodding his appreciation.

"Did you have any trouble on a personal level?"

"Not really," he said.

Chester patted him on the back. "See there? I knew you could do it."

On his way to the door, Ben turned and said, "I'm going out on the town tonight. I need to unwind."

"That's okay. Just stay away from the places you used to patronize."

Ben bobbed his head.

He stopped at the public library after leaving the safe house and caught up on the news. Rifling through back issues of the New York and London dailies, he searched for any mention of the assassination, and didn't find any.

Two hours later, he left and picked up a turkey on rye and a side dish of potato salad at the deli near the parking garage. Flecks of snow fluttered under a somber twilight on his way to the garage. The two goons followed him home.

Later that night, he led them to Leon and Eddie's, a swing club on Fifty-Second Street. He hadn't been there in years, well before Chester would have been following him, he thought. He wanted to stand out, meet people, talk to someone, and kick up a little dust on the dance floor. Decked out in his fine threads, he felt his dignity returning.

The joint was jumping. A colorful big band played a lively version of *Pennsylvania 6-5000*. Dressed in red jackets and black pants, three horn players bobbed their upper bodies and instruments in unison to the beat. Two girls in sleek black strapless dresses backed a male singer in a black tux. The pounding drums and pulsating bass stood out. A boisterous crowd jammed the dance floor, tables and booths, with a sizeable gathering at the bar near the entrance. Ben had found his elixir; he felt alive, the dark clouds of Oslo dissipating.

He grabbed a waiter and ordered a gin and tonic. "Ben," a voice cried out, somehow overriding the din. He jerked his head and saw a vaguely familiar face grinning and waving. The name Jack flashed in his mind. Ben didn't really know the guy. Jack was sitting with a woman and another couple, all of whom eagerly eyed him. He didn't recognize any of the three. Jack motioned him to join them and the others egged him on. It was that kind of night. He gave Jack the right-o sign and gestured for the waiter to deliver his drink to their table.

Jack introduced him to his gang by first names. Frank, Connie, and Luann, a blond sitting next to Jack. It had been almost a year since he had stepped out – two, since he had done so frequently – and he hadn't expected to run into people who knew him as Ben. He thought of

Chester's reaction and thought of leaving for another club. He brushed off the imagined criticism. Ben relished the idea of being himself again, if only for an evening. He had earned it. He needed it.

"Do you dance, Ben?" Luann said. He nodded and she glanced at Jack for permission. Anything for his buddy Ben, he said, or words to that effect. Luann jumped to her feet while Ben tried hard to place Jack's face, curious as to how they had become such good friends. He decided they hadn't; that Jack was drunk.

And so the evening went. The girls took turns sharing Ben. Occasionally, Frank and Jack ventured onto the dance floor. Mostly they just drank and cut up, keeping the gin and tonics coming for Ben. More than he could handle; he let them back up. At last, both couples ended up on the dance floor together. Ben caught the stare of a woman two tables down. A pretty brunette with brown eyes in a black dress. He had seen her on the floor with different partners and now she was alone. He gestured for her to join him on the dance floor and she accepted.

Their hands met on the edge of the dance floor. "I'm Tammy," she said. He went with Nick, hoping to limit the damage. "I thought I heard them call you Ben?"

"What, that guy? He's drunk. I don't even know him."

"You didn't correct him," she said.

"When a man is buying, I don't want to embarrass him in front of his friends. He can call me anything he wants."

Tammy laughed. "Okay, Nick."

They spent the next half hour dancing. Not much was said between them. She asked him if he lived in Manhattan. He told her he did, that he had an apartment "in the village." She asked if he meant

Greenwich Village. Yes, he said, and she told him she was from New Jersey. He got the clear idea that she wanted him to ask her back to his apartment. He let the opportunity pass, hoping she wouldn't press the issue. He just wanted to have fun.

Then he spotted the skinny goon at the bar, the one who drove the Chevy tail. He was sucking on a cigarette and nursing a drink.

Ben felt his party balloon burst. He wondered how long the man had been there and whether he had overheard anyone refer to him by his real name. His suspicions drifted to Tammy. Was she planted on him? He tried to recall when he first saw her that evening. He wasn't sure. Not in the first hour, he was fairly certain. He wondered if he was being overly paranoid. What could she want from him? She wasn't asking him anything. Maybe she planned to do that later, after he took her home with him. It then occurred to him that *not* taking her home also had its consequences. She was attractive, alone, and they had hit it off – at least on the dance floor. Why wouldn't he, unless he was stuck on Marsha. Was Chester testing him?

When the song ended, he invited her to have a seat. Jack and his gang had left, so he escorted her to their empty table. Someone had drunk his gin and tonics. He ordered more drinks and sat with his back to the bar, not wanting to tip off the skinny interloper that he was wise to him. He wanted to pump Tammy and figure out if she was up to something besides a night on the town. The band played *Tuxedo Junction* in the background.

"What do you do for a living?" she said.

"I'm a writer."

"Oh." She seemed impressed. "What do you write?"

"Right now I'm translating some stories by Anton Chekhov."

Her eyes glassed over. "Who's that?"

"He's a Russian author."

She squinted as if trying to place the name, trying to be sociable; she clearly didn't care.

"I have a boring job. Let's talk about you. What brings a Jersey girl to the island?" She shrugged, flashing promiscuous eyes. "A good time. Looks like I've come to the right place." She paused. "You're a good dancer."

Ben thanked her and said she wasn't too bad herself. Their drinks arrived.

"What made you pick this place?" he said.

She shrugged again. "Perhaps it was fate." She raised her eyebrows and seductively drew her drink to her lips. Ben noticed for the first time that they were rosy and plump, very kissable, igniting a few sparks in Ben. An image of Marsha doused the flame. Amused, he took a break, stirring his drink. He had only taken his eyes off her for a moment.

"Are you married?" she said.

An odd question, Ben thought.

He shook his head. "You?"

She grinned and slid her left hand on the table top, displaying a bare ring finger.

He held up his, and she laughed. Ben detected a subtle irony in the laugh.

"Don't look now but a man at the bar seems to have an interest in you," she said.

"Maybe it's you he's interested in," Ben said.

She fidgeted. "He's wasting his time, if he is; he's not my type."

"What type is he?"

"He looks like a private detective. I thought a jealous wife might have hired him."

"Nope. Not me. No wife. No girlfriend."

"So then we can leave together," she said. It was a challenging question, not a statement.

"We could. I could take you home...or I could take you back to my apartment."

"You won't be disappointed if you do," she said.

He took another drink, mulling over the situation. He saw both risk and opportunity; he just needed to think it through.

The band finished playing *Tuxedo Junction*. Her eyes shifted back toward the bar.

"Oops," she said. "It looks like we're both in the clear. He's leaving." Ben observed a subtle sigh of relief in her and got the idea she was the one with a jealous spouse.

The band struck up *In the Mood*. He reached for her hand. Let's dance and then we can go back to my apartment. She sprang out of her seat, beaming.

* * *

Chester's men followed them back to his apartment and he took Tammy inside. Upstairs, he crossed the living room, pulled the shades, and drew the curtains.

"You really are a writer?" she said, looking at his typewriter and strewn papers.

"Yeah. Look around. No pictures of wives or girlfriends, either."

"I believe you," she said, but scanned the living room anyway.

Ben turned the lamp off, leaving only the faint glow of the entry light. He began to unbutton his shirt. "Where do you prefer to sleep, on the couch or in the bed?"

A confused look overcame her. "What?"

"Listen, I had fun with you tonight but I don't want to sleep with you."

"Then why did you bring me here?"

"I didn't want to disappoint the private dick."

"But he left," she said.

"He might have caught you staring at him. Who knows why he left, but I'm sure he didn't go far. He might even be parked on the street right now."

"I... I don't under..."

"It's complicated. Don't ask."

She sighed, her hands on her hips, her mouth open in shock.

"You said I wouldn't be disappointed if I brought you here," Ben said. "So please be a sport and I'll treat you to a nice breakfast and get you home in the morning."

Her befuddled look turned into a bemused smile. She shook her head and then collapsed onto the couch. "The couch, I guess." She broke into a surreal laugh.

He patted her on the shoulder. "Thanks. I'll get you a blanket and pillow."

CHAPTER NINE

Ben was just thinking that he hadn't seen any sign of Chester's tail for a full week when he spotted Billy Ray standing on the corner. On his way to his parked car and then to the library, he continued his course – and his train of thought.

The surveillance had been round the clock for five days, closely for two more and then it became sporadic. They hadn't seemed too interested in tracking down Tammy. When he dropped her off at a subway station the following morning, they had stayed on Ben's trail, not hers.

"Shine, mister?" Billy Ray was waving a shine rag in a wide arc above his head, grinning broadly. It was the first day of spring, a pleasant day, and the first time he had seen Billy Ray since November. He was probably ready to get back on the dole, get those fins coming in. Ben was certainly ready to dish them out.

"Have you ever worked other places?" Ben said. Billy Ray finished applying polish and reached for his brush.

"Yep, I tried 'em all, most of 'em, lookin' for the hot corners. I ain't been nowhere since I got this one last summer, though."

"So you used to switch around?"

"Yep, sure did. That's why I got the wagon." He nodded at the metal contraption that contained his equipment. Faded splotches of red paint revealed the original color. A weathered brown had taken its place.

"How about the Garment District, Eighth Avenue, up around West Twenty-seventh Street? Can you go that far?" speaking about the corner streets nearest the safe house.

"If the money's right, I can go anyplace." After a beat he peered up, a sly grin on his face.

Ben laughed. "Yeah, you're definitely going to end up owning this city."

* * *

Three days later, the window shade of the safe house was up. The next day Ben parked his car on the north side of Eighth Avenue, east of Twenty-seventh, and crossed over, purposely avoiding a direct pass of Billy Ray who was set up and with a customer on the corner. It was three fifty-five in the afternoon, five minutes before the time designated for the meeting.

Chester was already inside. He crushed out the cigarette he was smoking and opened his attaché case. "I have an assignment. You leave in a week."

The meeting lasted fifteen minutes. When Ben left the building, he veered to his right, again avoiding contact with Billy Ray. He felt the attention of Chester, peering through a crack in the shade.

The hairs on the back of his neck stood up. It could have been his imagination, of course, but the anxiety was real, the concern warranted. He knew the consequences for himself and swore upon the altar of God that he would kill Chester if anything happened to Billy Ray.

He left the boy at the corner for the rest of the week, steering clear of him and not drawing his attention on his daily five o'clock runs to check the window shade. During that period, he didn't observe any surveillance and finally concluded that it was safe to pull him back. On his next trip by the safe house, he timed his drive-by to catch a red light across from the shine stand. Billy Ray spotted him and Ben discreetly flashed his index finger, signaling him to return to his original spot the next day, one of three rotating locations they had settled on.

The next day, Ben stopped for a shine. Billy Ray told him that he had observed no one following Ben, either at the corner in the Garment District or that day by his apartment. "The man," he said, had been dropped off by a black 1937 Chevrolet four-door sedan on the north side of Twenty-Seventh Street and had walked to the building that Ben had gone to.

"He went right on by me."

"Did you ask him for a shine?"

"Sure did, and he walked on by like he didn't see me, but he know'd I was there, jus' he couldn't be bothered by a colored boy. I paid my dues on the rocks; I know the look."

"I bet you do," said Ben.

"When he come out," Billy Ray said, "the '37 was right there to pick him up. I hollered at him again, and he walked on by again. And he needed a shine. I seen that the first time he went by."

Billy Ray said that Chester was picked up at four thirty-five, which was about twenty minutes after Ben had left the building. Billy Ray's description of the driver and vehicle matched that of the driver and black car used by Chester when Ben had first met him.

When Billy Ray finished the shine, Ben rose. "I'm going to be out of town for a couple of weeks. Switch your locations every couple of days. Go to the number two spot next. Keep your eyes peeled and I'll find you when I return. Be here the next day after you see me."

He reached inside his pocket, pulled out a twenty dollar bill to cover the previous and coming weeks. Before showing it to him, he said, "Have you ever seen a twenty dollar bill?"

The boy's eyes popped wide, as Ben was afraid might happen.

"Pretend it's only ten cents and I'll give it to you."

Ben spent the rest of the day shopping. Topping his list: a second automobile. And not just any automobile. He put principles aside and bought a Ford. A barely-used 1939 black deluxe sedan. It came with whitewall tires, but he swapped them out.

He stored the other items he purchased that day in the trunk of the Ford and then rented space in a garage and parked the car there.

CHAPTER TEN

Ben sat at a table with his mission colleagues outside a restaurant on the Montebello Embankment adjacent to the river Seine, across from the magnificent Cathedral of Notre Dame. He sipped from a glass of Margaux and choked down the blather of his Number One, who tried in vain to convince Ben where he should position himself the next day.

Ben pursued a parallel train of thought. He yearned for the terse and respectful Frenchie, and wondered where he was? Had he been banished or done away with for missing Oskar Krager? Of course, he might not even speak French, contrary to the image he had evoked in Ben. He wondered what he should name his Number One. He was a cantankerous, short, nearly-bald, ugly man, who turned uglier with every word. When nothing better came to mind, he christened him Popeye, from the comic strip character. He had already named his Number Three, a fair-haired, well-proportioned, blue-eyed lad, who had a dashing air about him. Ben instantly thought of Dolohov, the Tolstoy character in *War and Peace,* and it stuck.

Ben sneaked a peek at Dolohov, hoping to get his take on Popeye's rambling critique. His attention was diverted by a young lady who sat alone and stared at him from the next table. Their eyes met and she flashed a flirtatious smile. Bored and annoyed with Popeye, he returned the smile. Dolohov perked up, glanced over his shoulder at the girl, and returned a telling look to Ben, who then gave up on the girl and took another sip of his wine.

"What do you have to say to his argument?" Dolohov said to Ben.

"I understand what he would do if he were me, but he's not me. I'll be tucked among the trees on the grassy knoll between the hotel and the river. I like the spot. I feel safe there. I can keep my mind on my business instead of my back. As far as the lighting goes, I had my sight with me last night, so when I told him the lighting was fine from there, I meant that the lighting was fine from there."

"He adds an extra fifty yards, maybe more, to his escape route," Popeye said. "Maybe he doesn't appreciate how quickly the Paris police can respond."

"He knows the consequences for not escaping," Dolohov said to Popeye and then to Ben, "Don't you?"

"Well put," Ben said to Dolohov, not hiding his irritation with Popeye.

Popeye shrugged, giving up. He extended his hand for Ben.

"Don't worry about it," Ben said, giving Popeye a sincere look but not his hand.

"Anything else?" Dolohov said to both of them.

"Whoever gets a clear shot fires first, right?" Popeye said to Ben.

"Agreed," Ben said. Chester had briefed him that the normal rule calling for Number One to fire first was off due to the heavy pedestrian traffic and the need to fire at ground level.

Dolohov, who had turned from Popeye to Ben, flipped an inquiring look back at Popeye, as if repeating his question, *Anything else*? Popeye shook his head. Dolohov gave the same expression to Ben, who said he was done.

"Alright then," Dolohov said, scooting his chair back. He wagged a finger at Ben and spoke softly. "No girls tonight, lover boy," and winked.

Ben laughed. "She started it. I was just being polite." He glanced at the young lady who still had her eyes on him. She flashed a coy smile.

Dolohov caught the exchange as he rose to his feet. He leaned over and whispered in Ben's ear. "Time to go."

Ben downed the remaining bit of wine in his glass. He waved goodbye to the girl, pushing back his chair and rising.

* * *

Twenty-four hours later, he squatted behind a tree near the Quai de Bethune on the Ile St. Louis across the Seine from the landmark La Tour d'Argent an elegant restaurant atop a seven-story building, and waited for his target to emerge. Keeping a careful watch on the sidewalks and street behind him, Ben cradled his Mauser 98K in his arms and replayed Chester's briefing: *The target is Henri Beauchamp, a high-ranking member of the French government who is secretly working with the Nazis to bring about an armistice and subsequent collaboration with the French. Naturally, France's support of the alliance is critical.*

It sounded plausible to Ben. Then Chester had added: *This is the last time I'm bending the security rules for you.*

In the future I will only show you a picture of the target.
Ben told Chester that he understood and didn't have a
problem with it. What he meant was that he was
convinced of Chester's connections with both American
and British militaries, not that he now trusted his
information.

Ben stared at the penthouse windows of the fancy
restaurant where his target was dining and wondered
what the panoramic view must be like for Monsieur
Beauchamp, or whatever his name really was. Unable to
afford eating at the high-end restaurant as a student,
Ben had never been inside. He had read and heard about
its fantastic views, though, and envied anyone who
could afford such a dining experience – until now he
had, that is.

A limousine with small French flags on each front
fender came into view and roused Ben fully alert. As the
target's transport eased up to the curb outside the
restaurant, Ben checked behind him, saw that it was
clear, and rose. He assumed a firing stance against the
tree, using a low limb for support, and put the front
doors of the restaurant in the cross-hairs of his faintly lit
telescope.

A couple strolling the quay passed in front of the door
and obstructed Ben's line of sight. His view cleared
momentarily only to be blocked again by another
passerby. The wisdom of having two shooters from two
different positions became crystal clear to him when he
considered that Popeye's view was being similarly
obstructed by the same pedestrians, only at different
times.

Beauchamp emerged from the restaurant and popped
into Ben's sight, merrily engaged in conversation with

his peers who walked on either side of him. He pulled on a glove as he strode toward the open door of the waiting limousine. Ben fired. Two impacts struck Beauchamp, one in his chest, the other in his neck. The sound of Popeye's discharge hit Ben's ears a moment later.

Beauchamp slumped against one of his peers who called for help. He and the other man shoved the man's limp body inside the automobile, and the limousine sped off.

Ben dropped down to the ground. Hysterical screams and shouts in the vicinity of the assault could be heard across the river. He checked behind him, found the area clear, and flung the rifle under a nearby bush. He jumped to his feet and ran to the broad sidewalk to his rear. The moment he reached it, he slowed to a brisk pace, headed west toward the Tournelle Bridge. Popeye had been positioned on the other side of the bridge.

Ben rolled through the escape plans etched indelibly in his mind, suppressing panic and the urge to run, his pulse quickening. They would take separate taxis to a pre-arranged destination on the outskirts of Paris where they would rendezvous and board a French military truck that would take them to Marseilles. A fishing trawler would then deliver them to the Island of Corsica, where they would board a British naval vessel.

Ben neared the bridge. A police van suddenly appeared from the Quai de la Tournelle and swerved hard onto the bridge. Ben saw two civilians and a police officer in front of the restaurant all pointing fingers in Popeye's direction. The police officer was also running toward the bridge, his pistol drawn. Popeye, who for all his lecturing on the subject was no closer to the bridge than Ben, did an abrupt about-face. Ben froze, not wanting to draw attention to himself, which, so far at least, had not occurred. All eyes were on Popeye.

The police van screeched to a halt barely half-way across the bridge. Three officers piled out as the van rocked to a complete stop. Two of them aimed their weapons at Popeye, one a rifle, the other a pistol. The third officer pointed a pistol at Ben and hollered for him to raise his hands. A fourth officer – the one on foot who had run onto the bridge – aimed his pistol at Ben.

Ben slowly raised his hands, his mind racing, his heart pounding. He didn't have time to reach into his pocket for the cyanide capsule. A hellish fear struck him. Where's Dolohov, his Number Three? Ben was much more concerned about a bullet from a sniper's rifle than one from pistols almost fifty yards away. In a near-panic, he scanned the area in search of Dolohov.

Suddenly a fusillade of explosions broke loose, sounding like a string of firecrackers let loose. Smoke engulfed the guns trained on Popeye – who fell to the ground, lifeless. The smoking weapons whipped Ben's way. He now had four guns pointed at him, with two policemen inching toward him, their pistols ready to fire.

Two shots split the night air in rapid succession, and both men crumpled in mid-step. Bedlam erupted among the remaining three officers. Conflicting orders were shouted, weapons wildly brandished, officers pulled in different directions, ducking and searching for cover while also searching for the unseen threat. Ben stood his ground, his hands in the air. He saw the terror and desperation in their eyes and did not want to add to their confusion, causing them to shoot indiscriminately.

He let the scene play out, prepared to bolt.

Another shot rang out. The policeman with the rifle buckled at the knees and collapsed.

The two other officers fell behind the cover of the van, taking their eyes off Ben and aiming them in the direction of the Tour D' Argent, the general vicinity of their attacker.

Ben lowered his arms and retreated, walking backwards, slowly at first, not wishing to draw attention to himself and while gathering information before striking out. Onlookers on the other side of the bridge had their attention stuck on a third story window in a building across the street west of the restaurant. Two policemen on foot in front of the restaurant fired pistols repeatedly at the window, shattering glass. After a short lull, Dolohov popped out in plain view, aimed his rifle toward the policemen, shot and killed one of them, and then disappeared just when bullets from the guns of the two officers behind the van ripped into the building.

Everyone Ben could see, in vehicles and on foot, were fully engrossed in the action involving Dolohov. He spun on his heels and slipped away, headed east, sneaking peeks over his shoulder as he melted into the Paris night.

Dolohov reappeared through the window and exchanged another round of bullets with the police officers. Debris all around Dolohov dislodged and flew off. Meanwhile, the lone officer in front of the restaurant fell to the ground. Ben looked back toward the van behind which the two policemen had taken cover. One was reloading his pistol. The other lay on the ground beside him, motionless. That was the last image he saw. Out of view, he began running.

He heard only the blare of sirens in his wake; no more shots were fired.

* * *

Ben leaped inside the French military transport truck almost thirty minutes later, vaulting over the raised tailgate. A few minutes later a sprinting Dolohov clambered aboard and motioned for the driver to leave. "Only two," he said, holding up two fingers. "Go!"

Ben, who had seen Dolohov coming and had lowered the tailgate for him, now lifted it. Dolohov dropped a canvass cover, enclosing them. The truck took off, and the two men settled on benches that encircled the bed of the truck, seated across from one another, Dolohov catching his breath.

"You were great back there," Ben said.

Dolohov gave him a weary look. "I guess Number One was right about the Paris police responding quickly."

"Who shot him?" Ben said.

"Not me. They must have thought he was going for a gun. You were lucky he did. I was trying to make up my mind which of you to shoot first. And I was lucky to out-shoot pistols at close range with the telescopic sight on my rifle."

Dolohov grabbed a blanket lying near him, bunched it up, and fell onto it. He took a deep breath and let it out, shaking his head in apparent disbelief. He glanced at Ben. "Wake me if anything exciting happens."

Ben laughed. Dolohov grinned and then closed his eyes.

After the truck had reached cruising speed on the open highway, Ben grabbed a blanket. Somewhere between Paris and Marseilles, he too fell asleep.

* * *

They next spoke at sea, aboard a French trawler. Ben leaned over the railing on the bow of the boat, basking in the briny, mid-morning breeze.

"Do you play cards?" he heard Dolohov's voice behind him. Ben turned. Dolohov riffled the cards, displaying them.

"No, I...I don't play," he said, and Dolohov's face sagged. "I was just thinking about what you said last night about us being lucky. I was lucky alright, but not you. Your courage and skill is what saved us."

Dolohov sloughed off the compliment.

"All in a day's work, huh?" Ben said.

"You could say that. You did your job and I did mine. However you want to look at it, we now have time to kill and a deck of cards. I'll teach you how to play."

"How do you do it?" Ben said. "Kill someone you don't know, see one of our own men gunned down, then fall asleep and get up the next morning wanting to play cards."

"Don't think about it. That's the ticket: don't think about it. If we weren't doing this, we'd probably be stuck in a foxhole someplace. You'd still be killing people you don't know and watching your own men get gunned down. Plus, you'd get ordered about all day long, the food is lousy, and the pay stinks. If you want to think about something, think about that."

Dolohov began walking off and jerked his head for Ben to follow him. "We can talk at the table while I deal the cards. No one's down there."

Ben followed him, and when they arrived in the small cabin below the deck, Dolohov took a seat at the table and started dealing the cards. Ben held up his palm as he sat across from him. "No, not for me."

Dolohov sighed and pulled back the cards he had dealt to Ben. He re-shuffled and dealt himself a hand of solitaire, as Ben pondered Dolohov's *don't-think-about-it* philosophy. His memory somehow led him to recall the time he had confided in Marsha about the plight of David and Michael. It had brought him great relief. Keeping it inside had resulted in torment. Isidor's rules of security had prevented him from opening up sooner and Chester's rules of security now prevented him and Dolohov from conversing freely. It was then that he hit on the "ticket" for him. Personalizing relationships. That was the difference in his outlook on dating before and after getting to know Marsha. She had forced him to get to know her – or to take a hike. And ever since, he preferred being with her over any other women he had been with, even when he hadn't so much as kissed her.

He then saw clearly how the rules of security, preventing people from getting to know so much as the other person's name had degraded him and made the job – already difficult – even more difficult. The simple act of naming people – unconsciously undertaken – had helped personalize the job, making life a little more bearable, keeping him from dropping into some spiritual abyss.

An amusing idea struck him.

"I'm glad we talked about this," Ben said. Dolohov gave him a glance but kept playing. "Because it caused me to realize something."

Dolohov stopped playing and stared at Ben, a blank expression on his face.

"We're people. You and I. Not numbers."

Dolohov straightened. An uneasy skepticism replaced the blankness.

"They do this on purpose...with all those rules, I mean. It's designed to de-personalize us so it doesn't matter who you kill, who goes in with you and who comes out alive. Relationships do matter, though. I feel better just having talked to you about it."

Appearing confused, Dolohov said, "I just asked you to play cards."

Ben snickered. "Look at us. Here we are in the middle of the Mediterranean Sea. We just got through risking our lives for each other, yet we don't even know each other's names."

Dolohov's face tightened, and he shot Ben a steely-eyed glance. "You think too much. I warned you about that."

"Actually, I do know your name. You're Dolohov."

His head flew back. "What's that you say?"

"Dolohov."

Dolohov laughed. "Whatever gave you that crazy idea?"

"I named you. I name all the people I work with."

He ogled Ben as if he were nuts.

"It's true. I name people according to the first impression I get of them, and you reminded me of Dolohov."

"Who's that?"

"A character in the novel *War and Peace*."

"What's he like?"

"He's like you. He was bold in battle, too. He even played cards."

"Oh yeah? That was the first thing you thought about me?" Ben nodded. "Well then, I think I'll name you Lover Boy, because that was the first thing I thought about you."

Ben laughed and extended his hand. "Nice to meet you, Dolohov."

"Same to you, Lover Boy. Now, let's play cards."

"I told you, I don't play."

"Put a lid on it, will you? With your brains, you can learn."

CHAPTER ELEVEN

B en arrived in New York on the second Thursday in April, a cool overcast day. He squeezed through a small opening in the door to his apartment. The wadded paper he used as a security check was still wedged in the crack. Apparently no one had entered while he was away. He let some air into the room and changed clothes, slipping on his wrist watch and retrieving his keys for the '37 Chevy.

He drove to the public library, and on the way stopped at the safe house to raise the window shade. The first newspaper he checked was the New York *Daily News*, the one in which he had Billy Ray place his ad. He looked for a reply, and saw none. It had been three weeks, and he expected something within a month.

The next item on his agenda was to find accounts of Germany's attack on Oslo, something he had heard whispered on the U. S. Navy ship he had taken across the Atlantic. Germany now occupied Narvik, the key transshipment port for Swedish iron ore. Chester said the assassination of Krage was designed to prevent Swedish ore from reaching Germany.

He confirmed the rumors. Electrically controlled mines guarding the inner harbor of Oslo were taken out of action by unknown persons, which allowed the easy entrance of German ships into the port. Germany had taken Norway and now controlled Narvik. He then ran across an article in the *New York Times* that filled him with outrage. A high official with the U. S. Department of Navy stated that the Nazi's "Fifth Column" – organizations of native sympathizers acting as saboteurs on behalf of the enemy – was operating in Holland, Norway, and Poland before Germany invaded each country.

The article said the United States Senate planned to hold hearings into the "alleged treason" in Norway. Ben broke out in a cold sweat. He wondered whether Chester – and he, in turn – were part of the "Fifth Column," advancing the Nazi cause, possibly even working for them. Memories of the British planes that chauffeured him to Norway and into France, and the British and U.S. ships that had helped him escape those countries, flashed through his mind, confusing him.

All the more reason for him to implement his plan.

Before he left the library, he looked for reports on the Paris assassination. Once again, the print media were silent.

When he left the library, he pulled into the garage and parked next to his new Ford. He opened its trunk and retrieved the items he had purchased prior to his Paris trip. He organized them for the next day, then jumped in, started the engine, and drove off. He parked the car along the southbound curb of Seventh Avenue, near Twenty-Seventh Street, a half block from the exit of the West Side subway exit, and a block and a half from the safe house. He locked the car and took the subway back to the Village.

* * *

Now in disguise, Ben spotted Chester's car in his rearview mirror. Ben now sported a moustache and black-rimmed glasses, and wore a dark gray pullover and a black leather jacket. Rain also helped obscure him.

He straightened in the seat of his Ford and slipped it into gear, his foot on the clutch, timing his takeoff from the curb.

As Chester's car went through the intersection, the traffic signal at Twenty-seventh turned yellow. Ben whipped the steering wheel and stepped on the gas. The light turned red and he came to a stop three cars short of the intersection. Chester's car pulled over in front of the safe house on the next block.

Chester emerged from the building under an umbrella. The traffic light at Ben's intersection turned green. Chester opened the front passenger door, closed his umbrella and ducked inside, just as the two cars in front of Ben began moving. Ben released his clutch and began inching forward, almost two car lengths behind the car in front of him.

Chester's driver signaled to pull into traffic and the two cars in front of Ben kept going, forcing Ben to yield, and placing him directly behind Chester. Ben saw inside the vehicle and recognized the features of both men. Chester's driver glanced into his rear view mirror, a mere fifteen feet or so away. Ben could see his eyes. His heart raced. A bead of sweat dripped from his forehead down onto his nose.

The driver's arm popped out the window, signaling for a lane change. His eyes lowered from the mirror. Apparently, he planned to turn left at Twenty-Sixth Street.

Ben relaxed some, feeling victorious for having passed his first test. Chester's car changed lanes. Ben allowed a car in the other lane to pass before slipping into that lane himself. He took a moment to check his surroundings. Everything seemed to be in order, no sign of Chester's goons. His confidence rose and his pulse settled. He could now tail Chester with one car as he had been tailed with two, using many techniques he had learned from Chester and his agents.

At the intersection of Twenty-Sixth, Chester's car turned left and the car in front of Ben went straight. Ben prepared to turn left, but had to yield to northbound traffic. He entered the intersection, stopped with his left arm out, and waited for the intersection to clear. He kept an eye on Chester's car. By the time Ben was able to turn, Chester was halfway down the street. Ben sped up to close the gap. The rain slackened.

Chester's car went straight through the intersection at Seventh Avenue, the light turned yellow while Ben was still two car lengths short of the stop line. He stomped on the gas.

The light turned red as he entered the intersection. Cars in two northbound lanes began moving forward but suddenly stopped. A pedestrian entered the walkway from the south curb. Ben started to hit the horn, but the pedestrian noticed Ben's car and abruptly pulled back. Ben sped through the crosswalk.

He slowed to match the flow of traffic and picked up Chester's car. Two cars had come between them, but Chester remained in the same far-left lane that Ben occupied. The rain slowed to a drizzle, nullifying the need for his wipers. Chester's were off, but Ben kept his on.

The light turned green and Chester's car crossed the intersection and changed lanes. Ben slowed and yielded to a car on his right, then broke into the lane, drawing a horn blast from another vehicle. He was three cars back of Chester. The traffic slowed and Chester's car began a right turn on Broadway. Ben signaled for a right turn. He caught up with Chester after Broadway curved off to the right, just past Pine Street, and settled into a comfortable routine.

He followed Chester left on Exchange Plaza, and left again at William Street until the car suddenly decelerated and veered toward the curb. Ben slammed on his brakes. They locked up, the wheels began skidding, and his car slid on a collision path with Chester's. Ben was terrified. He eased up on the brake, swerved to the left, and skated by Chester's car, missing it by less than six inches. Horns behind him and to his left blared. Keeping with the conventions of New York City drivers, Ben blasted his horn and threw his hand in the air, directed at Chester's driver, and sped off, his heart in his throat.

A quick glance into his rear view mirror gave him the information he needed: Chester had stepped out of the car and was approaching the entrance of the New York Bank Building. The light ahead turned yellow, and Ben came to a stop. He looked back over his shoulder and saw Chester enter the limestone building.

The light turned green and traffic begin to move. Ben spotted Chester's car making a right turn onto Pine Street. He relaxed, and wiped the sweat from his forehead with his sleeve, then rolled the window down and switched on the radio. *Deep Purple* by Larry Clinton and his Orchestra was playing, Marsha's favorite.

CHAPTER TWELVE

Ben jotted down the information he saw in front of him on a piece of paper, and closed the book. Sitting at the viewing table in the Hall of Records, he gathered up both volumes of the property records he had borrowed, and returned them to the counter. The room consisted of a long counter and five huge viewing tables. Three clerks busily worked behind the counter taking written requests and calling out names when records requested by them had been pulled, picking up returned volumes, and answering questions from people standing in line.

Ben went to the end of the line.

When his turn came, a plump, middle-aged lady pleasantly asked, "May I help you, sir?"

Ben handed the clerk a piece of paper on which he had scrawled the name of the owner of two buildings, the safe house and a three-story duplex on the Upper East Side, on Fifth Avenue, to which he had followed Chester numerous times over the past two weeks, going there from the Bank of New York Building.

Franklin Trust Assets, Limited, Postal Box 28, Nassau, Bahamas, the note read. She glanced at the note and then at Ben. "I'm trying to trace the owner of some property and I came up with that," Ben said. "How do I find out who owns or runs that company?"

"Write them a letter."

"Of course," Ben muttered, trying not to look stupid, his mind racing for an intelligent follow-up question. He knew from standing in line that people in the queue could hear his conversation and – if they were bored as he had been or were just plain nosy – were listening.

"Is there another way to find out?" Ben asked. "Just in case they don't respond. I don't do this for a living."

"You would have to go to the Bahamas and check their public records. But countries like that don't have much in the way of public records. In other words, save your money."

Ben suspected she was right. It only figured that Chester and his people were clever enough to block easy discovery, especially from an amateur investigator.

"Sorry," said the clerk. "Is there anything else I can help you with?"

Hat in hand, Ben thanked her and left.

CHAPTER THIRTEEN

Sitting in the Grand Central Newsreel Theater, Ben watched the images of the German Army taking Holland and Belgium, followed by the invasion of France. France signed an armistice with Nazi Germany almost ten weeks after the assassination of Henri Beauchamp. He recalled Chester telling him that the purpose of eliminating Beauchamp was to prevent an armistice with Germany. Maybe the killing bought ten weeks of time and forced Germany to attack but he was skeptical. He feared he saw a pattern emerging. An ominous pattern. A mission to eliminate an important figure in order to prevent a specified harmful event was followed by that event. Perhaps the Paris mission, like the one to Oslo, was a failure despite Chester's laudatory comments and financial reward.

The newsreel and Ben's musings brought to mind the words of President Roosevelt given in a fireside chat two weeks before the French armistice:

We know of the new methods of attack. The Trojan Horse. The Fifth Column that betrays a nation unprepared for treachery. Spies, saboteurs, and traitors are the actors in this new tragedy.

That was the second mention of the so-called Fifth Column by a high-ranking official. Both came after one of his assignments. Both assignments occurred mere weeks before the Nazi hammer fell on an ally. Grave misgivings fell upon him, dampening his willingness to proceed. He left the theater under a starlit sky, considering his accomplishments and objectives, and comparing them with the harm he might be facilitating.

The exercise led him to a dead-end. He was convinced that Chester had the resources to assist him one day to rescue his brothers, and he had partially performed his end of the bargain; he didn't want to leave his credits on the table and walk away empty-handed. He was afraid to question Chester or protest for fear of how he might react. He was reminded of their first training session when Chester became almost maniacal when Ben absent-mindedly waited at the door for Chester to leave the safe house with him. Ben was still under Chester's thumb. And the fact was, he didn't know that he was part of any Fifth Column. Neither official, and none of the press, had even mentioned the assassinations.

He decided to play the Ace of Hearts.

When he reached his car, he headed home, driving by the safe house. "Dammit," he said, slamming the steering wheel with an open palm.

The shade was up.

CHAPTER FOURTEEN

Ben pecked at his typewriter. At the top of the page, centered and capitalized, he typed, ADVERTISEMENT. Below that he typed the line: *Penn Station connection. Looking to Buy or Rent. London.* Further down the page, he centered and capitalized, *INSTRUCTIONS*, and then typed the following: Please run in the Real Estate Wanted section every Friday for eight weeks.

He then pulled the sheet out of the carriage, folded it, and stuck it in an envelope. He stuffed a five dollar bill inside and then sealed it. On the outside of the envelope, he printed in ink, *Ad + Instructions for Ad.* He placed the envelope inside his right dress shoe. He looked outside. It was still raining. As Billy Ray would say it, when it rained, he "packed it in." Ben carried his dress shoes out the door, anyway. Maybe it would stop raining by the time he returned from the safe house.

* * *

"I don't know if you keep up with the news," Chester said, "but this so-called 'Fifth Column' has really interfered with our plans."

Ben was sitting across from Chester at the kitchen table, and almost fell out of his chair.

"Yes," Ben said, "I've seen all the news on it and was concerned that our work in both Oslo and Paris seems to have gone for naught. Even the Senate plans to hold hearings."

"That's all well and good. The Senate should look into it, but that's all a bunch of bureaucracy. We're going to cut through the red tape. We've identified dozens of key saboteurs inside Norway, France, Holland and Belgium, and we're going to dispense with them.

"I told you to expect a lot of action, and this is it. We're sending you inside these countries on a series of assignments. The operation will last for the foreseeable future, many months. The action will be practically nonstop, until we clear them out and gain an upper hand. You will be gone weeks at a time. I may very well have to brief you by courier on some of the assignments, meaning you might not even return between engagements. When you do return, it may be for only twenty-four or seventy-two hours or a week.

"It will be dangerous, more dangerous than before because now you will be going into occupied territory. Your compensation will be doubled, in some cases tripled."

Ben's attention latched on to "*going into occupied territory.*"

"Does that mean you can now get me inside Germany as well?"

As Chester crushed the cigarette he had been smoking, he shook his head. "No, not at all. Germany's borders are completely sealed, and have been for a few years. They've only just taken these other territories. They haven't had the time or the resources to seal their borders to that degree. We have identified huge, gaping holes in the borders of these countries through which we can easily pass, mainly with low-flying aircraft.

"You will be trained to jump onto and off of these specially designed aircraft without their having to come to a stop. The landing strips we'll be using are no more than open fields, and are rarely long enough for landings and takeoffs to and from a complete stop. In some cases you will be met by partisan forces who will escort you into target zones; in others, you will travel on foot. The training and experience you receive will prepare you for an eventual incursion inside Germany to rescue your brothers."

"When do I get started?" Ben said. Chester lit another cigarette.

"I will brief you daily for three days and you will leave on the fourth day." Ben nodded.

* * *

The rain stopped during the briefing, and Billy Ray was set up on the corner as Ben drove by. He parked and went inside his apartment. He decided that his dress shoes didn't need a shine, after all.

PART IV

May 1941 - January 1942

CHAPTER ONE

B en sat alone dozing in the cargo bay of a Soviet Air Forces plane, soothed by the drone of its engines, when the whirr and clank of the landing gear dropping stirred him from his half-sleep. The engines whined as the plane began its descent. That meant he was in Finland and would soon have company. He moved into position against the sliding door, one hand on the latch, the other braced against the fuselage.

The plane slammed to the earth just as Ben opened the door. The door banged shut, and Ben's legs flew out from under him, jamming his right wrist as he fought to hold on. With a sharp pain shooting up his arm, Ben regained his footing and the plane settled onto a true course, bouncing and jerking over the open field. He braced his legs and right arm and again wrenched the door open, his left arm carrying most of the weight, holding it open. He craned his neck and peered into the semi-darkness. He spotted two men running on a course to converge with the decelerating plane.

Ben stood in the doorway, braced himself using his left hand against the fuselage and extended his right arm. He instantly recognized the first man. Frenchie grabbed his arm at the elbow, and then lunged as Ben simultaneously heaved. Frenchie dove headlong into the plane's cargo bay. Ben immediately righted himself and reached out for the other man, who vaulted and grabbed Ben's wrist in one movement, causing a stabbing pain that shot up his arm. Ben screamed and let go of the fuselage with his left arm, grabbed the torso of the man and fell backward. They landed in a heap, as the plane's engines revved to complete the touch-and-go. Frenchie snatched the man's legs and hauled him in. The plane accelerated and Frenchie closed and sealed the door.

Gasping for breath, Ben leaned against the fuselage, holding his throbbing wrist. The plane lifted off the ground, and the smoothness of air replaced the turbulence of the uneven ground.

"You okay?" Frenchie said.

Ben tested it, moving it side to side. Painful and limited in range, he pressed down on it with his left arm, approximating the weight of his rifle, and flexed his trigger finger. No pain at all; complete ease of movement. "It still works," he said. He shook his head. "That was a rough one."

Frenchie agreed.

After Ben had caught his breath, he checked his wrist again. It was doing a little better already. Nothing serious, he decided. He shook it for Frenchie, who was watching. "It's okay." Frenchie nodded as though relieved. Ben gave him a close look. "So, we meet again."

Frenchie flashed a crooked grin that turned into a frown as he displayed two fingers, as if acknowledging he had been demoted. Ben laughed. He was glad to see that Frenchie had a sense of humor. He was prepared for more banter when he became aware of a hostile glare fixed on him from Number Three, who sat in the shadows of the dimly lit bay, almost invisible. He was four or five inches shorter than Ben, and thinner, wiry. Ben noticed his tight, compact body when he pulled him aboard. He was fair-haired with sunken, cold blue eyes and a malevolent demeanor.

He named him "Ghost."

He decided not to permit Ghost to dampen his mood – or his camaraderie with Frenchie.

"I'm glad to see you here," he said to Frenchie. "I wondered what might happen if I miss." Frenchie laughed, and Ben laughed with him. Ghost's nostrils flared, the muscles around his jaw tightened.

"That was a joke," Ben said to Ghost, trying to lighten him up.

Ghost abruptly lunged at Ben, grabbed the front of his shirt and twisted. He bared his teeth. "Listen, pretty boy. Cut the shit." A lump of Ben's shirt was twisted in his fist. He let loose of it with an angry shove. "And don't miss!"

Ben met Ghost's glare of intimidation with a confident half-smile. He wasn't looking for a fight; he just wanted to make a point. Ghost backed down.

Ben exchanged glances with Frenchie, whose face showed nothing.

* * *

Ben stood outside the main portal to the Kremlin, a compound of churches and cathedrals, historic towers, government buildings, palaces, monuments, and the Alexander Gardens. Engaged in his site survey, he caught himself partly observing, partly recalling his civic lessons. The city of Moscow was built around the Kremlin, a name that is derived from the Russian word for fortress. And it once was a medieval city, a fortress on a hill above the Moscow River. Long ago, Moscow grew miles beyond the walls of the Kremlin, laid out in a series of concentric circles that surround the old city. In times past, the Kremlin was the citadel of the Tsars; now it was the seat of the Soviet government. His target would emerge the next day from behind the gate in Savior Tower on the northeast side of the Kremlin, across from Red Square.

He envisioned two motorcycles emerging, driven by Soviet soldiers followed by a convertible limousine that carried his target, a Soviet Army General. Another pair of motorcycles took up the rear. On foot, Ben traced the route the target would take on his way to the airport northwest of the city. He walked through a section of the city named Kitay Gorod, heading northeast on Ilinka Boulevard and then winding around a loop in the street where the general would meet his demise.

Twenty-two hours later, Ben's vision became reality. The lead motorcycles entered the loop, followed closely by the limousine. Onlookers lined the streets, straining to glimpse the dignitary in the motorcade, perhaps thinking it was Stalin. Ben had a better view, from atop a six-story building.

He fired his Mosin 91/30 sniper rifle, striking the General in his upper chest, a little off target. Another explosion ripped the air, which now filled with shrieks and screams from the hysterical crowd. The General's head blew backwards. The target slumped in his seat and the motorcade screeched to a halt. Appearing confused and terror-stricken, the four soldiers on motorcycles desperately searched in all directions for the source of the shots. Ben scooted across the roof and escaped down a fire escape in the rear of the building. The shrill wail of a siren erupted amid the sound of gunning motors.

The three men rendezvoused inside a vacant building and ripped off their peasant clothes, cramming them into travel bags they had stashed there the day before. They squeezed into Soviet Army uniforms and, running, boarded a Soviet military bus that had just come to a halt outside. The bus whisked them away. North of the city, it dropped them off and they scrambled into the cover of a stand of birch trees, changing back once more into their peasant clothes. They ditched the travel bags and hid out until well after dark.

Around eleven that night, a black sedan pulled to a stop on the road adjacent to them. A flashlight flickered off and on, three times. They piled inside and were taken to the Leningrad Railway Station northeast of Moscow, arriving one half-hour prior to the departure of the Red Arrow, an express train to Leningrad. At the station, the men separated.

Thirty minutes later, Ben made his way to the platform, just as the first of the train's three whistles blew. As he approached the train, a Soviet Army officer stared at him suspiciously. Ben ignored him, maintaining a carefree outlook. He was confident that there had been no witnesses; and without witnesses, they had no descriptions.

When he reached the short boarding line, Ben casually turned and caught the officer still staring at him. The officer walked toward Ben, slowly at first, but then picked up his pace as if he had come to some conclusion about him. Clearly, the officer intended to confront him. Ben felt trapped in line with no place or time to run.

"Hey! Hey, you!" the officer yelled in Ben's direction. Steam from the train hissed, partly drowning out his cry.

Ben continued to ignore him. In front of him were two people standing in line to board the train and a conductor who was checking tickets. None of them turned or paid any heed to the shouting officer. The conductor cleared the first passenger, leaving only a woman in front of Ben. She presented her papers and ticket.

"Stop that man," the officer yelled again, louder and with more determination.

The conductor cleared the woman. She took a half-step, then stopped and turned toward the shouting officer. Ben shoved his papers into the hands of the conductor who looked up at the approaching officer, and back at Ben. With a befuddled expression, he hesitated.

Ben turned to address the threat behind him.

The charging officer threw an angry finger at Ben, who shrugged his ignorance.

At that moment, Ghost appeared out of a group of people lingering on the platform, waving a cigarette at the officer, grabbing his attention. "A light, Sir," Ghost said, rapidly approaching the officer. Rattled, the officer pulled up about six feet short of Ben, his attention fixed on Ghost.

Ben seized the moment. "See," he said to the conductor, reaching out for his papers.

As he began studying them, Ben sneaked an anxious glance over his shoulder.

"A light, Sir," Ghost said. "I need a light." He waved the cigarette in the face of the soldier, who flailed at Ghost. "Get out of my way," he said.

Ghost skillfully parried the arm with his left. Simultaneously, a stiletto slipped out of his right sleeve into the palm of his hand and Ghost jammed it under the officer's ribs. The officer stiffened as if having a seizure, his face contorted. He sputtered and fell into Ghost, who took him into his arms, the knife nowhere in sight.

"You may go," the conductor said to Ben, returning his papers. Ben thanked him and took the papers. At the same moment, he heard Ghost cry out.

"Heart attack!"

Both he and the conductor abruptly turned. Ghost gently lowered the officer to the ground and knelt beside him. "Heart attack," he yelled to onlookers. "Call for an ambulance."

The conductor left Ben to board and ran to the officer's aid. The people milling about the platform, who apparently had been saving their final goodbyes to loved ones until the last whistle, and who had previously been unaware or disinterested in the Army officer's actions, now took note of him, gasping and gawking. A crowd quickly closed around Ghost and the fallen officer.

Ben eased his way onto the train as the whistle blew for the second time.

He took a seat next to a window on the platform side of the train and watched what was unfolding. The crowd had thinned by the time the whistle blew for the third and final time. Ghost was still attending the man. Three emergency personnel ran toward them, two carrying a stretcher, the other a medical bag. Ben heard the sound of pressurized air releasing. The train shook and the screeching of metal on metal began. The train began to move forward.

Ghost said something to the emergency personnel as they arrived and then ran and leaped onto the moving train.

Ben craned his neck, hoping to see the faces of the medical people when they learned the man had been stabbed. He was wondering how long it would take them to piece together the facts and realize that the Good Samaritan was really a killer. The train left the platform, picking up speed. It was too late for authorities to stop the train, but they had plenty of time to call ahead to Leningrad. By then they would have a description of Ghost and his connection to the station killing – and to the assassination. Police and soldiers would likely be awaiting them.

He thought through the possibilities and prepared a strategy for each.

Ben thought of Frenchie. He looked over the car and finally spotted him on the other side of the aisle, two rows up, apparently already asleep and unaware of the episode on the platform. He had no idea where Ghost had settled. He considered waking Frenchie and consulting him, but dismissed the idea. He would worry about it later if and when the train stopped. It was midnight and he was tired.

He closed his eyes and drifted off. In the mist of memory, Marsha wandered back to him, breathing his name with a sigh.

* * *

Ben awoke the next morning as the train reached the outskirts of Leningrad, meaning it was close to eight o'clock. The sky was bright and mostly clear. Peace and calm was all he saw. He reviewed his predicament with a fresh view, and considered whether to stay on board. If he was going to jump, he needed to be doing it soon. He opted to stay on board.

The train pulled into the Moscow Rail Terminal in Leningrad about fifteen minutes later, the train snorting and hissing as it slowed. And then his worst fears were realized. The station was swarming with uniformed men, both police and military. He grew restive, his heart pumping rapidly. Too late to abort now, he felt trapped.

As the train shuddered to a stop, uniformed men closed in on the exit doors. Ben rose. He cast his eyes at Frenchie who wore an uneasy, puzzled look. Ben gestured for him to keep his distance, and he entered the aisle. He took a deep breath, composed himself, and stepped off the train. Soldiers were demanding papers from the passengers and peering into their faces. Ben pulled his papers. He projected an air of innocence, hoping for the best.

He showed his papers to a soldier on his right. The soldier gave him the once-over, checked the papers, and then shoved them back at him. His attention was already on the next person in line.

Outside the station on Neva Avenue, Frenchie sidled up to him. "What was that all about?"

"I think they're looking for Number Three. Have you seen him?"

"No. Did he even get on the train?"

"I saw him get on, but he had an incident with a soldier on the platform." A taxi pulled up to the curb. "Here, let's get out of here." He took Frenchie by the arm and guided him into the taxi, jumping in behind him, notwithstanding their instruction that they travel separately. Frenchie didn't object.

* * *

Two hours later, Ben and Frenchie stood alone in a clump of trees next to an open field, waiting for the low-flying, twin-engine Soviet military plane circling overhead to get into position for a touch-and-go landing. The plane banked northward, straightened out, and began a steep descent.

"Get ready," Ben said. "Here she comes."

Frenchie looked over his shoulder. "I guess we lost him."

"Yeah, I guess so."

The plane touched down, and the side door slid open. The two men bolted from the trees and dashed toward the middle of the field. An officer in a Soviet uniform stood in the doorway ready to assist them. Seeing that he ran faster, Ben angled west of Frenchie's trajectory. "You first," he yelled. Frenchie veered toward the open door, leaped and grabbed the edge of the doorway with his right hand. The officer, a co-pilot, grabbed his extended left hand and pulled. Frenchie sailed inside.

Favoring his right wrist, Ben motioned for the co-pilot to step aside. The moment he did, Ben dove through the door, landing outstretched on the metal deck with a painful thud. He felt two hands at his waist lift and hurl him the rest of the way inside.

"Look!" Frenchie yelled.

"Stay down, there's one more," the co-pilot shouted, and Ben scrambled to his feet, peered out, and saw Ghost sprinting toward them. Ben and Frenchie reached out, grabbed his arms, and pulled him aboard.

"All in," the co-pilot yelled to the cockpit. "Take it up." He helped Ben and Frenchie close and secure the hatch before heading back to the cockpit. The plane lifted off.

When they were aloft and alone, Ben turned to Ghost. "How did you get through the dragnet back at the station?" he asked in Russian.

Ghost glared at him and didn't respond, which reminded Ben of Ghost's behavior going into Russia. For some reason Ben had thought that things would be different now. Apparently not. He turned to Frenchie.

"You should have seen what happened at the Leningrad Station in Moscow, on the platform."

Frenchie perked up.

"Number Three took out a uniformed military officer who was on to me," Ben said, sneaking a peek at Ghost, still catching his hateful glower. "The officer was coming after me when our comrade here stepped in his path and dropped him like a bad date."

Frenchie grinned and glanced at Ghost, who looked as if he was about to blow a gasket. Frenchie wiped the grin off his face, obviously sensing trouble. He shrank back.

Not Ben. He had only begun. "He hollered, 'Heart attack,' and people standing around bought into it. The conductor even ran off to get emergency care for him. And, it was true. He really did have a heart attack. I saw it. His heart got attacked by a knife. No one else saw what happened; he was so quick and smooth."

Ben threw Ghost an admiring look and Frenchie's eyes rolled in his direction. Ghost was not amused. He shot daggers at Ben.

"So, thanks for saving my life back there," Ben said to Ghost, whose taut jaw muscles rippled, his livid eyes locked fiercely on Ben.

Ben turned to Frenchie and said, "That's his way of saying, 'you're welcome.'"

Diplomatically bowing out, Frenchie lowered his eyes and turned away. Ben glanced at Ghost who continued to seethe. As with a wild mustang refusing to submit, Ben intended to ride the hateful bull crap out of Ghost.

Ben stared into his eyes and felt the force and blackness of Ghost's glare. Perhaps he could stare him down, perhaps not, but he was going to try. He switched to English: "You are one, scary, cold-blooded bastard."

Ghost uncoiled like a rattlesnake, striking out with a pistol in his hand that had appeared out of thin air. Ben kicked his face, Ghost fell backwards, and Ben dove for his gun hand. With a violent twist, he slammed it against the hull. A stabbing pain shot up Ben's right wrist. He let out a scream. Ghost groaned as his hand smashed into the steel fuselage. The gun popped out of his grasp and flew through the air, clanging to the deck.

Ben lunged for the pistol, but Ghost lashed out and struck his jaw with a vicious left hook that stunned Ben. When he shook the cobwebs loose, he saw Ghost diving for the gun. Ben slammed his right elbow into Ghost's ribs with all his might and then hooked his left arm around his head, grabbed his chin, and snapped it back. Ghost wailed, falling short of the gun by inches.

The door to the cockpit opened and the co-pilot stepped out and yelled, "What's going on? Hey, knock it off you two." Frenchie jumped up, blocking his path.

Ben grabbed the gun with his right hand while keeping a strong hold on Ghost's twisted neck. As soon as he had a good grip on the pistol, he jammed the barrel up against Ghost's skull. Ghost let up. He didn't buckle or show any fear, just common sense.

"Put the gun down," the officer demanded; Frenchie told him to stay out of it.

Ben gritted his teeth, nose-to-nose with Ghost. He was angry enough to kill – and still might; he hadn't made up his mind. What seemed like minutes passed. Neither budged. As Ben's breathing calmed, his objective for confronting Ghost came into focus. He may have already achieved it. He just wanted to make it clear they had reached an understanding.

He spoke measuredly, in English. "If you ever come at me again, I'll kill you. Do you understand?"

Ghost didn't say anything, but his eyes did: message received. Ben slowly released the pressure of his grip, the barrel of the gun still pressed against Ghost's head. Ghost didn't move a muscle. Remembering the spectators, Ben turned one eye to Frenchie, who was standing next to the co-pilot, his palm up, warning him to hold off, his eyes on Ben. The co-pilot didn't move. Ben returned his full attention to Ghost. He let go of him and moved back against the side of the cargo bay, his eyes and pistol on Ghost. When he was settled, he lowered the pistol.

Ghost slithered back to his original spot, scowled at Ben and then shrunk back into his own world. His scowl was one of self-preservation, no longer threatening.

The co-pilot ducked back into the cockpit and closed the door.

Frenchie saluted Ben with his eyebrows, then took a seat and closed his eyes.

CHAPTER TWO

Ben handed Billy Ray his dress shoes. "I'll pick these up tomorrow," he said, and took a seat for a shine of his walking shoes. Billy Ray nodded, taking and placing the shoes under his wagon.

"There's an envelope inside the right shoe. Wait until after I leave to take it out. Later today, I want you to go by the *Daily News* building. Remember that place?"

Billy Ray was rubbing in polish, and didn't look up. "Uh-huh, that's when I put the ad in the paper."

"Right. We're going to do the same thing. The ad and the instructions are in the envelope, along with the money for the ad. What's left over is for you."

Billy Ray started bobbing. "Yeah, that's the kind of music I like to hear."

Ben smiled, and made a casual scan of the area. "If you don't jump up and start dancing, I have more of your kind of music." He motioned for Ben's other shoe, and Ben switched shoes.

"I got to get into my shine, that's all," Billy Ray said. "You jus' keep hittin' those notes, you'll see."

"In the left shoe, there's a telegram. You know what that is?"

"Ain't that a message?"

"Yes, Western Union. You know how to send one?" He didn't. Ben asked him if he knew where the Holley Hotel was. What, did Ben think he was stupid?

"I want you to go there and send a telegram. The note inside the envelope contains the message to send and who it goes to. Just go into the lobby and tell the man behind the counter that you want to send a telegram, then hand him the note. He'll know what to do with it. The money to send it is in the envelope, plus a little extra for you."

Billy Ray double-tapped Ben's shoe with added gusto, as though punctuating Ben's music with a drum beat.

He flipped the polish tin into the wagon and reached for the brush. "Got them chollies comin' home to Billy Ray."

Ben laughed.

"What's it say?" Billy Ray asked as he began buffing Ben's shoe.

"It says Happy Birthday and it's signed by B.R. Montclair."

"B.R. That's like my name, Billy Ray."

"You can pretend it's your name, but if anyone asks for your name just tell them Billy Ray. Don't tell anyone your last name is Montclair. If you have to explain anything, just say you're delivering a message for someone and leave it at that. It's none of their business. If they ask too many questions, walk away. We can try it again somewhere else."

"Who's it to?" Billy Ray said.

"It's going to Charles Montclair for pickup at the counter of the Western Union station in Atlantic City. All that means is that someone by that name can pick it up. You can pretend you are sending your dad or your uncle a birthday greeting if you want, but don't tell them that."

Billy signaled for Ben to switch shoes.

"I've got one more errand for you," Ben said, taking down the shined shoe and replacing it with the other one. "I need you to go by the building on Eighth and Twenty-seventh later today. Look at the fifth window from the corner on the second floor. Which one did I say?"

"The fifth one, countin' from the corner."

"What floor?" Ben said.

"Second floor. Is that where the man goes?"

"Yes. But that's not important. Here's what's important," Ben said. "The window shade on that window is up today. Ride by tomorrow after three o'clock and it will be down. I want you to see the window shade up and down so you know exactly what I mean some day when I ask you to keep an eye on the window. Are you getting all this?"

Billy Ray nodded. "Yeah, ain't much to it."

"I'll pick up my dress shoes after you do that and make sure everything went okay."

Billy Ray finished the shine, and Ben rose to pay him.

"When does your school let out," Ben said.

"Next week. Why?"

Ben shook his head. "Just curious, that's all."

* * *

Chester took a drag on his cigarette as he finished reading Ben's report. "One of the pilots said you got into a fight with Number Three," Chester said, exhaling. "I don't see any mention of it in your report."

"I didn't think it was important," Ben said.

"What was the problem?"

"I don't remember."

Chester stared at Ben, taking another puff. He blew it out. "I can always make sure you two don't work together again."

"That isn't necessary. We reached an understanding."

Chester snuffed the cigarette, exhaling a cloud of smoke. "Very well." He placed Ben's report in a satchel and pulled out a wad of cash, handing it to Ben. He then slapped Ben on the shoulder. "Good job, as usual," and then waved his hand, signaling that Ben could leave. When Chester got into his car fifteen minutes later, Ben was on his tail, driving his '39 Ford and wearing his disguise.

The driver dropped Chester off at the Bank of New York Building. Ben parked up the street in view of the William Street doors, listening to his radio. An hour and a half later, Chester emerged and walked to the curb. Ben started his engine. Chester's car arrived moments later, and Chester hopped in. Ben followed the car to South Street where it turned left and pulled to the curb near the pier. Chester got out and the car took off. He entered a building almost a half block down the street. Ben parked his car. Forty minutes later, a man emerged from the same door that Chester had entered.

It was Ghost.

* * *

"Western Union," the voice on the other end of the line said.

Ben was calling from a pay phone. "My name is Charles Montclair. I'm expecting a telegram."

"I'll check. Hold on, please." Later, the voice returned. "Yes, we have something for you. It's for pick up at the counter."

"Thank you." Ben hung up the phone. He didn't go to Atlantic City; he didn't have to. He knew Billy Ray could send a telegram, which is all he wanted to know.

CHAPTER THREE

A mild breeze blew through the windows of his Ford, as if to emphasize the perfect spring day it was. Ben parked along a side street with the rear bumper of his car very close to the car behind to obscure his out-of-state license plate. He nervously bided his time. He knew school would be out soon because buses and cars already lined the driveway that arced in front of the school, the only elementary school in Rocky Mount. He hoped she taught there, otherwise he would have to ask around. The town was tiny; the city limits sign put its population at 1,366. A stranger asking questions would stand out, as did his black-on-yellow New York license plate.

So many things rushed through his mind, each one stood out and took prominence over the others. He wondered whether Marsha still had feelings for him and, if she did, how she would react to his need for secrecy. Chester crossed his mind. The thought of the window shade to the safe house going up sickened him, and also reminded him to call the Roger Smith Hotel in Washington, D. C. and check for a telegram from Billy Ray before he settled in for the night. He went over again for the thousandth time what he would say to

Marsha and how she might react to seeing him. As his joyous visions played out, he stopped and reminded himself to maintain his decorum and security so as to not create a spectacle that people who saw them together might remember.

A school bell rang, rousing Ben from his reverie. He sat upright, his pulse suddenly racing, his stomach queasy. Children burst through the doorway and suddenly filled the air with laughter and playful shouts and screams. They began filling the buses and cars, swarming the sidewalks, heading north and south. Ben kept a close watch out for grown-ups emerging from the white double doors with one eye on the parking lot. After all, she might have a car now or be riding with someone who did. A boyfriend maybe? That prospect sickened Ben as much as that window shade going up.

A steady stream of cars left the front of the school, intermixed with the buses, and the mass migration thinned to a trickle. And then Marsha stepped out, carrying books – alone. She cheerfully waved to various children as she walked off. Her radiant face tugged at Ben's heart. For a moment the whole experience seemed surreal, as though he wasn't really there seeing her. Then reality sunk in. His heart was pounding like a bass drum. Then he realized that tears had welled up in both eyes. His palms were sweating. He pulled a handkerchief out of a pocket and wiped his eyes and hands. He drew in a deep breath.

When the children had cleared and Marsha was walking alone, he started the car. Before pulling forward, he made a final check for unwanted attention, then let out on the clutch. The car began moving. He steered it onto the street and drove up behind her. He pulled over to the curb alongside her, and stopped. She turned her head and then did a double-take. Her eyes burst wide.

"Ben!" she screamed.

Ben threw open the door and motioned for her to get in.

She jumped in, dropped her books, and grabbed him in her arms, washing away all his pent-up fears and concerns. Ben squeezed her tightly. She moved to kiss him, but he cut her short.

"Where can we talk so no one will see us?" he said. "I've got to get this car off the street."

She balked, suddenly confused. "Quickly, I'll explain later."

She thought hard for a second and then brightened. "I know. A cabin in the hills where daddy used to make moonshine. Even the revenuers couldn't find it."

"He *made* liquor? I thought you meant he drank it?"

"He did that too."

Ben laughed. "Perfect. Good ol' moonshine boys," spoken with the best hillbilly accent he could muster.

She giggled. "You'll fit right into these parts."

He put the car in gear and started to pull away from the curb, but held up. "I hate to ask you to do this, but as we go through town, I need you to duck down out of sight."

She hesitated and Ben grimaced apologetically. "Alright," she said, then scrunched down into the seat well.

"I'm sorry," Ben said.

"No, please don't be. I don't mind."

From that position, she directed him west of town. After they had reached the city limits, he told her the coast was clear, and she twisted back into her seat and directed him along a narrow, curving state road through the village of Ferrum, then had him steer north on a winding gravel road. Any time a car or pickup came near, she either ducked down or turned away.

She asked him how long he planned to stay.

"Until late Sunday night, I hope. I have to call in daily, including later today. Don't let me forget. If I'm wanted back in New York, I have to leave no later than midnight."

Marsha frowned, and Ben reached out for her. She snuggled up next to him. "How did your family emergency turn out?" she asked.

"There was no family emergency," he said.

She straightened.

"The truth is, I'm engaged in highly classified activities that I can't discuss. No one is supposed to know, especially you. I'm not supposed to have a romantic relationship, so I lied to you."

"Is that because of the war in Europe?" She then snapped, "No, you don't have to say any more," and settled against him, pulling his arm back over her shoulder. "I figured it out soon after you left. With your intelligence and knowledge of the German language and culture, I'm sure you were an attractive candidate..."

Amazed at her deduction, Ben thought to himself, *Am I the only person in America who believed President Roosevelt when he said we weren't involved in the war?*

"... and I know how strongly you feel about ..." she cut herself off. "Oh, what about David and Michael. Are they still in prison?"

Ben told her that he had heard nothing further about them, which visibly saddened her.

Twenty to thirty minutes after leaving Rocky Mount, Marsha told Ben to turn off the highway onto an overgrown dirt road choked with weeds. They took the unmarked, rutted path several miles up into heavily forested foothills until they reached a dilapidated wooden gate. Marsha jumped out of the car, opened it for him to pass through, and then closed it behind them. They drove through the woods, up and over a ridge, forded a creek, and then continued until the pathway ended.

"Park on the other side of those bushes, next to the boulder," she said. "We have to walk the rest of the way, unless you want to talk in the car."

He marveled at the remoteness of the location, which he had to admit was just about ideal, given his situation. He parked the car and turned to her. "I first want to finish the wonderful greeting I interrupted, if you don't mind."

She smiled and leaned in to him. He took her in his arms, and they kissed.

When they separated, tears were flowing down Marsha's grinning face, reminding him of sunshine breaking through stormy clouds. He wiped a tear away with his thumb. "I worried that you might have forgotten about me," he said.

She shook her head and hugged him tightly. "I thought of you every single day. I knew you would come back to me one day. I just knew it."

"In the mist of a memory I wander back to you," he sang, and she joined in: "breathing my name with a sigh."

"Oh, I can't believe you remembered that," she said. "I thought about that song a million times, every time I thought of you." Ben told her he had, too, ever since hearing the song on the radio one day and remembering it was her favorite song.

She led him to the cabin, a one-mile trek through the woods and further up the mountainside. The word cabin was too generous for what he saw before him. It was a large, one-room mountain shack, put together with clapboards, spit, and a promise. The weather had long since worn away the spit.

Behind the shack was a falling-down outhouse, with its door fallen off and lying on the ground, foot-high weeds growing around it. Further off in the distance stood the still, an assembly of five huge tanks set on concrete blocks and surrounded by barrels, buckets, and jugs. A long pipe and several hoses were still lying around. It was obvious, more care and resources had been put into the construction of the still than the sleeping quarters.

"It seems to be in pretty good shape," he said about the still.

"I've still got daddy's recipes for corn whiskey and apple and peach brandy, if you want to give it a go."

Ben laughed. "No thanks. I have enough suspense in my life."

She took him inside the shack, which was a mess. Dirt, dust, and even leaves littered the floor. There was a full-sized bed with a moldy mattress, a pot-bellied stove, a sink, a homemade kitchen table with wobbly chairs, and a shelf full of metal cups, dishes, and silverware. A chest of drawers made of a sturdy hardwood was the nicest thing furnishing the place. Ben opened a drawer, and pulled out a pair of overalls and a pair of faded red long johns with a buttoned flap in the rear.

"Oh, I like these," he said, displaying them. "I wonder if they fit."

"I'd pay a month's salary to see you in them."

"I'm sure you would." He folded them and put them back.

"Well, what do you think?" she said.

"The location is sublime. Otherwise, it's..." he glanced about him, straining for an adjective, "... kind of *rustic*."

She laughed. "I know it needs some work, but I have linens and other things at the house; we can spruce it up."

"Aha," he said. "I know what's missing. A bath."

"We've got that, too. There's a creek not far from here." She pointed in the general direction of the still. "You can skinny-dip."

The term threw him.

"Don't tell me you've never gone skinny-dippin'?" she teased.

"I've never bathed in a creek if that's what you mean."

"City folk. I'll explain it later. We better get started cleaning up."

She made a list on paper she had brought for that purpose, and marked an "M" next to the ones she would pick up from her house and a "B" for the ones Ben would purchase.

The former category included food, bedding, cleaning utensils, and toilet paper. The latter included a new mattress, two lanterns, kerosene, dishware, and lye (both for scrubbing inside the shack and for use in the outhouse).

"I need to keep my car off the streets as much as possible," Ben said. "I have a New York license plate and it seems to catch attention."

"I can see that it would," she said. "Maybe it's best that you shop in Roanoke. You can drop me off in Rocky Mount and I'll drive my car and meet you back here." She told him she not only inherited her daddy's house but had bought a car with the remainder of her trust fund. She volunteered to pick up supper for them both from a restaurant, promising him he would enjoy the local cuisine. "You'll return for the food, if nothing else."

She sketched a map with driving instructions to Roanoke and each store Ben needed to visit. "By the way," he said. "Is there a pay phone nearby? I'll call in from Roanoke today, but I'll want something closer for tomorrow?"

"Yes, there's one in Ferrum," she said. "Exactly one."

* * *

He saved the call to the Roger Smith Hotel in Washington, D. C. for last, and anxiously dropped sixty cents in the coin slot as instructed by the operator. "Hello. I'm calling to check on a telegram that may have been sent to you for my pickup," he said when a male voice answered the phone. "Charles Montclair."

"Let me check," said the voice. After ten or fifteen seconds he returned. "No, Mr. Montclair. I'm sorry but there aren't any messages for you at this time."

Ben heaved a sigh of relief, thanked the man, and hung up. He let out a muffled whoop and punched the air. A ton of pent-up emotions vanished from his shoulders.

* * *

He waited for Marsha on the grassy lane, out of view of the highway. She arrived soon after sunset and they returned to the shack carrying food, paper plates, plastic forks and cups up to the shack. Having eaten only snacks purchased at gas stations since his breakfast at the hotel in Washington, D.C. where he slept the night before, Ben was famished.

Over a heavy oilcloth red-and-white checked tablecloth, they ate cornbread cakes, Southern barbecued pork, and coleslaw, all in the glow of a single kerosene lantern.

"Absolutely delicious," he said, savoring every bite.

She was pleased. "I still owe you one for the Russian meal you made me. The next time you visit, I will make you a banquet of my favorite Southern foods. I don't want to spend my time in a kitchen this weekend."

"I look forward to it," he said.

They spent the next four hours trekking to their cars carrying supplies, cleaning the cabin as best they could and re-making it into something warm and cozy, in a very "rustic" sort of way – or at least as close to that as they could make it.

Standing back and admiring the finished product, he asked her what she thought.

"You're my guest, so if you like it, I like it," she said. He said he did.

With a long day of driving and all the work, Ben was tired – and grimy. He asked her to show him to the bathing area. He grabbed a bar of soap, a towel, and some clothes to change into and she escorted him, carrying the lantern. Twenty feet or so downstream from the still, in a clearing brilliantly lit by a nearly full moon, the brook emptied into a pool about eight feet across. Moonlight shimmered off its surface. The sound of frogs, crickets, and the call of a whippoorwill added to the idyllic ambience. Tensions he didn't know he harbored drained from his body. He felt limp, more relaxed than from a dozen rubdowns. The idea of a career making moonshine and never returning to New York crossed his mind. He was awestruck.

"Beautiful, isn't it?" she said.

"Heavenly. How deep is the pool?" he asked.

"Three and a half to four feet," she said and then warned him, "It's a mountain stream and it's very cool. Jump in, don't mosey into it."

He looked for one of the nearby boulders to set his things on.

"I think I'll join you," she said. "I brought some things, just in case. Go ahead and jump in. I'll be back in a jiffy." She walked off, taking the lantern with her.

The lantern was not needed in the clearing. The moon cast a glow so bright he could see his shadow as he walked. He undressed down to his boxer shorts and jumped in. She was right. The chill of the water shocked him to the bone. He yelped and vigorously splashed about, shuddered, and fought for his breath. His body adapted to the temperature in a grueling couple of minutes, and he began washing up.

Marsha returned wearing a robe and her shoes. She kicked off the shoes and let the robe slip off her shoulders. To Ben's complete, but ecstatic surprise, she stood on the ledge, naked. Not only was he surprised at her uninhibited behavior, but he wondered how she had managed to hide such a beautiful body all this time. He was dizzy with the sight, and more than a little aroused.

"*This* is skinny-dippin'," she said, and dove into the water.

She rose to the surface near Ben, shook off the chill and stood against him, smiled sweetly and gave him a soft kiss on the nape of his neck.

Ben's reaction was strong, and predictable.

* * *

They were awakened the next morning by a deafening din, the sound of thunder and heavy rain beating down on the corrugated tin roof. Ben gave Marsha an incredulous look. And then the terrible racket caused by the storm became a secondary issue. A dollop of water splashed on his tilted forehead, and Marsha laughed at his expression. "Oops," she said

They suddenly became aware of leaks in other parts of the shack, too.

Ben threw the covers back, and they jumped out of bed, scrambling for receptacles. They raced to keep up. Before long the shack was cluttered with pots, pans, cups, and glasses. The storm passed after an hour or so. The leaks continued for another ten or fifteen minutes.

They spent the rest of the day tearing down the leaky corrugated tin sheets and replacing them with new ones.

CHAPTER FOUR

Hertzberg Jewelers, street number 156. Ben compared the name and street number to the advertisement he was holding. Hertzberg *Jewelers, 156 Atlantic Avenue, Newark, New Jersey.* Ben had underlined the words, *connection* and *London* in the ad which ran June 20, 1941 in the *Daily News.* He folded it and slipped it into his pants pocket. His hat, jacket and tie lay in the passenger seat of his Ford. The weather was sweltering, his windows were wide open, and his unbuttoned white shirt's sleeves were rolled up. The fabric stuck to his back, wet with sweat.

He made a final scan of his surroundings, and saw nothing unusual. He was concerned about a possible stakeout of the jewelry store. Meeting and trusting someone new involved inherent risks.

He drew a deep breath, then grabbed the door handle and shoved.

He entered the jewelry shop to the sound of ringing bells. A gray-haired, bespectacled man assisting a woman with his back to Ben, turned his head.

"I'll be with you in a minute sir," the man said. "Please feel free to look around."

"Thank you, I will."

Four glass display counters in the center of the small shop formed a square, in the middle of which was an open space where the shopkeeper now stood. A pendulum wall clock hung on the back wall beside a small interior window with a counter. A work table and shelves were visible through the window. Two ceiling fans moved the air, which made it feel a lot cooler than outside.

Ben looked over a display of rings.

A few minutes later, the man said to his customer, "Think about it while I help that gentleman," and he approached Ben with a pleasant smile. "Thank you for your patience, sir. How may I be of service to you?"

Feeling compromised by the presence of the woman who, though seemingly preoccupied, was within hearing distance, Ben decided to stall. He pointed to a ring that had attracted his eye. "Is that an engagement ring?"

"It could be. Is that what you're looking for?"

"No. I'm a confirmed bachelor," he said. The woman at the other end of the counter raised her eyes, which validated Ben's instincts. He smiled at her, and she shied away. "I was thinking more like a birthday present for my sister. That's aquamarine, isn't it?"

"Yes, and a very fine one. It is museum quality, so are the diamonds. Let me show it to you." He removed the ring from the display and handed it to Ben. He said it was an art deco ring in a platinum setting with a brilliant, point nine-carat center gem framed by four round diamonds totaling point-four carat.

Ben inquired about the price. "Six hundred and fifty dollars," the man said.

That was a lot for a sister, Ben thought. "Expensive, yes," the shopkeeper said. But a bargain for such rare quality, I assure you. May I show it to you or do you have another price range in mind?"

The woman said she had made a decision and the shopkeeper looked at Ben for an answer before excusing himself. "Yes," Ben said. "Let me look at it while you finish with her."

"Thank you again for your patience," the man said to Ben, after closing the sale with his customer and returning to Ben. "What do you think of the ring?"

Ben stalled until he heard the door's bells. He then reached into his pocket. He unfolded the advertisement and laid it on the counter, watching closely for the man's reaction. "Actually, I'm responding to this ad in the *New York Daily News*."

The man's eyes widened and his face turned serious. "Oh." He pulled it closer, then peered into Ben's face, as though comparing his features to a description he had been given.

"Do you have anything else to show me?" he said, letting go of the advertisement and cautiously putting away the ring, his hand quivering.

Ben said he did, and reached into his shirt pocket and produced the torn half of the Ace of Hearts.

"Excuse me for a minute, please. I'll be right back." He walked through the back door and reappeared a minute or so later, holding what seemed to be the other half of the card. He held out his hand for Ben's portion and then put the two side by side on the counter. The two halves matched perfectly. He beamed and extended his hand.

"My name is Avron; I'm the proprietor of the store. Come with me," he said, walking toward the back of the store. "I have something for you."

Avron escorted Ben into a cramped office space, leaving the showroom door open. A desk, chair, and filing cabinet took up most of the floor space. Neatly stacked shelves surrounded an open safe on the front wall. Avron reached inside the safe and extracted an envelope.

"This is for you."

Ben took the unmarked envelope.

"My instructions are that you will give me a response in the near future. My wife also works here. Don't give me anything in her presence. Get my attention, then go to the diner four doors down." He pointed west. "Buy a newspaper and order a cup of coffee, or whatever you like, and I will join you within minutes. Place whatever you have for me inside the newspaper and when you leave offer me the paper or give it to me if I ask you for it."

"What do I do if she's here but you aren't?"

"Ask for me and tell her you have been dealing with me regarding a purchase and you would prefer to work with me. She will respect your wishes and tell you when I'm expected."

"Sounds easy enough."

Avron saw him out the door. As they passed the aquamarine ring, Ben stopped and pointed to it. "About that ring: If other people saw it on a young woman's finger, might they think it was an engagement ring?"

Avron gestured equivocally. "Not if they knew her birthday was in March, I wouldn't think so. She can always clarify it. Usually announcements accompany an engagement. Anyone who knows a woman knows whether she's engaged."

Ben nodded, lost in thought.

"If you want the ring, tell me and I'll sell it to you for what I paid for it, which is five hundred dollars."

Ben was impressed with his generosity, and thanked him. "I'll let you know."

* * *

He drove to the first gas station he saw, asked for a fill-up, and ducked into the restroom, locking it. He tore open the envelope and deciphered the contents.

Great to hear from you. Brothers alive and well, circumstances considered. Information two months old. I assume you are employed. Is it safe to meet outside New York? Security is top priority. Use extreme caution. Where and when? Give me one month's lead time, minimum. Let me know by coded return letter. Hand deliver only to the person who gave you this. Communication channel is via courier who personally delivers secure envelopes to & from me. Slow but safe. Still, don't talk about your job. Next key words: Emerald and Glasgow.

Ben shredded the letter into tiny pieces and flushed them down the toilet and then left in search of the closest stationery store.

* * *

Parked against a curb, Ben scratched out his encoded response.

Thanks for family news. Am alive and well in NY. Travel often for weeks at a time. Availability difficult to predict and subject to sudden change. Have much to report. Have freedom of movement in and around NY. Up to six hours travel distance. Example: Washington D.C. Not sure of solution. Schedule several meetings over a two-month period? I will show up at first opportunity. Please advise.

He stuffed the message into a sealed envelope. He placed his raw draft in the glove compartment with the leftover writing supplies he had purchased at the Five and Dime. He returned to the jewelry store and dropped off the envelope.

Afterward, he pointed his car south and drove to Rocky Mount.

Chapter Five

Ben was nursing a cup of coffee at the bar of the Raleigh Hotel in Washington, D.C. when he heard the unmistakable voice over his right shoulder. He didn't look up.

"How late are you open?" Isidor said to the bartender while casually placing his left hand on the bar near Ben, exposing to him a small wad of paper. Ben made a furtive scan of his surroundings as the bartender answered. The few people in the bar looked to be in another world. The bartender himself had gone back to polishing glassware. Isidor thanked him and pulled away. Ben cupped the paper wad, slid it over to his cup, and then made sure no one was looking before picking it up. He finished his coffee, then headed for the men's room.

Wait ten minutes, then walk to 13th Street, take a streetcar to New York Avenue, and from there take a taxi to the Silver Theater on Colesville Road. Nearby is a soda fountain in a store named People's Drug. Treat yourself. I will watch for a tail. Return to the Hotel by 2 p.m. and sit in the lobby. If you see me pass through by 2:15, no tail and we meet at 9 pm in Rock Creek Park near the Kennedy Street entrance. If you don't see me in the lobby, *bad news. Pick up instructions in Newark tomorrow noon.*

* * *

"Let's walk and you can tell me your news," Isidor said softly as he got within hearing distance of Ben. It was a lovely evening. There was a full moon and the temperature had to be at least seventy degrees.

"I'm an assassin, working for an arrogant son of a bitch who goes by the name of the brand of cigarettes he smokes." Isidor seemed astonished. "Chester Field. I don't know who he really is but I have his residence address and know he works out of a bank building in Manhattan. I have a full report," and Ben patted his abdomen, striking the package.

"Do you know anything about this operation?" Ben said.

"No," said Isidor. "We suspected there was an assassination unit somewhere and that they were looking to beef it up back in '38 when we cut you loose."

"Who are they?" Ben asked.

Isidor briefed Ben on the nexus among the private Wall Street intelligence networks, factions within American and British military intelligence organizations, and the Zionist Mossad Section B. "Allen Dulles is the chief Wall Street intelligence officer, while a man by the name of Jack Philby is the principle agent for London financial interests. Eli Traynor is liaison for the Mossad."

"Chester is not Dulles," Ben said. "I found his picture in the library. They're not at all similar in appearance."

Ben handed off his report when they passed beneath the thick foliage of a clump of trees, blocking out the luminous night sky. Isidor unbuttoned his shirt and shoved it in. "Do you give the address of the safe house, your apartment..."

"Everything," Ben said, cutting him off. He didn't report his connection with Billy Ray, his two cars, Marsha, the translations he was working on, and other things he didn't consider relevant. Ben told him how Chester had recruited him by promising to help him rescue his brothers and how he had become convinced of Chester's credentials by his access to U.S. and foreign military resources used to get him in and out of other countries.

Isidor appeared dazed and confused over the extent of military resources employed, particularly British ships and planes, asking more than once, "Are you sure it was British military?" Ben was certain. "The details in my report will convince you."

"My dear friend," he eventually said, "with the information you have now provided me, we can analyze and discover, if not right away then with a little work, exactly who authorized the disposal of British military resources to Chester's people. We'll fit the pieces of the puzzle together and determine their channels of communication, who is involved, and then either eliminate them or monitor them to our advantage. Without your having taken this job and going out on these missions we would have nothing.

"At some point we'll have the means to rapidly transmit information about an assignment shortly after you receive it, analyze it, and, depending on the circumstances, either allow the hit to happen or thwart it in some way that doesn't compromise you or this operation. The possibilities of what we can do with your intelligence are endless, and I hope we'll get you on the inside of their operation before long. We need to identify their chain of command and expose them, bring them to justice, and end their ability to manipulate governments and profit from the wars they foment.

"Let me also share with you some highly confidential information: I am working for, and you are, too, as an extension of me, a patriotic faction within British military intelligence, the SIS. In April of '38, a secret intelligence office was opened in New York, in the Rockefeller Center, named British Security Coordination, or BSC. A Canadian and Great War hero for the British, William Stephenson, runs it. He has direct access to both Churchill and Roosevelt. The major purpose of the office is to coordinate British and American intelligence and steer control of America's intelligence apparatus away from Wall Street and other private interests that are motivated by profit, not the best interests of our countries and their citizens. The BSC is secret but official. Its underlying purpose is to destroy Nazi influences in America and disrupt pro-Nazi business deals. It does this through a publicity effort, instigating governmental investigations.

"I am now going to share with you something I knew when we last met in London but didn't tell you. This is the most highly classified operation SIS has, or so I've been told." Isidor then disclosed to Ben the existence of the wiretapping unit. "But this unit is highly *un*-official. Only two people know about it other than you and me: the man I work for and the head of SIS.

"The objective of this unit is to uproot the influence of Nazi profiteers in American foreign policy and put an end to their aid and support for the Third Reich. The idea is to phase out these unofficial, covert operations after the unit has succeeded in cleaning out the Wall Street bandits and then merge its resources into one centralized intelligence office to succeed the existing BSC.

"A recent development, however, threatens our plan. Dulles and his gang at the State Department somehow got wind of BSC and are planning a public relations campaign to drive out the Brits. My point is that our toehold in this country is very tenuous, and slipping, which makes your position all the more valuable, valuable beyond words. On your shoulders might rest the survival of your brothers and many other Jews in Germany, as well as help return control of the intelligence and foreign policy operations – and thus the militaries – of both the British and American governments to the duly elected representatives of our people."

Ben felt pride replacing concern; his qualms began to melt away. He felt a new burden, but he also felt empowered. "This is great," he said. "Just what I needed, Izzy."

Isidor smiled and slapped his shoulder.

"How long do you think it will take to set up the support system?" Ben asked.

"Months. It will occur in stages, beginning tonight. I want to do some personal investigating now that I'm in the country; check out the safe house and other places listed in your report, maybe a few other things. When I get back to London, I'll get all the information analyzed by pros and determine how best to organize communications and support systems. The channel through the jeweler is far too slow for us to analyze the information before you undertake a mission, but until we come up with something better we will continue to use it."

Reaching into his shirt pocket, Isidor said, "In case we lose touch again." He held out two pieces of a torn playing card, this time the Ace of Spades. "Here." He handed half to Ben, putting the other half back in his pocket.

Ben spent the night at the Raleigh Hotel, and rose bright and early Friday morning, hopped in his Ford and crossed the Potomac River into Virginia to spend Labor Day weekend with Marsha.

CHAPTER SIX

"Let me show you a picture," Isidor said, handing Ben a photograph of a man exiting the New York safe house. "Is that Chester?"

It was the middle of October. It had been six weeks since they last met in Rock Creek Park. Ben had driven him to a remote promontory on the Virginia side of the Potomac and parked overlooking an arched bridge and Georgetown on the other side. The late afternoon sun slanted through the windshield. Sir William had provided the photographs to him with the request that he obtain confirmation from Ben before he went any further with the investigation.

"Yes," Ben said.

"His real name is Major Louis Mortimer Bloomfield."

"Major? In whose Army?"

Isidor shrugged off the question, putting the photograph away. "Look past anything you see on the surface of this man, my friend. He's full of contradictions. He's a married man, but a practicing homosexual. He's a major in the U.S. Army, but he never went through the service's training or rose through the ranks. He's Chester, but he's Louis. His emergence as a global player came through his affiliation with a powerful international law firm in Montreal, Phillips & Vineberg. Before 1936, he was the attorney and controller of the Sam Bronfman liquor and drug fortune. Bronfman was a whiskey maker and wholesaler who made his fortune during prohibition and was – and still is – closely connected to organized crime. After the end of prohibition, Bronfman expanded both his territory and product line – to include illegal narcotics."

He presented another photograph. Ben gasped. The reaction answered Isidor's question. He grinned. The man in the picture was Ben's Moscow target. "Suicide," he informed Ben. "According to official reports."

Ben laughed. "Suicide? There were at least three hundred people in the streets that saw him assassinated."

Isidor shrugged. "They didn't write the reports." He gestured for Ben to drive on, putting away the second photo. "Let's get moving." He looked over his shoulder, scanning their surroundings as the car began rolling. The coast was clear.

"Was he friend or foe?" Ben said.

"Hard to tell. He's Soviet military intelligence, GRU."

"Right. Glavnoye Razvedyvatelnoye Upravleniye."

"I'll take your word for it." He returned Ben's smile and continued. "I'm told the British had him on a watch list. The Soviets signed a secret nonaggression pact with Hitler soon after learning of the Saudi oil deal with the Nazis. He apparently knew the source of the Soviet intelligence. SIS suspects a mole, but it could have come straight from Philby or Dulles. Or the reason for the hit could have been unrelated. There's been a lot of intrigue and turmoil inside the GRU lately over the pact with Hitler. The chief of the GRU, who was against the pact, was arrested in July and shot the next day without a trial, only a few weeks after your mission."

"What about Krager and the others," Ben said.

"Our preliminary investigation doesn't show an Oskar Krager as part of any Norwegian shipping line, nor a French Henri Beauchamp." He reminded Ben that the main purpose of his trip was to confirm that Chester and Bloomfield were one and the same, that he wasn't prepared for much more on this trip. He returned to that subject.

"Bloomfield met with Dulles and Philby shortly before the Arlosoroff assassination but how he knew either man is unclear. A few years later, in 1936, he suddenly became an intelligence officer in the British Army working directly with British General Orde Wingate in Palestine. They set up and secretly trained special night squads within the Haganah, the grassroots Jewish Army. An illegal army. British policy forbade military support for either the Arabs or Jews. Bloomfield trained the night squads to carry out assassinations and engage in terrorist actions against Arab raiders.

"His introduction to Wingate came through the SIS, apparently the result of an indirect referral from Philby. In his former role as the head of SIS in Amman, Transjordan, he helped form the Arab Legion, which is now funded by King Saud and has its own version of night squads committing terrorist acts against Jews in Palestine. Notice how both sides of the conflict are pitted against one another by basically the same people. Meanwhile, the person who negotiated with moderate Arabs to peacefully coexist as one nation was eliminated."

"They *want* conflict," Ben said, only partly a question.

"Conflict is profitable. Perpetual conflict is perpetually profitable."

CHAPTER SEVEN

Ben arrived in Rocky Mount before the post office opened that Saturday. He opened Marsha's mailbox, using the combination she had given him, and inserted a penny postcard of the Washington Monument. The unsigned card was addressed to her. When she saw the card, she would know he was at the shack.

He planned to catch a nap. He had been up late with Isidor, and didn't cross back into Virginia until almost midnight, catching nearly three hours' sleep in the car along the roadside, once on Route 211, and again on Route 11.

The final twenty-five miles, from Roanoke to Rocky Mount on Route 220 had been easier only because he knew a bed was not far ahead.

* * *

The smell of coffee roused him from a deep slumber. He shook the cobwebs from his head and Marsha came into focus, sitting at the table, reading. She lowered the book and grinned. "Good morning, Sunshine. I mean, afternoon."

Rising to his elbows, he asked: "What time is it?"

"A little after two," she said, closing the book and standing up. She leaned over and kissed him on the forehead. "Coffee's brewing. You have time to jump in for a bath, if you want."

The thought of chilled water made him shiver. He needed it, though, to clear his head. He felt hung over. "Yeah, I suppose I should." He threw the covers back, and swung his feet over the side of the bed, then groaned, rubbed his eyes, and stretched, yawning.

"Here," she said, tossing him a towel, which he missed. A bar of soap was not far behind. "Hey," he hollered. He bobbled it but managed to hang on. He could tell from her barely suppressed laugh that he must have looked like a klutz. He laughed with her and then sprang from the bed, grabbing and playfully squeezing her. He snuggled against her, kissing her on the neck, before suddenly breaking away.

"You'll get yours later," he said, on his way for his toiletry kit on top of the dresser.

"Promise?"

"You can bank on it."

When he rounded the shack, she pressed against the screen window over the stove. "I brought a picnic basket...unless you want breakfast. I thought we could picnic in the mountains. I know the perfect spot."

"Picnic," he said without looking back.

* * *

The sweeping vista was breathtaking. Miles and miles of rolling hills, mountains in the distance, with a forest ablaze in autumn colors in the foreground under a bright blue sky.

They were standing on the very top of a small mountain, under the rustling red leaves of an old oak tree. The air was fresh and surprisingly warm.

"Beautiful, isn't it?" Marsha said.

"Absolutely sublime. I've never seen such a magnificent sight." He drew in a deep breath, and took it all in. "I've never felt this good in my entire life. Everything is perfect: the weather, the location, the view... and most of all, being with you."

"Oh, Ben," Marsha sighed.

"It's true." She was holding a blanket, prepared to spread it on the leaves. "Here, let me help you."

They sat on the blanket, the basket in front of them. He put his arm around her and together they took in the spectacular view.

"I've been coming here every year since I was a small child," she said. "My daddy used to bring me and we would sit here for hours. He taught me the different colors for each kind of tree. This is a pin oak," referring to the one they were sitting under. "They turn red, as you can see, but they can also be russet. The yellow one over there is a cottonwood," and she named a dozen more trees visible from their blanket. "It's so lovely and peaceful; I could sit here all day. And I do sometimes."

He reached for the basket. "What do you have in here? I'm starving," opening and rummaging through it as she began to answer.

"Fried chicken ..." she began.

"Umm, smells good." He took over. "Potato salad, carrots...oops. What's this?"

She peered over the edge of the basket, curious. He pulled out a small felt-covered box and presented it to her with a puzzled look, a ring box.

She gasped, her eyes and mouth wide. She looked from the box to him and back, slowly taking hold of it. A mixture of surprise, joy, and playful reproach settled on her face, as she began to open it and then paused. He gave her an encouraging nod, and she flipped it open, revealing the art deco ring with the large aquamarine surrounded by diamonds which sparkled brilliantly in the sunlight.

"Oh, it's beautiful," she said, taking it out of the case and placing it on her ring finger. She stared expectantly at Ben as tears began to well in her eyes.

He took her hand in his and looked deep into her eyes. "Ti viy-desh za me-nya?"

Another gasp. Her hand rushed to her mouth in astonishment as the tears began flowing down her cheek. "Does that mean what I think it means?"

"Yes. Will you marry me?"

She threw herself at him, wrapping her arms around him. "Yes, yes, a thousand times yes." She pressed her lips against his and they kissed, then embraced and kissed again. Time passed, more than a couple of minutes. When they finally parted, she reached for a napkin out of the basket and began wiping her tears, admiring him between swipes. His own eyes teared up when he saw her still-beaming face, and the same radiance he saw in the university library the day they met, which now seemed so long ago. He was in love with her he knew, and now realized he had been from the moment he first saw her.

He took her in his arms and held her tightly. She was now his. He kissed her on the forehead and said, "Thank you."

After their emotions had settled some, Ben braced himself and took on a somber tone. "This has to be our secret. You can't tell anyone you're engaged."

"I know. I don't mind that. What happens between us is all that matters to me."

"Since your birthday is in March, I thought you could begin wearing it openly then, and perhaps tell people it was a birthday present to yourself."

"Or say nothing at all. It's my birthstone, is all anybody needs to know." Ben mulled it over briefly and then gave a satisfied nod. She knew the people here and their ways better than he, and he trusted her judgment.

"Except when we're together out here," she said. "And every night when we're apart. I'll slip it on before I go to bed and dream about you." A glint appeared in her eye, and she sang: "*In the mist of a memory you wander back to me; Breathing my name with a sigh. When the deep purple falls...*"

Ben pulled her next to him and gently squeezed. He felt his eyes moisten again. He didn't want to think about being apart.

When the deep purple falls over sleepy garden walls...

CHAPTER EIGHT

Ben took a break from his translation project to prepare an answer to Isidor's message, which he had picked up from the jeweler yesterday. Isidor had the new operational plans and was ready to meet and go over them, plus some new intelligence. He wanted three dates one week apart, in case Ben was unable to appear on the first one or two.

He was sitting in the reading room of the library, a notepad, pencil, and several books spread before him, two of them open, one written in Russian, the other in English.

His current routine brought him to the library daily. First, he would visit the newspaper room and catch up on world events – and also make a quick scan of the classified advertising section of the *London Times* to check for signals from Isidor.

Ben started with January 5, 1942, jotting down that date. That was the first day he would be available. Today was Tuesday, December 16, 1941, and he planned to leave Thursday to be with Marsha. Her school let out on Friday, but he wanted to arrive a day early. He had a surprise for her. She was off through Sunday, January Fourth. He wanted to spend the entire period with her.

Ben could meet Isidor in Washington D.C. on his way back.

He wrote down January 13 and 20, then ripped off that section of the notepaper and stuck it in his shirt pocket. He would encode the message later. He now only needed to make his connection with Billy Ray. He scanned the reading room, looking for him, and then checked his watch. Three fifty-five. Billy Ray had another five minutes.

This was the system they had worked out for the winter months so Ben could continue to take his secret vacations. Billy Ray came to the library once each week.

Ben went back to his research, re-orienting himself to the Russian words listed on the notepaper and then digging into the translated work in front of him. His project was to see how other translators – ones he respected – translated certain Russian words and phrases into English.

Five minutes later, his mental alarm clock sounded. He checked the library floor again, and this time saw Billy Ray sitting at a table on the far side of the room, his head buried in a book. Ben passed over him and finished his scan, looking for any unwanted attention. Seeing none, he headed for the men's room.

Billy Ray walked in while he was washing his hands, taking one of the stalls. Ben took his time, waiting for the only other occupant to leave, then took an envelope out of his pants pocket and shoved it under the stall door.

"Chollies from Santa," he said. "Merry Christmas."

Billy Ray laughed.

CHAPTER NINE

Ben crossed the Rocky Mount city limits late on Thursday as planned. He had stopped in Philadelphia to shop for presents after having first dropped off the coded message for Isidor in Newark. He didn't mind sleeping in the cabin for one night. The mere thought of doing so, however, sent a shiver through his body. He recalled the first cold spell in November when he was forced to change his routine there. Sleeping there in the winter had not been a problem; the pot-bellied stove provided more than enough heat. The rough part was the bone-chilling trip to the outhouse. Not just the walk to and from it, which was horrible, but the time inside was no picnic, either. Chamber pots would work, but not in the presence of a woman. Bathing in the pool was out of the question; heating a tub full of hot water was way too much work. This called for some creative planning. They conspired to meet at the shack on Ben's first day back and steal away to Marsha's house after the streets of Rocky Mount had rolled up, with Ben curled up on the floor of the back seat of her car.

He recalled the first time they put the plan into action, around midnight on a Saturday. He felt the car roll to a stop, heard the car door open and Marsha exit. A few minutes later she opened the back door, and leaned in, as though she were taking something out of the back seat. "It's clear now," she whispered. Ben crawled out, crawling on his hands and knees through the opened back door. Moments later, Marsha came in and closed the door, before erupting in gales of laughter. He came out of the memory chuckling.

He had also reached the post office. He parked four spaces from the front door, next to the pay phone. He first dropped off a post card in Marsha's box, this time depicting the Gettysburg Civil War battlefield, and telephoned the Raleigh Hotel in Washington.

When a clerk answered, he said, "Do you have a telegram for Charles for Montclair?" He had to repeat the name, but then the clerk put the phone down to check."

"Yes, Mr. Montclair. You have a telegram for pickup."

Ben didn't say anything, but his heart sank. He heard a voice that seemed far away, and it took him several seconds to realize it was the hotel clerk's. "Excuse me," Ben said.

"I can read it to you and save you the trip, if you like. There are only two words."

What was the point? he thought to himself, but his mouth said, "Please."

"The message is from B. R. Montclair. It says, Merry Christmas."

Merry, my ass. "Thank you."

* * *

He arrived at the shack laden with packages, and somehow managed to open the door without dropping any. He meant to carry out his plan to surprise Marsha, to cut and decorate a tree, and to arrange the presents. He was not prepared for her to surprise him.

On the table stood a Menorah with the head candle and eight others, one for each night of Hanukkah, standing proudly, ready to be lit. Surrounding it were wrapped presents, a bottle of wine, dishes filled with chocolates, nuts, paraffin-wrapped cheeses, and crackers – and a Driedel, a child's spinning top. He hadn't seen one since 1932, in Munich, when he last celebrated the Holiday with his brothers and Adam's family. He recalled playing a game with Adam's children and felt his eyes moisten.

There was also a note. He opened it. Happy Hanukkah. *I know the first day of Hanukkah was on the 14*[th] *this year, but I thought we could push it back five days and celebrate them all. I love you, Marsha.* She obviously had done her homework; they hadn't discussed Hanukkah. He wondered what would happen if he didn't return to New York, but knew the answer.

He placed his packages on the bed and started a fire, then lit the kerosene lantern and went outside to find a small fir tree. He found an axe in the tool shed next to the still, cut down a tree, and decorated it with tinsel and glass ornaments after setting it on top of the chest of drawers. He arranged the presents under the tree and those that didn't fit there he placed next to the chest. By then, it was midnight. He had to meet Chester at three p.m. the next day. He gave himself another half-hour.

He poured a glass of wine and opened the presents Marsha had left for him, feasting on cheese and crackers. He stuffed some candy and nuts in his coat pocket for the trip back to New York. Then he wrote a note to Marsha, thanking her for the Hanukkah display, the treats and gifts, and telling her he had to leave for duty. He had told her he would return as soon as possible but that he suspected he might not be free again until after the New Year.

"Until then, I will keep you in my thoughts and dreams. Love forever, Ben."

CHAPTER TEN

"Lisbon?" Ben repeated.

"For strategic reasons," Chester said, lighting a cigarette and taking a drag. "I need you on the Continent so we can move you in and out of European countries more quickly using fewer resources now that America has joined the war." Chester's whole demeanor suggested some military-like control over him: he was resolute and spoke as though Ben had no choice but to obey, which, combined with the sudden, dramatic change of plans, rankled and confused him.

"I don't speak Portuguese."

"You won't need to. You won't be doing any jobs inside Portugal and I understand that people of many nationalities pass through Lisbon. Most of them speak English and you should, too, while you're there. Lisbon is ideal for our operation because it is the central city and port of a neutral country with a long coastline and plenty of open fields, which makes it easily accessible for unobserved entries and departures into and out of the war zones of Europe."

As Ben struggled to come to grips with the sudden change, Chester took on a more conciliatory air. "Not only will we have more of an impact on the outcome of the war with you in Lisbon but we will be better positioned in the event an opportunity to go inside Germany appears. An opportunity could come and go in less time than I could ship you there. So you should view this as an opportunity rather than a setback."

Ben took in and let out a deep breath through his mouth, resigning himself to his fate. "When do I leave?"

"First thing in the morning," Chester said. "This afternoon, and for however long it takes, I need to go over the new operational guidelines: how we communicate, how you conduct yourself in and out of Lisbon, and so on. All you will need is a travel bag. Don't worry about the items in your apartment, I'll pack and store them for you. I plan to re-sell your car. I paid for it. A driver will pick you up at six, and a plane will be ready for you at Bennett Field in Brooklyn by six-thirty."

"I'll need more time than that."

"Why?" Chester said.

"Why? Less than 24 hour's notice? I want to think it through and make sure I have something to do in my spare time, like reading and working on my translations." Ben tried to come up with some logical excuses without betraying his true motive, which was to alert Isidor and Marsha. "What about a typewriter? And books? Can I take them with me?"

"You're allowed one large item, such as a trunk or a duffel bag, in addition to a carry-on travel bag. So take with you whatever will fit inside them. Whatever else you need, I'll either have it delivered to you in Lisbon or wire you the money so you can buy it there."

"I need to buy a trunk."

"I have one you can use. I'll have a driver drop it off at your apartment later tonight."

Ben saw no way out. He threw up his arms. "Okay. I guess I'm going to Lisbon."

"Good," Chester said, crunching out his cigarette. He reached for his briefcase. "Let's get started."

* * *

Ben started his car and pulled away from the curb, leaving the safe house. It was twilight; the streetlights had just come on. There was just enough light to tell a police radio antenna from a regular one. He was being followed by Chester's goons. He wondered whether they had tried to follow him from his apartment, which is how the surveillance had worked in the past: the window shade went up and they picked him up on his way to meet Chester the next day. If they had tried to do that this time, they would know he hadn't come from his apartment. Instead, he had come from the parking garage where he had switched from the Ford to the Chevy, having arrived in New York later than planned. Not that it mattered; he was entitled to leave his apartment and have a night life – just as long as they hadn't seen him in his Ford. He dismissed that concern as he replayed his arrival to the city.

The more important question was, why surveillance now? He hadn't seen any for months, more than a year now. He had kept a careful eye out for tails on Tuesday through Thursday, as he prepared for and left on his trip to Rocky Mount, and was convinced there were none. Isidor himself had checked for tails on Ben in D. C. Perhaps he and Isidor had been found out. But if that were true, wouldn't Chester have *dispatched* him, as he had called the ultimate penalty for breaching security?

He pictured Ghost getting that assignment, and relishing the role, like the wolf dressed in grandmother's clothing upon seeing Little Red Riding Hood. It didn't add up; there was more to it than what Chester had told him.

He attacked the mystery from a different angle, taking a hard view of the reason for his sudden transfer. Reason One: he was prevented from meeting Isidor or even notifying him that he was headed to Lisbon. Reason Two: he would no longer be able to visit Marsha or notify her that he was leaving the country. He could write her from Lisbon, but if the relationship were known by Chester, the letter could be intercepted and Chester might take further measures to ensure the relationship ended.

He took up the second reason. Chester didn't *dispatch* him for the security violation, but then, he would lose one of his best men if he had Ben killed, and he didn't need to do that. The transfer solved that problem. Ben began to soften in his outrage. He had broken the rules by seeing Marsha. Banishment to Lisbon was a fair penalty. No need to kill him, just separate them. Fair enough. He could live with that. She was his. She would be there when he returned. His times with her had been the happiest of his life. It had all been worth it. In hindsight, he would have made that deal: seven months with Marsha in exchange for leaving the country when America officially entered the war.

And so, he came to be at peace with the separation from Marsha. As long as Chester left her alone, that is. If he touched even one hair on her head, he was a dead man. He surely knew that: he had taught Ben to kill for reasons unknown, imagine if Ben had a reason. No, Chester would have to kill Ben if he went down that road and, if he planned to kill Ben, why bother her? She was not a spy; she was only a girlfriend – or a fiancée, depending on how much Chester knew.

Isidor was another matter. He *was* a spy. Moreover, he was a spy directing his forces at Chester and his operation; he *was* Chester's enemy. A connection to Isidor made Ben an enemy. The punishment for that was death. Chester would have him killed for that, beyond a doubt.

Except, perhaps Chester might plan to first ship him overseas and kill him quietly, out of range of British and American agents lurking in and around Manhattan and watching over Ben, for all Chester knew. A whole new reason for paranoia unsettled him. Maybe that fate awaited him in Lisbon.

Ben calmed himself down and searched for an innocent reason for the surveillance. Chester's excuse for shipping him to Lisbon, after all, was reasonable. Easier access to European countries. And he liked the idea of having an opportunity to go inside Germany on short notice. Maybe Chester was just being security conscious, making sure the Nazis weren't onto what he was doing and able to track his transfer. But that didn't really ring true.

Ben reached his apartment and another idea struck him. He parked and went inside. He wrapped his palm around the brass door knob. It was cool to the touch. He tightened his grip. He rotated his wrist. The knob slowly turned. He heard a click, then stopped. He leaned on the door. It moved. He pushed, applying only enough pressure to gradually open a gap of less than seven inches. He reached in and flipped a switch. Light spilled into the hallway. He squeezed through the gap. Halfway through, he craned his head around the door.

The wad of paper was lying on the floor.

CHAPTER ELEVEN

Isidor put the finishing touches on his cable. He was in his room at the Roger Smith where Ben had failed to show for the third week in a row, and didn't signal that he had received an assignment. Isidor had a bad feeling about this; something had gone wrong. He wanted to travel to New York and sniff around for Ben, and indicated that in his report to Sir William. The cable was in code.

Sir William was standing by waiting to hear whether Ben had shown, an unusual display of interest on his part, which added to Isidor's sense that there was a serious problem.

Isidor went to the lobby and handed the bell captain an envelope, a dollar bill on top.

"Please deliver urgently," he said.

The concierge accepted it with a dignified bow. "Certainly, Mr. Franks."

"I'm expecting a quick reply. Please get it to me the instant it arrives. You will find me in the lounge or in my room."

He received the same bow, same response. Isidor thanked him, and headed for the lounge. He bought a copy of *The Washington Post* on his way and ordered a beer once he arrived, then settled into a booth along the far wall.

He was engrossed in an article about Great Britain examining mails carried by American transatlantic airliners, cutting the last communication channel by which Germans in North America could send money and securities to the Reich, when he heard the bell captain say his name. He looked up. About twenty minutes had passed.

"This just came for you, Mr. Franks," his hand extended.

Isidor took the message and reached into his pocket for another tip. That done, he folded his newspaper, gulped down the remainder of his beer, rose, and went to his room to read Sir William's reply.

Imperative you not go to NY based on information you lack. Request you return immediately. Cable me a time and date when we can discuss situation.

CHAPTER TWELVE

"**A** nasty habit, I know," Sir William said, as he finished packing the light honey-colored bowl of his meerschaum pipe. He struck a wooden match and its sulfurous smell was quickly replaced by the sweet aroma of burning tobacco. Sir William shook out the flame and settled into one of the cottage arm chairs, crossing his legs.

"I suppose I should get right to the point."

"Please do," Isidor said.

"Ben may be a casualty of a political war that has erupted between Dulles and his Wall Street cronies and President Roosevelt. Unfortunately, British intelligence is the cause of that war, in their view, and to be quite candid about, they're right. By that I mean our intelligence office in New York, the BSC. You might recall me telling you that the BSC is run by William Stephenson, a Canadian who has direct access to both President Roosevelt and our Mr. Churchill, and that it's been working to expose and end Wall Street's profiteering and the flow of Saudi oil to the Third Reich." Isidor indicated that he did.

"Splendid, then I shall jump ahead and point out to you that aiding Hitler before America entered the war is merely scandalous, whereas aiding Hitler when he is an enemy at war is treasonous."

"Of course, it is," Isidor agreed.

"President Roosevelt shares your view. With our detailed evidence, he turned to an ally in the U. S. Senate, a fellow by the name of Harry Truman, and he opened an investigation. John D. Rockefeller, Jr., Allen Dulles, Jack Forrestal of Dillon Reed, Prescott Bush of Brown Harriman...the whole lot of them, were on their way to the gallows.

"And then the executives of a Dulles client, Standard Oil of New Jersey, told the Justice Department that Saudi Oil would be cut off if criminal actions went forward."

"Really?" said Isidor, who was beginning to see the shape of the threat to Ben.

"I'm afraid so," Sir William said. "Mr. Roosevelt has recently advised us through Mr. Stephenson that he cannot win a head-on political battle with Wall Street. Instead, he wants to give them what they think they want: the BSC office. He proposes that we convert it into a new centralized intelligence agency, controlled by a person appointed by the President, a person who happens to be a close ally of Mr. Roosevelt's, a confidant of Mr. Stephenson and a personal friend of C's. The chap's name is Bill Donovan. He's in London as we speak, going over our organizational and administrative channels.

"As part of the deal, Mr. Roosevelt shrewdly proposed that Dulles be given a key role in the new agency."

Isidor recoiled.

Sir William sprang forward, his elbows on his knees and a sparkle in his eyes.

"But think about it. One, how can they refuse the offer? They want control of our operations. Fine. Take it. Two, we have a stationary target; we can monitor his actions from above and below. Mr. Donovan, from above, and Mr. Stephenson, from below. Mr. Stephenson will continue to oversee our most sensitive covert operations, including the wiretap unit, which both the President and Mr. Donovan – whom we have now brought into the loop – have permitted to continue."

"Ah," Isidor said. He caught himself stroking his beard.

"I think it is absolutely brilliant," Sir William said. "That is, when one considers our circumstances...our operations being under attack, and all that.

"Be that as it may, I want to impress upon you the magnitude of the political battle and the animosity Dulles has for British intelligence activities in New York. Bloomfield, the real name of this Chester fellow who oversees Ben, is apparently reporting directly to Dulles.

"We suspect that Dulles ordered Bloomfield to increase security on all his men, especially Ben, due to their prior suspicions of our hand in the falsification of his college records years ago. We don't know what's happened to Ben. Perhaps they discovered his connection to you after they clamped down on security and got rid of him. Or perhaps their new security measures restricted his movement so much that he was prevented from meeting or signaling you. One thing we know for sure is that the battle between Dulles and BSC is so intense that it is not safe to go looking for him. In fact, we considered that they have set a trap to see if anyone does come looking for him."

"I see your reasoning," Isidor said. "It all makes sense."

"Splendid. I thought you would agree."

Sir William reached for his pipe and tobacco pouch.

Isidor was still saddened. He heaved a heavy sigh.

Sir William paused loading his pipe. "Take heart, Mr. Franks. He's a bright fellow. He was isolated before and managed to keep his head and later contact you. If he's alive and still in business, he will do so again. I also plan to keep an eye out for movements on British vessels by civilian saboteurs or spies. We have identified some of the persons who facilitated the use of British military resources for Bloomfield's missions and we're keeping a close eye on them. A very close eye, indeed. We want to know whether they were their employees or unwitting agents, and precisely where their orders originated. I'll let you know if I come up with anything."

PART V

May 1942 - May 1944

CHAPTER ONE

" **A** merica has become the center of the democratic world and the Zionist movement must focus its activities there. Not just with diplomacy, which is required, but we must systematically enlist broad public support for our aims. Because America will be anything but isolationist after the war."

Emanuel Neumann was speaking in the high-ceilinged grand ballroom of New York's elegant Biltmore Hotel. More than five hundred delegates were present, their attention glued to the elderly Zionist statesmen, one of the pioneers of the movement. The second day of a six-day conference, the date was May 9, 1942. Isidor's eyes drifted to the crystal chandeliers, then onto Rabbi Stephen Wise, who sat across from him at the same table. Wise was the head of both the American Jewish Congress and the World Jewish Organization. He was seated next to Dr. Chaim Weizmann, his long-time friend and confidante and President of the World Zionist Organization and Zionist executive in London. Isidor had traveled with him to New York, along with a small contingent from the office.

The vast majority of delegates were Americans. Dubbed the Extraordinary Conference of American

Zionists, Dr. Weizmann had initiated the gathering, along with David Ben-Gurion, the Labor Zionist and chairman of the executive committee of the Jewish Agency of Palestine. The purpose of the assembly was to create and demonstrate Zionist unity. Isidor knew that Ben-Gurion's strategy was to stage a coup d'état, obtain control of the World Zionist Organization and then break with the British and take a militant stand in Palestine. The only question he had was how the American delegates would react. Would they embrace or reject the leadership of Ben-Gurion over Weizmann and Wise?

"We have nothing to gain from a continued partnership with Britain, whether in London or Palestine," Neumann continued, creating a buzz, a few cheers – and widened eyes from both Wise and Weizmann. "England has failed the Zionist movement."

Weizmann shifted uneasily in his seat. Wise's lower jar tightened; his brow furrowed with indignation.

"The leadership of the Emergency Committee," the speaker meant Wise and Louis Lipsky, who also sat at their table, two chairs to Wise's right, "has failed us."

Wise, Lipsky, and Weizmann exchanged glances, mixtures of surprise and resentment showing on their faces. Their growing consternation was solidified by cheers and an increasing buzz from the crowd, almost excitement. Neumann made a call for a reorganization of that body, and concluded by saying, "If we can effectively mobilize our forces and talent throughout the country, if we go in now for an all-out effort for winning the battle of America, there is a good chance we can win the battle of Palestine, and open the doors to immigration and land ownership."

The delegates erupted, many rising to their feet. Weizmann looked a little pale. Wise did a slow grind with his teeth. Apparently they hadn't seen it coming.

The theme was repeated. Rabbi Abba Hillel Silver roused the hall of delegates with his oratory zeal. There was no future for a British-Zionist link, he said. "The British Empire is on the brink of dissolution in Asia and worldwide." A burst of applause. "British colonial rule in Palestine is a tangled mess." More applause.

The electricity of anticipated change spread through the room, and Isidor found himself wondering how he could faithfully relay to Sir William what he was witnessing. Not everyone applauded. Rabbi Wise was wooden, his eyes politely riveted on the speaker. Isidor wished he knew the man's thoughts. If the rabbi didn't see how he could maintain his leadership position, Isidor would point it out to him later at their scheduled meeting.

Isidor began doodling on his notepad.

"If there is to be a cutting of the Gordian knot," Silver continued, "if there is to be a new start for a Jewish Homeland, the hand that will wield the knife, I believe, will not be in London, but in Washington." A rousing ovation. The delegates cheered, at least most of them. But only a handful in the know, like Isidor, understood the aptness and depth of the metaphor. At that very moment, the entire Jewish underground in Palestine was being drawn together for a Jewish war of liberation against the British. The plans drawn, the implementation begun, approval was secondary – and presumed.

Isidor had mixed feelings about the likely result. He strongly favored the end of immigration restrictions and giving the British government a slap in the face for abandoning the Peel Plan to partition Palestine into two states, as agreed by Weizmann and moderate Arab leaders in 1938. But he didn't trust Ben-Gurion to pursue the rescue of European Jews.

Isidor tore off the sheet he had been scribbling on and wadded it up. He started thinking about his report to Sir William, and wrote. *Britain out. America in. Negotiation with the Arabs out. Militancy in.* He would fill in the details later. There remained only a glimmer of hope.

* * *

"This report was smuggled out of Poland last week," Isidor said, handing it Peter Bergson. "Seven hundred thousand Jews have already been killed. Hundreds of thousands more are being rounded up from all parts of the Nazi-occupied territories, crammed into train cars, and deported to Polish camps for mass extermination in gas chambers. The Nazis call it 'The Final Solution.'"

Both Bergson and his companion, Eri Jabotinsky, had agreed to meet secretly with Isidor in his hotel suite. Isidor first met the men in Poland in 1938. He was the son of Ze'ev Jabotinsky, the leader of the Revisionist Zionist Alliance, the person who vigorously opposed the Transfer Agreement and boldly took on the Labor Party at the 1933 Zionist Congress. Bergson and Jabotinsky held a grudge against the Labor Party leadership over their attempt to frame Revisionists for the assassination of Chaim Arlosoroff.

Isidor did not want to be seen conspiring with the men. He worked for Mossad, Section B, Eli Traynor's intelligence unit, which was aligned with the Haganah, the Jewish military, and its leader, David Ben-Gurion.

Isidor's plan was to get the report of The Final Solution into the hands of Weizmann and Rabbi Wise for them to use as a strategy to win over the conference and avert a takeover of Zionist leadership by Ben-Gurion.

Isidor got the kind of reaction he expected. Both men were appalled and angry.

"Does the Zionist Executive know about this?" Bergson said between clenched teeth as he skimmed through the report.

"No," Isidor said, " but I've arranged a meeting for both Rabbi Wise and Dr. Weizmann. I want you to present the report to them."

Bergson stopped, lifted his head.

"You need to be the front man," Isidor said. "I will be more effective in the background."

"What about Eri? We're together."

Isidor turned to Eri.

"You know I support you. I supported your father. I think your presence, however..."

Jabotinsky cut him short. "Enough said. I agree. The political wounds are still fresh for me as well." To Bergson, he said, "Listen to him, whatever he says."

"What's the plan?" Bergson said to Isidor.

Isidor laid it out. Afterward, he reiterated the need for diplomacy. "You have to understand that these men are elderly and have different views on ..."

"Yes," Bergson snapped. "They're murderers. They're responsible for this," he waived the Polish report in the air. "They killed the boycott of German goods and saved Hitler's ass."

Isidor's heart sank. *I knew this was a bad idea*, he thought. But then, Bergson changed his tune. "I'm saying to you that I know what you mean: diplomacy."

"They are powerful men despite their flaws," Isidor said. "Rabbi Wise has a personal friendship with President Roosevelt. He can pick up the phone and meet him later that day."

"We have connections, too," Jabotinsky said. "All over Washington."

"And in Hollywood," Bergson added. "I'll do this for you, Isidor, but Eri's right, we don't need them. And I won't compromise my honor for those cowardly gasbags. We get them to set aside politics and we rescue the Jews of Europe. Period. End of story. They're either on board or they're not."

"Promise me one thing," Isidor said. "Present the report and tell them of your plan to spread the word through your connections in Hollywood and Washington and let me take care of the diplomacy. I beg you not to express your private views."

"Of course. I can be diplomatic when I need to be."

* * *

"You want a report? Here," Bergson said, and dropped it loudly onto the table in front of Rabbi Wise. He was responding to Wise's lament that he had gone to the press with rumors of mass executions but had been rebuffed without an official report to show them. Bergson's intense gaze bore into the eyes of Wise, who was visibly shaken and exchanged private glances with Weizmann. They were gathered around a marble-topped coffee table in Weizmann's hotel suite. The rabbi and Louis Lipsky sat on a sofa on one side of the table. Isidor and Weizmann were seated in arm chairs at the ends, and Bergson sat across from the rabbi.

Isidor cringed and then cleared his throat. Bergson glanced at Isidor out of the corner of his eye, then forged ahead. "That was smuggled out of Poland just last week. Seven hundred thousand Jews have already been slaughtered."

Isidor grabbed him by the arm. "Excuse me, Peter. Let the rabbi express himself. If the press tells him he needs something official and the State Department hasn't given him anything, then we can correct that. Perhaps the rabbi can present your report to his contact at the State Department." The crimson in Bergson's face began to fade. Isidor wanted to stall and let his composure fully return. He turned to Wise. "Who is your contact there?"

"I've been dealing on this issue mainly with Undersecretary Welles."

"Perhaps you can present the report to Undersecretary Welles, then."

"What's this say?" Weizmann said, referring to the report. Isidor gave the men an overview of *The Final Solution* and then said, "Here's your chance to take a leadership position, gentlemen. Leadership. That's what's needed in this time of horror and atrocity." Isidor looked from Wise to Weizmann, studying their reactions. "This is how you stave off Ben-Gurion. You are our only hope for statehood obtained with honor and clean hands, standing up for our brethren in Europe who are helpless and cry out for us. Hear their cries. Rescue them."

Wise glanced at Weizmann who nodded slowly showing his agreement. Isidor was prepared to remind the rabbi of the time when they had first met, in Prague in August 1933, at another crucial point in the plight of European Jews. Wise had backed down then, allowing the Transfer Agreement to gain approval and, for all practical intents, allowing Hitler to remain in office. But he felt he had struck a chord with him and decided to keep it in reserve.

Wise held the report. "I've been getting reports of killings, but nothing systematic or on this scale. It defies imagination, which is one of the problems I've run into when trying to sell it to the press. I've needed some proof, something official. I can take this to the State Department. I like Isidor's idea."

Isidor stole a glance at Bergson, who seemed pleased with the progress apparently being made.

"Ben-Gurion is aware of this information but has been soft-pedaling it," Isidor said. "Jews in Palestine know practically nothing about it. The *Duvar*, a daily newspaper aligned with Ben-Gurion, ran a story but included Nazi propaganda claims of exaggeration in the same article." He pulled from his portfolio a copy of a newspaper article and handed it to Wise. "See where it quotes Josef Goebbels," he said, referring to Hitler's Minister of Propaganda. Wise raised his eyebrows and nodded, then passed the article to Lipsky.

"As Peter said, he plans to disseminate the news widely in America. I've done an informal poll of the delegates here at the conference and people were outraged when they heard the news. They want something done about it. This can be the issue that unites Jews across the world, and you can lead them. Adopt this issue and you can maintain your leadership positions. Otherwise, you heard the applause; I think Ben-Gurion will ..."

He was interrupted by a fusillade of raps on the door. Lipsky said he'd get it. He rose and took two steps, then halted.

The door sprang open. In barged Ben-Gurion with Traynor in tow. "Gentlemen, I hope I'm not intruding," Ben-Gurion said.

Everyone rose. Wise invited them in. "No, of course you aren't. You're always welcome. Please, pull up some chairs and seat yourselves."

Isidor stepped aside and offered his chair to Ben-Gurion. He greeted Traynor who joined him, standing next to the coffee table.

"Thank you, Isidor," Ben-Gurion said. "Nice to see you."

"And you, Sir," Isidor said, bowing slightly.

Ben-Gurion unbuttoned his suit jacket and took a seat. "I thought we should talk about unifying the conference," he said, looking from Wise to Weizmann. Only then did he notice the presence of Bergson who, along with Jabotinsky, was one of his staunchest critics. His eyes narrowed into a suspicious glare, then began roaming the room, landing on the Polish report and the *Duvar* news article lying on the table. Isidor casually shifted his hand to the back of Bergson's chair, anticipating trouble. He poked him, hoping to remind him to play it smart.

Rabbi Wise spoke. "Peter Bergson, here," waving his hand at Bergson, "brought us this report from inside Poland as confirmation of the mass extermination of Jews under control of the Nazis, as part of Reich policy called *The Final Solution*. Are you aware of it?"

Ben-Gurion, who had given Isidor an icy stare while Wise was speaking, replied, "I've heard such reports. A tragedy, if true."

"I intend to investigate the report with the State Department," Wise said, "and, if I verify it, I will do everything in my power to put an end to the slaughter. It was this sort of tragedy we had in mind preventing with the worldwide boycott of German goods back in '33."

"Naturally we too will work to verify the reports," Ben-Gurion said. "And we will do what we can to rescue Jews and aid the Allies. For those who want to emigrate and settle in Palestine, that is. Frankly, I could care less about the rest." Bergson gasped, tightening up as if prepared to jump out of his chair. Isidor's fingers dug into Bergson's shoulder. "Bear in mind, gentlemen, that Zionism is above all. We must do everything so that the *Land of Israel* becomes the *State of Israel*. Sometimes leadership requires a blunt assessment of a situation be made, even a catastrophe, in light of the objective one seeks."

He turned to Isidor. "About the cries coming from your country," his words laced with contempt, "we should recognize that all of the Allied nations are spilling much of their blood, and if we don't sacrifice any blood, by what right do we merit coming to the bargaining table when they divide nations and lands at war's end." Isidor felt Bergson's muscles stiffen, and dug deeper into his shoulder. "Therefore, it is silly, even impudent on our part to ask these nations who are spilling their blood to spend their money and go into enemy countries in order to protect our people – for only with spilling our blood shall we get the land."

Bergson sprang from his chair. "Murderer!" he screamed at Ben-Gurion, who jumped to meet Bergson's assault head-on. Isidor dove for Bergson, caught the back of his collar and jerked on it. Traynor stepped between the two men, shoving Bergson backwards.

Isidor wrapped his arms around Bergson's chest and neck just as he lunged forward, throwing his arms up in a desperate attempt to escape from Isidor's grasp. Isidor held tight and twisted, shoved, and wrestled Bergson toward the door.

After a step or two, Bergson stopped resisting, but turned and snarled at Ben-Gurion, wagging his index finger.

"Murderers! All of you! You're in cahoots with the Nazis, you always have been, and you'll rot in Hell with them!"

Isidor slammed him against the door, freeing his right hand to turn the knob. The door swung open and Isidor flung Bergson through it. Isidor followed, closing the door behind him.

"Now look what you've done," Isidor said.

"We don't need them. I don't need them."

"You're wrong. We *do* need them."

"We'll see about that." He spun on his heels, and Isidor grabbed him.

"Listen to me. Go, cool off, and meet me in my room tonight. I'll help you, even if you go it alone, but trust me, you don't want them as your enemies. They can hurt you. They can hurt our cause. Okay?"

His nostrils flared, Bergson gradually regained control of his temper. "Okay," he finally said.

Isidor patted him on the shoulder. "It's history now. Don't worry about it."

When he returned to the room, a hush fell over the men gathered there, all eyes on Isidor. "I'm sorry about that, gentlemen. I should not have let him present the Polish report to you, but, as you can see, he has it; he plans to go public with it, and is quite passionate about his cause. I thought you should know about it, and now you do."

"Indeed," said Ben-Gurion, who then returned his attention to the men gathered around the table, his eyes pausing and connecting with Traynor's.

CHAPTER TWO

Isidor strolled through Washington Square, taking in the sights and making sure he had not been followed, then trudged down Sullivan Street toward West Third. The weather was on the cool side, especially in the shade, which there was plenty of. He gazed at the lush treetops, a rich green under crystal-clear blue skies. Now that the Biltmore Conference was over, he had people to see and places to go. First on the list: he needed a shoe shine.

When the street corner near Ben's Village apartment came into view, he caught sight of the boy whipping a brush at the feet of a seated customer, on the southwest corner, in front of an Italian restaurant. Ben had only told Isidor that a shoe shine boy who worked on the corner of his street had helped him deliver newspaper ads and watch the window shade. He didn't give his name or describe him, or mention him in his written reports. Isidor had spotted the boy when he came to New York after meeting Ben in Rock Creek Park in Washington.

Isidor slowed his pace, timing his arrival to coincide with the customer's departure. Meanwhile, he took in the scenery, the pedestrians, the storefronts, the cars on the street. He saw no signs of surveillance. He knew he was taking a risk by venturing into Ben's former neighborhood, but considered it minimal as long as he didn't approach Ben's apartment. Sir William had arranged for a sweep of the general area by agents from the BSC's covert operations branch and they found nothing out of the ordinary. There was still no confirmation that Ben had vacated his apartment, but it was assumed he had.

Standing on the corner and taking in the sights with a visual scan from left to right, he watched the customer pay for his shine. Isidor crossed over, longing for an Italian meal when, lo...a boy waving a rag in the air grabbed his attention.

"Shine, mister?" the boy said.

Isidor turned to him and held up his finger, altering his course toward the boy, whose face lit up as if he had won a prize. Isidor chuckled.

"What's your name?" Isidor asked after he was seated and the boy was slapping on black polish with a rag he had dipped into a tin.

"Billy Ray Williams. What's yours?"

"Isidor."

"Isidor?" he said, looking up, brightening. "Never heard that one before."

Isidor laughed. "Not many people have."

A minute into the shine, when they were all alone, Isidor said, "I'm looking for a dear friend of mine who used to live down the street. His name was Nick."

Billy Ray froze for an instant, resuming his polish with less vigor. "Nick?" he finally said. "What's his last name?"

"He only went by Nick, or Nicholas."

Billy Ray gave him the silent treatment. Moments passed, then he tapped the tip of the shoe he had been polishing, signaling for the other one. He gave Isidor a stony glance during the transfer and then returned to his business.

"Nick told me about you. He liked you. He said that you had warned him that men in two cars with police radio antennae were following him when he first moved to the Village and that you used to run errands for him, like placing advertisements in the newspaper."

Leery black eyes peered up at him, but Billy Ray didn't say anything. He continued polishing.

"I'm worried about Nick. He was supposed to meet me in January but he didn't show up. I was hoping you could help me find him."

Billy Ray slowed his polish. "Supposin' I could, what you want to know?"

"I want to know when you last saw him and any other clues you can give me. I also want to know if you've talked to anyone else. Does anyone know you used to help Nick?"

Billy Ray tapped the toe of Isidor's shoe and put away the polish tin. He grabbed the brush. His movements were slow, contemplative. "The man knows," Billy Ray said, as he began to brush and glanced up.

Isidor figured out that he meant Bloomfield, the man Ben knew as Chester, and he described him to Billy Ray.

"Yeah, that's him."

Isidor asked how the man knew, and Billy Ray said, "He says he seen my spyin' on the window and then seen me do the telegram when the shade went up."

Isidor asked when that happened, and Billy Ray said, "The day before Christmas." *Christmas?* Isidor thought.

The window shade went up on Christmas Eve? Where did Ben go for Christmas? Billy Ray was still talking. "He nabbed me on my bike when I was ridin' home after the telegram, and made me get in his car."

"How did he make you get in the car?"

"He says he could put me in reform school if'n I didn't tell him all I did for Nick." Billy Ray stopped buffing Isidor's shoe, talking directly to Isidor.

"Keep shining my shoes," Isidor said, and again scanned the surroundings as Billy Ray went back to work. "What did you tell him?" Isidor asked.

"I played it cool and jus' cop to spyin' on the window and the telegram that one time. He says he knows I did one to Atlantic City, so I cop to that one, too."

"Did you tell them about placing ads in the papers?" Isidor said.

"Nope. Like I said, I played it cool on all that." Billy Ray tapped Isidor's shoe and motioned for the other one.

"Did you ever see Nick again after sending the telegram the day before Christmas?"

"Nope. I never seen him again. His car went, too. He jus' quit the scene, sudden like."

Isidor let out a deep breath, mulling over all he had heard. A curious idea struck him. "How did you know when to watch the window in the winter? I forgot to ask Nick how you did that." Billy Ray said he met him in the library once a week.

Isidor asked: "How long had you been doing that?"

"We only jus' start doin' that," Billy Ray said.

"Do you remember when you started meeting him at the library? It might help me figure out what happened to him."

"When it got too cold to shine," Billy Ray said.

"So, last year was the first winter you did that?" Isidor said.

"Uh-huh, that's what I'm saying."

* * *

Isidor arrived back at the Biltmore a half hour before his scheduled meeting with Bergson and Jabotinsky. He recalled the meeting with the Jewish leaders and wondered what could be salvaged from it in light of the results of the conference. The Coup d'Etat succeeded: David Ben-Gurion and the Zionist executive in Palestine, rather than Weizmann and the London executive, were designated to lead the Zionist movement and determine policy toward the British.

There was not a single resolution about saving Jews in Europe passed. The only mention – his blood began to boil with the recollection – was: *This Conference offers a message of hope and encouragement to our fellow Jews in the Ghettos and concentration camps of Hitler-dominated Europe and prays that their hour of liberation may not be too distant.* Ben-Gurion could pray; Isidor would act.

Plan B, which had been pre-approved by Sir William, was now in play.

He stopped at the front desk before heading back to his room to finalize his preparations for the meeting. "Any messages, please, for Isidor Franks."

The clerk checked and found something. "Yes, Mr. Franks. A cable from London." He handed it over and Isidor thanked him.

Expecting a reply to his report on the Biltmore Conference, Isidor decoded the message in his room, reading it as he did.

New information. We may have found your man. Cable time and date for briefing. Good show on Biltmore activities. Making the best of a bad result.

CHAPTER THREE

"Have you ever killed a man?" Ghost snarled at Rookie, their Number Two, whose baby-face showed no hint of experience in life, let alone clandestine operations. The contrast with the cool and steadily reliable Frenchie, the man he was replacing, was striking, even unsettling. The three of them, Ghost, Frenchie, and Ben, had been on a series of assignments throughout Crimea, mere steps ahead of the German Army, and Frenchie had fallen in Sevastopol.

They were seated in the lobby of the Intourist Hotel in the heart of Stalingrad, their site surveys out of the way. Approaching ten p.m., they not only met for the purpose of finalizing their plans for the next morning's shoot but hoped to catch a glimpse of their target who was scheduled to arrive from Moscow at any time.

"Don't answer that," Ben interjected, but it was too late.

"I was a sniper in the Red Army and had more than two hundred kills at the siege of Leningrad."

At the mention of Leningrad, Ben perked up, wondering how recently Rookie had been there and desiring first-hand news from the still-besieged city. But that could wait. It would have to. As Number Three, he was in charge and had a near-mutiny on his hands. Ghost had goaded Rookie into committing a capital security offense by talking about his background.

"That's enough, both of you," Ben said. He glared at Ghost.

"Snipers have an army by their sides," Ghost said to Ben. "Look at his hands, they're trembling. He's going to get us all killed."

"I'll be okay in the morning," Rookie said.

Ben remembered his first job in Oslo, how he had not been able to sleep the night before but had somehow managed to compose himself for the job and, in fact, had out-performed the far more experienced Frenchie. He also wondered how he had looked to Frenchie and High Pockets, and how he might have reacted had either of them challenged him the night before, as Ghost had just done to this boy. Knowing that Rookie was a battle-tested sniper allayed any of Ben's concerns and should have taken care of Ghost's, too. He suspected something else was gnawing at Ghost, something related to their reversed roles. He was prepared to chalk off Ghost's testy mood to the sweltering temperature of the hot August night, which had come down from a high well over one hundred degrees to around the century mark, and was accompanied by a debilitating humidity.

"See there," he said to Ghost. "He'll be okay in the morning."

"And if he isn't, can you pull the trigger?"

"So that's what this is about? You think I can't do my job."

"Can you?"

Ben held his ground, searching for the appropriate way to mollify Ghost when he was roused by a bustle in the lobby. He looked up and saw their target striding through, dressed in business clothes, and accompanied by two men on either side of him.

"There he is," Ben said in a hushed tone, looking away to avoid all three of them being caught staring at once.

"So we're on," he said when their target had cleared the lobby.

Ghost snarled at Rookie: "Go to your position but don't shoot."

"Don't listen to him," Ben said. "You know your job. Be prepared to fire. Number One might not have time for a second shot."

"I won't need a second shot," Ghost said.

"Then we have nothing to argue about." Ben rose to his feet, ending the meeting.

* * *

The next morning Ben crouched on the roof of a department store on the northeast corner of Red Square, about one hundred yards away from the Intourist Hotel from which their target would soon emerge. He gauged the mild wind from the west and considered the different firing vectors that he would have to take into account. Firing west across Red Square, in the general direction of a five-story office building where Rookie was stationed, was the most likely direction he would have to fire. That shot would not be affected by the wind. He calibrated his Mauser 98K rifle scope for the front door of the building, one hundred and fifty yards away. He looked to the northwest, at Railway Station Number One, where Ghost was positioned, and calculated the windage for an unlikely shot in that direction. The range was four hundred yards. He wouldn't have time to adjust his scope, but he needed the information so he knew how much to "aim off" his target to compensate for its current setting.

Then he waited, his rifle cradled in his arms.

Finally, a Red Army staff car came into view on the west side of Red Square, headed southeasterly, toward Gorky Theater. Ben glanced at the rooftop of the five-story office building and saw Rookie's rifle barrel peek over the roof edge. Too soon, but better early than late. He glanced at the railway station and saw nothing. He was confident that he could have swung his rifle up, looked through its scope, and still not have seen the master assassin.

The target's vehicle turned at the end of the square onto Lenin Avenue and turned again on Mira Street in front of a department store, headed toward the Intourist Hotel at the other end of the square, to which Ben now turned his attention, expecting the man to step out from the hotel at any moment.

The car passed by the *Stalingrad Pravda* newspaper building, moving in front of the post office, closing on its destination. Their prey emerged from the hotel. He turned, facing his approaching ride, which was pulling to the curb. He took a step, his last. His body jolted sideways. The crack of a rifle shot split the air. Still on his feet, the man's head snapped backwards. Another blast sounded. The body free-fell to the ground.

A smattering of pedestrians in the area scurried for cover – except for one. A man on the street corner nearest the victim pointed to the top of the office building across the square, to Rookie's location. Two soldiers jumped out of the army staff car, drew weapons from holsters, and followed the witness's finger, sprinting toward the building. Unable to see Rookie at that moment, Ben aimed his rifle in the general direction of the building, prepared to fire.

Pedestrians on the other side of the square re-directed the soldiers to the backside of the building. Rookie must have dropped down the fire escape, as called for in his escape plans.

Within a minute, sirens blared from every direction. The soldiers reached the office building, disappearing from Ben's sight. Another minute passed. A whistle blew, a shot rang out. They came from behind Rookie's office building.

Two police cars careened into view and screeched to a halt two streets west of the building. Cops piled out of them, guns at the ready. Ben shifted his position, shuffling along the edge of the rooftop, and trained his rifle in that direction. Gunfire erupted, a rapid stutter of shots.

A moment later an unarmed Rookie, his Number Two, popped into view, running easterly toward Lenin Avenue, looking over his shoulder. Ben sighted Number Two in his scope, settled the crosshair on him and then aimed off, taking into his calculation the increased range of an estimated two hundred and fifty yards. A pair of soldiers came into view from the east and blind-sided Rookie, spilling him – and spoiling Ben's aim. Number Two reached into his pocket while his captors struggled to subdue him. One hammered at his arm, apparently trying to dislodge the hand, as another soldier, grabbed his legs. Number Two bobbed in and out of view in Ben's scope. Another three policemen and soldiers arrived and piled onto the boy, ripping his hand from his pocket and pinning him to the ground, obstructing a clear shot.

Moments later, the captors hoisted their prize to his feet. Ben centered the cluster of men in his telescope, waiting for an open target. The captive's head wobbled among several, the sight of his torso completely obstructed. Ben rotated his rifle, and duck-walked, tracking their movement, anticipating a better glimpse. Almost a full minute passed without any more than a fleeting prospect. Frustrated, he looked over his telescope and took a broader view. He saw a police van parked on Lenin Avenue, its back doors wide, apparently waiting to haul Rookie. His escorts would have to turn a corner, at which time Ben would have a front view of the group, and likely a clean line of sight. He waddled on his haunches to a location that afforded the best view of the spot he expected Number Two would be open. He estimated the range, re-calculated the windage, and set his scope. He waited.

When they turned the corner, the prisoner was fully exposed, soldiers and police on either side, centered in the crosshair. Three more steps. Two. One. He squeezed the trigger. Number Two doubled over, clutching his gut, writhing. His escorts recoiled. Ben prepared for a second shot, but the phalanx closed on his slumping target, obscuring his sight. A bullet zinged off the edge of the roof, two feet from him, spattering fragments of concrete against the side of his face. He was being fired on. He ducked out of sight, and considered his options. He saw one.

With his rifle in tow, Ben scooted to the back of the roof and slipped over the edge.

* * *

Perhaps an hour later, he perched on a low-lying branch of a maple tree, hidden by the thick foliage of its leaves, reading the day's edition of the local newspaper he had picked up on his way out of the city. Nothing enlightening, just information about air raid drills, rationing, and general references to Soviet victories west of Stalingrad, which Ben knew from reading the London papers were untrue. The German offensive through the Ukraine now threatened the city itself. He folded the paper and wedged it between two branches, commiserating over Rookie's misfortune. He regretted Rookie's loss, especially by his hand, and knew he would never get to speak with him about the Leningrad siege. He should stick to his formula for success, anyway: complete focus on the assignment, avoiding distractions and extraneous actions; total alertness and observation of details; continually envisioning a positive outcome.

A flaming red sun began to set. The muggy heat, again well above one hundred degrees, refused to abate. When the wind blew, it came from the west, hot and dry, and brought no relief. The newspaper reported that no rain had fallen for two months. The weather was about the only topic in *Pravda* he believed. He longed for the sea breeze of the Mediterranean, which he would soon feel, or better yet, the mild evening breeze of the Atlantic Ocean that awaited him in Lisbon.

His thoughts were interrupted by the distant hum of an airplane engine. He dropped to the ground, landing with a thud. A low-flying, single-engine plane bearing Soviet military insignia came into view from the east and approached the meadow adjacent to him. The plane decelerated and descended. As Ben ambled into the meadow, he saw Ghost emerge from foliage about fifty yards downfield.

* * *

Ben felt Ghost's icy stare, and ignored it. They had been settled into the cargo bay of the plane for more than an hour, cruising smoothly, hearing only the steady drone of the engine. Neither had spoken. They never did, except when they had to. Ben had given up trying to be sociable with him. Occasionally Ben would make eye contact with him, even smile. Ghost hated that, and would always turn away or close his eyes. All Ben had to do to get Ghost to stop staring at him was to stare back, which he decided to do. He stared at Ghost, casually, without hostility. Ghost couldn't confront Ben with any emotion other than hatred. He probably hated that, too.

This time, however, Ghost didn't shy away. Ben instantly detected why. He wanted to know what happened to Rookie. He could ask, Ben thought. Why didn't he just ask? Because he lacked the social skills to do even that. Ben decided to make him speak, either that or make him die of curiosity; he refused to give in to Ghost's hateful stare-down. How odd that Ghost was not backing down or shying away. He must really, really want to know what happened to Rookie. But did he want to know badly enough to speak to him? That was the million dollar question.

Now that Ben had an opportunity to peek inside Ghost for the first time in two years, he seized it, studying him, admiring anew the attributes that had aided his survival, and wondering what made him tick. The master assassin was fearless and reliable as a Swiss watch, although, as Ben had discovered that morning, not infallible as a rifleman: his shot had missed the mark and Rookie had been required to fire after all. Except for that one error, he had never made a mistake and was always in the right place at the right time. He was the first person Ben wanted on his assassination team and the last person he wanted sent after him.

Ghost probably felt the same way about Ben, although he would never admit it, not even to himself. Deep down, he probably was glad to see Ben show up for an assignment, as long as Ben didn't have the Number Three role. Yes, there was definitely that proviso. Ghost liked to be in charge. And Ben was fine with that; Ghost was that good. His only weakness was that lack of social skills, especially dealing with someone like Rookie. It suddenly occurred to Ben why Chester had selected him over Ghost for the role. Chester also knew Ghost's limitations. Smart man, Chester. Devious, arrogant, single-minded, all of that, but smart. Without emotion or compassion for another living thing, Ghost was the perfect killing machine.

And then the killing machine spoke, startling Ben.

"What happened to Number Two?"

"He was captured. Now he's dead." Not known for sure, but close enough for this conversation.

"Did he take the pill?"

Ben shook his head. "I had to kill him."

A faint smile crept onto Ghost's face and then he settled against the fuselage and closed his eyes. Ben chuckled to himself. The reaction was high praise coming from Ghost. So, he was not quite a machine, after all.

Ben saw his own journey headed in the same direction. He was no longer as happy and care-free as he once had been. His anger over the plight of his brothers, and his forced separation from Marsha had dragged out and ate away at his innate optimism. He knew he would rebound once his brothers were freed, and once he was reunited with Marsha. His mood over his job was lasting; he felt himself descending into some kind of spiritual abyss. Killing someone no longer fazed him. In fact, he enjoyed the emotional high, the adrenalin rush, the power trip, or whatever it was, where everything slowed down and his perceptions intensified a thousand-fold. But each time he came out of the high now, he felt a little piece of him missing. And today he had killed a teammate, someone he knew, someone he liked, and admired. Rookie was a brave soldier who had defended Ben's hometown, his family, friends, and countrymen against Nazi invaders; yet killing him had not bothered Ben.

That realization disturbed him.

Now he saw himself – and Ghost – in a new light. He realized that once, however long ago it might have been, Ghost had been in all likelihood a decent person but this job had eroded that man, slowly perhaps, but surely, into something machine-like, almost soulless. And he knew that he too would eventually become such a man if he continued to kill. The memory of his father instructing him and his brothers in their faith returned in that moment and he realized something he wished he could share with his father. He knew now what the Commandment meant. Killing was not bad or evil because it was a *sin*; it was bad or evil because killing another person assumed authority we didn't have, and degraded the killer spiritually to a point beyond which there can be no healing, no redemption. Like Ghost, he could one day be unable to view the world and the people in it with anything other than contempt.

Ben hated Ghost, and was beginning to hate himself. He felt trapped, responsible in part for David's and

Michael's imprisonment. He had given his word and felt duty-bound to fulfill it. Yet he longed for Marsha and the days when he once taught and translated Russian literature and went to baseball games.

And the tears welled up in his eyes. And then they flowed.

CHAPTER FOUR

Upon his return to Lisbon, Ben opened up his apartment. It was hot and stuffy, and the fresh air flow immediately began to make a difference. At least Lisbon would be cool at night. As he stripped out of his shirt, he looked over the living room. The novel he had been reading, the French version of *The Count of Monte Cristo*, lay where he had left it, on the lamp stand next to his reading chair. A chess board was still set up on his writing desk, waiting his next move. A book entitled, *Chess Endgame Fundamentals*, lay beside the board. An average, infrequent player growing up in Russia, he had become good in Lisbon, playing daily.

He threw his shirt on the sofa and slid aside the board and chessmen. He replaced them with the typewriter that had been sitting on the floor. From a drawer he took a small stack of paper and placed it next to the typewriter, preparing to write his report. But first, he stepped out onto the balcony of the top-level apartment, third floor. In the Bairro Alto section of Lisbon, it overlooked the red roof tops of the hilly neighborhood and the flat central part of the city. He reveled in the panoramic view of St. George's Castle and the River Tejo, and drew a deep breath. The beep of a horn brought him closer to home. He looked down on the cobblestone street scene below: a lady nonchalantly crossing the street, an auto stopped to allow her to cross, and a smattering of pedestrians idly strolling the sidewalks in front of a row of shops. A trolley clanged in the distance. Peaceful and charming, it felt good to be back.

He looked north, to the second-story balcony on the other side of the street. A pot of daisies, yellow, white, and pink, hung from the wall. He was relieved it was hanging, and not resting below on the railing. He needed a break, at least for one day. Flowers up brightened the most dreary days. Flowers down meant a trip to the safe house, usually to pick up an assignment. Or a letter from Chester. But even that prospect had become predictable and maddening. No, you can't return to New York; no, now is not the time to go into Germany.

There were only two things wrong with Lisbon, otherwise he loved the city. It was an ocean away from Marsha, and there was no shoeshine boy on the corner. He felt trapped, much like he had when he first moved to Greenwich Village. The windows in the rows of buildings on both sides of the street seemed like a thousand eyes. Any passenger in any trolley, each shop owner in every business he entered, could be one of Chester's men. He didn't feel safe to play his half of the Ace of spades. He resigned himself to that fate months ago.

Thinking of Chester, he trudged back inside the apartment. He fed a piece of paper into the carriage and began pounding the typewriter keys. He wrote his report.

When he finished, he took a bath and stepped into fresh clothes, slacks and a white, long-sleeved shirt, unbuttoned at the collar, sleeves rolled up. No hat. He walked the five-block distance to the safe house, an apartment above a cobbler's shop, and bounded up the wooden stairs. At the top, he unlocked the door with one of two keys attached to a key chain.

Inside, the austerely-furnished room was hot and stuffy. Windows closed, shades drawn, the air was stale. He went straight to the kitchenette, inserted the second key into one of the white-painted cabinets and opened it. The cabinet was bare, but not for long: he tossed in the envelope containing his report to Chester. He raised the shade in the bedroom window, which opened onto the street, and then left the apartment, locking its door behind him.

His Stalingrad mission was officially completed.

He boarded a bisque-colored trolley and, hopping from one tram to another, wound his way to Cidade Baixa, the lower city section of Lisbon, to a café on Rua dos Sapateiros, where he dined at a sidewalk table, splurging. It had become part of his celebratory ritual in London. He started with soup, caldo verde, made with fresh shredded kale, potato, and spice with a smoky sausage, and ended with sea bass, followed by cherry liqueur. He took his time, savoring both the meal and the peaceful atmosphere.

He walked off the extra calories with a long leisurely stroll toward the river, to the Pelican's Roost, his favorite haunt. The tavern was a cross between an English pub and a Russian chess parlor. A large, rustic-looking establishment with a bar and six dining tables in the front, and three billiard tables and two dart boards in the middle section, very English. In the rear were three rows of card or gaming tables with naked light bulbs hanging over them, resembled a chess parlor Ben had visited in St. Petersburg as a teenager.

A dozen or so customers were sprinkled throughout the front two sections. Another dozen hung out in back, most of them gathered round one table. Laughter and excited utterances erupted from it, telling Ben that Joe was up to his old tricks. He grabbed a beer from the bar and ventured toward the noise, giving a friendly nod to familiar faces along the way. No names, just faces. He assumed they were all spies from various warring nations, just as he was sure they knew he was one. An air of camaraderie filled the room. He marveled at the culture and strange conventions of the tavern every time he entered. Ask no questions, no problem. Probe, a stiletto in the ribs, body dumped in a dark alley. Everyone understood and abided by the unwritten rules. Even the PVDE, Salazar's secret police, turned a blind eye. Antonio de Oliveira Salazar was the Prime Minister and de facto dictator of Portugal. No spying was allowed, in other words. Strictly enforced. The policy was good for the economy – and the spies.

In the back, the situation was as Ben suspected. Three chess boards, three opponents – now two, one was rising, licking his wounds – and one master, actually a grand master. That was Joe. He was the exception to the rule about names. He bandied his about. A hulk of a man, from his forehead and bushy black eyebrows down to his hands. Like everyone in the place, he spoke English, but did so with a heavy Russian accent. Overseas, many people called American men Joe. Obviously he was not one of those. Josef, perhaps, as in

Stalin. Either way, Ben found it funny, and he was sure Joe intended it to be so. A fixture at the Roost, Joe raked in the silver coins and paper currency next to the board that had been being vacated.

"Drinks," he said in his deep, booming voice. More cheers. He flashed a big grin at Ben, exposing a silver-capped front tooth that sparkled with the reflection of the light.

"You next," he said, holding up a finger. "One pawn this time."

Joe abruptly lowered his head, suddenly engrossed. One of his opponents had made a move, hitting his timer. A few seconds later, Joe gripped his black-squared bishop and pushed it down the board. Not only his hand, but his arm and whole body leaned into the move. Having been on the other side of the board, Ben knew that the physical manner of Joe's moves combined with his skill tended to overwhelm an opponent, if only briefly, but then, the moves added up. Ben found it helpful to recognize this feature of Joe's game. He got the idea that the current victim didn't; the man seemed to be reeling. The move completed, Joe slapped his timer.

A waiter arrived and began taking orders. Ben displayed his beer bottle, waving him off.

"No," Joe bellowed, wagging his finger at Ben. "I insist."

Ben knew better than to argue. Another beer it would be.

Joe's other two opponents fell in short order, each defeat causing an outburst of kudos, jeers and condolences, shouts and whistles. Joe pocketed the money and ordered more drinks. Another outburst.

Ben finally had his turn at the table. One-on-one. The extra boards and half the gathering having spread to other tables. They agreed on fifty Escudos, and placed their bets, laying both bank notes and coins one either side of the board. Joe cupped a pawn in each hand, inviting Ben to pick. He chose white. When the board was set, Joe leaned on his elbows. "You take," he said. Ben removed the black queen's pawn.

He recalled his first game with Joe, on a chilly day in February. After watching Joe mow down several opponents, he had refused to play the chess marvel. Joe egged him into playing by telling him he could pick any piece of his and remove it. "Any piece?" he said. Almost in jest, and still not having accepted his invitation to play, Ben picked up Joe's queen. Joe curled his lip, adopting a forlorn look, but then shook it off and said, "Sit." A buzz swept through the tavern, and within seconds of accepting the invitation, a throng had descended upon the table, more than the number of patrons in the whole joint moments earlier. It seemed as if people on the streets had received the word and poured in. The hoopla reminded him of the buzz surrounding the Joe Louis-Max Schmeling boxing rematch in Yankee Stadium in '38. The results were similar, too. Both Joes won. And Ben had thought he was a fairly good player. After that humiliation, he purchased a chess board and instruction books, having made a vow to play Joe even-up before he left Lisbon. An unrealistic goal, he at least had lowered his handicap. The last time they played, Ben won playing white with a two-pawn advantage.

More importantly, the undertaking had pulled him out of his doldrums. He sat around bored stiff for two months after arriving in Lisbon, moping. No assignments, nothing. He even started smoking cigarettes before he decided to venture out and find some sort of life. That's when he stumbled upon the Pelican's Roost.

Joe motioned for him to make the first move, and Ben quickly cleared his mind, leading with his king's pawn. They played to a draw. Ben took a break and played a rematch. As black, he was beaten again. He ate fish and chips before heading home.

After nine o'clock, it was dark outside when he reached the trolley stop, joining a small gathering that began to swell when a street car turned the corner, and walkers rushed to catch it. The car lurched to a stop, and the waiting crowd bunched together, clearing space for the new passengers. A middle-aged lady standing to Ben's right bumped into him. She squeaked and with a deep voice said, "Excuse me." Ben was more startled by the voice than the bump. It had a ring of familiarity. As he turned to meet it, a figure passed, brushing up against his right arm. A hand grabbed his and pressed an object into his palm. He formed a fist, clutching it, and then twisted his neck to see who it was. All he caught was a glimpse of the back of a man walking off, mingling with a group of other passengers stepping off.

He couldn't see the face. He didn't have to. The voice, the frame, and the aura added up to only one conclusion: it had to be Izzy.

He clenched his fist and clamped down on his sudden jubilation. He tried, but was unable to quell the bounce in his step boarding the trolley.

CHAPTER FIVE

"Did you come from Stalingrad?" Isidor asked when they met two hours later in a dimly lit, one-room apartment above a tailor's shop on the shore of the river Tejo in the Alfama district of Lisbon.

"How did you know?"

"A KGB agent was assassinated outside his hotel in downtown Stalingrad three days ago and we know there was movement of two civilian personnel on British planes in and out of Malta coincident with the incident."

"Whose cause did I help?"

"I was told people at SIS cheered when the news crossed the wire."

Ben found that comforting; he felt something lift from his shoulders. The idea of killing for a just cause: a novel concept. It made a difference for his self-image.

"The target eliminated in Stalingrad was believed to have been a German double-agent connected with a vast intelligence network through the Ukraine and in Moscow who SIS had given the code name 'Peggy,'" Isidor said.

Ben told him he had done a series of assignments in the Ukraine, and Isidor added, "I'll get the details later and report them to London for analysis, but I suspect your targets are somehow related to Peggy's network.

"Hitler plans to attack Stalingrad," he continued. "This time the Soviets are preparing for it." He told Ben that an independent British intelligence network and a separate intelligence network operating out of Switzerland, both with connections inside the German high command, had warned the Soviet Union in the Spring of 1941 that Hitler planned to attack Russia in June of that year. The intelligence wasn't heeded. Someone within the Soviet general staff (STAVKA) misled Stalin into believing that the intelligence was part of a British plot to bring the Soviet Union into the war.

"As a consequence," Isidor said, "The German Army rolled over the Soviet borders and had a clean shot to Moscow. Now Stalin and STAVKA are listening. Operation Blue is a secret German plan. The original objectives were to capture the Caucasus oil fields and sever the Volga river lifeline of the Soviet Union, not to attack Stalingrad. Hitler changed the objectives and decided to attack. Stalin has issued orders to prepare the city.

"This is a significant development. Had Peggy discovered that information, it would have been passed on to the German high command, if British assumptions are correct.

"All of this means that the people issuing orders to Bloomfield, who financially propped up the Reich and profited from both sides of the war, have turned on Hitler and are throwing their support to the Allies, to the Soviets in particular."

Ben wrinkled his brow, puzzled.

"It appears they want an East-West balance of power in Europe as part of the outcome, but we lack the intelligence to make a firm conclusion at this point," Isidor said.

He shifted gears, telling Ben he had brought with him a tawny port wine that was delicious and offered a glass. Ben accepted and ambled to a window and peered out as Isidor uncorked the bottle and poured.

The district they were in was a hilly maze of narrow lanes, cramped dwellings, and den-like shops, resembling what Ben imagined Istanbul or Cairo might look like. The inky blackness of the river to the south framed the view.

"Here," Isidor said, handing him a glass. Ben took a sip. He agreed, it was delicious.

"How did you find ..." Ben said, interrupted by Isidor simultaneously asking him what had happened to him in New York, with neither completing his question. They laughed and then Ben answered first. He was shipped out with no advance warning, and put under tight surveillance, he said, going over the details with Isidor, whose demeanor showed concern.

"Were you involved in anything that might have given rise to their suspicion?"

Ben was taken aback; the question came from left field. "What do you mean?"

"Any activities that Bloomfield might have stumbled onto, keeping the wrong kind of company, breaking his security rules..." His voice trailed off, giving way to a probing expression.

Ben thought of his trips to Rocky Mount but dismissed their relevance. He didn't want to go into it. "No," he said, turning and tipping his glass.

"If you think of something let me know, because we need to know what happened. It's possible our covers are blown."

Ben spun back to face him, alarmed.

Isidor told Ben of the backdrop of his sudden departure, about the push by the State Department to run the British out of New York and take over their intelligence apparatus after uncovering covert operations being run on them. "They ended up getting the BSC office but not the critical operations center. The British helped the U.S. form a centralized agency, and brought in Allen Dulles to run it. It has changed names already, and is now called the Office of Strategic Services, OSS for short. We've wondered whether they found out about our operation, yours and mine. Or possibly they just beefed up security and decided not to take any more chances with you, so that shipping you out was designed to sever any *possible* connections to British Intelligence. I know Dulles and Bloomfield have transferred their base of operations since then, but the timing...the suddenness...the surveillance..." He didn't finish the sentence. "I need to know if there was something else that might have justified their actions, so they can be accurately evaluated."

Ben turned away, taking another drink, mulling it over.

"If it will help jog your memory," Isidor said, "I was in New York in May. I got my shoes shined."

The wine glass almost fell out of Ben's hand. "He talked to you?"

"After I assured him I was your friend trying to find you. It wasn't easy."

"What did he say?" Ben said.

"He said Chester caught him watching the window and ..."

"What? When? Did he hurt him?"

"He didn't hurt him," Isidor said. "He scared him, or at least he tried to. The boy is very streetwise. He handled it well and only admitted to what Chester already knew," Isidor said.

"Which was?"

"After he saw the window shade up, he rode his bicycle to a hotel and sent a telegram..." Isidor paused, "...to Washington." He paused again. "On Christmas Eve." His expression said he was owed an explanation.

Ben set the glass on top of a book case near the window. He ran his fingers through his hair, mumbling, "Oh, boy." He didn't understand why he found it so difficult to disclose his secret to Isidor. He saw no rational reason to hold on to it, especially now that their covers may have been blown. He needed the support and analysis of Isidor and SIS. He decided to spill it.

"I was seeing someone. My fiancée."

Isidor recoiled, his face contorted. Apparently he had considered everything but that. And then his eyes opened wide. "Aha!" he said. "A woman!" He prayerfully threw up his arms, his head back. "They'll do it every time."

Amused, Ben shook his head. He could tell Isidor was being facetious, apparently relieved to hear an innocent explanation. He put his arm around Ben. "A fiancée, eh?"

Ben nodded. "Yes. She's wonderful. I can't wait for you to meet her."

Isidor congratulated him. "It might not have been the smartest thing you've done, but I'm happy for you if you're happy."

"She lives in western Virginia," Ben said, "a long way from Washington. Do you think Chester knows?"

"You must assume he knows about the relationship and plan accordingly," Isidor said. It is foolhardy not to. I say that as a dear friend, knowing you're not a fool." He reached for the wine bottle and began to pour himself another glass, muttering under his breath. "Well, you're in love, which is the same thing."

Ben cracked up. He had Isidor top off his wine glass, giving him a one-armed hug and then told him about meeting Marsha at Columbia, Chester's admonition, and their reunion.

"He knows," Isidor said.

"Do you think he would do anything to her?"

Isidor shook his head. "No, he won't hurt her. Unless you become a problem. You were smart to tell me. Now I will keep her in mind. If we need to, we can protect her, move her if necessary."

Ben thanked Isidor, then asked how Isidor had found him.

"My handler at SIS traced your movement to the Lisbon area of Portugal, and I hunted for you in and around Estoril, a village up the coast.

"Bloomfield is tied to Dulles, who is now part of the OSS, as I mentioned. The OSS has an office in the Palacio Hotel in Estoril, but Dulles lives in Bern, Switzerland and runs the OSS office there. He still has his hands in the New York OSS office. He runs an inner clique that handles covert actions for the OSS and gives Bloomfield free rein of agency resources. A lot of intelligence activity for Allied countries is planned and coordinated out of the Estoril office, and we discovered Bloomfield spends a lot of time in the area. I hunted there but later got a tip about the spy hangouts here in Lisbon. I spotted you in the Pelican's Roost six weeks ago."

Isidor said he had followed Ben prior to approaching him in order to learn his routine, to see what kind of surveillance he might be under. "You're clean outside of your neighborhood. The cobbler below the safe house is a courier and cutout for your control officer, Bloomfield, the man you call Chester." Ben understood the term cutout to mean an intermediary used to transfer information and only knew the source and destination of information. "He delivers and picks up messages for you at the OSS office in Estoril and occasionally meets with Bloomfield. He's also the one who lowers and raises the flower pot. He doesn't live in the apartment, but he has access to it."

Isidor grabbed his portfolio, which was lying on a table under the dim orange glow of a shaded lamp, and then steered Ben into a kitchenette area, and flicked on an overhead light while talking. "I don't know if you're being watched in your neighborhood, but the opportunities for it are endless. All the apartments and shops...it's almost impossible to monitor." Ben said he'd recognized that, which is why he never tried to contact him.

Over a wooden table, Isidor said, "Let me show you a photograph."

"Ghost." Ben whispered the moment he saw it. "Where did you get this?"

"He lives in Cascais, a little fishing village a bit further up the coast from Estoril. I followed a man who had met with Bloomfield at the Estoril Casino, which led me to a safe house in Cascais where I took the photograph."

"He was with me in Stalingrad, and throughout Ukraine," Ben said.

"Before the war, he was an international hit man for organized crime elements connected to the Bronfman outfit, clients of Bloomfield's Montreal law firm. He's a Russian immigrant. His Russian name is Yuriy Helvas. His adopted American name is Jerry Helms."

Isidor then showed him a photo of Frenchie, whom Ben identified and said, "He was killed on a job in Sevastopol.

"He's another Russian. He immigrated to Corsica around 1935 and got hooked up with the French Corsican underworld. Heroin production, which connects to..."

Ben finished his sentence. "Bronfman."

"Precisely," Isidor said. "Bronfman to Bloomfield to Dulles. We used to think the guy I worked for, Traynor, the head of Haganah intelligence, was doing the recruiting for this assassination unit, but it appears not to be the case."

He clarified for Ben that the Haganah was the Jewish military in Palestine. "Apparently Bloomfield recruits and controls his men and Dulles provides American and British military resources through his connections and also takes care of the security, background investigations and ..."

Isidor cut himself short. "Which reminds me of something. In '38, when we had to let you go, we learned something I can share with you now, although it is still highly classified. We discovered a document in the hands of Haganah intelligence that came from Allen Dulles's Wall Street intelligence unit. Dulles must have been investigating you, which means you had already been selected as a likely recruit by Bloomfield. They discovered that your university records had been falsified and suspected SIS was responsible. Not too many outfits have that capability. Their report was sent to Traynor's unit. We later discovered that David and Michael were being held as political prisoners. Because we know the Zionists have shared information with the Nazis before, it is possible that Dulles or Bloomfield gave the information to Traynor's unit for them to relay to the Nazis to apply pressure on the Nazis so they would hold your brothers as political prisoners. I thought about that after you described to me how your recruitment went."

"Couldn't the Nazis have discovered the falsified records independently?" Ben asked.

"Highly unlikely. They would need willing agents inside government agencies like the FBI or State Department. University administrators wouldn't permit it any other way. Not only did SIS get the records cleaned, but they kept them clean for five years. The Nazis don't have that kind of resource inside America."

"I wonder if he really plans to help me rescue them, or if he's just using me," Ben said. "I've been thinking about giving him an ultimatum. Maybe I should make him deliver on his promise before I do anything else for him. What do you think of that idea?"

"I think you should. I was going to suggest that later tonight, in fact," Isidor said. "I have some information you can use to support your demand."

Ben's mind drifted. He shook his head. "If I verify Chester did that, he's a dead man."

Isidor put his hands on Ben's shoulder. "I have a better way for you to get even."

Then there came a quiet, but distinct rap on the door and Isidor put his finger to his lips. He glanced at his watch. "Just a minute," he called out. Whispering to Ben, "I ordered some food and drink. That must be it." He clicked off the kitchen light and ushered Ben in there, out of sight from the door, and then answered it. He returned carting a large tray. He asked Ben to get the light, and placed the tray on the table, pushing aside his portfolio. "It was supposed to be here an hour ago. Help yourself."

Meats, fresh fruit and vegetables, eggs, bread, cheese, a red wine, and water filled the tray. It looked good. Ben dug in.

Isidor told Ben that the original plan of the BSC in New York was to monitor Dulles and the Wall Street profiteers and then when America entered to war, to instigate investigations and have them prosecuted for treason and shut down. "The plan worked, for about two months," he said.

"After the attack on Pearl Harbor, U.S. Senator Harry Truman convened an investigation into the traitorous deals, the Truman Committee. After a month or so, the investigation was suddenly dropped. Not for lack of evidence but because the Dulles brothers had one of their clients threaten to interrupt the U.S. oil supply if the investigation continued. They extorted the government, in other words. At roughly the same time, February of '42, the assistant Attorney General of the United States stormed into the offices of Standard Oil of New Jersey in Rockefeller Plaza and outlined federal charges against the company, demanding $1.5 million in fines and control of its Nazi patents. The Standard executives pointed out that the entire war effort was fueled by their Saudi oil and it could be stopped. The charges were dropped. The fact is, neither America nor Britain can prosecute a war without oil. Their countries were already rationing gasoline for their citizens."

"Unbelievable," Ben said. "Those are the people I should be assassinating." He laughed. "Look at me. My solution is to kill everybody. See what this job's done to me?"

"Killing them would be the easy way out for them. Exposing them and bringing them to justice is what they deserve. Our plan is to gather evidence and prosecute them for war crimes after the Allies win the war. We're all over Dulles. That's how we know about the plans to end the war with a balance of power. He's also juggling corporate books, using Swiss holding companies to hide the collaboration of Wall Street banks and corporations with the Nazis and planning to pull out Nazi scientists and selected party leaders and Nazi gold and assets. They have the war's end game all planned out. We're on to them and they don't know it, or at least they don't know how much we know. That's what I'm told anyway."

Isidor finished eating, poured himself a glass of wine, and doused the kitchen light. "Let's sit in the comfortable chairs," he said, heading toward the living room. Ben sensed a change in Isidor, something serious. They settled into the living room, Isidor under the orange glow of a dim lamp by the apartment door.

"Earlier in the year, in May, a report was smuggled out of Poland. Among other things in the report was a gas, a cyanide-based insecticide called Zyklon B that is manufactured by a chemical company largely owned by I.G. Farben. Farben is the second largest shareholder in

Standard Oil, next to Rockefeller, and a partner of Standard Oil in various patents and projects. Isidor's look turned grave. "The Reich is using the gas to exterminate Jews."

Ben gasped; the air went out of his lungs.

When Ben recovered enough to take in more information, Isidor apprised him of Hitler's Final Solution. He then went into the actions being undertaken in the U.S. by Peter Bergson and others, to publicize the ongoing atrocities and muster public support for a massive rescue action. He related to Ben a story about a successful bribery offer by Rabbi Michael Ber Weissmandel to the SS Lt. Col. Adolf Eichmann to obtain the release of thousands of Jews in Slovakia. "We're trying to expand on his success and have extended a request to Eichmann through intermediaries for the amount it would take to obtain the release of all Jews in Nazi-occupied territories. If the Soviets defeat the Reich at Stalingrad, Eichmann might start thinking more about life after the Reich.

"If you can get Bloomfield to help rescue your brothers, we can not only discover Dulles's contacts inside the Reich but we can learn their methods and possibly rescue many more."

Ben felt rejuvenated, determined. "I'm in. Is this the information you had for me? Can I use this?"

"No, you can't use what I've told you. They might trace it to me. But *The New York Times* did an exposé on the mass killings. I will get you a copy. Try to find it yourself, in the meantime. It was just published a day or two ago."

CHAPTER SIX

"You're demanding me to expose our resources inside the Reich at a crucial time in the war," Chester said.

"I exposed *my* resources, my life," Ben said, "so I could earn the chance to save my brothers. If we wait until it is safe to use your resources, they may be dead. You owe this to me. We had a deal."

They were meeting in the fishing village of Cascais, a short electric rail ride west of Lisbon, in a two-room office suite above a restaurant. It was a safe house. Ben recognized the front of the building from the picture taken of Ghost by Isidor.

"Where do you get your information?" Chester said. The question was loaded, laced with subtle suspicion.

Ben produced his copy of the *New York Times* article. "There is also the BBC radio report I mentioned in my letter."

Chester had his eyes on the article as Ben spoke and didn't respond.

When he let loose of the article, he said. "Yes, and I found out the BBC report was based entirely on a German-American Alliance report. It hasn't been officially verified. Neither has the Peter Bergson report been verified, which is what this article is based on," Chester said with a sweep of his hand.

Ben bore into Chester, "Nor have the reasons for any of your assignments been officially verified."

Chester flinched. "What do you mean by that?"

"I mean the basis of our bargain has been trust, not officially verified reports," Ben said. "I trust the reports I'm hearing. They have the ring of truth. I didn't challenge your reasons for doing the jobs you asked me to do and I don't want you to challenge my reasons for wanting to go inside Germany now."

Chester doused the cigarette he was working on. He reached for another one, but then tossed the cigarette package on the desk he was sitting behind and rose. Ben was across from him. Chester circled the desk, then leaned against it, facing and studying Ben.

"I've put a lot of thought to how we could rescue them and I concluded that we will need to go inside Germany on some kind of test run before we do the actual rescue attempt. I've come up with a plan that might work. The truth is, the resources required are simply not available to me at the moment. If the Russians defeat the German Sixth Army at Stalingrad, then everything changes. Only then does it become possible. Can you work with me on that time table?"

"If I have to."

Chester nodded, lit a cigarette, and exhaled. "Until then, are you available for any jobs?"

"No," Ben said.

Chester pursed his lips. "Why not?"

"Because I'm not in the right frame of mind. I'll get everyone killed. Even if I have to wait four months to go inside Germany, you will find me any day of the week at the newsstands, listening to the BBC for more news, or somehow worrying or thinking about my brothers. I'm no longer an asset for you. I'm a liability – until we get them out of Germany."

Chester blew out a stream of smoke. "Let me ask you something, and please be honest with me."

"Go ahead," Ben said.

"If we get your brothers out, are you going to be in the right frame of mind?"

"After I do a little celebrating, I will be," Ben said, smiling.

Chester was not amused; he stared at Ben, studying him. He took a drag, then rose and returned to his desk chair. "I hope you understand that the resources we need are not at my beck and call. The people who give the green light on a project like this think in terms of risk and benefits. Going inside Germany on your time table, as opposed to theirs, creates a greater risk. I will need to sell them on a benefit to justify that risk. Do you follow me?"

Ben didn't, and he got the feeling that Chester was hedging. "That makes sense," he said, hoping to draw him out.

"How do you suggest I sell it?"

"Easily," Ben said. "You tell them they've already achieved a hundred times more benefit than the risk you're asking them to take. Starting with Stalingrad, where I helped make a Russian victory possible, and working backward: Forty-two successful missions. Forty-two times I risked my life. Forty-two times I carried a cyanide capsule in my pocket, prepared to bite on it. I'm one of your best men. They got all that in return for what they're now risking. And you might add to that:

you promised to do this for me three years ago. I assume you're dealing with honorable people."

Chester grinned. "Yes, yes. All true. Unfortunately, high-ranking military intelligence officers are charged with a war to win and they answer to politicians. They look forward, not backward."

"You knew that when we made the deal," Ben said.

"I said it had to be the right time."

Ben snapped. "It *is* the right time, because we're running out of time and soon won't have any at all."

"I heard you the first time," Chester said.

"Then what are you driving at?" Ben said.

"Let me put it to you another way," Chester said, crushing out his half-smoked cigarette and leaning forward. "I know how to sell this. They're making future plans, even beyond the war. There will always be a need to maintain a balance of power among nations in order to prevent future wars."

Ben somehow managed to control his emotions. He shrugged. "Then do that."

CHAPTER SEVEN

"**G**ood luck, men." Ben and Dolohov's chauffeur spoke for the first time. He had picked them up at a hotel in Bern that morning. They were in Bern to be fitted for their clothing, and photographed for their travel papers. The car was pulled off to the side of a country lane in northern Switzerland, its engine running. They were standing by the open trunk. Inside were two rifle cases, duffel bags, and one picnic basket. Dolohov grabbed the basket, cradling it by the handles in one arm, and picked up one case and bag. Ben took the rest.

"Take care," Ben said, as the driver dropped the trunk lid.

The car roared off, kicking up snow from the shoulder of the gravel road. "Talkative fellow."

Dolohov chuckled. "Let's get off the road."

The Soviet Union had defeated the German Sixth Army at Stalingrad in February 1943. It was now March; six months after Ben had issued his ultimatum to Chester.

Ben looked around them. He saw rolling hills, vineyards, and a vast expanse of open space, not a single farmhouse or dwelling. A thin layer of snow carpeted areas not exposed to the sun. Lake Constance was visible far in the distance. On the other side of the lake was Germany. He shuddered; they were that close.

"That must be the trail," Dolohov said. On the north side of the road, to the right, a visible trail snaked across the landscape. "How about the trees? Let's get organized first." Ben nodded, starting off toward a grove of tall, bare oaks.

In the trees, they opened their duffel bags. Ben went through his. It contained two sets of clothes, one civilian, one a German Army uniform; identification papers, both military and civilian. He opened the civilian papers, a German Railway guest worker document with his picture affixed. Friedrich Mueller, it said. Nazi stamps were on both sides of the paper. He checked the military papers: Major Friedrich Mueller was photographed in an Army uniform.

They didn't have a Number Three, a first for Ben. No explanation had been given. He wondered if Dolohov knew why. "No Number Three," he said, as he dug through the bag, half statement, half question.

"Night shoot, I guess," Dolohov said.

True, Ben thought. But they would return the following morning by train. He recalled the assignment in Moscow when Ghost came in handy, and said, "I feel naked without a Number Three."

Dolohov paused, looking up from his bag. "There you go thinking again. I warned you about that."

Ben laughed. He liked Dolohov. Loyal soldier, wind him up, give him his orders, and let him go. No muss, no fuss. Get in, get out, play some cards.

They decided to lunch before heading out, and dug through the basket. Sandwiches, potato salad, vegetables, and a thermos for each of them. He opened one: coffee, steaming. He took a sip. Fresh and tasty. Eating utensils, napkins, and a jug of water also were inside. He opened one of the sandwiches and took a bite. He studied his map as he chewed. Dolohov did the same. An "X" marked where they had been dropped off. They were to take the pathway visible from the road. Three miles to the "R," the rendezvous spot. It doubled as a firing range. They needed to familiarize themselves with the French MAS-36 and its cartridges and zero in their rifles to the iron sights, no scope, since they would be firing at night.

They made it to the firing range with an hour to spare. A wide open area, buttressed by a steep incline. They set up targets at one hundred yards, zeroed in their sights, and then "faced off," as Dolohov called it, betting their thermoses of coffee on a ten-shot match. Close, but Ben won. He poured a half cup of coffee out of Dolohov's thermos and handed the thermos back to him. "You owe me a beer when we get back to Lisbon."

When the sun dipped over the horizon, they changed into their German Uniforms, hiding their Swiss travel clothes under a bush. Dolohov took from his travel bag a large white sheet and spread it in the center of the field and waited under a tree nearby. Within minutes, a single-engine Messerschmitt bearing Wehrmacht insignia and flying low came from across the lake, circled, and landed. They hustled aboard, toting their bags and rifle cases, jamming them into the two cramped seats behind the pilot. Once they had settled in, Ben gave the thumbs up and the plane began to taxi. It lifted off, and within minutes they had crossed into Germany. Ben felt a triumphant surge in his chest. Then anxiety crept in, too; entering Germany meant possible resistance, anti-aircraft fire.

As the Swiss border and daylight fell behind them, he began to relax and become acclimated to the reality of being in enemy territory – and focused on his mission.

"Hang on," the pilot said, as the plane began its descent. Ben took the warning to heart. Below them was pitch blackness. He grabbed the arm rests and braced his legs. The plane hit the earth with a thud and ricocheted off, then struck again, tilted to the right. They tumbled and bounced, eventually settling into a bumpy deceleration, and came to a halt.

Ben threw his duffel bag out first, and then slapped the pilot on his shoulder. "Great job," he said, "and thanks," then climbed out of the plane. Dolohov handed him the rifle cases, tossed him his bag, and then dropped down with his gear in hand. The two of them scurried off the narrow landing strip to a stand of trees.

Ben spread his coat to shield the red light from Dolohov's flashlight as both men studied their map. They agreed on their position and set off to the west. Ben stepped off seventy-five yards, adjusted his direction slightly and spied a grassy lane in a small clearing, pointing. They took the lane into the woods where they found a two-door Opel with Army insignia on its sides and an Army license plate waiting for them. The keys were in the ignition. Dolohov opened the driver's door.

"How about a lift, Major Mueller?" Dolohov said.

"Please, Lieutenant."

* * *

Ben lay in a cluster of bushes in the wooded embankment approximately one hundred yards from a major weapons factory. Light from a full moon illuminated the divide and reflected off a carpet of snow, clearly revealing: the main entrance; a wide lane bordering the factory; an enormous, sparsely filled parking lot; and an idle railway spur. An occasional gust of chilly air swayed the brush and branches, breaking the otherwise dead silence and creating an eerie ambience.

He waited until the unmistakable image of a large, fat man, dressed in a fur-collared overcoat, emerged from the main entrance. Ben aligned the iron forward and aft sights on his rifle with the target and tracked him as he walked to the edge of the lane, under the wash of a street lamp.

The man glanced in both directions, evidently on the lookout for transportation that, according to Chester's notes, would not arrive.

The loud report of Ben's rifle split the silence, and a bullet slammed into the chest of the man, who buckled, but didn't fall. A moment later, another shot rang out from a spot about fifty yards south of Ben. Their target keeled over. No one came to his rescue.

Ben tossed the rifle into a gully and slipped away into the night.

* * *

In civilian clothes, they boarded a train in Stuttgart, presenting their German Railway Identity Documents. Not the slightest suspicion seen. They sat in the same car on opposite sides of the aisle. As the final boarding whistle blew, a Gestapo officer, a Major, entered the car and walked down the aisle. He peered into Ben's face and then Dolohov's as he passed. Not good. Ben looked over his shoulder and saw the Major settle into a seat three rows back of Dolohov. He pivoted forward before the officer could catch him staring.

They changed trains at Mannheim, bound for France through Saarbrucken. The Gestapo officer was close behind them. He boarded the same train, same car. They had seen it coming. "I'll take the back," Ben whispered. Dolohov nodded and peeled off, taking a seat near the front.

Ben kept walking, taking a seat in the rear of the car. The Gestapo officer seemed unfazed; he dropped into a mid-car seat and scooted over next to a window. Ben removed his hat and used it for a makeshift pillow, closing his eyes.

* * *

The early morning sun shone on the planks of the railway station platform. A thin layer of ice covered the portion not hit by the sun's rays. The usual bustle and movement of attendants, porters, and people arriving to greet the train were visible. Ben saw no soldiers or Gestapo, his main interest. The train's wheels screeched and slid to a stop, its sharp whistle blared the cobwebs out of his mind and stirred even the soundest sleepers awake. Steam rose from the tracks and, combined with the morning haze rising from the planks, clouded Ben's view of the station. He remembered the Gestapo officer and snapped his head, searching for him. He spotted him in the same seat, looking out the window. Through the departing passengers, Ben caught glimpses of Dolohov, still at the front of the car. Their eyes met. Both had attention on the Major. Ben wondered what would happen if one of them left the train, and considered doing just that, but then a new danger arose, dwarfing the old one.

Two men dressed in Gestapo uniforms stormed onto the coach. They had the vigor and determination of men on a mission. They seized upon Dolohov. "You," the tall, mustachioed one shouted, pointing and jerking a thumb in the air. "Come with us." Dolohov slowly lifted his frame. Ben tightened his grip on the arm rest, ready to bolt, calculating, trying to read Dolohov.

Mustache greeted the Gestapo passenger as he passed by. It was a respectful greeting, said to the uniform and not the man, which Ben interpreted to mean that they didn't know each other. He continued down the aisle. His eyes landed squarely on Ben. "You. Come with me." He grabbed Ben by the arm to speed his rise. Then he pushed and shoved him to the door, herding him off the train.

When Ben landed on the platform, Mustache's partner was mulling over Dolohov's papers. "Your papers," the Mustache demanded of Ben with a final shove, clearing a pathway to the train steps. Ben caught Dolohov's attention. A shift of his eyes told him that he would take his man, if the document inspection didn't go their way.

"You boarded in Stuttgart, didn't you," Ben's captor said, an accusation, not a question. Before Ben could answer, they were interrupted by a voice behind them. "Lieutenant."

Ben craned his neck to see the Gestapo passenger walking toward them. "These are my men. I'm escorting them out of the country. They are guest workers who are no longer guests of the Reich. And we boarded in Ulm, not Stuttgart." He presented a document. "Here are my orders. You will see that the names match those on their travel papers."

Ben sneaked a peak at Dolohov, whose eyes were narrowed, his look incredulous.

The orders shown the arresting Gestapo officer must have been convincing. He snapped to attention upon returning them. "Very well, Major Schmidt."

Ben stood tall, gazing at the confident face of the Gestapo Major and placing three fingers on his cheek for Dolohov and sneaked him a wink.

CHAPTER EIGHT

Inside the Alfama flat, Isidor handed Ben two photographs and looked over his shoulder, standing next to the shaded lamp. Ben pointed to one of them: "Dolohov."

"And the other?" Isidor said. The second picture was of a man dressed in business attire, leaving the same building shown in the first photograph. The dim light reflected off the shiny surface of the man's face. Ben picked up the picture to take a closer look.

He drew a blank and shook his head. "I've never seen him."

Isidor returned to his chair, saying, "We had pictures taken of all the debarking passengers at the Bern train station." He was referring to Ben's return route. "Based on your prior description of Dolohov, we picked him out and followed him upon his return to Lisbon. He checked in to a hotel after the two of you met for drinks and flew to London the following day.

"He met the second man two days later, at the building you see in the picture. His name is Colonel Clay Shaw. He works out of the London branch of OSS. We don't know too much about him right now, but people are working on it. They also hope to discover Dolohov's true identity and background. I'll let you know when I find out more."

"Was my information from inside Germany helpful?" Ben said.

"Yes, incredibly so I've been told. My SIS contact was quite pleased and asked me to give you a 'jolly good show.'"

Ben smiled, gratified. He took a seat on the sofa, across from Isidor. "You said you could help move Marsha. I want to do that before I go back inside Germany."

"Okay. What's going on?" Isidor said. This was their first meeting since Ben met with Chester. In the interim they had been communicating by dead drops, and Ben hadn't told him about his new deal with Chester. He did now.

"I have no intention of working with him anymore. I said what I had to say in order to save my brothers. I can't do the job anymore. I'm burnt out."

Isidor let out a long breath and scratched his beard.

"Please, don't try to talk me into staying on, if that's what you're thinking," Ben said. "My life is with her, not him."

Isidor threw out his hands. "My dear friend, how do you plan to do this? You don't break a deal and just walk away from men like Bloomfield and Dulles."

"I know," Ben said. "I'm working on a plan. I was hoping you could help me."

Isidor sighed, shaking his head. He rose and began pacing, his head bowed. Finally, he said, "Why don't you hold off on a firm decision until after you get your brothers out."

"No," Ben said. "My decision is firm."

"Please, hear me out," Isidor said. Ben gave him ground. "I understand your decision about the job. You're burnt out. I think you can later tell him that and plead for a desk job."

Ben started shaking his head. "Please, just listen to me," Isidor said.

"I'm done, Izzy. I can't stand him, and I hate what he and Dulles are doing. I'd rather shoot them than work for them, and I'm done shooting people."

"Okay," Isidor said. "Get your brothers out. Let's talk about Marsha." Ben perked up. "I've already done some ground work. We've got someone stationed in a flat across from yours. We've logged your routine, when your lights go on, when the windows open, when you go for a walk, and so on. We can carry on a charade for three, four days; keep an eye on the flower pot for you. I have a little more work to do, but I can set her up in London with layers of security so that it will be almost impossible for anyone to get to her."

Ben jumped out of his seat, grabbed Isidor and hugged him.

Isidor held up his hand. "All I ask in return is that you hear me out after you rescue your brothers."

"Deal," Ben said.

CHAPTER NINE

Ben drove slowly. Marsha's car was parked in her driveway. He kept moving, hoping to catch a sign that she was home without attracting attention from her neighbors. Three kids were playing hopscotch on the sidewalk across the street. One looked up, a boy, maybe ten years old. He stared, first at the gas rationing sticker in his windshield, then at Ben. The red paper sticker with the letter "C" signified someone important for the war effort, such as a doctor. There weren't too many of those, especially in rural areas deep in southwest Virginia. People noticed, even kids. They wondered who you were to merit it. Some looks were resentful. So the sticker was both a curse and a necessity; it entitled Ben to buy enough gasoline to make the round trip from New York.

As Ben drove by him, the boy's attention went to his license plate, reminding him of the second problem associated with his car: a yellow on black 1943 New York registration. The boy returned to his game. Ben quickly surveyed the street before taking another peek at Marsha's house and found it clear. He glanced over his left shoulder and caught a glimpse of a figure in back of the house, working in the yard. All he saw was a white blouse, tan shorts, and brunette hair, but that was enough. As he continued down the street at a steady speed, he reassessed his strategy.

He had arrived in Roanoke in the wee hours of Saturday morning, a half-day behind schedule and way too late to drop off a postcard in her mailbox for a Friday evening pickup. To save mileage, he found a hotel and got some sleep. The next morning he took a bath, dressed, and ate breakfast. He stopped at a public phone to call her, but she hadn't answered.

He checked his rear view mirror. The children were still there, playing. He didn't want anyone to see him go into Marsha's house. He grew impatient, and stepped on the accelerator.

He found a parking spot next to a church three blocks away, and backed it in close to the church, hiding a view of the license plate from the street. He removed the rationing sticker and hid it under the passenger seat, slipped out and locked the car doors. He walked toward Marsha's. He took a back street. He negotiated his way through a grassy lane into Marsha's backyard and stood under a shady tree next to her back porch, shielded from her neighbors, with a clear view of her garden. Marsha was bent over, hoeing the top soil, her hair down over the left side of her face. He was close enough to make out the aquamarine stone on the ring. A smile came to his face.

She rose to catch her breath, brushing her hair back – and froze. Her hand went to her mouth. Ben quickly put his finger to his lips, darting his head left and right. She glanced over her shoulder, all around, then threw down the hoe and ran to him, lunging into his open arms. She squeezed, then leaned back to kiss him. Tears rolled down her cheeks. He wrapped his arms around her and kissed her back, but only briefly. He let go, worried about their privacy.

He checked the surroundings, didn't see anything, and motioned toward the house. "Can we go inside?"

She nodded. "Stay here. I'll let you know when it's clear." She started to walk away, but held back and leaned into him. She kissed him and gave him a quick squeeze. When she reached the porch, she peeked around both sides of her house, then motioned for Ben, holding the screen door wide. He dashed inside.

She fell into his arms. He relished the softness of her skin against his face, the fresh smell of her hair, and the fullness of her body. He kissed her and held her tightly. He finally released her and put his hands on her shoulders. "Let me look at you," he said.

Tears still filled her bright, sparkling eyes.

"Okay," she said, wiping her tears and grinning.

He took her hand and pulled it away, shaking his head. "Uh-uh, you're beautiful just the way you are." He felt his own tears. He reached for her left hand, holding it by her finger tips, raising it.

"I never take it off," she said.

He kissed her hand. "I never want you to."

* * *

After they were reacquainted, she asked how long he was staying.

"I leave tomorrow." She frowned. "I know," he said. "I want to go to the mountain cabin after it gets dark. I dropped off some things there this morning that I need to give you. I also want to get my car off the street."

After night fell, they retreated to the shack, taking both cars. They arrived just before a storm front moved in. The temperature dropped sharply and rain pelted the corrugated tin roof, bringing back the memory of their first night in the cabin.

"That was so funny..." Marsha said, laughing so hard she had trouble saying it. "You were still half asleep and a big drop hit you right between the eyes. I remember your face..."

She laughed uncontrollably, doubled over. "You were..." she couldn't get it out.

"And then all the pots and pans ..." Ben said.

"And cups and glasses... the coffee pot," Marsha added.

After they settled down, Marsha rubbed Ben's shoulder, and sighed. "I had so much fun coming here with you. I think about it all the time. I always start laughing." She leaned over and hugged him.

"Me, too," Ben said. "My memories of being with you kept me going, believe me. Someday I'll tell you about it."

He kissed her. They were sitting on the edge of the bed. He put his arm around her, as she snuggled up against him.

Ben was reluctant to spoil the mood, but knew he had to. He took a nervous breath. "When does school let out for the summer?" he said.

She leaned her head back, an inquiring look on her face. "Ten more days. Why?"

"How would you like to go to England?" he said.

She lit up. "Really? With you?"

"Really," he said.

"When?" She said.

He took a deep breath, pausing. "Tomorrow, Monday at the latest."

"What?" she said. "Monday? I still have school." She made a face, confused and incredulous, and then a realization began to dawn on her. "You're serious."

"Yes, I am serious.

"What's happening, Ben?"

He rose from the bed, his hands in his pant pockets. Standing squarely before her, he spat it out: "I'm about to leave on a mission inside Germany to rescue my brothers."

Marsha's mouth fell open; her expression was a mixture of shock and elation. She jumped to her feet. "This is... I don't know what to say. Can you do that? Isn't that incredibly dangerous? I mean, that would be such a relief if you could get them out, but...Why do I have to leave here for you to do that?"

"I've already said too much. I wish I could explain, but I can't. Not now. I plan to take David and Michael to London, and I'd like you to be there."

"Will you be going there?" she said.

"Not right away, but eventually.

"How long?" she asked.

"It could be two months, it could be six. I don't know."

"Well, that's not so bad," she said, cozying up to Ben and wrapping her arms around his waist. He took her in his arms. After a few moments, she raised her head slowly, a wary look in her eyes. "Ben, am I in danger?"

"No. No one is in danger. If you go to London, you will be perfectly safe."

Her arms went limp, and Ben pulled her close, hugging her. "Listen, I'm going to work any problems out. That's my plan. I just don't want to take any chances."

"What kind of a problem are you talking about?" she said.

"It has to do with my job. I want to quit my job and there might be a problem doing that. Please don't ask me anymore. The less you know the better. And don't worry about your job. I've got plenty of money."

"I don't care about money," she said. "I only care about you – and us."

"I'll be fine," Ben said. "If you only knew what I've been through the last four years...trust me, you wouldn't worry about me. You'll be fine, too. I have very powerful people set up to take care of us, all of us, David and Michael, too. I have no support for you here."

She burrowed against him, her arms wrapped around him, and he enveloped her. She settled her head on his shoulder. He kissed the top of her head. "We'll be fine. Even here, you'd probably be okay. But I just don't want to take any chance, that's all."

He held her and rocked her gently for a couple of minutes. "It won't be long and one day soon we'll be together forever," he said. "The worst is over."

She finally broke the silence. "I could call my lawyer and have him sell my house. I guess I could tell the school that I had an emergency come up...what was yours, a family emergency in Leningrad?" A sly grin creased her face. "Did that work?"

"It worked with you, didn't it?"

"I guess it did for a day or two, anyway."

"That's all we need," he said. "Have a seat and I'll go over my plan. Let me show you something." He retrieved the small case that he had hidden under the bed. He set it on the table and opened the clasps. He held up two stacks of cash. "Here's two thousand dollars." He pulled up a key and a passbook. "This is a key to a safety deposit box in a London bank, and this is a savings account passbook. In the deposit box are cashier's checks. In all, there's a little over a hundred thousand dollars."

Marsha could hardly believe him. "One hundred thousand dollars. You have a hundred thousand dollars?"

"No. *We* have one hundred thousand dollars. This is our money. I have plans for some of it, so don't spend it all before I get there."

She laughed. "I couldn't if I tried."

Ben pulled up a chair, took a manila envelope from the case. "Here are your travel instructions."

He went over the plan to put her on a bus to Jacksonville, Florida, where she would board a yacht chartered to take her to the Bahamas. From there she would board a British plane that would take her to London.

When he had finished, he ran his fingers through a shock of hair that had fallen over one side of her face, and pushed it back. "Are you really okay with this?"

She gave a brisk nod. "Yes."

"I'll make up for all the inconveniences I've caused you, I promise."

"You already have," she said.

He took her in his arms and kissed her in earnest.

CHAPTER TEN

On his way to the SS Training Camp, Ben passed the final landmarks on the map he had memorized: eight grand buildings, white with red roofs. Ahead was the southwest gate to the camp, through which he had to pass to reach the adjacent concentration camp. He was in the small city of Dachau, a quaint, picturesque city about ten miles outside Munich, with a population of about thirteen thousand.

Along with the fine lawns, stone walls, and black iron-grilled gates. It looked as though he might have been approaching a girl's finishing school in a New York suburb. The day was mild, the mountain air fresh. It was all so neat, so orderly, so beautiful. So very disgusting.

He peered into the rearview mirror of his jeep at the military transport truck behind him, the dutiful Dolohov at the wheel. He pointed at the gate on his left; Dolohov flashed him a thumbs up.

As he downshifted and slowed to make the turn he felt a tingling in his hands. This was it. The past four years led up to what lay ahead: a double gate under a stone arch. Above the arch, the Nazi Eagle perched over a wreath-encircled Swastika. Three Army sentries manned the gate. He tightened his grip on the steering wheel to steady his nerves, and drew a deep breath. Not since Oslo had he been so overwhelmed before an assignment.

With his heart racing almost out of control, he went over for the hundredth time the cover story Chester had given him, testing under fire his ability to remember who he was, or rather who he was supposed to be: Sturmbannführer Franz Biederman, an SS doctor. The SS rank was the Army equivalent of Major. Dolohov was his aide, a Junior Storm Leader, the Army equivalent of a Lieutenant.

He heard Chester's voice and, under his breath, repeated his words in unison: "You are in charge of a very highly confidential medical testing program to be run on selected Jewish prisoners. You report to Himmler, himself. All of the eighteen persons on your list either are imprisoned at Dachau currently or will be transported to Dachau prior to your arrival. Your papers indicate that you will further transport them to a secret medical facility." Don't forget the anecdotes, he reminded himself: Trained on these grounds by former Commandant Eicke in 1934.

He pressed the clutch and brake pedal, bringing the jeep's wheels to a stop.

A soldier with a clipboard greeted him. Ben presented his papers. "Major Franz Biederman," he said. With the live action, his nerves began to settle.

"Ah, yes. Here you are," the soldier said, his finger running down a sheet of paper and coming to a stop. "Welcome Herr Biederman." He saluted, and Ben returned it.

"The lieutenant is with me," Ben said, gesturing toward Dolohov.

"Of course, Herr Biederman." He threw a hand at the gate and said, "Let them pass." The large wooden doors immediately began to open inward. As the jeep rolled forward, the soldier with the clipboard stepped back and motioned Dolohov to pass.

On the other side of the gates a new round of jitters attacked Ben. Chester's final words about the eighteen prisoners came to mind. "All of the eighteen who are still alive, that is." The image of Chester's eyes falling during a heavy pause tormented him all over again. "The names on your list were passed on to the proper authorities. I do not have any current information about their status."

He caught the jeep accelerating, and let up on the gas. He picked up Dolohov in his mirror and synchronized their speeds, forcing other thoughts from his mind.

They drove down a tree-lined lane and crossed over the Würm River, a concrete-lined canal which bordered the western edge of the prison compound, and separated the training and concentration camps.

They soon reached the gatehouse and main entrance, a large, two-story building with a red roof, through the middle of which a brick road led through black wrought iron gates.

A machine gun in a tower atop the gatehouse pointed toward the inside of the camp. Other well-tended buildings were visible alongside the compound which was, itself, surrounded by high, barbed wire-topped fences that stretched as far as Ben could see, the line broken twice by watch towers.

Ben parked the jeep outside the compound in front of the administrative building. Dolohov parked nearby and followed him inside.

He presented his papers to a soldier sitting at a receptionist desk. "I have orders for the Camp Commandant, please, Colonel Martin Weiss." His SS rank was the next higher than Ben's, a Senior Storm Unit Leader, equivalent to Lieutenant Colonel in the Army.

The soldier glanced at the papers. "Yes, Herr Biederman, he's expecting you." He made a call from a telephone sitting on his desk. "Major Franz Biederman has arrived, Herr Weiss."

Ben stole a glance at Dolohov, who seemed to be thinking the same thing: smooth as ice.

"He'll be right with you Herr Biederman," and a moment later a door opened behind him. A tall, lanky officer appeared through it, greeting Herr Biederman. He was holding a small package of files, bundled with strings, a folded piece of paper stuck beneath them. The clerk handed his commander the papers Ben had presented. Weiss gave them a cursory glance and returned them to Ben, introducing himself. In turn, Ben introduced Dolohov as his aide, Lieutenant Schneider.

"The prisoners are gathered in the gate house awaiting your arrival. Here's a list of the ones we are able to provide you, and their medical files," Weiss said, handing over the bundle.

A tremor coursed through Ben. He saw the ribs of maybe a half dozen files. He accepted them, fighting to maintain his composure. "Is this the list of names?" referring to the folded piece of paper.

"It is," Weiss said. He continued speaking as Ben pulled out the list and handed the files to Dolohov. "Unfortunately, I only have six of the Jews given in the instructions I received."

"Six!" Ben said, as his nervous fingers fumbled unfolding the list. "There were supposed to be eighteen."

"I realize that, Herr Biederman. Only eight of the eighteen were still alive when I received the list." He spoke with a detached calmness, which added salt to Ben's agony. "And two of them died in transit from other camps." Seeking the transfer of inmates from other camps was a device designed to further disguise the true purpose of the mission. His words barely registered with Ben whose attention was transfixed on the list. He was horrified. Michael's name was not on the list.

His hands, then his whole body began to tremble. He fought to remain calm, tightening his muscles until the veins in his neck almost burst. Weiss stared at him, bewildered. Then Ben let loose, giving Weiss the full brunt of his emotions.

"How can you be so blasé over a monumental blunder like this? I report to Himmler himself." Weiss recoiled, his eyes bulging from their sockets. "We cannot run our experiments on only six people," Ben said.

"Does it have to be a certain eighteen? I can give you more Jews."

Ben felt his composure returning. He straightened his uniform and calmed himself, much to Weiss's relief, who tightened his lips into a half-smile. "I will get you twelve more," he said.

"Give me twenty more."

Weiss raised his brows, his smile turning into a frown.

"In case any die in transit," Ben added with thick sarcasm.

"Ah, good point," Weiss said. He turned to the clerk. "Get me the files of twenty Jews who are fit to travel and have the guards bring them to the gatehouse."

"Yes, Herr Weiss," the clerk said. "Right away, sir."

As the clerk got busy, Weiss took on an apologetic tone. "Can I get you some coffee, Herr Biederman?" Ben looked at Dolohov. "And you, too, of course, Herr Schneider." Dolohov shrugged, and Ben nodded. Weiss escorted them into his office and ordered three coffees over the phone. Pastries, too, after clearing it with his guests.

"Have a seat, gentlemen," he said, gesturing toward two chairs in front of his desk. "What part of the country are you gentlemen from?"

"Munich," Ben answered, as he sat.

"Berlin," Dolohov said. Ben knew from Isidor that Dolohov could similarly answer questions about his city of origin. Before receiving a commission in the British Army, he had lived in Berlin as a teenager where his father had been a diplomat in the British Foreign Office.

"Munich?" Weiss said to Ben, reaching for a cigarette on his desk, and offering one to each of his guests. Ben nodded, waving off the cigarette. Dolohov accepted.

"So you're familiar with the area?" Weiss said.

"Of course," Ben said. "I did my SS training here in Dachau."

"Is that a fact?" Ben sensed that Weiss was just being friendly, even conciliatory, not trying to trip him up. No matter, the fact was verifiable according to Chester. Training camp records would show the attendance of Franz Biederman, medical doctor.

"Yes," Ben said. "I trained under Obergruppenführer Theodor Eicke, in '34, may he rest in peace." Eicke had been killed in action earlier in the year.

"Yes, indeed. A tragic loss to the Reich." Weiss rushed his words, taking up what had clearly interested him.

"Thirty-four? Then you must have met Obersturmbannführer Adolf Eichmann."

"We were classmates."

Weiss expressed his admiration for Eichmann, acknowledged by Ben, then rattled off a number of other names from that period. Ben indicated knowing most of them, and even threw out a few himself, names provided by Chester. He began to feel uncomfortable, though; the depth of his cover story had been reached. Fortune intervened: the coffee and pastries arrived. He used the change of pace to steer the conversation in another direction, as they consumed their refreshments.

"This is my first time back," Ben said. "The camp has expanded tremendously since then."

"Indeed," Weiss said. "I should give you a tour. It's now like a small town, with stores, a movie theater, a post office, restaurants, a community center, even a swimming pool."

"Really? Ben said. "All that." Weiss nodded. "Do the men still go to Munich for fun?"

"Some do," Weiss said. "There are more women there."

Ben showed his interest to Weiss, and shot a licentious glance at Dolohov.

"Because of the war," Weiss said, "there are three women for every man."

"Three?" Ben said, extending his lower lip, nodding thoughtfully. "In my day, the best I did was two."

Weiss did a double-take, and then allowed himself a broad grin. Dolohov got it right away. His sparkling eyes went from Ben to Weiss and back. Ben noted to himself that both men had a more favorable opinion than Adam of that sort of activity, as he recalled the morning Adam barged into his apartment unannounced. Adam came unglued and lectured him almost their entire walk to the store for the family meeting he had called.

Just then a rap on the door interrupted them, and the clerk stuck his head through the door. "The prisoners are ready, sir." Weiss thanked him and then turned to Ben, who was rising.

"We should talk more about your methods, Herr Biederman. In the name of medicine, of course."

"Of course, Commandant."

* * *

Weiss had them back the truck around to the gatehouse and its iron gates. Dolohov did the driving while Ben walked with Weiss toward the gates, pulling up when they reached one of two stone walls, both about a meter high. Only then did Ben see the sign on the gates, also in iron, clearly enough to read: *Work Brings Freedom.*

Weiss motioned for Dolohov to stop the truck as he neared the stone walls. Two prison guards who had come from the gatehouse propped rifles they were carrying against the side of the truck and helped lower the truck's rear railing, pulling a ladder in place. They then grabbed their rifles and hustled into positions along the brick lane, about five feet apart, where one signaled. Ben's eyes followed the signal to the tower above the gatehouse and saw a machine gun aimed on the pathway between the gatehouse and the truck. The gunner behind it signaled his readiness. The guard then motioned toward the gatehouse, saying, "Bring the prisoners."

Ben drew a deep breath, his pulse quickening. Dolohov joined him and Weiss, and Ben turned, standing obliquely, not wishing to give David a straight look at his face but also keeping an eye out for him. Two prison guards came into view, pulling and pushing forward prisoners whose sight caused Ben to wince. They looked like something from a horror movie, more like skeletons in rags than human beings.

One after another were herded like cattle toward the truck. Gaunt and frail, despondent and servile, they shuffled forward. Four women were in the group, according to the final list given Ben, but he could not tell them from the men. All the prisoners wore striped denim prison garb, defeated faces, shaved heads, and an assortment of patches on their pants, including the yellow triangles Isidor had spoken about when they first met in New York, signifying their status as Jews. A black number on a white rectangle below the triangles identified their prison number. Ben referred to his list of prisoners being transferred and found David's number and began looking for it while also keeping an eye out for a red triangle on top of a yellow one, recalling that bit of trivia from Isidor; it identified them as political prisoners.

Ben's attention was captured by a guard accosting two straggling prisoners, striking one with a hard thrust of his rifle butt. Ben glowered at the guard, turned to Weiss, and barked, "Herr Weiss, please order your guards not to harm my patients."

"Do not touch the prisoners," Weiss shouted, and Ben nodded his appreciation, then resumed his search for David. His eyes focused on someone who vaguely resembled David. He checked the number on his pant leg and noticed an inverted red triangle upon a yellow one, forming a six-pointed star. He re-checked the number against the one on his list allocated to David. They matched.

He took a closer look, appalled at the sight. A pathetic package of skin and bones and hollowed eyes, he marched mindlessly toward the truck, passing Ben, oblivious to the world around him. It was difficult for Ben to equate this man to the handsome, fit person he had last seen, attired in finely tailored clothes, an open, friendly face, eyes keenly aware of his surroundings.

His eyes filled with tears and he must have gasped or made some sound, because Weiss turned to him, a perplexed look on his face. Ben turned away abruptly, toward Dolohov, who likewise seemed confused.

He heard Weiss's penetrating voice. "Is something wrong, Herr Biederman?"

Ben spun to face him. "These prisoners are in no condition to travel. Have they even eaten today?"

"Of course," Weiss said.

Ben snapped back. "What have they eaten?"

"The same as every day. Soup and bread. This is not a country club, Herr Biederman. Food is scare. You should know that. The German people must be fed first, after all."

A whiff of an aroma passed through Ben's nostrils. He looked around and took a deep breath in an effort to identify the odor. "Is that bratwurst I smell?"

"That is for the staff, not the prisoners," Weiss replied.

"Get these people some of the staff food," Ben said, shouting.

"Herr Biederman!" Weiss yelled back. "The staff only eat meat twice per week as it is."

"What else is being prepared for the staff?"

"Sauerkraut and potato salad, I believe. I'm willing to have some of each given to your patients, but not the meat."

"I want one bratwurst for every four patients, Herr Weiss. That is not a request."

"Herr Biederman, that is not part of my orders and I outrank you."

Ben leaned into his face. "Get them the food!" Now!"

Weiss backed down, and began issuing orders to a couple of the guards, who immediately snapped into action. Meanwhile, Ben glanced at Dolohov who stared at him in shocked silence. The last of the prisoners had boarded the truck.

After the guards had rushed off, Ben thanked Weiss. "I shall report favorably on your assistance." He saluted, spun around, and headed for the cab of the truck, grabbing Dolohov by the elbow. "Let's be off, Herr Schneider."

As he passed, Dolohov whispered, "Are you trying to get us shot?"

Ben pulled up. "Get in the truck. I'll catch up." He reversed course. "Herr Weiss, a word please." Weiss took a step or two in his direction. "No hard feelings I hope. It's just that I take my work seriously, perhaps too seriously."

"I'm not used to taking orders from subordinate officers, Herr Biederman. I do my best running this camp with what few resources I am allocated."

"I'm sure you do. I'm sorry I got carried away. We're both trying to get by with too little these days." They chatted about the tough times the Reich was experiencing, and while they did, the food was delivered for the "patients."

"It would also help," Weiss added, "if I was given more information. We have a hospital on the grounds and SS doctors who perform medical experiments on the prisoners. No one has explained to me why you need the prisoners in the first place."

"Herr Weiss, I can assure you that your hospital has neither the equipment nor the security clearance for this project. I can say no more."

As the truck pulled away, Weiss seemed to lighten up, consoled.

"The rigors of our job aside," Ben said, "I plan to return to the area in the fall. If you show me around the training camp, I'll show you some of my methods in Munich."

Weiss glowed. "Yes, let's do that." He held out his hand, and Ben shook it, and then saluted him, giving him a crisp "Heil Hitler."

Ben then hustled to his jeep and drove off, catching up with the truck as it pulled to a stop at the outer gates. The railing up and flaps down, he couldn't see the prisoners, but imagined them gorging themselves with potato salad, sauerkraut, and quarter pieces of bratwurst, and wondered what they might be thinking about their destinies. Did they have the faintest idea that they would soon be free? Or, more likely, were they considering this their last meal?

* * *

Ben drove the jeep off the road and deep into a stand of trees north of Machtenstein, a small Bavarian town northwest of Dachau. He braked, jumped out, and ran toward Dolohov, who bounced the truck over the field not far behind him. With flailing arms, he guided Dolohov under and around the low-lying branches, toward the inner sanctum of the wooded area. A military transport truck driving across an open field would be hard to explain. Dolohov brought the truck to a stop. He jumped out and helped Ben quickly camouflage the truck with brush and tree branches reserved for the task, and did the same to the jeep. Only then did they take a breather and check their watches and timetable. They had another two hours until dusk and the arrival of the transport plane that would land in the field beside the trees that sheltered them.

Dolohov pulled out a deck of cards, jumped upon a fender and asked Ben to join him in a game on the hood of the truck. Ben waved him off.

"Not right now. I want to check on the patients. I hope we haven't lost any."

"Righto. Don't take all day," Dolohov said.

Still in his SS uniform, but without the hat, Ben threw open one of the canvas flaps and peered in. Scared and confused, the passengers cowered at the sight of Ben. He scanned the lot, searching for David. He spotted him leaning against the frame of the canopy, listless. Ben bounded over the railing into the bed of the truck, anxious that David might have passed away. He kneeled beside him and found his pulse. David stirred, his eyes opened, looking directly at Ben, then closed. Ben lifted him upright and sat beside him, gently laying David's head and shoulders onto his lap. David's eyelids fluttered, then opened. He stared at Ben, showing no apparent recognition. Ben felt the glare of the other passengers and raised his head, catching their befuddled looks. He gave it little thought, instead returning his attention to David, who stared at him with vacant eyes, then drifted off to sleep, the movement of his chest barely perceptible. Ben softly stroked his cheek, and wept.

A minute or two later, maybe longer, he became aware of whispers, a commotion of sorts, and looked up. He had forgotten his other passengers and now saw them caught up in the spectacle before them, an SS officer sobbing over a Jew whom he held lovingly in his arms.

The canvas flap on the back of the truck suddenly opened. Dolohov peered inside, gawking. Before Ben could muster his thoughts for a response, a light seemed to have gone on for Dolohov – who until that point had not shown the slightest curiosity in the purpose of their mission. He lowered the flap.

One of the passengers woke one of the others with a fervent zeal, as if desiring to share with him the incredible sight. The quiet stir grew to a lively buzz and soon the entire lot of them were fully alert, alternately staring spellbound at Ben or exchanging puzzled looks with one another, coming out of their shells and regarding him less as an enemy and more of friend. Ben dropped his gaze onto David. A tear dripped from his eyes onto David's face, and then another one fell. David stirred, then awakened. For the first time, Ben saw some life in the eyes focused on him. David's face twisted into a puzzled look, and then gradually gave way to an inquiring one. "Ben?" David said, his voice sounding from deep in his throat, raspy and faint.

One of the passengers sat upright in his seat, and Ben recognized the face. It was Ernst Beckner, a respected businessman from Munich and customer of the family store.

"Is that you, Ben?" David asked again.

Fighting back tears, Ben nodded.

Ernst announced to the others in an excited state, "It's Ben Komorosky, a Jew."

David eked out a smile, apparently recognizing Ben. He leaned over and pressed his sobbing face against David's, kissing him on the cheek.

A hush fell upon the truck, all eyes fixed on him. He saw in their faces pent up emotions of joy, grief, anxiety, and curiosity. He relaxed his hold on David and brought himself under control so he could address them.

Ernst beat him to it. "Where are you taking us, Ben?" The other passengers perked up and leaned forward.

"I'm taking you...," he choked up again. "I'm taking you to freedom."

The passengers burst alive with cheers, gasps, shouts and cries of joy. David managed a grin and squeezed Ben's hand.

CHAPTER ELEVEN

"At least, David might live," Ben said after thanking Isidor for his commiseration over Michael's death. "Chester has permitted me to stay by his side until he is fully recovered. We're taking them to a Royal Navy hospital in Malta on a British hospital ship. We leave in two days."

They were in the Alfama flat, shortly after Ben's return to Lisbon.

Isidor asked whether David had said anything about the reason he and Michael had been held as political prisoners and not released when their papers came in, and Ben told him he hadn't. "I tried, but he's not up to talking about Dachau or Michael. He couldn't even read his confidentiality agreement." The intelligence community was demanding that freed prisoners desiring entry into either America or Great Britain sign a pledge never to discuss their rescue. "Ernst Beckner is the one who told me how Michael died."

When Ben had finished his debriefing, Isidor took from his case an unopened letter and handed it to Ben. "From Marsha," he said. Ben snatched the letter and asked if he had met her. Isidor hadn't and explained that he and his contact at SIS decided to establish three different layers of cutouts separating her from the intelligence agency for her added protection. He said that communication between her and Ben should occur infrequently for that reason, and that he should give his reply to her letter before he left the apartment.

"It's important that she hear from you now. While you're reading and preparing a response, I'll go for a walk and get some fresh air," he said, taking a pad of paper and a pen from his brief case and laying it on the table.

Ben opened the letter as Isidor walked out.

Marsha said she was doing "quite well" and that she loved London except for being apart from him and her friends back home, but that she was making friends under the alias she had adopted. She ended the letter with surprising news.

"P.S. I am beremenna."

Ben laughed out loud, and started writing.

My Dearest Marsha,

Great news! We can back-date our marriage, I guess, in order to avoid explaining our extraordinary circumstances. (Joke – I'm not concerned about impressions and I know you aren't either.) For some reason, I am stuck on the name Sarah for a girl. Do you approve? You can name the boy, as long as we give him the middle name of Michael.

I have both wonderful and tragic news. David is alive and free from the Nazi barbarians, though I am told by his doctor that it will take him months to recover. I intend to remain by his side until he fully recuperates, at which time I will accompany him to England where he has already been approved for entry. I know you will understand. When will I reach London with David? Of course, I'm not sure, but I do hope it's before your delivery date. Mid-February, right? Perhaps for the Holidays. That would be nice, to finish up those interrupted holidays two years ago.

The tragic news is that Nazi guards killed Michael – in so many words. He died of typhus, but when he first complained of being ill with a fever the guards refused pleas to take him to the camp hospital. Instead, they ordered him and his supporters outside and made them march in a cold rain for several hours, until Michael passed out. Only then was he taken to the hospital where he died a few days later.

The stories I have heard from those eyewitnesses able to talk about their experiences inside that prison are incredible, utterly inhumane and horrifying. I will share with you the gist of some of them so you can relate to what David and Michael endured. Some I could never repeat. Of the various classifications of prisoners, Jews received the worst treatment in the camp. They were often beaten by both the Nazi guards and German prisoners, the criminals, who were assigned to supervise them. Jews were given the hardest work details and were fed far less food: only a small portion of a loaf of bread that had to last three days, a barley drink in the morning, and watery soup for dinner. They were not issued gloves, underwear or coats, despite the harsh winters, and they slept in overcrowded barracks on straw.

How I came into possession of this information, who I spoke with and how David gained his release, and where I am now or soon will be cannot be discussed now, if ever.

I am told that communications to and from you are risky for both of us, and, therefore, that you should not expect to hear from me unless something of great urgency arises. Rest assured, however, that I am and will be safe, healthy, and in no danger whatsoever in the coming months, since my only task is to nurse David back to health in a safe, secure zone far from any battlefield.

Please also know at all times that I love you beyond measure and am constantly thinking of you and, as soon as David is well enough to understand, I will spend my days singing your praises and preparing him to meet my princess – and the mother-to-be of his niece or nephew, our child. I long to hold you and kiss you.

All my love,

Ben.

Isidor returned soon after Ben finished sealing the envelope. He handed the letter to Isidor and excitedly announced: "I'm going to be a father."

CHAPTER TWELVE

Ben lived in military housing and spent most of his time at the hospital, often falling asleep at night by David's bedside. During that critical period little was said, even when David was awake. In Lisbon, David had broken down crying and became distant and distraught for hours when Ben mentioned Michael's name or the Dachau prison camp. In Malta, much to Ben's surprise, David couldn't remember anything about the rescue or their trip there. Ben had learned from his experiences there not to talk about anything but the present, to minimize conversation, and when they did talk, to keep it light and positive.

"Have you heard from Adam?" David repeatedly asked him, and each time he did, Ben gave the same answer.

"The last I heard he and his family were doing well." Actually, Ben had had no news since before the siege of Leningrad and wondered himself. He didn't ask David whether he knew about the siege.

"That's good," David would say.

One morning as he walked through the lobby of the hospital heading for his flat, Ben caught sight of a man sitting in a chair peering over a newspaper at him. What struck him most about the man was a white hat with a three-inch black band, one of the signals Isidor told Ben to be alert for. He approached the man. "Excuse me. Do we know each other?"

The man reflected, then shook his head. "I'm sorry, you must have mistaken me for someone else."

"I see. Perhaps it was the hat. It looks familiar."

The man sat up and closed the newspaper, holding it with one hand. "Ah, well I dare say it must be popular. I get so many compliments. I found it in Lisbon."

"A diamond in the rough," Ben said.

"Precisely." The man set the newspaper down, lifted the hat off his head and, displaying the inner band, spoke about the hat as proudly as the milliner who had made it might have.

"Notice the fine detail. Even the stitching of the leather band is..." Ben saw the small envelope protruding from the band as the man continued talking. "Here," he said, offering the hat to Ben. "See for yourself."

Ben took the hat and removed the envelope from the band with his left hand as he inspected it, nodded, and handed the hat back to its owner, palming the envelope in the process. "Very nice. If I pass through Lisbon, I'll keep my eyes out for one."

After the man returned the hat to his head, Ben stuck his left hand in his pants pocket while extending his right to shake hands with the man. They shook, and he went back to his newspaper while Ben departed the hospital.

When he returned to his flat in the nearby hamlet of Rinella, Ben opened the envelope and read the coded message from Isidor. It gave the description of a fisherman who sold his daily catch from a stall at the fish market in Valletta, the capital of Malta, across the Grand Harbor. Two miniature British flags on crossed poles adorned the frame of the stall. Ben was to go there to drop off coded messages and to check in each Thursday morning to receive incoming messages, presenting his half of the torn Ace of Spades to the proprietor on his first visit. Their messages would be quickly transmitted in code on a secure radio frequency by a trusted intermediary. *Use this channel if at all for important news only.*

* * *

On Thursday Ben made his way down to the Senglea strand, the coastal strip on the peninsula below Rinella, and crossed the harbor by ferry to Valletta and the fish market. He spotted the right fish stall by the crossed flags and by Isidor's description of the man working in the booth. He bought a half kilo of fresh mahi-mahi, or lampuka as the Maltese called it. When ready to pay, he took a quick look around. The area looked clear. He presented the fisherman with a five pound note, on top of which he had placed the torn half of the Ace of Spades.

The fisherman peered into Ben's eyes as he took the note and card. "I'll change it for you." He leaned over a currency tray on a stack of wooden crates with his back to Ben. Meanwhile, Ben took in the sights, letting his eyes roam. Again he saw nothing. When he returned his attention to the fisherman, he saw an extended hand. "I look forward to doing business with you, Matey," he said, giving Ben his change and taking the note in one smooth movement.

Ben tipped his hat. "I'll see you next week."

* * *

In November, more than four months after his arrival in Malta, David was able to get out of bed and walk short distances up and down the corridor with Ben's assistance. By the end of the month, his appetite started returning and he began putting on weight. His energy level began to increase and his span of attention broadened to the point he could play a few hands of gin rummy. His doctor said that his vital organs had finally begun to function well, and that he had turned an important corner in his recovery. For the first time he was able to give a good prognosis and estimate when he might leave the facility – two to three months. That time frame put their return beyond Marsha's expected delivery date.

On Thursday, Ben delivered his first message to Isidor, updating him on his brother's improved condition, giving him an estimated departure date in mid-February, and asking him to pass on the news to Marsha, along with his regrets that he would likely not return in time for the birth of their baby. He ended the message with: *No other news. Subjects of interest still not broached.*

By January, David and Ben's short walks in the hospital had turned into long walks outdoors, and their talks became more meaningful. "I would like to share a secret with you," Ben said on one of their walks. They stood on a promontory overlooking an expanse of the Mediterranean Sea and Grand Harbor, in which were British warships, including an aircraft carrier at the entrance and a destroyer in Rinella Bay, across which lay the city of Valletta.

David looked at him expectantly.

"I have a fiancée."

David lit up and asked Ben to describe her, which Ben did in glowing terms, to which David replied, "She sounds wonderful. Is she Jewish?"

"No, but she once asked to go to temple and she lit the candles for me during Hanukkah."

David chuckled and put an assuring arm on his shoulder. "She must be something special if she got you to settle down. When do I get to meet her?"

"As soon as you can travel. She's in England." Because the conversation had gone so well, Ben decided to take it a step further. "In fact, by the time we arrive you will also get to meet your new niece or nephew, and I, my son or daughter."

"Oh, really?" David said with a mixed reaction of surprise, delight, and confusion.

"We wanted to get married first, but...well, it's a long story that I can't go into right now. When I said I was telling you a secret, I meant it. Izzy knows, but you're the only other person I've told."

David assured him that his secret was safe.

Ben then told him about the money he had saved and about his plan to invest part of it in a high-end clothing store in London, something along the lines of the one David had in Munich.

He looked at David, wondering whether he remembered the store and, if so, whether its memory caused him any pain. "That's a good plan," David said. "Maybe I could handle your books."

Knowing that the assets David managed to transfer out of Germany would not buy his own store, Ben went on. "Actually, I wasn't planning on doing any of the hiring or managing. What do I know about the business end of it? I just want to put up the money for it. I will need a partner; someone capable of running a store as well as you ran yours in Munich." He stopped and turned to David. "Someone who will be an equal partner with full control."

David was spellbound. His eyes became misty. The weight of five and a half years in prison, the loss of his business, the death and mistreatment of his friends, and the tragic end to Michael's life, all seemed to start lifting from his heavy heart.

* * *

On the second Thursday in February, Ben made his weekly trip to the fish market, selected some fresh fish, and paid for it. A wadded envelope accompanied his change. He stuffed it all in his pocket, concealing his delight.

He had not received a message from Isidor since first opening up the communication channel and had been anxiously awaiting news about Marsha. He returned to the ferry with a bounce in his step.

Ben had more shopping to do on the other side of the harbor before returning to his flat, which was the only secure place he could read the message. He speedily finished his shopping, which consisted of picking up two bottles of Maltese Chardonnay in a shop on the Senglea strand, buying fresh vegetables from a horse-drawn cart in Rinella and handing it all to a neighbor by noon, in time for her to prepare Lampuka pie, a delicious dish made with onions, tomatoes, spinach, capers, and olives. She also made freshly baked hobz, a crusty, flavorful bread which she rubbed with tomatoes, herbs and capers and toasted as a kind of crostini. The two of them had come to an arrangement in which Ben purchased the food, she prepared the meal and they divided it, half for her and her husband, the other half for Ben and David. The delicious meal had been an instant hit and had quickly become a Thursday tradition, not to mention having provided a solid cover for his weekly trip to the fish market.

After shopping and turning over all but one bottle of the wine to his neighbor, he finally made it to his apartment, and opened the message.

On February 8 Marsha gave birth to a baby girl. She named her Sarah Michelle. Mazel tov! The baby weighed seven pounds, eight ounces, was nineteen inches long, has dark hair and brown eyes, and is beautiful. This from the mother who reports that she came through the birth with flying colors. She sends her love. More good news. Have received word from the home front. All survived the siege. They were made aware of your health and the fate of the other two. Have you still no word from our mutual friend?

Over the Lampuka pie, hobz, and Maltese Chardonnay at David's bedside, Ben shared the news of Sarah's birth, and told David that the siege of Leningrad had ended and that he had received word that their parents and all of Adam's family had survived it.

"That's wonderful news. So, they've finally beaten back the Krauts?"

"You knew about the siege?"

"The Nazis eagerly shared the news of their victories. We also got news from other sources, new arrivals and whatnot."

Ben noticed, first, that David had volunteered information for the first time about his experiences inside the camp, and second, the ease with which he had spoken.

He then chose his words carefully.

"David, do you know why you were not released when your emigration papers came in?"

"Yes. We were marched to the gatehouse about a week after we arrived and shown the Soviet papers by the foreign minister, Alfred Rosenberg. He said that you and Isidor Franks were spying against the Reich for a foreign government and wanted to know where you were or he wouldn't release us, and we refused to tell him. I mean, I refused to tell him. Michael still thought you were in London."

"Did Rosenberg say which foreign government?" Ben asked.

"No."

"Did he say why he thought Izzy and I were spies?"

"He said your German travel papers indicated that you were going to America to attend Columbia University but that you never showed up there and that you didn't live at the London address you used for correspondence with me – and that's the sort of thing that spies do."

"Did he mention anything to you about my records at Columbia University being falsified?" Ben asked.

David mulled over the question before answering. "No," he said and then brightened.

"That's what puzzled me. He said you didn't go there, but Isidor came to the store and told me that you did go to the school as originally planned. Did you?"

"Yes, I went to school there, and graduated. In fact, at the time you met Rosenberg at the gatehouse, I was teaching there."

"Then why did he say that? It sounded like he looked for you at the school and didn't find you."

"He must have only asked for me at the school," Ben said. "We had my records expunged to make it more difficult for them to find me. He must not have looked beyond that." He thought for a moment before adding, "Our plan to protect me from the Nazis worked. I'm deeply saddened that it was used as an excuse to hold you and Michael. I feel very bad and guilty about that." He bowed his head.

David, who was lying in bed, propped up by pillows, sat up.

"Nonsense. I refuse to listen to you talk that way. You did your best to get me to leave Germany. You risked your life to save me. Please, you are not to blame."

Ben patted his hand. "Thank you. I accept that regarding you. But what about Michael?"

"He could have left, too. Let me share something else with you. After conditions started getting really bad inside the camp, I told Michael I had more information about you and asked him if he wanted me to tell the authorities. He refused. Do you want to know why?"

"Yes," Ben said.

"He said he felt as though he were contributing to your and Isidor's fight against the Nazis by not telling them anything. He thought that was more important than his suffering. We both did. And look, you saved the lives of twenty-four Jews."

Twenty-four of the twenty-six people rescued survived; two didn't recover.

Ben reached for David's hand and began to cry. When he had partially composed himself, he thanked David for telling him; that he now thought of Michael as being a hero, not a victim.

David smiled.

After a moment, he added, "And do you want to know something else you were right about? Rosenberg *is* a pig!"

Ben laughed through his tears.

* * *

The next day, Ben dropped off his report to Isidor:

Nazi authorities did not know school records falsified. Just said I never attended and that I did not live at London address. Said you and I were spies for an unnamed foreign government. Subject has been cleared for discharge. Will provide travel plans when received.

When he returned to the hospital, David was gone.

CHAPTER THIRTEEN

Ben ran to the nursing station. "Where's my brother? He's not in his bed."

Startled the nurse at first stammered. "I don't...well, now that I think of it, there was a Colonel and two civilians who wanted to see him. I believe he's still with them. I'm not sure where they went. Should I find out for you?"

"Please. It is really important to me, if you don't mind."

"I can do that," and off she went. After five minutes or so she returned with the news that David had been taken into a conference room. "A soldier standing outside the door said he had strict orders not to allow anyone to disturb them, so I suppose you will have to wait until they're done."

"Did the soldier say how long they would be?"

"I'm sorry, he didn't, and I doubt that he would know from the look of him." Ben thanked her for her trouble and retreated to David's bedside.

An hour later, David returned to the hospital wing.

"What was that all about?" Ben asked.

"Ah, good. I'm famished." David had his eyes on the tray of food sitting on a stand by his bed. "They were

British military intelligence officers. They said it was a routine interview that they needed to conduct before I leave the hospital. It was routine. Do you mind if I eat while we talk."

"Go ahead. What did they talk about?"

David propped himself up and pulled the food tray over his lap. "They asked me about my stay and the camp and had me sign some papers promising never to talk about the rescue. They said all the persons rescued have had to do the same thing."

Ben relaxed. "Did they give you a copy?"

"No, but they said a copy would be provided me when I leave," David said between bites of a tuna sandwich.

"What kind of things did they ask about your stay in the camp?"

"Everything. How we were treated, work detail, how Michael died, the guards. They also wanted to know why we were labeled political prisoners."

"Really?" Ben said. "What did you tell them?"

"Basically the same thing I told you, that they wouldn't release us because they thought you were a spy against the Reich and wanted to know where you were."

Something didn't seem right for Ben. "Are you sure they were from British military intelligence?"

"That's what they said. One of them was dressed in a British Army uniform, a Colonel. The other two were in business attire. One of those two spoke German and only translated."

"Did they go into details about why the Nazis thought I was a spy, or for what country?" Ben said.

"Yes. They asked all the same questions you did. They even asked if Rosenberg said anything about your school records being falsified."

A red flag shot up for Ben. British military intelligence didn't need to ask that question. At least, not the people Isidor was aligned with.

"What's wrong?" David said.

"Nothing," Ben said. "I was just surprised that their interview was so detailed. Finish your meal. I need to take care of some chores at my apartment."

* * *

Ben fired off a report to Isidor:

Our subject was interviewed by people claiming to be British military intelligence who inquired about the political prisoner status in detail. Asked if Nazi authorities mentioned my school records being falsified. This isn't good, is it?

When Ben returned to his apartment, a British soldier was waiting for him. He verified Ben's name and handed him an envelope. "This message is urgent. I have orders to await your reply."

"May I read this in private," Ben said.

"Certainly."

Ben went inside his apartment and opened the envelope. It was a message from Chester.

Your services needed. Arrangements being made to ship the two of you on British cruiser. You are to board by 8 p.m. this evening and spend the night for departure early tomorrow. You will arrive in Portsmouth, England, on the eighteenth where you will be picked up and escorted to a London hotel with reservations in your brother's name. That concludes my end of the deal. You will be met at the hotel and taken to the airport to be flown to New York.

Ben blew his top. "That dirty son of a bitch." He wadded the message and threw it against a wall as hard as he could. He was thinking of the time when he was banished to Lisbon and was prevented from contacting Isidor. Only this time, Chester's order not only put in jeopardy Ben's plan to see Marsha and the baby, but also undermined Ben's whole escape plan. He dropped into the sofa and cursed again. "That dirty rotten bastard." He stewed and calculated, his mind awhirl, searching for a solution. Stymied, his attention eventually returned to the message and his realization that he hadn't read it all. He retrieved it, and read the ending.

You will be met at the hotel and taken to the airport to be flown to New York, scheduled to arrive on the afternoon of the twentieth. Meet me at Hecksher Playground in Central Park, ten p.m.

"Damn," he said, wadding the paper and throwing it against the wall again. This time it bounced back to his feet. He gave it a swift kick and then fell back into the sofa, dropping his head into his hands.

CHAPTER FOURTEEN

They arrived in Portsmouth, England in a bone-chilling, drizzle, a foggy morning, not fit for standing on the deck as the ship entered the harbor or for being seen by someone looking for him from the dock. Besides, the crew usurped the obvious spaces, lining all the weather decks in their dress uniforms for an impressive homecoming display. The ship's band was playing; the crowd was cheering and blowing kisses; little kids were jumping for joy. It was quite a spectacle. Ben had goose bumps, and not from the cold. He could almost imagine the whole pageant was just for him, and he was sure each of the crew members felt the same way. They hardly noticed the foul weather.

David's eyes glistened with tears, and Ben thought he knew what his brother was going through. He patted him on the back: "Welcome to your new home."

After the ship was moored and the formalities had ended, two men wearing British army uniforms came aboard. "They must be our escorts," he said to David. "Let's get our stuff." A messenger arrived at their cabin door just as they had picked up their bags.

"You're presence is requested on the quarterdeck," the sailor said, and he led the way.

Two British Army officers greeted them there. One was a major, the other a lieutenant.

"David Komorosky?" the Major asked.

"That's David," Ben said. "I'm Ben."

The major gave his hand for a shake and introduced himself as Major Benning. Both Ben and David shook his hand. "And this is Lieutenant Marshall."

"Good morning, gentlemen," Marshall said, and another round of handshakes occurred.

"We are your escorts," the Major said. "We have a car on the pier waiting. These men will carry your bags," gesturing to two burly sailors who were standing behind them.

"Shall we go?" Both he and the lieutenant turned and gave way for David and Ben to lead them down the gangway.

On the pier, a man wearing civilian clothes stood next to an Army staff car, watching their approach. Ben kept a careful eye on the pier, hoping to see a signal of some sort from Isidor. Had there been a plan to communicate, it probably had been aborted. Ben thought the same thing when the ship had stopped in Gibraltar and he had gone ashore, hoping he would be slipped a note or that some other kind of contact might be made. Security had been too tight.

That left the hotel for his last hope.

The sailors loaded the luggage in the trunk of the staff car under the direction of the lieutenant. The man in civilian clothes introduced himself as Robert Phillips, with British military intelligence, but Ben knew better. He remembered the face from a picture Isidor had shown him in Lisbon. He was Clay Shaw, London office of America's OSS Office.

Both military men sat in the front, the lieutenant behind the wheel. Phillips followed Ben into the car, taking a door.

"Did you enjoy your trip?" Phillips said to David, leaning forward. Ben interpreted for David in German and said to Phillips, "His English isn't so good. He said he liked the cabin and the food, but not the waves when we reached the Atlantic."

Phillips laughed. "He should try a destroyer." Ben gave Phillips a knowing smile, and then passed his comment to David, adding that destroyers are smaller and bounced more.

"No thanks," David replied.

They were headed to the Goring Hotel in the center of London, the major said. He had turned in his seat. "It's a very nice hotel near Buckingham Palace."

The car rolled to a stop in front of the hotel a little more than an hour later. The driver piled out and motioned for a porter. He opened David's door. As David stepped out of the car and Ben began to slide across the seat, the major took Ben's arm. Ben stopped. "My orders are to leave for the airport in twenty minutes," he said. Phillips turned to Ben.

"I'll see you in twenty," Ben said to the major, then scrambled out of the car.

A bellman pushing a hand cart arrived. "All of them?" he said to the lieutenant who was standing by the open trunk.

"No, just these," the lieutenant replied, pointing. "Just one of them are staying."

Ben rushed to intervene. "That one goes, too," he said, pointing to one of his bags. "My bag, but the contents are his."

The lieutenant nodded and said to the bellman, "And this one."

Ben walked quickly to catch up with David who had stopped and turned at the hotel door. Phillips was on his heels. Ben paused.

"Are you planning to follow me to his room?" Ben said. If he did, Ben was thinking they should rally the rest of the British Army, because he wasn't going to allow it.

"No, I'll wait in the lobby."

"Thank you," Ben said.

In the lobby, Phillips sat back as Ben and David approached the registration desk. Ben's eyes danced through the hotel in search of a signal. He saw nothing.

A short queue at the registration desk disappeared in less than a minute. Their luggage had arrived, and the bellman was standing by, waiting for a room number. David stepped up to the desk and gave his name to the clerk. Ben checked out the beautiful interior of the spacious hotel, beginning with the ceiling, nodding his head approvingly. He still didn't see what he was looking for.

The desk clerk handed David a key for a room on the sixth floor. He was explaining the hotel services, and Ben was listening over David's shoulder, knowing David didn't have a clue what he was saying. He whispered in David's ear, "I'll explain it later."

A voice vaguely familiar to Ben caught his attention. "Any messages for room four-twelve?" Ben glanced to his right. A man was speaking to another desk clerk.

"Four-twelve? I'll check for you," the attendant said.

Ben could not see the front of the man's face, but he noticed his hat: a white hat with a wide black band, just like the one he had seen at the British naval hospital in Malta. He then placed the voice. His spirits lifted, he returned his full attention to David.

As the porter led David and Ben to the elevators, Ben glanced over his shoulder and saw Phillips and the lieutenant seated in a pair of leather chairs. Phillips pointed to his watch. Ben bobbed his head.

In David's room Ben tossed his travel bag on the bed, opening it. "If you see Marsha before I do, give her all this." He ran his fingers across a stack of letters to her, identifying them. "The rest of the things in here are presents for her and Sarah. I have to run a quick errand.

"Don't let anyone in the room while I'm gone and, if anyone calls for me, tell them I am in the restroom, if they persist. I won't be long."

He stepped into the hall, closed the door behind him, and looked both ways. All clear. He saw an exit sign likely indicating a stairway, and headed for it, jogging softly on the balls of his feet. He made another check when he got to the door, saw nothing, and opened the door, and went down two floors, two steps at a time. He opened the door a crack and peered into the corridor. He waited for an elderly couple to enter a room, then stepped into the corridor.

He tapped on room four-twelve. In a second or two the door opened, an inch. The man who had been wearing the white hat in the lobby peeked through the crack, then pulled it open wide, tilting his head sharply indicating Ben should enter quickly. Once inside, the man reached inside his jacket, saying, "We meet again."

"Thank God," Ben said.

He accepted a sealed envelope from the man, who said, "I was told there would be no reply," and reached for the doorknob. "I'll check the hall before letting you out." He stuck his head out the door, looking both ways. "It's clear," he said, stepping out of the way. "Go quickly."

Ben slipped out.

* * *

"Wait a few hours after I leave and then call that number from a public phone," Ben said to David, after returning to his room. He was sitting on the bed next to David and speaking in hushed tones. "It's a law office. Ask for the name on the note. He's Jewish and speaks Russian. He'll put you in touch with someone who will sneak you out of the hotel and connect you with Marsha."

"You pulled it off." David said. He had a big grin on his face, and Ben could tell he *really* wanted to meet Marsha and the baby, which gratified him. Ben just winked.

"I need to help you memorize the name and number before I leave." He looked at his watch. "I have eight minutes, so let's get with it."

CHAPTER FIFTEEN

They met at the Essex House Hotel in a twenty-sixth floor room overlooking the south end of New York's Central Park. The walls were beige-colored; an ornate chandelier cast a warm glow. Ceiling-to-floor pleated drapes across a north-facing window were tightly drawn.

Ben had just arrived and tossed his coat and hat on the king-sized bed. Isidor told him that David had been taken to a safe and secure location already, which was the news Ben wanted to hear. "He's got a brand new identity with fresh citizenship papers, and he'll get to meet Marsha within the next few days. Everything went perfectly, and he's doing great."

Ben thanked Isidor.

It took that long to put him in touch with Marsha because of the levels of security and cutouts in place, Isidor explained. Again, great news to Ben. The more security for her, the better. He began to relax for the first time in more than a week. He was now free to make his move. He wanted to hear what Isidor had to say before making a final decision, though. He owed him that.

Isidor gestured at one of the covered windows, the one closest to the bed, walking toward it. "Show me where you're supposed to meet," he said, making a slit in the drapes barely enough to peek through, and not enough to be seen from the street. And that part of the room was dark.

Ben peered through the slit. Heavy storm clouds hung over the park and darkened the early evening sky. "Over there," Ben said, stepping back to let Isidor see the southeast section of the park from his vantage point. "About three hundred yards north, maybe a hundred fifty inside the park, going that way." Ben gestured to the east. "In a playground. You can't see it but that's the general area."

They moved away from the window. Isidor motioned for him to take a seat.

Isidor set his large frame on the sofa and kicked off his shoes, resting his left foot on the coffee table. Ben took the arm chair. Isidor asked about David's stay in Dachau and his recovery, and they chatted for another thirty minutes or so.

Eventually, Isidor set his foot down. He leaned an elbow on the arm of the sofa, and gave Ben a forlorn look.

"He knows about us, doesn't he?" Ben said.

"Are you talking about David's interview?" Isidor said.

"Yes. What happened?" Ben said.

"Two of the officers who interviewed him were OSS, Dulles' men, including the one who did all the German translations. Our SIS man doesn't know the language, so we were duped. OSS was in charge of rescue security, getting the confidentiality agreements signed, so their presence was not out of the ordinary. Their questions about David's political prisoner status were."

"What were they after?" Ben said.

"We think they wanted to know what the Nazis knew about your spy activities so they would know what got reported back to you. That's one thing. Maybe they sent the report about your college records having been falsified to the Nazis with the intention of having your brothers held but weren't sure whether their report made it to Alfred Rosenberg.

"Or something more sophisticated may have occurred. Maybe they wanted to know whether I knew about the report, which I could only have discovered in one of two ways, both of which connect me to SIS as a double agent. Either from the BCS covert operations in NY or from access to Traynor's personal Mossad files. I didn't have the authority to have gained access through channels. If I know about it, it is only because I am a double agent for SIS."

"How would they have determined that through David's interview?" Ben said.

"By asking him what you asked him on that subject?" Isidor said.

"David didn't mention them asking that."

"David probably wouldn't have recognized what they were up to," Isidor said. "They're professionals. They can run circles around someone like David who doesn't know intelligence techniques and doesn't have a devious nature."

"So then our covers are blown?" Ben said.

"No, my friend. My cover is blown in that event, not yours," adding that he was a double agent, working for both British military intelligence and of Mossad, Section B. "What do you think Chester wants with me?" Ben said.

Isidor reached for a pitcher of ice water and a glass on the coffee table, speaking as he poured. "He either has an assignment for you, as he said in his cable, or he has something else up his sleeve." He offered Ben a glass of water and when Ben accepted he poured another one. He downed about half the glass, set it down, and leaned back on the sofa.

He gave Ben a studied look and leaned forward again. "Let me give you a broader picture of what we in London think is going on. You need to know this."

Isidor then told him he believed Chester, whom he called Bloomfield, merely suspected an intelligence link between them, saying that he still thought Ben had been shipped out of the country under surveillance as a precautionary measure, and put into a fish bowl in Lisbon where he could be watched closely, all as a result of Dulles and his gang at the State Department having discovered that British intelligence was leading covert operations against them in New York.

"We believe his discovery of the shoeshine boy watching that window shade for you set off alarm bells," Isidor said, "but that he had already planned to ship you out. They cannot connect you and me in Washington that weekend, because I was in London at the time. He may have figured out that you were going to Virginia to see Marsha.

"If so, and if he has done any follow-up, he will have found out that she moved out very suddenly last May...before the school year was out. His conclusion will likely be that you have a relationship with her, not that you are any sort of double agent.

"In Lisbon, they would have learned the same thing that they learned when they first put you under surveillance in New York – that you were *not* engaged in intelligence activities." He paused, finishing his glass of water. "I am also confident that they have not witnessed us exchanging information.

"They have always known about our activities inside Germany and our connection afterward, my friend. They have always suspected us working together for SIS. And we've always been smart about it, cutting loose from one another when they got hot on our trail and re-connecting when things cooled off.

"We think they have long range plans for you. The current SIS prediction is that the major financial players are manipulating an Allied victory with the Soviet Union sharing in the spoils, setting up an East-West balance of power in Europe. Your Russian background fits nicely with their vision of the world's future. They also want a State of Israel controlled by the Haganah and the Mossad so they can maintain turmoil in the Middle East and continue to profit from both Jews and Arabs.

"The only danger for you is your connection to me if they have discovered I'm a double agent. If they know that, they will have to deal with that problem before they invest further in you."

"How would they do that?" Ben said

"We can talk about that later," Isidor said. He leaned forward and lowered his voice. "Here's what you need to know." Ben edged forward in his chair to hear him clearly. "This is a closely guarded secret. Separate it from everything else you know. You don't know what I'm about to tell you." He paused when he was done, waiting for Ben's acknowledgment.

"Okay," said Ben.

"I once told you that Dulles was being monitored. The British are working with the U.S. Treasury Department to bring Dulles and the financial supporters of Hitler to justice after the war. At first they were stymied. Dulles was too sharp. They had the American consulate in Switzerland and his personal courier wired. Nothing incriminating was found. And then they found a secret telephone line between his office and the head of Swiss intelligence. Wonderful stuff came from the wiretap on that line. The head of Swiss intelligence was an informant to German intelligence and German industrialists. Everything fell into place after that. British code breakers quickly deciphered their communications and we came into a gold mine of information.

"Literally.

"Gold.

"The movement of capital out of Germany. Since the fall of Stalingrad, Germans in high places, even members of the Reich, foresee an Allied victory in the war, and Dulles is helping them move their assets, in addition to helping British and American financial investors pull out their capital, or at least to be in a position to pull it out. All that information has been forwarded to the U.S. Treasury Department, to a special office overseen by the secretary himself, Henry Morgenthau, who reports directly to President Roosevelt. The president is adamant that the bankers and industrialists be prosecuted for war crimes after the peace treaty is signed.

"His plan is, first, to prosecute the German bankers, and then the German industrialists. Morgenthau, as a third step, will unleash the wiretap evidence showing that the Nazis had hidden their stolen assets in Swiss banks with Dulles's help, creating a public outcry to prosecute British and American businessmen, bankers and industrialists for their aid to the enemy in a time of war, which is treason.

"Roosevelt is targeting not only the Dulles brothers but others, including industrialists like Henry Ford, the Rockefellers..., a bunch of them. His intention is to forever break the power of Wall Street and the City of London over American foreign policy."

Ben felt a spark. He recalled the feeling he once had, of being entirely caught up in a quest for justice. The initial goal was to bring down Hitler through a worldwide boycott of German goods, and then, when that failed, to build a cover in New York that might later be used to investigate and expose the titans of Wall Street who had financed the rise of Hitler. Yet today it was only a spark. The fire was no longer there. He loved seeing the sparkle in Isidor's eyes, though. He grinned.

"Good stuff, eh?" Isidor said.

"Yes, it is," Ben said. "I hope they will get the justice due them."

"The intelligence gathered through you contributed to our success. You are an essential part of the team." Isidor slapped Ben on the knee.

A few seconds went by and Isidor's convivial face turned serious. "The problem is, someone leaked the news about the wiretaps to Dulles. He's scrambling to undo the transactions, cover his tracks, and redirect the German assets out of the Swiss banks. Already some assets have been diverted to Belgium, but we've lost the trail." He gazed into Ben's eyes.

"We need to get you inside his office."

Ben was crestfallen, unsure how to respond. Finally he said, "I want to be with Marsha – and my daughter. I can't do without her in my life, I'm sorry, I just can't."

"You can have a family and still work for them."

"How? The bastard said I couldn't."

"Bloomfield's married," Isidor said. "So is Dulles." He rolled his eyes. "Neither one of them acts like it, but they *are*. Being on the inside is not like being in the field. Most of them have families. And they don't go after each other's families when there's a falling out. They might get rid of the agent, sure, or haul him up on espionage charges, but they don't go after his family."

"What if they do know you're a double agent?"

"They can remove the danger by removing me."

His comment staggered Ben like a blow to the head.

"Yes, you heard me right. If anyone has been found out, it is me. I'm the one who has to go. Give me up if you have to, so you can gain access."

Ben let out a sarcastic snort. "Forget it. I'll do no such thing."

"I'm serious. The overall objective is more important than one man. You might end up being our final hope for bringing them to justice. Besides, old Izzy is a pretty clever fellow, no? Don't worry about me. Just confess, if that's what it takes. Tell them everything you know. Let the chips fall where they may."

Ben chewed on his words for a moment, and then dismissed Isidor's idea with a wave of his hand. But Isidor was steadfast; staring in stony silence.

"Besides, who would I report to?" Ben said.

"To no one, right away. You would need to rebuild their trust in you. But when the time is right, to someone trustworthy at SIS; to my direct handler, if need be, assuming he also survives this crisis. I personally vouch for him. I also vouch for his boss, the head of SIS, who will be the person responsible for controlling you if my handler goes down."

Ben heaved a heavy sigh, and sank into his chair. He looked at Isidor, who was staring at him in a friendly yet serious way, holding his message in place. Ben dropped his eyes, strumming his fingers on the arm of the chair. He turned to Isidor.

"Can we order some food and talk about this later?"

Isidor's face brightened. "Good idea."

CHAPTER SIXTEEN

Ben ducked behind a tree to shield himself from the bitter wind. Chester was late and he was freezing. He cupped his bare hands, blew hot air into them, and rubbed them together. When he looked up, he saw Chester in the distance, his face hidden in the shadows. The frame and arrogant gait of the man was all he needed to see. Ben stuck his hands into his coat pockets, his right hand settling on the handle of his revolver. As Chester slowly approached, and his face came into view, Ben saw a frigid stare, a look he had only seen in him once before: the same shiver now shot up his spine, lifting the hairs on the back of his neck.

Then his survival instincts kicked in. Fear was his enemy. He heaved it aside, steeling himself. He refused to be intimidated.

New game. New rules.

He mimicked Chester, ambling toward him, at the same pace, with the same demeanor. The cold north wind blew against his face, barely registering.

As the gap closed, a faint smile appeared on Chester's face. Ben returned the friendly gesture and gently pressed his fingertips against his revolver. Chester stopped and casually looked to his left and right, as though checking to see whether Ben was alone – or perhaps to see if his men were in place. Ben followed his gaze in both directions. He saw nothing but pitch blackness and bare tree branches bending in the howling wind.

"Hello, Ben."

"Chester."

"How are you?"

"I'm fine. And you?" He noticed that Chester was empty-handed. He had no assignment for Ben. He had another agenda entirely.

"What's wrong?" Chester said. "I'm not armed, if that's what you want to know."

"I thought you had an assignment for me."

"I do. But I wouldn't hand it out here, in a park."

"Okay, I give up. Why are we meeting here in the middle of the night?"

"The last time we talked you were worried about your brothers. I wasn't sure if you were really up to working for me now."

"We had a deal. You kept your end of it and I intend to keep mine."

"Because I've been thinking about that," Chester continued, as if not hearing Ben. "In terms of really being fair to you. I started thinking: 'Ben doesn't like this kind of work. He wanted to get his brothers out of Germany. That's the motivation I tapped into when we first met. And now he's achieved his objective. I should be honest and fair with him. He's done everything I've asked of him. Maybe he doesn't really want to do this. Why hold a man to a deal he doesn't like?'"

"Actually, you're wrong. I want to do this. Maybe I wasn't into it that much when we last met, but I was frustrated. I knew that Jews inside Germany were being exterminated, and I couldn't concentrate on anything else." Chester's glare bored into Ben as he spoke, trying to see into recesses of his mind. If Chester meant to intimidate him, he had failed. If anything, Ben was annoyed, but didn't let it show. He kept speaking, sincerely. "I told you I would be grateful if you helped me rescue them, and I am. I now see my job in a different light. You were right about everything, the resources at your disposal, the results of my work, stemming the Nazi ..."

"Don't play games with me." Chester's mood had turned on a dime.

"What are you talking about?"

"I know about Isidor Franks," he shot back.

Ben recoiled. His defenses and composure evaporated. He felt a deeper chill, from Chester's icy glare. He struggled to regain his bearings.

"I know what's going through your mind right now," Chester said, taunting him. *"How much does he know?"* He leaned into Ben as he spoke. "You're wondering, *'Does he know...'"* Now eyeball to eyeball, his smoker's breath in Ben's nostrils. *"'Where Franks is? Right now?'"*

Chester sprang back, his eyes remaining locked on Ben's. Clearly, he knew the answer to his question. Ben caught himself. No, Chester was only projecting that. He had knocked Ben off balance, but Ben was recovering. He felt a surge of confidence return.

New game. New rules.

He felt a smile come to his lips knowing that, ultimately, he had the upper hand.

Chester dropped his eyes, scuffing a small patch of old snow with his shoe, as if he didn't care whether Ben believed him or not. He looked to the heavens, and then became his old self again, the man who used to meet Ben at the safe house.

"I'm going to level with you," he said. "I like you. I've said it before. I meant it then and I mean it now. I don't want to send anyone after you. I really don't. Work with me to plug the security holes and I'll write this off as Franks taking advantage of you for his own ends. What I want from you are straight answers."

"I don't know what you're talking about."

"Don't try to outfox me, Ben."

"I wouldn't dream of it."

"Then don't." Chester threw his face at Ben, shouting. Like lightning, his face was contorted into a mask of fury, his eyes squinting, his lips pursed. Ben just looked at him, their eyes locked. In that moment, however long it lasted, Ben sensed in Chester certitude. He knew *something*. He had a plan. He would execute the plan. A deadly seriousness came through his gaze, giving Ben's next decision the weight of life or death.

Ben relaxed, yielding to Chester.

"Give me straight answers," Chester said, "and we can fix things between you and me. This is your last chance. One lie and I walk away."

"What do you want to know?" Ben asked.

"Who else have you talked to?"

"No one, just Franks."

"What about your brother, David? You spent all that time with him in Malta, and on the boat. Didn't he ever wonder how you got inside Germany?"

"If he did, he didn't express it."

"What about Marsha?"

The name struck Ben like a sledgehammer.

Chester lifted his head, peering down on Ben in a knowing, almost fatherly way. He drew a deep breath, patiently waiting for a reply, letting Ben twist in the wind. Ben studied him, wondering how much he did know. Chester was implacable. Not a crack. Chester's warning replayed in Ben's mind. *One lie and I walk away.* "No," he finally said. "Nothing."

"But you did see her after I told you not to, didn't you?"

"I did. Not right away, but I did."

"What'd you tell her you were doing?"

"Only that I was doing some secret work for the government. She's patriotic, like most people. She accepted it and never pried. She's no threat to you or your organization.

"Where is she now?"

"She has nothing to do with this," Ben shot back, displaying his own fury.

"As a lover and a confidante, she has plenty to do with it. You put her in this position..."

"That's right. I did. It was my mistake, but she's no threat to you. She's not a *confidante* on matters that concern you or your organization, no more than your male lovers..." The last part slipped out and Ben tried to reel it in, his lips mumbling some inaudible nonsense. Chester shriveled, his face a twisted kaleidoscope of emotions: anger, embarrassment and shock.

Ben held up the palm of his hand, searching for the appropriate words, but none came. Meanwhile Chester composed himself, cleared his throat, and puffed himself back onto his agenda. Ben continued, softly. "She knows nothing, and I'm not going to tell you where she is. If you want to hurt her for some reason..."

"I don't want to hurt her."

"Or use her as leverage against me."

"I don't want that, either." Chester started to say more, but Ben cut him off.

"Then you don't need to know where she is. This is about Franks, isn't it?" Chester didn't say anything, instead focusing on Ben, thinking, and eventually agreeing in a subliminal way. He crossed his hands below his waist, one gloved hand in the other. Ben took that as a positive signal that they had reached an accord with which he could live. "I understand your need to know about Franks," he said, "and I'm willing to cooperate with you to that degree."

Chester bobbed his head. "Okay, let's do that. Where's Franks right now?"

"He's here in New York. Do you want to know where he's staying?"

Chester stared into Ben's eyes for a while and, without lifting his gaze, drifted off. He shifted his jaw from side to side, wriggling his thin black moustache, and then re-focused on Ben.

"No. That won't be necessary," he said. His soft words carried an ominous undertone, driving bile into the pit of Ben's stomach.

Chester slapped his arm around Ben's shoulder. "You're a smart man, just like the Ben I know. I'm glad you decided to come clean with me. We'll fix things and put it behind us. Like I said, I like you and I want to work with you."

The hell he did, the bastard. Ben nodded, shaking lose a smile, playing along.

"Give me a day or two, and I'll get back with you on that assignment I have. I might have some more questions in the meantime. If I do, I'll get in touch." With his arm still around Ben, Chester began to escort him out of the park.

Ben stood firm, which startled Chester.

"No. You're a company man. Your plans don't include working with me."

Chester eased back his arm and stood erect.

"I also know you're not going to send anyone after me or the people I love, including Franks, but that's only because you can't afford to."

An odd mixture of concern and incredulity came to Chester's face.

"Everything I know or have done has been written down. I plan to send you a copy. I sent a copy to someone else in a sealed package, with instructions not to open it as long as I'm alive; but if anything happens to me, that person is instructed to open it, make copies, and publish it worldwide. That person will forever remain unknown to you, but if I live a peaceful life, the package will be destroyed, unopened."

Chester leered at Ben, calculating, unsure.

"I'll talk to Franks about our discussion," Ben said, "tell him it's over, and get him to walk away, too. You won't have to worry about leaks. The holes will be gone and there'll be nothing for you to plug. Everyone walks away."

Chester kept his mind locked on Ben's, again trying to penetrate it. A light suddenly went on in his eyes; a slight grin cracked his face. Very subtle, but perceptible. And then it grew. First a chuckle, then, implausibly, laughter.

Ben was mystified by this reaction, unsure whether to play along and laugh with him. "Ah, never trust a spy,"

Chester said. "We both pretended that we had come clean, but we're still lying to each other."

The flesh on Ben's hands and face began to crawl.

"I don't think you've written anything," Chester said. "Maybe you plan to. Otherwise, why did you come to this meeting pretending you were ready to go on another assignment?" He paused, glaring at Ben. You need more time."

"You're wrong," Ben retorted. "The reason Franks is in New York is because he wants to know what my next assignment is. That was going to be the end of it for me. Then I was going to give you a copy of my manuscript."

Chester briefly considered. "Well, now that I know your plan, let's have it. Give me my copy."

"I will. I'll get it and give it to you. How about tomorrow morning? At eight, same place."

Chester smirked. "How about I go with you now and get my copy, so we can be done with it."

Ben faltered, his bluff called.

"I'm sorry it had to end this way," Chester said.

Chester turned, and began walking away.

The cold north wind whipped through the park, pelting Ben's back, howling. The branches above him creaked.

The implications of Chester walking away became quickly clear. He envisioned a bullet splitting his skull that second. He scrambled for the nearest tree and threw himself against it, hugging it, his frantic eyes darting from one hiding spot to another as he shuffled around the perimeter of the tree, in search of a rifle barrel.

All he saw besides trees and shadows was the fading silhouette of Chester, who never looked back.

A black car driving north on West Drive pulled to the curb, under the soft white spray of a streetlight, and Chester angled toward it.

Almost a minute had passed, and Ben had not been fired upon. That meant Chester had some other plan for him. The plan for Isidor, on the other hand, was clear. Ben craned his neck around the tree trunk and watched Chester climb into the car. Soon the car was out of sight.

Izzy.

Ben burst into a mad sprint.

CHAPTER SEVENTEEN

He arrived at Central Park South at a dead run and came to an abrupt stop just short of the street, his chest heaving. A phone. He needed to get to a telephone and warn Isidor.

He re-checked his options, using the time to catch his breath. Central Park South was lined with skyscraper hotels, most of them between Sixth and Seventh Avenues. The Essex House was out of the question. That's where Isidor was staying. Assassins were likely stationed outside it. The idea crossed his mind that Chester had expected Ben to warn Isidor, possibly going directly to the Essex on foot, giving Chester two targets at the same location. The Hotel St. Moritz was the closest.

Stationary, and his oxygen partly replenished, he began to think more clearly. He began thinking from Chester's point of view. Why let Ben get away unless he knew where he would go? Ben would warn Isidor, that's certain, but he would be smarter than to return to the Essex. He would warn him by telephone, and the closest public phones were in the hotels on Central Park South. Ben concluded that Chester would station men in the park, in the trees midway between Sixth and Seventh, leaving the entrances to every hotel within two hundred yards an easy shot, even at night. He snapped his head westward, searching the edge of the park for movement or likely perches. He came up empty.

East-west traffic came to a halt, and Ben went for it, racing and weaving toward the St. Moritz, his head bowed. He reached the other side of the boulevard in one piece, his heart pounding. Twenty feet of open space to go. He gave it all he had. He reached the door and burst through it, causing a spectacle inside. He bent over, hands on knees, heaving for air. His side was splitting. A few moments later, he straightened and raised his palms, signaling to onlookers that he was okay. He spotted a bank of pay phones and moved toward them; reassuring his audience he was really was okay.

Order in the lobby was restored by the time he reached the phones. He latched onto the furthest one. He was still gasping for air when he dropped a nickel in the slot, taking from his pants pocket a note containing Isidor's hotel phone and room numbers. The phone started ringing. Ben turned his back to a man three phones down, cramming the paper back into his pants. The Essex Hotel operator answered. He spit out Isidor's room number, then cast a nervous glance at the lobby. Nothing unusual. Then at the phone bank. The man near him was still there, absorbed in his conversation, laughing.

The phone in his hand rang again, and was picked up. Isidor answered.

"They know about you!" Ben said in an urgent whisper, glancing over his shoulder at his phone mate who showed no reaction.

"What happened?"

"Chester knows everything. He even knows where you're staying."

"Did he say how he knew?"

"No. Just get out; just get out, any way but the front door. Don't go out the front door."

"Does he have men covering the front door?"

"I don't know where they are, but they're out there somewhere. You need to go."

He felt his voice rising and glanced over his shoulder. The man had turned his back to Ben, still gabbing and carrying on.

"Slow down and tell me what happened."

"I'll tell you later. Just get out of there and meet me where we planned."

"Tell me something, anything. I need information, not commands," Isidor snapped.

"He knows about you. He said your name. He knows you're in New York and where you're staying. I know he's got men laying for you by the way he talked and acted."

"What about you?"

"It's all over. He's going to send people after me, too. They're probably set up by my... Do we really have to talk about this now? Please leave." He was about to say, by his car.

"I'm looking out the window right now, and–"

"Dammit, Izzy! Get away from the window and listen to me! You won't see them. They might be three blocks away."

A stir in front of the hotel lobby grabbed Ben's attention. He turned. Two police officers were talking to a clerk.

"It might be better for me to call a taxi and go out the front," Isidor said. "It's only ten feet to the curb and there's a canopy over the entrance."

"Cops. I have to go," Ben hurriedly said. He started to hang up, and then it suddenly registered with him what Isidor had said. "No, don't go out the front!" he said into the mouthpiece before hanging up. He wasn't sure whether Isidor heard him.

Ben turned and saw the clerk point him out to the cops. He searched for an exit, saw a door, and made a beeline for it.

"Hey, Mister! Stop!" one of the cops yelled.

Ben raced down a corridor, the cops in hot pursuit, guests gasping and shrieking and stepping aside, leaving him exposed. He saw a door to his right and tore into it, propelling himself through. It opened to the kitchen. He spotted a rear door and sprinted for it. The kitchen door behind him crashed open.

"Stop! You're under arrest. Stop, or we'll shoot."

Ben reached the back door, grabbed the knob and flung it open in one motion, and then dove through it, slamming the door behind him. He found himself in an alleyway. To the right was Sixth Avenue. A taxi came into view, heading north toward Central Park South. "Taxi," he screamed at the top of his lungs, dashing for it, waving his hands.

The taxi came to a screeching halt the moment Ben hit the sidewalk. He made a mad scramble to the cab, and landed inside, snapping the door shut just as the two cops exited the restaurant, pistols drawn.

They caught sight of him and broke into a hard run, waving their arms and pistols and mouthing for the taxi to stop.

"Where ya' headed, pal?" The cabbie said, as he took off.

"Union Square," Ben answered, not that he wanted to go there. He wanted the driver to turn right on Central Park South, which would be quicker than a left turn. "Turn right–"

The driver turned and shot him a nasty look.

"I have to catch a train and I'm running late."

The cab was moving forward, but the driver was looking at Ben. "Then tell me to step on it. Don't tell me how to get there."

Ben heard the cries of the cops, muffled by the sound of traffic in the enclosed cab, but still audible. He leaned forward, hoping to block the driver's field of vision, and raised his voice to drown out their cries. "Step on it. And watch where the hell you're driving, please."

"Now you're talking." The driver turned in his seat and hit the gas. The cab lunged forward. Ben kept talking. In addition to the screams of the police, horns behind them started blaring, maybe in an attempt to get the driver's attention. Ben raised his voice.

"That wind's a killer. Goes right through you. Must be quite a storm that's hitting us. Any idea of the temperature?" He thought of a radio, additional noise. "You got a radio?" He did. Ben saw it as the words came out.

"Freezing," the driver said. "I don't go by the degree bullshit. It's either freezing or it ain't. How much it's freezing don't matter."

The light at Central Park turned yellow. They were still one car back, the car in front of them just entering the intersection. Ben gripped the seat. His right hand was resting on the top of the front passenger seat. He found himself willing the driver to run the light, his fingers digging into the seat. He began to panic. He peeked over his shoulder. The cops were in hot pursuit, closing in. The sound of sirens came from somewhere behind them. He couldn't tell from which street, probably Seventh Avenue, the next street to the west.

"Step on it." He yelled, commanding him. The driver had just let up on the gas.

"Hey, pal. It's red." He was twisting in his seat. Yes, now it was. He could have beaten the eastbound traffic into the intersection. The driver's eyes widened, suddenly locked on to something past Ben's left shoulder.

"Holy shit," he said.

Ben slid across the seat, reaching for the door handle, and throwing it open. "Sorry. Gotta go."

He zigzagged through the two lanes of standing northbound cars, crouching and weaving, his hands leaning on stopped car hoods for leverage. The southbound lanes came alive with accelerating traffic. He darted between on-rushing cars in the first lane. A cacophony of squealing brakes and angry horns blared. Sirens and police officers were screaming behind him.

In the center of the two lanes, a huge old Packard was barreling down the street. Ben stomped his heels into the pavement and leaned back like a matador. The Packard whizzed by, brushing his coat. He jumped into the final traffic lane, the instant it passed him by, baring the palm of his hand to the driver of another moving car as he pressed forward. The car screeched to a stop, its horn a steady blast, as Ben scooted by within inches of the right headlamp. He hit the sidewalk in a flat-out run.

He turned left on Central Park South toward the Hampshire House. In front of the hotel a taxi driver was taking luggage from his trunk. An elderly woman stood on the sidewalk, waiting. The driver closed the trunk. The driver's door was open, the motor running. Ben stole a glance over his shoulder. The cops had just turned onto Central Park South. He darted into the street and leaped inside the cab, behind the wheel.

The cabbie dropped the luggage he was carrying. "Hey, you asshole. Get the fuck out of my cab." He dove for the front passenger door and swung it open just as Ben slammed the car into gear and squealed off. The cabbie hung on for dear life, scrambling to catch up and jump in. The two cops who had been chasing Ben had come to a halt on the sidewalk, their guns drawn. With all the commotion and attention he was attracting, another fleeting thought passed through his mind: two assassins were likely perched on the other side of the boulevard, a short one hundred yards or so away, the side of his head a perfect target through the glass window.

Tires screeched behind him. He braced himself for impact and gunned it. The cabbie's legs flew out from under him. Dragged for about five feet, he let loose a final invective and fell away. A bullet ripped through the backseat passenger's window, shattering it. Tires behind him screeched, a horn to his left blared, and a car swerved into the westbound lane, clipping the front fender of the cab as it went by. A second shot rang out and struck the passenger side of the cab.

Ben spotted an opening in the westbound traffic and yanked on the steering wheel. He stomped on the gas pedal, spinning and skidding the cab into a full U-turn, setting off another chain reaction of braking tires, swerving automobiles, and honking horns. Two more pistol rounds cracked.

Splat. Splat.

One struck the door post behind Ben's ear, the other hit the back door. The taxi rocked from side to side and settled in the far lane, putting distance between him and the officers. Seconds later, he was out of their range altogether, driving in front of the Essex House Hotel.

* * *

Inside his hotel room, Isidor cradled the phone, clinging to Ben's warning; digesting and picking apart the skimpy information he'd shared. His suspicion focused and refocused. Did Dulles and his men trail him to New York? Did they really know where he was? If so, wouldn't they cover the back as well as the front of the hotel? Might they come straight to his room? He grabbed his overnight bag, which was packed and ready to go. He doused the light, then twisted the doorknob, slowly cracking the door. He peered through the small opening and, seeing nothing, gently widened it and stepped into the corridor. It was empty and quiet. He made for the stairway, hustling.

When he reached the ground floor, he saw a smattering of people meandering about, guests mainly, and a couple of hotel employees, not professionals in his estimation. He began to relax and gravitated toward the back of the hotel. He found an exit door and pushed it open. The cold night air hit his face. He saw a deserted alleyway, but then pulled back, closing the door. He felt a rising uncertainty. He recalled Ben's final words, "*Don't go out the front,*" and pondered his dilemma. His instincts told him to do one thing; Ben told him to do another. He had learned never to go against his instincts; he hadn't learned the same lesson with regard to Ben. As much as he respected Ben's intelligence and experience, he sensed in him an emotional reaction, as if he had panicked and possibly bought into Bloomfield's double-dealing. It sounded as if he had no evidence that men were stationed anywhere and was only speculating. Again, he thought, why would he not cover both the front and back? He briefly considered going out a side door or a bottom floor window, but dismissed it. Why not cover the entire hotel? That's what he would do were he Bloomfield. He then considered hiding out, perhaps finding a vacant room, bribing a clerk for a key without having to register. The sound of police sirens outside prompted him to dismiss that idea. He didn't want to be trapped inside the hotel; he preferred to leave on his terms, trusting his instincts until solid information dissuaded him. He turned and headed for the front doors.

In the lobby by the doors, he approached the bell captain and handed him a dollar bill. "I need a cab," he said.

The bellman accepted the bill and summoned a bellhop. The bellhop snapped to attention and raced over. "Hail this gentleman a cab," the bell captain ordered.

"Yes, sir," the bellhop replied, and reached out for Isidor's traveling bag.

Isidor pulled it back. "No, I'll carry it." The bellhop registered his surprise, but gave in when Isidor insisted. When he was out of earshot of the captain, and the bellhop was almost to the front door, Isidor called him back. "Come here," he said. He had a dollar bill in his hand, and showed it. The bellhop retreated, an eager look on his face.

"Yes, sir?" He reached a tentative hand for the bill, and Isidor let go.

"I'll wait inside while you flag one down. When it pulls up to the curb, open the back door for me and I'll run out and jump inside." The man was nodding, willing to please, but clearly puzzled. "It's cold outside," Isidor added.

"Yes, sir, it sure is." His puzzlement gone, his servility back in full bloom. He corkscrewed his body, ready to bolt.

"Here," Isidor said. He turned over his bag. "Throw it in the back seat."

"What about the trunk?"

"Either one."

The bellhop scampered off, and Isidor watched him through one of the three glass doors, standing back a few feet. The sound of multiple sirens outside grew louder, deafening each time one of the doors opened. A gust of arctic air also swooped into the lobby with each opening.

One cab was already sitting against the curb just outside the door, and a second one, flagged by Isidor's bellhop, was pulling over. Isidor began gauging his run, and saw only five or six steps. He liked his chances. Once he was in the cab, he would conveniently drop something and lean over to pick it up, remaining out of sight until the cab cleared the area. His taxi pulled up to the curb behind the first cab. The driver got out and popped the trunk, then grabbed Isidor's suitcase. The bellhop stepped quickly and opened the back door and motioned for Isidor, standing by and holding onto the door.

Isidor waited for the driver to climb behind the wheel and then opened the door and quickly stepped outside. Gunshots exploded. Isidor fell back, stumbling, at first thinking he was being fired upon, but then realizing the shots were coming from down the street, to his right. He looked in that direction and saw a taxicab swerve dangerously in front of traffic, into a U-turn. The sound of two more shots split the air, striking the fleeing cab. The shots came from pistols brandished by two policemen standing on the sidewalk at the other end of the street. The bellhop and other pedestrians on the street stopped and stared.

His back plastered against the glass door, sheltered under the hotel's sidewalk canopy, Isidor saw his opportunity. He bolted toward the open back door of his cab.

CHAPTER EIGHTEEN

A s Ben sped beyond the range of the officers who had finally ceased fire, twin police cars, marked NYPD, appeared on Seventh Avenue, on the other side of the Essex House Hotel, trying to bust through the intersection onto Central Park South. Ben caught sight of a man running from the entrance of the Essex. Izzy! At that very moment, rifle fire erupted, two shots in rapid succession. Isidor's head snapped back, his chest sank, his legs buckled and he fell in a crumpled heap, lifeless.

It froze his heart, sucked the air out of his lungs. He choked, gasped for air, struggled to refocus on his own escape. The sound of squealing tires snapped his attention back to the street. He slammed on his brakes and squealed to a halt. Horns blasted. Two cars behind him collided, then another. The two police cars, sirens wailing, broke through the intersection and rounded on to Central Park South. A bellhop and others on the sidewalk in front of the Essex were frantically gesturing and pointing to where Isidor lay.

The police cruisers pulled over, one behind the cab Isidor had run toward, the other alongside it, and double-parked.

Stuck in traffic, and still stunned, Ben watched. Tears welled. The officers who had fired upon Ben converged on the scene, one of them shouting, furiously waving his gun arm in the air at the double-parked unit, pointing at Ben with the other. Traffic in front of Ben started to crawl forward. He banged the steering wheel, cursing for the traffic to move. He kept one eye on the scene surrounding Isidor. One of the foot policemen reached his body and knelt. The patrol officer from the double-parked car had just stepped onto the pavement when his attention went to the cop who was pointing at Ben. He turned in Ben's direction. Their eyes met. The officer sped toward his car as traffic began to move forward. The left lane opened. He jammed on the accelerator and whipped the cab into that lane.

He crossed Seventh Avenue, glancing in his rear view mirror. The double-parked officer was on his radio. Ben switched lanes again, hit the gas, and passed two cars, then ducked back into the left lane. He caught a green light at Broadway and flew through the intersection. He reached Tenth Avenue and turned left, cruising toward Lower Manhattan. For the moment, he was without a tail. A reprieve he knew wouldn't last. He felt his body relax. He tried to take stock of his situation, but haunting images of Isidor being gunned down overwhelmed his senses, the horror of the scene jolting him as it replayed in his mind. He pounded the steering wheel with his open hand, crying, "No, no, no," and sobbing uncontrollably. "Why did you go out the front?"

He caught himself falling deeper and deeper into despair. He had to concentrate. He rolled down the window, letting in the icy air. He flipped on the radio, got a music station, and cranked the volume up. A Bing

Crosby tune was playing. He began to come around. He slowed for a red light, rolled the window part way up – he was shivering and lowered the volume. The music suddenly stopped, a news announcer's voice cut in.

We interrupt this broadcast for a news bulletin received from the New York City Police Department. Minutes ago, a man was gunned down outside the Essex House Hotel in Manhattan near Central Park. The murderer, who is believed to be a Nazi saboteur, escaped in a stolen yellow taxi cab. He was headed west on Central Park South when last seen, and is armed and dangerous. Anyone with information should report it immediately to the police.

He heard the distant cry of a siren. He looked into the rear view mirror and saw flashing red lights bearing down on him, weaving in and out of traffic. His light turned green and cars ahead of him started to inch forward. He spied a break in traffic to his left, stepped on the gas and darted into the narrow passage, the siren louder, the red lights closing in on him. Cars behind him started parting, clearing the way. A few in front of him followed suit. He kept a heavy foot on the pedal, picking up speed, splitting through the parting traffic, weaving in and out of lanes.

The police cars kept gaining, now less than a block behind him. Ben was up to fifty miles an hour, and accelerating. An intersection was ahead, a green light. The cab was pushing fifty-five, more and more cars pulled off the street. He drifted into the right lane. The police car drifted with him, only about three car lengths back, then two. Ben slowed to fifty, letting the police car close within one car length, and then made a hard left into the intersection.

The rear of Ben's taxi spun out, the cab careened sideways. He whipped the steering wheel into the slide, breaking the skid, and then downshifted into second gear. The cab fishtailed through the intersection, righting itself near the curb of the far lane. He stomped on the gas, accelerated to about thirty, and then rammed the transmission into high gear and sped off. The police car behind him had lost ground, but was still behind him. Another cruiser with flashing lights and siren raging appeared out of nowhere and fell in line behind the first.

Ben tore down the street, bouncing around slower cars, laying on his horn, losing ground to the cops. Another intersection loomed ahead. The green light changed to yellow. A lone auto in his lane slowed to stop. He swerved into the right lane and leaned on his horn. The light turned red. He glanced in the rearview mirror. The police cars were right on him. He rammed the gas pedal into the floorboard just as the cross traffic began moving into the intersection. He gripped the steering wheel with both hands and hit the intersection at sixty.

The sounds of burning rubber and angry horns erupted from both sides as Ben hit the midway point. A second later he shot through the intersection. A tremendous clash of metal on metal sounded like an explosion behind him, followed by squealing tires and a long series of collision aftershocks.

He let up on the gas and sailed down the boulevard, temporarily freed of any pursuers, and then turned right at Eighth Avenue. He drove south two streets, to Twenty-Second, and turned left. He pulled the taxi into the first alleyway he saw, broke, slammed on the brakes and bailed out as the car rocked to a stop. A pedestrian ran at him, hollering: "Taxi. Hey, taxi," then came to a standstill, his befuddled face out of joint.

Ben hollered over his shoulder, "You can have it. The keys are in the ignition. I'm done with it." He ducked down the alley, his arms and legs pumping all the way to the end. He pulled up before he exited on Twenty-Third and checked behind him. He saw nothing but the stolen taxi just as he had left it, its door hanging wide. Panting, he peered out from the alley onto the street, glanced in both directions, then slipped onto the sidewalk, going east. He hailed the first taxi he saw, and climbed aboard.

"Third Avenue El," he said. The cab took off.

Music played on the radio. "Pretty cold out there, huh?" the driver said, peering through the mirror. He had probably heard the same news report Ben had heard earlier, but wasn't obviously suspicious or on the lookout.

"Yeah," Ben said. He heard distant sirens, and tried to place them. "The wind rips right through you." They were probably emergency vehicles rushing to the scene of the crashes. He winced at the recollection of the gruesome-looking wreckage in his rear-view mirror.

"They say a blizzard's moving in," the driver said. "Should hit full force in a few hours. Gale force winds and heavy snow, then temperatures below zero.

"That's what I hear, too" Ben said.

"I'm about ready to call it quits. Business is already thinning out." Ben nodded. The driver was talking to him through the mirror. "How about you? You done for the night?"

"Yeah, way past done," Ben said, turning away. He wanted to keep his eyes on the streets and think through his next steps, not converse. The driver must have taken the hint; he started drumming his fingers on the steering wheel and shut up. Ben began his furtive search, looking for flashing lights, keeping track of the sirens. This section of town was peaceful. He began thinking about his Ford, how to approach it – whether he *should* approach it. The key question was whether Chester knows about the backup vehicle.

A further bulletin on the Essex House Hotel murder. The words from the radio set off an alarm in Ben. He snapped alert, shifting in his seat. *The suspect abandoned the stolen taxi on Twenty-Second Street between Seventh and Eighth Avenues and...*Ben felt the stare of the driver and glanced into the mirror. He saw a pair of wide eyes flinch from view, a hand darting for the radio.

"News," he said, tuning out the station. "Damned depressing. Always somebody getting killed, or something. I ain't got time for that crap. I have enough trouble with the streets of New York." A charade. He was a lousy actor. A jazz station took over, and the driver leaned back in his seat, tapping the beat on the wheel. "You know what I mean?" he looked in the mirror, once again composed.

Ben didn't reply. His eyes shifted from the driver in the mirror to a radio dispatch unit and a hand-held mike. The cab had just crossed Fourth Avenue and Third was his drop off.

He reached his hand into his coat pocket, pulled out his revolver and then switched it into his left hand. He made sure the driver saw it, and felt it. He pressed the butt of it against the man's shoulder.

"Hey, take it easy, pal. I got a wife and kids."

"Give me the mike," Ben said, reaching out his free hand.

The driver handed it to him, and Ben yanked it lose from the unit, and then threw it on the floorboard of the front passenger seat.

"I wasn't going to call you in. I swear I wasn't."

"Now we both know it." Ben put the gun away and settled back in his seat. "For what it's worth, I didn't kill anyone. My best friend was the one who was murdered and someone's trying to pin it on me. You'd run, too, if you knew what I know."

The driver kept his eyes on Ben. "Yeah, well it ain't any of my business. Here's your stop." The cabby pulled to the curb. Ben reached into his pocket.

"Thirty-five cents," the driver said.

Ben handed him a five dollar bill. "Keep the change."

As Ben stepped out, the cabbie hollered after him. Ben stuck his head back in before closing the door. The taxi driver said, "Hey, good luck. Okay?"

Ben nodded, "Thanks."

The taxi drove off, then Ben went to the station and purchased a token. As he waited for his change he noticed a poster pasted on a wall. It pictured Uncle Sam pointing his finger at the viewer, and read: *I Want YOU, Stay and Finish the Job.* A mordant chuckle escaped his throat.

His thoughts again turned to Isidor, who also wanted him to finish the job. A terrible sadness swept across him, bringing more tears. Had he stayed to finish the job, would Isidor still be alive? He didn't know. What he knew was that he had lost a true friend. He remembered Isidor's story, the Pogrom in Kishinev, and saw in him an unwavering, brave, and selfless commitment to a cause inspired at the age of six, and a life that became an ongoing fight against tyranny and oppression. He had a heart of gold, an undying love for his fellow Jews. He was a great man, a strong man, stronger than Ben.

"Sir. Can you hear me?" The lady had his change. She seemed perturbed.

"Sorry." He accepted the coins, a dime and nickel, and walked off. The taxi was nowhere in sight. That had been his main objective, to lose the cab. He bought the token as a ruse. No way was he getting on that train.

CHAPTER NINETEEN

Ben surveyed the garage where his Ford was stored and the surrounding area. He had just gotten off the subway at Sixth Avenue and Forty-Second Street and was standing on the southwest corner of the intersection, waiting for a light so he could cross. Retrieving the Ford was a calculated gamble. The only sure way to know if Chester knew about it was to approach it. If he lived to drive it away, he would have his answer. He knew where he wanted to go to write his story, his insurance policy. With the Ford, he would have enough gas to get there; his rationing books were inside.

Plan A was to retrieve the car and escape New York. Plan B was to keep walking, find a flophouse and lie low for a few days.

For his survey, he took the perspective of Chester planning an assassination, setting up a triangle. Numbers One and Two would form a triangle with the front of the garage. Bryant Park and the Public Library were the most likely spots; they both had plenty of trees and hidden space. They were awfully close to the garage, though, just across Forty-Second Street. But then, the area was not well lighted and the shooters would need to identify him. The strong gusts of wind were also a factor.

He considered where he would station snipers if he were planning the mission. He decided that he would put Number One in a grove of cedars on the Fifth Avenue corner of the library, at ground level. The buildings on the opposite side of the street would block the brunt of the wind and, besides, the line of sight would parallel the wind, eliminating it as a factor. He would put Number Two in Bryant Park, directly across from the garage. The western edge of the park made for a better angle with Number One but was too near Sixth Avenue; an unobstructed wind crossed the sight line. He zoomed in on those two spots for signs of concealment – and saw nothing.

The light turned green. He stepped into the intersection amongst three other people, laying back, using them as a screen, maintaining his watch on the two likeliest spots. More than merely observing, he strained to *sense* the potential danger. Did he *feel* a presence? He reached the other side still uncertain. He made a ninety degree turn after stepping on the curb, prepared to cross Forty-Second. His screen broke down; only one person remained with him.

He nestled himself on the left flank of a middle-aged man who was a foot shorter than him – and they were under the bright wash of the corner streetlight. His exposed head would look like a huge pumpkin to a marksman. A prickly sensation spread down his neck and arms. Time stood still. What was only a few seconds seemed like an eternity.

But then the light turned green and no shots had been fired.

He stepped from the curb, his nerves humming from the tension. As he crossed the street, he took a couple of deep breaths and exhaled slowly, then thought. The moment of truth had arrived, Plan A or Plan B? Did he turn right when he reached the other side and go to the garage, or go straight?

He envisioned himself stationed in the library cedars and considered what he would be waiting for: to clearly identify his target, of course. He recalled the Oslo assignment. He had been instructed to get a good look at the *face* – not a profile – and to wait for him *to exit* the hotel, not to watch for him to appear on the street. Perhaps his killers were on guard for a man with his face to either approach or exit the garage. If so, where exactly? What spot? He recalled the Stuttgart assignment, his only night shoot. He had been instructed to wait for the target to reach the curb under the light of a street lamp, the point where the subject's features were most visible, the aim most reliable.

On the corner, two steps ahead of him, was another brightly lit streetlight. The next most well-lighted spot between him and the garage was a round orange and white neon sign that protruded from the garage over the sidewalk.

He pulled the brim of his hat lower, his coat collar higher, walking with his head bent, his eyes wandering, still deciding. He stepped on the curb. One step forward, two steps. He abruptly turned right. A rush of adrenalin ripped through him, his pulse pounding. He felt naked, isolated, and exposed. He resisted the urge to run, knowing it would make no difference. It might even serve to erase a last doubt in the sniper's mind as to his identity. The rhythmic sounds of his leather heels striking concrete seemed extraordinarily loud; he heard his footfalls even above the pounding of his heart. And then he left the glow of the streetlight. Once again, no shots had been fired. His anxiety began to abate. Moments later, he reached the shadows between the corner and the garage. He passed by the deli he had often patronized years ago. The windows were dark, the store now vacant.

Moments later, he was staring from the shadows at the orange and white flush of the garage sign, about to enter its ambit – the last opportunity for would-be assassins to strike before he entered the building. *Watch over the garage, not the street*, he could hear Chester instruct his operatives. *Less light, but fifty yards closer – and a better triangulation. Sooner or later he will go to his car.* The last concept was the strongest argument for Plan B. Chester couldn't stake out the area with marksmen twenty-four hours a day for two or three days. But it also argued for a stakeout, not a team of assassins. Watch the garage, follow him, and then send in the assassins – or radio the cops. He cringed; the obstacles seemed insurmountable if Chester knew about the Ford. The image of Chester leaving the park, and never looking back, resurfaced. He was confident for a reason. The idea daunted him, and he quickly squashed it. *One step at a time*, he told himself. First, the garage.

His right foot entered the orange neon wash, and the anxiety returned, the quickened pulse, the thumping heart. His lower half was now aglow with orange tint, making his black pants look navy. Another step, his chest was in the eerie light. Another step and the neon glow washed across his face, what little was exposed. His pace had quickened without his being aware of it. He scurried the final steps, hurling himself into the inset entrance. He grabbed the knob and twisted it in one motion, and bolted through the door.

George McEwing was on duty, a feisty Irishman. He jumped to his feet. He had a magazine in his hands and was shaken. "Jimmy!" he said, when he realized what was going on. Jimmy was Ben's Ford name. Also used on his ration coupons. James, actually. James Wilson. "Thought I'd never see you again."

Ben was shaking the snow off his hat. "I got delayed."

"I'll say. The boss gets nervous when you go past what's paid for. You only paid for four months. It's been nine. Legally he can sell it to collect the rent."

"But you didn't?" Ben was on the verge of panic.

George's body reaction said no. "I'm just telling you..."

Ben took a breath. "I know. So let's square-up." He reached for his billfold. "Anything else going on I should know about?"

George curled his lip, thinking hard. Thinking was not one of his better skills. He finally shook his head, "No, just the money." Ben took his words to heart, because if George knew something, it would have shown. He was beginning to feel good about his chances for escape.

He came current with the rent and threw in a tip. George found the keys and then hooked up the battery. "Tires could use a little air," he said when he got to them. Ben had his head in the trunk, going through it to make sure everything was still there, especially the ration coupons and the "C" sticker. They were under the floor mat where he had left them. He looked to see how bad the tires were. George kicked them again so he could see. Not too bad.

"I'll get them later. I want to get on the road before the snow piles up."

He closed the trunk and slid behind the wheel. He turned the ignition and the car sprang to life. George watched him back up, waving the clear sign. When he came even with George, ready to drive forward, the redheaded man shook two fingers at him, his way of saying, "See you later." Ben refrained from telling him that, with any luck, he wouldn't return.

"Take care," was all he said.

He drove down the ramp that took him to Forty-Second Street. He was less concerned now about being shot. He was mainly on the lookout for a surveillance team, although he did notice his muscles tightening as the car rolled to a stop at the sidewalk in plain sight of the eastern portion of Bryant Park. He was no longer bundled up as he had been entering the garage; his topcoat was folded in the passenger seat, his hat tilted back. He crouched in the shadow of the recessed driveway, the orange flush of the neon sign only reaching the auto's hood. He thought about pulling the hat brim down, but didn't. If his car was under surveillance it wouldn't matter.

He eased up to the sidewalk, full into the neon wash. A second passed and no shots, meaning there wouldn't be any. He took a deep breath, checking the sidewalk in both directions. It was empty. The snow was really coming down now. He waited for the westbound traffic lanes to clear, watching out for cars with two-way radio antennas, and then moved forward, turning right.

Traffic was thin, much lighter than an hour ago. He did not see any signs of surveillance. He turned on the radio, keeping his eyes peeled. He made a left toward

Spring Street and the Holland Tunnel, but took a few detours along the way. His confidence continued to rise.

He finally called off the watch and crossed under the Hudson River into New Jersey. He had escaped. Chester didn't know about the Ford. And if he didn't know that, he didn't know about the mountain shack. He knew about Rocky Mount and he knew Marsha no longer lived there. He didn't know Ben had a reason to return to Rocky Mount. Chester couldn't send men after him because he didn't know where to send them. And he only had a few weeks to do it.

On the outskirts of Newark another news bulletin interrupted the radio program he was listening to. He quickly turned up the volume.

The New York City Police and Federal Bureau of Investigation have issued a joint statement. The man wanted for the Essex House Hotel murder was captured and later killed when he tried to escape. The murdered man has still not been identified and no motive for the killing has been determined. The FBI has assumed sole jurisdiction in the case because national security issues are involved. The FBI issued the following statement:

The Essex House murder is a matter of great concern to our nation's security as it involves elements of Hitler's Fifth Column, spies who covertly subvert democracy. Any persons who possess information about the victim and the reason he was killed are encouraged to contact the FBI. Persons wishing to remain anonymous may send written reports directly to the personal attention of J. Edgar Hoover, the director of the FBI in Washington, D.C., without fear of recrimination or reprisal.

A sense of triumph overcame Ben. He understood the message like no other person in the radio audience, because it was directed to him, *a person who possessed information about the victim and the reason he was killed*. He was being offered anonymity in return for a copy of his written report and a promise not to publish it if he is left alone. He figured he had out-foxed Chester, after all.

CHAPTER TWENTY

Ben entered the massive Department of Justice building through the Tenth Street entrance. He carried a small package under his arm, confident that his ordeal had finally ended. He marveled at the colorful murals, the striking mosaics on the ceiling, and the marble floors as he made his way to the office of J. Edgar Hoover. A receptionist there asked him if he had an appointment.

"No, but you may tell Mr. Hoover that I am a witness to the Essex House Hotel murder in New York last month."

She asked for his name.

"Please give Mr. Hoover the message. I'm sure that information will be sufficient."

Ben took a seat in the anteroom while she delivered the message. Less than two minutes later, a clean-cut, dark haired man with a square jaw entered the room accompanied by the receptionist, who referred him to Ben, who stood. The man approached and introduced himself as Clyde Tolson, an associate of Mr. Hoover. Ben held out the package.

"This is my eyewitness report, in response to your public announcement."

Tolson accepted it. "Will you please have a seat while I present this to Mr. Hoover?"

"Certainly."

Almost twenty minutes later, Tolson stuck his head inside the anteroom and motioned for Ben to follow him. He then escorted him to Hoover's office.

Hoover, who held a telephone to his ear, said something quietly into the phone and then lowered it. "Would you please be seated," referring to one of two impressive leather-upholstered chairs in front of his desk. He gave his aide a nod and Tolson departed.

After Ben was seated and the door had closed, Mr. Hoover pushed the base of the telephone to the center of his desk. "He wants to speak with you." Ben knew whom he meant. He put the phone to his ear, speaking first.

"Hello, Chester."

"Ben, I want to clarify our deal so there are no future misunderstandings. If we leave you and your family alone, then this report of yours will never be released, is that correct?"

"Leaving us alone includes me not dying mysteriously or unnaturally."

"That leaves us in a vulnerable position, don't you think? You could have a traffic accident tomorrow and through no fault of our own the report would be released."

"*Azoy geht dos*," Ben said.

"Excuse me."

"Yiddish," Ben said. "In English, it means: That's how it goes."

After a heavy pause, Ben added: "You're a smart man. Think about it. I could also have a traffic accident tomorrow caused by you and not be able to prove that it was through no fault of your own. Such a deal provides me no security whatsoever."

"Point taken," Chester said. "Let's move on. If you die a natural death, the original and all copies are destroyed, is that right?"

"That was the proposal I made to you in Central Park, but you rejected it when you had Isidor Franks killed. The current deal is that it will be released upon my death, even a natural one. So let's all hope I live to be a very old man and that your organization and the interests it serves have reformed so that what I have written is old news by the time it sees the light of day."

CHAPTER TWENTY-ONE

Ben stood on Pier 90 of the New York Passenger Ship Terminal watching the passengers file down the runway.

When Marsha got near the pier she handed the baby to David, who stood next to her. She broke through the crowd and ran to Ben, calling his name. She wrapped her arms around him and hugged him tightly and a long while.

He held her close, ultimately lifting her into the air, and then kissed her, for a long moment. She leaned back with tears streaming down her cheeks and looked into his eyes. She laughed. She saw the same thing in his face, a grin and flowing tears. She kissed and hugged him again.

When David caught up to them, he handed Sarah back to Marsha and spread his arms wide for Ben. They embraced. "You look absolutely fantastic," Ben said to him in German.

David replied in English, "Thanks to you, brother Ben, thanks to you."

Ben gave him an impressed look. "Wow. That is very good." He glanced at Marsha.

"She's a good teacher," David said.

Ben's attention fell on Sarah. Marsha held her up close to her face, and introduced her to Ben: "Sarah, this is your daddy."

The little girl smiled at Ben, who melted. He held his arms out, and Sarah reached for him, too.

Ben took her in his arms and looked into her smiling face. "Hello, Sarah." He hugged her, and kissed her check. "I'm your daddy, and I love you." Sarah flashed another big grin.

AFTERWORD

Isidor Franks and Ben Komorosky are fictional characters loosely based on two persons who formed part of the early Jewish resistance in 1933 Nazi Germany, working with the assistance of British military intelligence.

They later infiltrated the Zionist Headquarters and the Bloomfield-Dulles intelligence network operating out of New York in an effort to gain evidence of their war crimes and expose the British and American financial interests backing Hitler, and the deal that saved the Third Reich from financial ruin, the "Transfer Agreement."

Their story, and the information related to the assassination network, was reported to the author by an intelligence source claiming special knowledge, and may not be factual.

But the following facts are not in dispute:

- After the war, Major Louis Mortimer Bloomfield returned to the practice of law in Montreal, at his old firm, Phillips, Vineberg, Bloomfield & Goodman. In 1958, Bloomfield created Permanent Industrial Expositions, an import/export conglomerate, also known as PERMINDEX.

- After the attempted assassination of Charles de Gaulle in 1962, a French government investigation accused PERMINDEX of funding the assassination attempt.
- Colonel Clay Shaw left London's OSS office and later became the head of the International Trade Mart in New Orleans. The International Trade Mart was a subsidiary of PERMINDEX. In 1967, Clay Shaw was arrested, charged and prosecuted for being involved in the assassination of President Kennedy, but was acquitted by a jury.
- After the war, Allen Dulles lobbied for the National Security Act of 1947, which created the CIA and NSA (the National Security Agency). Dulles was appointed Director of the CIA and remained in that office until fired by President John F. Kennedy in 1963. His brother, John Foster Dulles, became Secretary of State.
- The CIA and NSA ran the basic military structure of the Cold War. The United States spent hundreds of billions of dollars fighting the Cold War.
- Allen Dulles served on the Warren Commission, which investigated the assassination of President Kennedy.
- The offices of I.G. Farben, a chemical conglomerate in Frankfurt, Germany became the Headquarters of Allied Reconstruction forces. Pursuant to the Marshall Plan, German industry was the first area of reconstruction addressed. While prominent Nazi leaders were later tried and convicted of war crimes at Nuremberg, I.G. Farben and other major industries that profited from the war were aided and assisted by Allied reconstruction forces and funds.

- I.G. Farben manufactured the gas, Zyklon B, used in the Nazi death camps to exterminate millions in the Third Reich's genocidal campaign against Jews, as well as gypsies, homosexuals, and other minorities.